American Fool's Day

American Fool's Day

Anthony Kishko

Cool Grove Press

Cool Grove Press, an imprint of
Cool Grove Publishing, Inc. New York.
512 Argyle Road, Brooklyn, NY 11218

www.coolgrove. com
For permissions and other inquiries write to info@coolgrove. com

ISBN 13: 978-1-887276-87-0
Library of Congress Control Number: 2022948135

Cool Grove Press is a member of
Community of Literary Magazines and Presses [CLMP]

Wholesale to the trade by Ingram/Spark

Media alchemy by Kiku

Cool Grove Press

This work is dedicated to EVERYONE

Table of Contents:

~I~

~II~

Episode 1

Zeroing

Who's there?

Hamlet I.i.1.

Dazed in fever, a well-dressed young man returns home, panicked and disheveled, stepping in through a blinding white hall. He'd been to a party . . . It went terribly wrong.

"What in the hell happened?"

Painfully, he's unable to recall the retreating details, like Orpheus climbing back from the forbidden corridors of the underworld—the labyrinthine chasm of dream—the ordeals of meaning. The land of the dead.

He looks behind. The disintegrating secret recedes, swept away under a subterranean tide. As if daunting angels are guarding his *Tree of Knowledge* with swords of fire, to ward off and censor the truths of memory, as few realize, *every angel is terrifying*. And what they guard . . . even-more so.

The wheel of life rolls. Sometimes it all goes sideways. Bristling through one debacle after another, he doubted any good would come from the night's earlier event. Attending with reluctance, little did he conceive the stark outcome.

Dried blood congealed to his brow . . . as if cut from a brush of thorns? Did he scale over a garden wall? Through the hedges? To escape? . . . As he ponders down at his scuffed shoes, their last shouts reverberate back to him:

"Suitor, that was the wrong one. What the f—?"

He fears if he sees back further he'll end up like Lot's wife—turned to salt while gazing at Sodom. *What carnage did he flee?*

A cancerous invasion of lurking terror. The more he concentrates backward, his pulsing migraine pounds in response with vengeance. Someone he knew just returned from Geneva. They worked at CERN: the European Organization for Nuclear Research, being the world's largest particle physics lab, the Hadron Collider/atom smasher Cyclotron.

The party—there was a celebration, about a new process . . . while whispered and frantic intelligence spread concerning a plot about an international conspiracy to sabotage the facility.

Here's momentary safety. A reprieve. At his hearth. The comfort of crimson walls to block out the world, sheathed behind the frayed velvet of sable curtains draped over a coffee-dark carpet. He wants to dive right in.

Dead roses glow under a smoked glass lamp of amber, hanging chained from the ceiling: Gothic in the dark room and autumn air.

The weathered grandfather clock pendulum tocks hypnotic. A photo lies upside down at his desk alongside an unsleeved record album.

A cracked computer screen phases through shots of galaxies from the James Webb Telescope as his world bends out of focus.

Distraught, seeking distraction, he turns on his old model television—*maybe some News* . . . and collapses on a pine-leather couch.

Chills ripple through flesh with tremors. Burning up—he pops three Tylenol, and a *Screwdriver.*

A black-and-white flick lights up the TV: spinning grainy texture—the vertical hold blurs and jolts, jumping its frame, the tubes fire up, through the tweaking electric snow, a film slicing authenticity of a gone world zaps and transmits through—it filters the after-resonance of a lost living past, as does the radiant afterglow heat of charcoal.

He thinks: *Does the universe, like film, preserve in data and energy an imprint? As in dimensions of ether: Edgar Cayce's Akashic records, the Omega Point —all that happens into eternity?*

Celluloid. Imprinted echoes of time. A ghost of reverb. The medium is a message and transference. Nitrate-coated emulsion freezes our shadows into frame-by-frame reeling shades. The sharp distillation of light pierces the ghostly residue projected vivid into caves. A metamorphosis of communique.

The jellied brain subsumed in a cottony apparatus, receives a transmitted movie, projected within an electric box to a cerebral vortex. Cognitive integration from image to conditioned mind. It imprints the psyche from Day One.

We crawl, awkward toddlers, towards its flashing summons. Its carnaval voices of commanding rhetoric and seductive hyperbole. A luminous monolith.

From this focalized network of conduits . . . Is thus, the film's archetype—its blueprint—still alive? Staging cycles of new timelines and quantum possibility? As its conditioned preservation gels to the receiving brains of millions.

Magic.

The spectrum coded in the montage of hypnotic dissociation, projected upon the now-abstracted other . . . His train of thought is breaking down.

But wait! Something's impossibly odd. The flick's main character, whom he's absently watching — *is* the Well Dressed Man *himself.*

Stunned—he jolts upright. Shock hammers his chest. Delirious, he can't stop the chain reaction of shaking terror, watching *himself.*

Should he call an ambulance? Will he have a heart attack? Or go insane? *The government must be recording this all as well?*

Where's the phone? What will he say?

Transfixed, this cinematic event "unreals" amid the sordid context story of some old-time motley Abbott & Costello caper —a Charlie Chaplin, Buster Keaton confused stunt-fest?

Lights strobe and viscerally flicker.

Gorgeous gals zing around across the squared ritual stage—*regal,* and devastating: carrying their vivacious aura of rhythm: Marlene Dietrich, Katherine Hepburn, Barbara Stanwick, Lauren Bacall . . . A surge of thought charges through the haze:

"Katherine Hepburn is about one of the coolest gals in the world."

It was like entering . . .heaven?

However—when the film's main character sees a beautiful actress—he smiles—then suddenly is struck—slapped, *by* the woman.

The Well Dressed Man *zones* into the TV—with a jacked-heart rate, furrows his brow, and drops his jaw—locked crooked and slack.

The ten-thousand pixelations constellated on the screen bleed through his eyes. The radiation scorches his retinas. Conducted and sponged into his neural tissues. Embalmed in a cocoon—an in-between state of electrified karmic limbo?

Exponentially perplexed by the genesis of his conundrum, he absorbs into this warped Zoner-land, while his mind tears into the grip of perception; as if it's another person, receding further away from himself.

He contemplates he hasn't used fluoride in years!—and doubts he accidentally brushed his teeth with Crest—to be the active side-effect cause of this epic delirium; this creeping infection.

Some marshaling force is pushing his "Id'" and consciousness backward (into his subconscious), or beyond? What compass can gauge the trajectory? There's increasing waves of seismic tremors. Sensationalized. Compacted into a decompositional suction. Unknown terms for an anomalous breakthrough.

There's a cognitive distortion of logic—a disembodied divorce from reality, yet intensifying his experience with a surrealistic logic. His IQ plummets with amplification of stupefied astonishment and a swirling restructuring of disassociating pieces.

A ponderous angst assaults him with punitive masochism—or is it passive aggressive sadism?—creeping its sling of incomprehensible weight, of mesmerized fear and guilt.

And smile?

Slam mister!

Katherine Hepburn delivers the man in the TV the best slap. The slap hits him so hard it knocks him clear out of his seat while watching from his own living room.

Strobing lights blast his brain in a seizure of a cerebral-palsy epileptic fit: Staggering up from the floor, drooling, he's alarmed to see the couch is gone. Along with the surrounding color.

Hepburn's reverberating slap propels him so mystifyingly hard—he finds himself transmogrified—as if—teleported alive within the seemingly black-and-white film. The *zonk* & *zttt* of the bulbs' glare momentarily blinds his dilating vision.

A youthful Bette Davis in a swimming black nightgown approaches. She slaps him. He stands speechless, just painfully smiling with cold sweat-hanging anxiety.

Pow! The onyx of her gown shimmers with hypnotic infinity.

"What the *devil* are you doing man?" she demanded. "You're *supposed* to be cleaning the pool! The *Pool* is not clean."

Her speech conveys utterances of sustaining pauses, with emphatic cadence of rhythmic impropriety and elevated diction. "*Wait* til I get *Joan* Crawford down *here* Mister. Damn. What the hell's the matter with you? Cat got your tongue? Why are you looking at me that way? Don't you know how to clean a pool? Honestly! Huh."

Bette, shaking with hyper mannerisms, puffs brazenly on a cheroot. She points across the way at an odd trio in a chaos of energy, clumsily gathering their things. They have: paints, ladders, brushes, brooms, soap, and a trained chimpanzee in white overalls.

"Theee*eese* men he*re* were supposed to do it!" she thundered, "—but they completely *fffffffucked* it up!"

Squinting towards the trio across the pool, he discerns, they're also decked in white overalls smeared with paint. One is crowned with a train engineer's cap, pupils rolling under forest-bushy eyebrows, black wire-rim glasses, chomping a cigar with a thick rectangular mustaches, trying to orchestrate diplomacy amidst the crew.

Next, there's a seemingly irate Italian with a Tyrolean alpine cap, cursing with hands flailing; and last, there's one with Goldilocks hair dangling under his paint-stained ragged top hat.

"Holy shit! Can it be? Is it really the M—?"

"You Mother*fff*—." Bette yelped—like some furious New England boarding school matron after a night with the sailors.

"And get this goddamned chimpanzee out of here!"

Little Caesar, the chimp, is hopping about with two stolen bathing suit tops, frenzied and mad with laughter.

"The Marx Brothers!? What in the holy mother of death . . . ?" thinks The Suit, amazed, free-falling in a bottomless pit of questions. He doesn't know whether to laugh with madness, or piss himself.

Groucho Marx is actually shuffling and animated: waving, gesturing, gesticulating, genuflecting, and fuming his goddamned cigar.

"You know what? Forget about it!" proclaimed Groucho. "Just forget it! The cow jumped over the moon. The silver spoon's on the loose. Let's go! Let's get the heck out of here! What do you mean—NO? Come on! Harpo, please! No *no no no no no no!* Please don't do that. Let's go home! What? Well—we'll find a home. Listen! Do you hear that? I hear sirens. Maybe it was the slap, ringing in my ears? It's an *odyssey*—emphasis on the odd. Haven't we had enough fun for today?"

Harpo Marx, with flailing Goldilocks, vigorously shakes his head forth and back.

"No? *Do you really think we're still getting paid?* Well, calm down. I'll find a way to get you a—What? A spaghetti dinner?—Well, alright then. And yes, with extra anchovies, of course! *And* a rhubarb pie. Sounds—exquisite. Mellifluous even," as Groucho rolls his thick brows to an invisible audience.

"Look! I'm begging you. I'm pleading, on my knees. Not again. Hey, get off me! *Don't you see the damage you've done?"*

Apparently, Harpo doesn't speak, as Groucho responds to Harpo's mute yet animated language of facial contortions and pantomime.

Harpo, a glazed, insane look in his eyes, beams and smiles sinister glee, wildly shaking his head with assent, exaggeratingly puffing his cheeks; then, sternly points with disdain-filled disapproval at Groucho and everyone else, gesturing for him to also take a look around.

"Okay, okay! The damage *we've all* done."

Harpo stands a moment, arms angrily folded, and nods with vindication.

"Alright. Stop. Listen to reason. For God's sake man! *Let's stay out of jail.* You forget? We made a deal never to return. Never I say. Think! Take a look—No. Wait. You know what—don't take a look. Eyes can be deceiving, obviously, in your case, comrade.

"Can you hear the women screaming? Well. Yes, I know you like that. But, they don't. Well, sure, oh yeah, some do. Sometimes. But not all the time. What? *Of course I loved your piano rhapsody.* Who knew? All this time I thought you only played harp. You took lessons? Ahhh, from that voluptuous virtuoso at the club? Then you gave *her lessons?* Crazy! No, don't demonstrate! Please. Hey! Stop that! *Get off! No, get off of me, not on me.* No, I won't dance with you. We came here to paint. Well, someone needs to clean this mess—we came to work—and look what happened? And for a whole three dollars a day! Not to give a performance, and a rowdy-dow.

"Hmm . . . there's the rub: maybe we should become—actors? We could be doing the rubbing—instead getting rubbed the wrong way? Apparently, it's impossible to concentrate around here."

Harpo whistles loud to babes hustling by. He's slapped, and responds with a dissolute grin of puckish wickedness.

Groucho snags Harpo before he pounces off, and shakes him: "You just can't help yourself? Snap out of it. If only you could play another tune. What can I say? It certainly was an unforgettable performance!

"Listen! Your fingers began unlocking ebony & ivory keys in a tranquility of notes, rising into *Fur Elise.* I wanted to cry. Then, you rumbled into the haunting chasms of Rachmaninoff. Stupendous! Bravo! *Bravo!*"

Harpo earnestly marches in place. Stops. Shades his eyes to scout far-off, then serenades an invisible violin. His hands *flowingly* make shapes of curvy ladies; he then leaps on a chair conducting an imaginary symphony. He grabs Groucho's cigar for a baton.

"Hey, give me that. Yes, maestro. Have a cigar! A fresh one. No? What? It makes you—sneezy? Well. Okay. But, when you started hoppin' on that Jelly-Roll Mortin ragtime jive—then brewed and boiled into a Boogie-woogie jam—fingers a fury, as Chico played beside you, *and* that flapper strode atop the piano—well, let's just say—things got out of hand. . . Look. *I know you're all wet.* I'm sorry! Come on, *don't* be mad. I just threw you in the pool because you really needed to cool down."

Bette yells "*You Fucks*!!!" with such command, authority, and nastiness, that it really puts the hook and jolt in the boys to scatter back in motion; doubly motivated to clear out.

"Who's going to pay for all this?" Bette hollered. "I'll sue. You should all be arrested and locked up off the street from decent society."

Groucho shouts from the other side, "Give the bill to the Well Dressed Man over there. Oh a' uh' hey, boss. Sorry about all this. You look impeccable though. Marvelous. See you back at the rendezvous," then Groucho scurries away and says to himself, "Wow. Some people just don't have a sense of humor. Things were great—until they went bad," and shouted, "Harpo, grab Little Caesar before he starts attacking the woman in the mink coat."

A bike horn honks, followed by an echoing slap.

The crew retreats as The Well Dressed Man spies a gang of delinquents: some black-eyed with bloody noses, wearing ragged oversized hand-me-downs, scrawny and lean, peek through the fence; one, with a propeller beanie, casts a fishing-pole line trying to snag the *hors d'oeuvres* tray.

"Are you *listening* to me?" Ms. Davis continued her tirade. "Fffucked up royally. Clean the goddamned pool! Soooooo, you're the one responsible for all this? What kind of shyster operation are you running here anyhow? *Are you a communist, Sir?*"

"Huh? What? Am I a—what? Excuse me?"

"Did you say you're associated with this Marxist brotherhood? You're a subversive! Well you'll never make it in this town once black balled and black listed. It all makes sense now. Knobbing with these low-types—birds of a feather! This is not the first time the piano ended up in the pool—that Curly bastard! What's wrong with men today? Look at this mess! Obviously you don't believe in hard work, or even morality. I'll see you hanged—by your dry necktie. What've you been up to? Swimming in Martinis? Getting slapped I see. Youuuu silly silly creature you. You— Maaannnn!"

There's a chorus of disruption as a bevy of hot bitchy voices clamor and rise with baby doll yeahs of "Yeahhhhh, clean the pool. Cleannnn the pool! Yeah, heyyy, come on! What's the big idea? *Why* aren't you cleaning the pool?"

The pool is cluttered awash in debris: submerged chairs, floating bathing suit tops, champagne bottles, a sunken piano, checkers, a book of Martin Heidegger's *Sein und Zeit/Being & Time, and* bananas.

The Well Dressed Man—*The Suit*—struggles to speak. He stutters something about his new suede shoes, polished and crisp to step under slender sun or moon, cabanas, verandas, band stands, or dim lighting—and his trim *Beau Brummel* custom-tailor threads—look out! *And* snazzy lapels—poorly expressing to Bette, he's *not* an irresponsible pool-cleaning entrepreneur.

A sharpening pulse knifes his chest. *Must breathe through the tightness.* The feverish knot. *Breathe.* Asking silently: could he be so blind to believe this disguise to get him through the illusions? Scene by scene? Where he's trapped, transported, where he's always been? Through the slice and cut of the slush piles swamped in and through the cosmic editing room?

His nose is bleeding. He grabs a handkerchief and his brain is smashed with a drift of perfume which glides like gossamer in a swoon of ether: *Chanel No. 5, Tabu* by Dana, *Shalimar,* Arden's *BlueGrass, Je Revien,* and still *tranquilizing* since its inception in 29—*Joy* by Jean Patou.

The Suit drowns dizzy, as if breathing ambrosia and nausea simultaneously. Scents swim drunkenly—broiling an already overly stimulated cerebral cortex.

Capillaries and synapses firing in a sheath of neural matrix connections. Axons thrum through infinitely *sinewed* density, right down to the buzzing quarks and popping electrons—blazing dendrites afire with the pulse of Afro-Cuban maracas, and congas in a mambo frenzy—a complete conundrum of the fight or flight response—the Sympathetic Nervous System's backed-up intensity of a centrifugal Adrenalin gush. But, where *to* flee? Who *to* fight?

A stoic-faced, mature fellow, pasty-skinned, enters the patio for some sun. Sporting a large French nose, sparse wispy hair, blank expression; walks on a leash what appears to be his pet penguin, strolling among the garden parlor aftermath of carnage, where actresses and models orbit and fuss.

The penguin walker passes a lounged row of flashy blondes and redheads who smartly epitomize the chic austere "prizes" of *Americana* in bikini candy. Technicolor seems to momentarily bleed through the shadowy gauze of black-and-white pale film. Stripes of cherry, white and blue bathing suits—some: warm-yellow like honey-lilies, spinning, but not toiling.

Their oil-gloss of tanning lotion reflects the sun—another shimmering hypnosis of infinity to *slide* into Eternity . . . Some gals prance about, clad elegant from cutting edge designs—streamline haughty in their imperious charades of strut and movement. Decked in jewel spark spider webs of sportswear, play-wear, etc. Ready for onset studio shoots, interviews, parties, rituals, initiations, occult sacrifices, Errol Flynn, Howard Hughes, or *Vogue* Magazine.

Thus the morose man with the penguin strolls through wearing big black shorts, black socks, his sun-lotioned nose, and a guinea T-shirt (his holiday garments). He places his penguin on a chair, then saunters over to the record player. He displaces the quiet croon of Bing Crosby—singing serene through the Victrola, until now, interrupted by his favorite album, the brazen needle roaring scratchy-loud—blasting a furnace of wailing New Orlean's hot Dixieland mad jazz.

A Brunette with short flapper hair throws off her clothes, jumps into a dance trot—then dives in the deep end, despite the disarray, swims to the bottom—and tries to play the piano underwater.

The rest of the lounge-side entourage of debutantes, not amused, accost the man playing this raging Dixieland jive-sound of figurative *trombones* sliding up women's skirts—and proceed to beat the shit out of the guy. They trounce and fuck him up royally: ironically, to the sound of drums skinned alive in a crashing fusillade of the holiday-basher's favorite song *Hold That Tiger,* hammering and walloped crazy like the Fourth of July.

The penguin hops into the pool and starts to cry. That's when the Keystone Cops arrive. Bette, before she struts off, points with irate aristocracy to the immaculately groomed man with a slap stained face—embarrassed and smacked in the wake of guilty carnage.

The squad of shaggy cops, stereotypically Irish, in over-sized uniforms, dump out of their paddy wagon and brandish their billy clubs at the traumatized Suit.

He, the zooted Suit, lost and zonkers, sends up a forlon prayer.

Episode 2

Pools of the Psyche

We are fools for Christ's sake . . .

—1 Corinthians 4:10

A miraculous ripple parts this reddened sea of Venusian hysteria as a person of ebony radiance approaches.

Decked out sleek in a slick tuxedo, *even better dressed* than the Well Dressed Man, who falls to his knees, at the Tux's feet, and blurts: "Holy Christ! Dear sweet lord Jesus."

The "Tux," a radiantly-graced black man with a Star of David pin on his lapel, sneers and chuckles in sing-song phrases, "Heh! Shucks. That ain't me, heh. *Maybe you need a church, Son.* What seems to be the problem? You look like you're in a really bad way." He facetiously gnashed his teeth to give a wincing grimace, larger than life, as he cynically looks around, and facetiously snarls: "*Reeeeaaal bad.*"

"Is there a way out? Could we activate the Wooden Soldiers to protect us?" The Suit pleaded.

"What are you talking about son?"

"Satchmo! How in the world could it be you? *What's going on? Why am I here?* Ya gotta save me! Where the hell am I? How'd it come to this? Am I such a bad person?" implored The Suit.

"Golly. You look pretty slapped around. Maybe—you're too nice of a guy?"

"Everyone is outta their minds," said The Suit. "Am I crazy? What's wrong? I'm having a breakdown. Aren't I? What's happening here? Help me! Please!"

"Ha. What's wrong? Boy, I'll show you what's wrong. Sit down, kid. Catch your breath and I'll explain."

Satch begins to unfurl a golden trumpet which stands out brighter than any of the grainy black-and-white lack of color that's saturated about them. "What's wrong is, most folks just can't get enough of this," he pauses—"or, they *juuuust* ain't gettin' it."

Satch Armstrong raises his trumpet high and strikes up a note. Bam! This is it. This is what's up. Two notes. Syncopated. The first lingering and longing for the second burst of staccato pointillism. Then a triad measured into a swung register of a low-up-down-higher combination—a triple octave stellar high-note even arch-angel Gabriel hears—warm and wavering in micro-tonal variation.

Brave vibrato blurs the spectrum in between articulate notes— playing with Time. Glissing in the sky. A kiss of wind. Swift tastes of bright and brilliant. A lazy hawk sailing the breeze. Like Johann Sebastian Bach in the clouds. Happiness. A Baroque jazz mystic warp, motionless moment: weightless—then slowly descending in a bluesy turnaround that starts to spill-out the main melodic theme in its snappin' vernacular.

The red-faced cops, momentarily halted by the music, snap to and begin to rush for The Suit with raucous importance. He leaps up, baffled to run, but Satch sits him back down, and smiles wide: pearly white. Each tooth is an ivory mountain where tempests of mellow-dee blow.

"Just hold on, Son. Don't you worry! Don't you fret! *Sure as jam ain't jelly, you'll never forget.*"

One loony Blue Meany was about to club them as Satch raises a trumpet towards the assaulting berserker, and Bam!

A note burst shot—*clean* swept that cop off his feet.

The Keystoners run to their fallen comrade, thinking he's been trumpeted to death. Satch lets out a volley of 32nd notes that stop those siren-freaked police dead in their tracks: like a happy Chicago gangster, with a Tommy Gun, on Valentine's Day.

Just knocked them over. He could kill a man with that horn.

Satchmo, as he launches into one long note, slows down time as the police freeze and then seem to move backwards. Satch is the hypersonic innovator of the modern world—transforming consciousness and the corny square-dance canned way people sang—and blasts a fresh complexity of music that's clearly tapped in and synchronous with the zeitgeist's exploding speed of new technologies, coinciding with breakthroughs in Physics by cats like: Schrodinger, Heisenberg, Einstein, Bohr, Bohm, Planck . . .

Disoriented, the cops stagger a bit, beaten and bruised. The mighty Armstrong, a herald announcing the Future is here, begins to jaw, haw and bellow, saying: "Okay, okay. I think you clowns done had enough. Leave this poor pool cleaner alone. And a One, a Two, a one- two- three! Swing it!"

The trumpet cheers a birth of breath and jazz's up the mass-acre with a catch-clickin'/foot tappin' shimmy. Weary cops dance helplessly and dangle and wave their fingers around, foxtrotting into a mosh-pit Charleston.

Those Keystoners were so spellbound stupid that they see tweeting birdy notes and stars orbit their brains long after *Satch* and *The Suit* slip away.

The crowning phrase that seals the musical spell is a line parted by Satch with such perfection that *everything* glows with him—Saint Louis Shakyamuni Bodhisattva Buddha, in the Nirvana now, whilst cherry blossoms shower down.

Later: Satch and *The Suit* are clackin' down the tracks to another crazy part of town—they lean off the back rail of a caboose, chattering in the steam-rollick fresco-thrill of modernity.

From the railcar a radio hums with the croon of drummer boy Bing Bowie: *"It's a god awful small affair, to the girl with the mousy hair . . . and she's hooked to the silver screen. But the film is a saddening bore, for she's lived it ten times or more . . ."* [1]

The Suit, confused by what he hears, is hazed in recollection. He stares into the horizon, and sees an image of Greta Garbo inexplicably passing through the poolside. This submerged recollection surfaces after all the drowning commotion, of her fixed at him with a sensual mourn of sad thoughtful eyes—boundless, ghostly, alien, and European.

Her mysterious Bohemian allure, seemed—ethereal, or esoteric—it doesn't belong in Hollywood Babylon. Or does it? She, a caged sultry angel, haunts him, with a key, beckoning—to freedom? A deeper enigma?

He wrinkles his forehead, contemplating how he didn't smile when he looked at her, so she didn't slap him when her eyes froze, and darkly met his.

Satch lights up a joint, turns to The Suit, and asks: "Heyyyy man. Wanna smoke a J?"

The Suit looks up alarmed, "Naw, that's okay. I'll pass. That stuff just makes me paranoid."

---

[1] "Is There Life on Mars?' <u>Hunky Dory</u>. Bowie, David. lp. 1970.

Episode 3

The Waiting Room

Echoes of the Broadway everglades—with her mythical Madonnas—still walking in their shades. Lenny Bruce declares a truce and plays his other hand. Marshall McLuhan, casual view-in, head buried in the sand.

Sirens on the rooftops wailing, but there's no ship sailing. Groucho, with his movies trailing, stands alone with his punchline failing.

Ku Klux Klan serves hot soul food, and the band plays *In the Mood*. The cheerleader waves her cyanide wand, there's a smell of Peach Blossom and bitter almond . . .

There's Howard Hughes in blue suede shoes, smiling at the Majorettes smoking Winston cigarettes. And as the song and dance begins, the children play at home with needles—needles and pins.

— *Broadway Melody* Genesis,

Satch and The Suit were up all night, trying to figure out what to do, and unravel The Suit's mystery.

Armstrong knew a decent flophouse to crash at on the Bunker Hill side of town—lots of dense Victorian mansions in disrepair turned to rentals—where folk can get lost, and don't pester with intrusive curiosity.

There's too many questions they don't even know how to ask, and few answers.

Satch is already besieged with problems. His first wife was extorting money from him, while his manager turned out to be a mobster who's ripping him off. "Dandy Ratshaw" signed him to a horrible tour, pocketing most of the profits and copyrights, and is now after him for more.

So Satch went *Awol*.

The world's greatest musician—ostensibly a fugitive on the run.

Meanwhile, The Suit doesn't know who he really is, as he's aided by who he thinks possesses super powers. Maybe the music is so good—it's all in his head? But Satch appears just as under the gun as he—up against demonic forces—an underground harbinger of Plutonic Underworld dark magic.

"Why don't you just spin-blast the hell out of Ratshaw with your horn? Take him down," said The Suit.

"Yeah, great idea, *Duke*. You really have some exaggerated notions about my divine trumpet skills. Even if I could—maybe the last thing I need is murder charges. I'm not the killing type. Weighs on the conscience. Weighs on my soul. I've seen it growing up on the streets, and got the high-tail out.

"It's one thing to knock some corny Keystone Cops around with *Good* music, with the breath of the holy spirit—for those naturally susceptible to rhythm and emotion—but my manager? The man is just pure *evil*. E-*vill*. Nasty! Mm mm *mmm!* A scathing poison stabs and burns the eyes to look at him. Once you see through his facade—and man, there's the rub—*if*—you see him first," Armstrong paused with a faraway stare.

"You alright, Satch?" said The Suit, who's now dis-royally dubbed Duke, by Armstrong.

"Listen," continued Satch, visibly disturbed by the subject. "I'm not the fearful type, but the veins constrict and strangle when Ratshaw's near. At first, it's *all* glamor. And charm. And magic. *Enchantment:* a hypnotic surface of illumination. But underneath it all, there's something—undefinable—something wrong—right out of the nauseous fogged up colorless abyss—a simultaneous vengeful hubris of Ahab with the terrifying white oblivion of the whale—a real coal and brimstone salesman, yet, as though on some secret, metaphysical hunt. He's a music agent, they're like that, sure, but he has *no* music in him. Deaf to it. He wanted me to sign contracts, in blood."

"Naw."

"Yeah. He tried to convey it with intoxicated humor, as if to laugh it off as a gag, but—you can imagine, I told him *hell no* to that voodoo malarkey. These people are stained with the black hand," Satch raised his own hand to say: "And I don't mean this. But let's worry about you for now."

Satch paces and ponders, then remarks, "Ahhh. So, I've been meaning to get back to my question. What's it you do with your life? What's your purpose? How do you earn a living?"

"There's lots of science jargon spinning in my head, but—I write, scripts—I think," returned Duke, the erstwhile Well Dressed Man.

"Oh? That explains a lot. Tsk tsk. That's just plain sad. Unholy-Hollywood? Starry-eyed? Is that what brings you here in this den of Delilahs, harems, and coy, sly rakes and shysters?—raking it up. Raking it in. Raking you out. Breaking your heart. Shimmy shim jam jive—sounds like I'd sing a song about it, but they'd have me tarred and strung up on a rail. A Satyricon of feasts in Sin it is. A good time for sure, but I do try to stay out of real trouble."

"How so?" asked Duke. "I've been thinking I'm trapped in Purgatory, but—"

"Well, I've seen my share of sin growing up in New Orleans. An epic hub of cultures, its diverging roots of music, circulated and mingled. The deep central heart and artery of America, it's Life itself—southern Black blues; folk strains from the Mississippi Delta, the sing-song preaching of Baptist ministers—the call and response of their choir and congregation, the Caribbean twang—its coruscating vibration of time, tribal dance, and drums which migrated in bloody ocean exodus from Africa—this consummating saga and symphony of pain cries out . . . There's Mardi Gras of course, and man, besides all that carnival variety, are Orleans folk just mad about the joyous martial fever of tight marching brass band parades!

"The Creoles were often West African and French colonials who intermarried of mixed race —they brought in a significant Opera and classical disciplined influence from Paris.

"Once the Civil War broke out, New Orleans was liberated from the Confederacy by the Union Navy early on; thereby it truly started to flourish with newfound freedoms. However, oddly enough, the catalyst of transformative change and fusion was caused by the racist Jim Crow laws instituted after the war ended. Lincoln was assassinated, and so Reconstruction failed. The South quickly regained its white supremacist laws and strangling grip.

"The southern Jim Crow laws shoved the bourgeois and aristocratic mixed race Creoles into segregation; thereby they were forced to associate with the darker quarters and persons of the city.

"Funny how fast racism becomes the great equalizer of class . . . That intersecting blend of Creole classical knowledge and discipline of reading and writing music, and the soulful power and rhythms of Black American blues, mixed, and thereby all these other elements became a profound elixir . . . And in a city of fun, you know what helped boil all that rock soup gumbo together?"

"Sex?" quipped The Suit.

"Damn straight. No doubt you're a romantic, and a hellcat. Well, you must understand houses of prostitution were a flourishing trade."

"Whore house entertainment?"

"Brothels all over Storyville—so they'd compete. The best had a darn good piano player. Not just to entertain, but to accompany or provide a sassy soundtrack to the entertainment the ladies were providing—if you catch my drift.

"Different kinds of fancy moves and such pyrotechnics would get an extra musical detail, so I hear. Jelly Roll Morton got his start that way."

"Jelly Roll," laughed Duke.

"Exactly."

"Figurative language."

"Figurative as action goes down, the piano speeds up the rhythm to compliment—or, if the customer, so to speak, was taking too long. You know, the original name for Jazz was Jass. Jasmine and ass? Anyway, somehow there's enough confluence of soul and spirit in that ancient melting pot to build a compelling synergy.

"But Hollywood? Sodom and Gomorrah reborn. And they shout at the gates. Slam Bam Floozy. Suzannah and Suzie. Knock knock knock at the doors. Let me in! Smoke Huffin' and puffin. Let me in, to where it's out. Where it's goin' down *down down down*. Drown in booze and ooze. Speakeasy and holler a profaned blasphemy of hallelujah hallelujah: Ho-zanna high in the lowest—hoigh-*dee high high high!* Rolling joy to the flash and flush of flesh. Open the dungeons to the torture chambers of soul. Boil in the swamp jungle carnival glue at the end of time— always just exploding off the edge of the present, which crashes into a new age at any sliced moment-less second of what they call—infinity."

"Damn Satch. That's deep. You're killin' me," said Duke.

"Yeah, it's a killer way of life that'll kill ya! I'm getting carried away. You don't smoke enough Reefer Tea, man. Accentuates the perceptions. Just testifyin'. Speaking in tongues. Wailing on the horn. Music. Poetry. Thought. Where does it come from?

"There's dense study, skill, practice and articulation involved. A discipline—but once performing, there's this light inside, like inspiration—in a fountain, the spirit speaks through.

"Then. There's New Orleans Voodoo, and the divine tug of war—symphony of saints and devils . . . I've seen it all, man."

Satch takes a swig of strong lemonade, and lights a joint, "So, what can we find for you in Hollywood?"

"I don't know if I need a scientist, or a psychologist. Probably both."

"Can't help ya there, though I know some hip cats."

"You know, I performed in a film—they made me dress up in leopard skins, like *I wuz some kind of jive Sambo King nigga Savage.* Ridiculous. These papier-maché milquetoast sons of bitches. They're lost in an illusion of a schoolboy mirage. Just like these shoot em' up Westerns they can't get enough of. They want the myth. I looked around the set, and said: *damnnnn.* I've survived and come up out of the short-lived battlefield streets of poverty and death.

"Man, try to dress me up like a fool, but I'm going to look and play like a king. They paid us, so we just wink to each other and rise above to take something home to the family. I said facetiously: *look at all these dark bone-in-the-nose Negroes. Why there's enough outfitted spear-chuckers in here for a Tarrr-zan movie.* Seriously. The sad thing is—turns out they just did a Tarzan movie; the studio wanted something to do with all those funky costumes. It's not like they fabricate many options for us swarthier skinned folk. These corn-on-the-cob cocksuckers . . . I don't want to give them the satisfaction of their intended ignorance. Cast not thy pearls to swine, so let them fly like shooting stars.

"I know in my heart, and I've a big one, most folk are good, but sleaze rises to the top with business and power. The big lie gets peddled down the generations. How do we eradicate this ugly heritage? After hundreds of years? What does one have to do? To be a man? To be human? To be a damned American? If I let it get to me, the music's joy of life that's meant to melt the poison snares of bigotry away would crack me in half. The gold sound of my trumpet turn sour, buried in some back alley, so they could stamp out our spirit. No way.

"They prick you to see if you'll bleed. And if you bleed red. How far can they push you? And how much indignation can they foster until they infect you with enough of their hate to provoke your curses, and fight back, so they can throw you back in chains. Hang you from a tree of hate. Can you begin to comprehend how hard it is?"

Duke shakes his head.

"Grace under fire. Composure under pressure. The humiliation. The robbery of life and treasure. They crucify us with *their* sins. Even as they raise holy bibles of righteousness above you as you're beaten. Then they kneel in their churches with imagined halos glowing above their sugared blessedness.

"Pride? You can't swallow that much pride. You'll choke. You have to transcend it . . . Grow taller. So tall that they have to look up from under your shadow. Ring out a creative heroism: let free a new empowering music to toll and echo like a salvation to redeem and overcome the world. Bring us all together. Hope for the next generation.

"Man, it's a war. But we fight with love. And forgiveness. A light to shine upon all. Otherwise I'd be dead in the gutter years ago. So, from stage to stage, and on that film set, I hemmed and hammed, but played it cool. I looked up to the sky, and launched a sound as high as I could. Blasted some heaven into that Sahara harem of silly. Something that millions of folk have never known before. A holy shot heard and seen around the globe to uplift their flattened and bland earth.

"No matter how they portray and betray us, to sellout and demean, a man's integrity and dignity in oneself, culture and music don't lie. Stand tall. A song to boom louder than all their tinsel of din. But that's why I've tried to get out of this bad contract I'm in with Ratshaw. I sure as hell don't want to be signed up for this demeaning corny shit. I'll perform under my own terms, thank you very much.

"Damn Satch, I don't know what to say . . ."

"Now you know. My vision spans the horizon. Leaders will grow. Strong generations rise. And leave this skeletal legacy farm behind. Withered in the dust. Scattered to the winds. Well then. I should introduce you to my friend Sweets."

"Sweets?"

"Yup. Sweets Pistachio: how people know him by. Actually his name is Mickey. Mickey O'Donnelly. Most know *of* Mickey O'Donnelly, but don't know who he really is. So Mickey prefers to go about as Sweets. Influential cat. More like a lion—even a rhinoceros—what can I say?—the man is a zoo. Has connections, which can be useful to you—the both of us. Knows the big Hollywood producers. He's adept at playing the game. Was a boxing champ in his youth. Few dare want to tussle a Charleston rowdy-dow with him, no way no how."

"Swell, I don't have a clue what to do. I'm with you, Satch."

Episode 4

Sweets

A strange thing happened to me in my dream. I was rapt into the Seventh
Heaven. There sat all the gods assembled . . . I was granted the favor to have
one wish. "Do you wish for youth," said Mercury, "or for beauty, or power, or
a long life? . . . Choose, but only one thing!" For a moment I was at a loss.
Then I addressed the gods . . . "Most honorable contemporaries, I choose one
thing—that I may always have the laughter on my side." Not one god made an
answer, but all began to laugh. From this I concluded that my wish had been
granted . . . for it would surely have been inappropriate to answer gravely:
your wish has been granted.

— Either/Or Soren Kierkegaard

The boys head out from Bunker Hill to Sweets's office. A convulsion of over-
hanging cloud thunders above. A cascade of rain punches down as they
run in and enter a large hall filled with coffins.

"Satch, this a—funeral parlor!?"

"I don't know man. Mickey's always into something."

There's a shadowy aura of sinking inevitability when thrust into a room
of empty coffins.

It's hard not to unconsciously picture oneself in one. All this warm pulsing
blood and fuzzy sunshine, then bam. Closed shut forever underground, *as the worms
crawl in, the worms crawl out. In your gizzard* . . .

"I'm getting the creeps. This is too spooky," said The Suit.

"Hey, watch your language."

Satch sees Mickey Sweets behind a desk piled with paperwork and hollers:
"Hey heyyy, Pops. Could I get me one of these big ol' death boxes with some cozy
plush lining? And a Victrola stereo buried with me, like a Pharaoh?"

19

Sweets pierces his eyes momentarily pissed-off through the stacks of pulp paper, then grins wide.

"Louie? That you? That voice! Heyyy Louie? How in the Samhain are ya?"

Mickey "Sweets" O'Donnelly, this burly mountain of a man, shoots up and walks out greeting like lightning: "Hello hello hello. How long's it been? Where you're going you won't need some cheap record player. Choirs of angels will jam on a strum frenzy of harps. You'll be the first chair star in Saint Peter's orchestra. Heh, I just hope I'll be able to peer up and hear you once in a while from that blast furnace I'm headed for."

"Aw, come on Pops, you ain't so bad," said Armstrong.

"Bad?"

"Well, frankly, you are pretty bad. But I've seen a heck of a lot worse."

"You just be sure," said Sweets, "to play loud as hell so I can hear you down there. Won't be hell anymore. Archangel Gabriel will just have to sit down and hand you his horn."

Satch lets out a stream of chuckles and huge smiles. They shake hands and hug like bears.

Sweets is a powerful man. Like a retired football lineman ready to call shots in a huddle and *hut-hut-hut hike!*—steamrolling anyone out of his way. A rounded, rotund, big-bone muscle character. Bull-doggish. A squarish and angular, ruddy-featured, bullish frame. Built like a brick bulldozer. Thin dark hair with gray streaks slicked straight back with Dapper Dan Pomade. Slight protruding jowl cheeks. Stern, occupied, and business-like, given to jovial outbreaks of animation. The Suit thinks Sweets reminds him of an actor—Jonathan Winters.

"Heh," thundered Sweets, "You know damned well you don't need one of these," motioning to the coffins on display. "I expect you to play at my funeral, but you'll never die. And if you do manage to pass on, man—you'll just levitate off the ground. Swingin'! *And when the saints, go marchin' in, when those saints- go- marchin'- in—*"

They break into song: *"I want to be in that number . . . Ha ha ha."*

"What could I do you for Satch?"

"Sweets, it's been nuts, my friend."

"Brother, when hasn't it?"

"I'd like to introduce you to the Suit."

"What kinda name is Suit?"

"Call him Duke. Duke the Suit."

"Duke Suitor, pleasure to meet you, Mister Sweets." Duke puts out his hand and Mickey O'Donnelly grasps it to shake, almost crushing with the forceful bear-claw of a hold. Duke winces trying not to show he's in pain.

"Hmm, how tall are ya Duke? How much do you weigh? What's your favorite color? We have a fantastic model over here—"

"No no no no no, heh, he doesn't want a coffin," said Satch.

"Gee son. Could've fooled me. You look like hell," Sweets said solemnly. "You're all pale, and ghostly. Not too happy? Guessed you're in the market for one of these? It's perfectly understandable. Too many binges? Heroin? Best gal leave you cold? Plenty of fly-high floozies flirtin' around to lasso all tangled and ripped-off with. But heck, sick of it all? Pick out something cozy and custom you could rest comforted, where your remains shall lie under the earth, and leave this sad sad life behind, while everybody else parties."

Sweets slaps him hard on the back with Paul Bunyan hands and starts to guffaw: "Ahhh, aw hell. I'm just fuckin' with ya kid."

Duke giggles uncomfortably. He notices the hymn books are written by William Blake?

"Just be careful about The Cheeze."

"The . . . *Cheese?*" said Duke.

"Yeah, he's an upstart honcho from out New York: Frankie Witz. With *The Wizard of Oz* coming out soon he's indulged in calling himself *The Wiz*. He's a wizz alright. As if "wits" isn't enough of an obnoxious moniker cognomen. Frankie is given to self-aggrandizing hyperbole. Loves to rub elbows with the uppity hoighty-toighty upper-crust, just to show off he's one of them. At least, to convince himself and others he's one, hobnobbing that scene. Otherwise he's mucking-up some advertising scam for free press. Or sniffing around what's hot. He'll buy out a good idea and make a mess of it. He'll steal it. Pervert it. Or worse, if he doesn't like what it's about, or if he doesn't like you, he'll buy it just to shelve it, block it, and bury you. Real petty crap. Shamelessly sadistic."

"Holy shit," exclaimed Duke.

"That's right. Spiteful prick. And he's got some power. You'll know him by his platinum-like aura and overly-spotlighted charm. Always craving that attention, like a junkie. Top of the slime. Beware! Frankie *The Cheeze* really turns on the charm. Full of promises. It's exactly how such a sleaze slithered and insinuated himself to get a foothold where he's at. That's why paradise is full of snakes."

"Ain't that the truth," said Satch.

"He's in with lots of grifters, attention-getters, organized crime, arms dealers as well as German bankers and industrialists—besides the caravan of vulnerable actresses and green investors, suck-ups, sycophants, shysters—low types. A crowning narcissist piece of work of the first order. The worst part is the tabloids fawn over him since he makes good copy—loves to gossip, spread rumors, tell audacious lies about his exploits to make him look good, as he denigrates others.

"Sells lots of magazines. Even buys lots of advertising so he's in even more magazines. Craves reading about his favorite hero—himself. So he dishes out cash to private detectives and slime-ball reporters to dig up blackmail. If he's a wiz at one thing—it's blackmail.

"Sometimes he bids out important events so he receives all the attention. Real tough guy. So tough that during the big war his daddy pulled strings so he wouldn't have to go fight."

"What a schmuck," said Satch. "I played at one of his parties once. Never again. Didn't appreciate overhearing comments like "darkie," "sambo," "boy,'" and worse, being mulled about. Dandy Ratshaw's one of his henchmen."

"Yeah," said Mickey, "he's so racist he calls blackmail: whitemail. Ridiculous phrase. What an idiot. Cheezy."

"How come no one has taken him down?" asked Duke

"Damned good question," said Mickey. "I'm no saint, but Witz is just rotten. Beauty is skin deep, but brother—ugliness is to the bone. I'd knock him off myself, if I could. As I said, he has so much "whitemail" on people floating around that if someone tried to take him out, he'd take half of Hollywood down with him. You know—his nouveau riche *ala Louis XIV* interior style mansion doesn't even have any 'real' art—mostly mirrors everywhere. They say he even has a gold mirror above his bedroom on the ceiling. Creepy.

"Now, if you'll kindly excuse me," said Sweets, as he stretches and makes loud cracking sounds swiveling his neck, "It's going to be a long night. It's swell to meet up, but listen cats—I've got billing to go over, and a biiiiig contract to sell this evening. There'll be caretakers, I mean uh, caterers and cocktails. It'll be a swingin' time. Maybe you fellas drop by? Once I settle business, we'll chat about what's possible."

Mickey O'Donnelly steps up into a large pillowed coffin, and lays down and sighs. "In the meantime," he says, "I need to get some shut eye. Been up all night. Workin' on my damnation, heh heh. I'll see you gentleman later."

Sweets proceeds to roll over as he closes the coffin.

Duke looks over to Louis who just shrugs his shoulders.

Episode 5

Toxic Candy

They'll sell you black is really gray
The sun is just the moon at day.
When you stalk through silver malls
You get to hoard the glitter that falls.
Hell & Heaven: . . .   Fool, fool!
You've got to pay for the bleeding dancer.—

Hell & Heaven Black Blabbath

Satch & The Suit return that evening.

There's a pyramid of champagne glasses stacked from the base of the bar counter. Ice carvings. A sextet band plays Dixieland and Swing. Oddly enough, an entourage of Air Corps/Air Force Generals, medallioned with heavy brass, smile smugly and mix about, including a young pilot, Fletcher Prouty.

Duke feels uneasy.

Sweets comments to the guests, and makes an announcement for their undivided attention . . .

The band plays a Mahler Funeral March: dark, solemn, turning sour. Off key, in a scratchy, anxious, dissonant insistence. The brass section churn with a mournful wah wah of plunger mutes pitch shifting the tones: biblical-like, but for some ancient sacrificial feast for Mammon or Beelzebub, as they may play back in ol' Babylon.

Is that a Shofar horn? Why is there a pan flute, and antler whistles?

Then the group, like a struggling locomotive, chug and hoot, get corny, and jazz-it-up, to grind into a sexier undertone of sin, and dance when—

Suddenly all the coffins begin to open.

"Holy Fruck!" yelped the Suit.

He spins 180 degrees on his heels to run and smack—crashes into a startled waitress serving hor d'oeuvres. The silver plate of caviar, champagne and deviled eggs splatter over one of the V.I.P. guests who just strolled in with his entourage—the soiled VIP fires off an expletive laden tirade.

"Cock schmucking fuckler putz . . ."

Terror burns a hole in Duke's back. A knife slice of hot blood vessels are ready to burst. His suede shoes slip up frantic over the caviar to dive for the door. A strong arm pulls his collar from behind—up into the air—impeding his desperate escape, and he's yanked a few leaps backward.

Sweets shakes Duke and smacks him, "Whaaat the ffffuck is your problem? What's wrong with *you*? Just cool out. Look!"

The Suit, throttled and confused, glances in fright about the room. He begins to discern what the coffins reveal. A vision beyond expectation, as a cavalcade of provocatively attired dancing girls rise from their plush graves.

A gush of perfume breezes the parlor. Smoke. Sweat. Candy. And Sex.

A redhead in wet leather with a German officer's cap steps out of the Crimson coffin.

A brunette in black girdle and garters from the Gothic carved wood special.

A buxom blonde in pink lingerie steps out of the modern streamlined model coffin.

The Suit violently shudders and cringes. Cold sweat breaks out on his brow. They even look like some of the gals from the pool, my god! He's painfully excited,

"Ohhh no, not again."

He shambled to break free and escape.

"Hey! What's with you?" Mickey griped in a deep voice. "What are you? *Gaaay?*"

Louis steps in to smooth things over.

Mickey Sweets whispers a shout of: "Who the funk is this guy? He ain't right. Why'd you bring this character to my place? Don't need anyone givin' my joint atmosphere. I'm trying to transact business."

Sweets looks at the Well Dressed Man and says, "You ain't right. I'll take you to the back alley and *show you what it's like*. You make no sense at all."

"Sorry Sweets. My boy here has been through some unconscionable trauma," said Satch. "He'll be fine, right as rain. Won't you Suit? Let's fix you up with a drink. How 'bout a nice Martini? Look at all this. I've never seen anything like it. Hollywood! And the military? Ain't America just too much?"

Sweets doubtfully raises eyebrows at the startled Suit.

Satch goes on, "Well, to tell the truth, my friend here had a run in with Bette Davis, Joan Crawford and her debutantes . . . There was a big misunderstanding, and Bette took it personally. Quite the spectacle."

Mickey's jaw drops, and says, "*Bette Davis?* Holy Jehoshaphat. Why didn't you say so? That explains it. She's cool, but land on her bad side—and man . . . That lady crazed on some tangent will make you run from hot tail anytime."

Sweets placed his arm around Duke in a grinning bear hug and said, "Come on kid, let's get you some smoked salmon and filet mignon. And maybe a Plain Jane who won't slap you silly. I got this Gal in accounting, she's a librarian—perfect!"

A camera snapshot bulb zttts and pops. A smokey blaze of burnt light leaves spotted impressions. *Say cheese?* Duke & Mister V.I.P. are now splattered for the newspapers. Headline: *Devil Eggs On His Face!*

Someone from the entourage hollers, "Hey this is a private event. No pictures. Confiscate that damned camera."

The photographer speeds off and slips out the back door before anyone gets to him.

Another coffin starts to tremble. There's a muffled honk and scream. A half-clad gal jumps out, then a haggard top-hat with crazed eyes leaps to follow.

Harpo Marx streaks through like a comet and bumps another waiter's tray of devilled egg and oysters from behind which spills onto the injured guest who'd already been surreptitiously spoiled in schmutz.

The VIP curses louder and carries on, confronting Mickey, growling out his furious ire.

"Sweets! What kind of indignity is this? I come out here to this soiree in good faith to what's been promised as a spectacular fabulous event—and this is the respect I'm showered with? No respect. None. And they're taking pictures! Look at this suit. The best tailors made me this, customized to precision. The *best* tailors— IN *THE WORLD*. Do you know how many clams I shelled out of my hard-earned fortune for this magnificent suit? You don't want to know how many I paid. *That's how much I paid*. The best tailors. From Manhattan—made—me—this—suit. I'll sue. This is how you treat a valued guest with respect? Garbage. I was promised it would be FABULOUS. This isn't fabulous. Does this look fabulous to you?"

"No Sir, " responded Sweets, contrite, while gripping a red fist behind his back.

A braying bahahaha yelps by.

"And where the hell did this goat come from? Jezebel Christ on a cross, Sweets. Is this a party, or a zoo?"

"Well—not really."

The irate VIP further emphasizes the egg and caviar stains on his clothes as waiters and his entourage furiously scrub them off.

"Forgive me," attempted Sweets to conciliate, "as we were unaware of your arrival. Absolutely not the most intended, fabulous moment, Mister —"

"Look, I'm the biggest name here. Not just some performing monkey actor. Can you think of anyone bigger? With bigger money?"

"Well—"

"Nobody makes a fool out of me. Do ya hear me Sweets? Nobody! I'm nobody's fool. In school they used-ta put a dunce's cap on me. I was no dunce as I clearly saw they were making me a fool."

"Clearly, sir."

"So I finally got up and kicked the teacher in the groin. Boy, did she see stars. Knocked her right over, let me tell you. I felt good about that. It was a life-changing event. I knew from that day forward I was going to shape my destiny. No woman, educated, teacher, or whomsoever from that day onwards would put me down as inferior without reciprocity. Now, listen! If that picture gets out I'll look like a laughing stock. Heads will roll. My enemies will gloat and laugh at me. At my expense. Do you know how expensive that'll be? To my reputation? I'm a tough sonofabitch, but I'm a sensitive man as well—did you know that? There's gonna be a few rolling heads rolling down Sunset Boulevard, right into the sunset, and off the edge of the world. Goodbye! Believe me. I'm not to be laughed at. I'm no laughing matter, for newspaper pulp fodder or otherwise. I hate the press. Want to strangle 'em. They're supposed to make a great man look great, not like a clown! *Do ya hear me?*" yelled the V.I.P., gaining in volume.

"Uh, yeah. I hear ya. Loud and clearly."

"Do I look like a clown? Do I look like some kind of a frickin' clown baby to you?"

"No, probably not. Look, please Mister—"

"Am I amusing? Am I invited here to be made an amusement of? I'll crush your whole family. And you! Mr. Suit? I heard Bette D. and Joan Crawford yapping about your destructive escapades. Why, you're a subversive. A communist! Hanging with Marxists? You'll regret you were ever born. Believe me. I'll make you feel like you never were, will be, or want to be born. We'll make a film about you called: *It's A Horrible Life*."

The V.I.P. storms off. One of his gruff entourage looks at Satch and Duke, and gives a signaled double hex of fingered devil's horns pointing at them. Grins. Then heads out.

"Dandy Ratshaw? Sonofa—" said Satch.

Sweets calls after them, "I'll make it right *Mr. Witz*."

"Mister—*Witz*?" nervously asked Duke. "That's—?"

"Yep. That's The Cheeze. Frankie Witz. I didn't invite him, but he finds his way around . . . Whoa. You've really stepped in it son."

Episode 6

Heady Waters

What fools these mortals be.

—*Midsummer Night's Dream* Shakespeare

When *The Cheeze* storms out, an actress in the entourage quickly accosts Duke and pulls him aside.

"I must tell you something," she said, dripping with a milky irresistible radiance, and eyes that see right through him.

"You're Hedy Lamarr?"

"Yes—"

"You kinda invented wi-fi," he said.

"Yes, I do appreciate you understanding I'm more than a dressed up doll, but what on earth are you speaking of? This is crucially important. There's little time. I was at that pool party fiasco of yours."

"It wasn't really my party," Duke said.

"Of course, I know. It started off a nice solemn day to read up on philosophy, but that didn't pan out. Nevertheless, I observed what happened—"

"Really. I didn't notice you there," he said.

"Hmm," she expressed with mock disdain. "Ladies buried in books surrounded by swimsuits rarely do. Anyhow, please pay attention."

Respectfully, the Suit said, "You're like one of the most beautiful—"

"Sir, do you need me to slap you?" as she mockingly raised her hand to strike.

"No, no; apologies."

"None required. Well then. I understand something radically strange has befallen you. It defies the known laws of science (emphasis on known), but I have an inkling it has heavy consequences for you. For the whole world, and the metaphysical fabric of reality. And I don't mean Coco Chanel. Something has changed. You must be aware. The Nazis have been abusing scalar and ether conceptual models from Nikola Tesla to be used in fantastic weaponry and anti-gravity—while channeling dark forces of the occult."

"What?"

"Hedy!" shouted Dandy Ratshaw. "Time to *vamanoose*. The Rolls Royce is here. Witz is so steamed he kicked the chauffeur out and is driving himself. These publicity weasels took another picture, I punched the photographer out cold. Don't they know this is a free country? Let's go. Now!"

"Damnit, I'm no one's prize poodle, but they have me in a compromised vice for contracting . . . and I don't like it for a second. It's difficult to get in touch with me. Greta will know."

Dandy grabs her arm, a thousand words pass from her eyes, and they're off.

Duke zones into contemplative introversion as he leans on the bar and grabs a Martini.

Bug-eyed Peter Lorre and dashing Errol Flynn bring up the rear, cackling and smirking along together as they slosh their way off.

Sweets calls out: "Flynn, you're with this . . . crew?"

"Sweets, you madman. Not really. But it's a gas. You know I'm a Tasmanian Devil descended from Mutineers of the H.M.S. Bounty. Witz and his scene is all like a low-brow conundrum wrapped in a sticky paradox. There's always fodder for a brawl—beauty pageant contestants—*who really want to win*, gangsters, pimps, journalists, tycoons, posers, and unbridled comic mayhem. It's—repugnant," laughed Flynn. "I'm hooked."

Sweets replied: "Eh, America. Sounds too much like my high school days, but run by the crowned dunce Sleaze of Nevernever Land himself."

Peter Lorre interjects with a nasally German accent: "The Sleaze Cheeze?" and giggled. "Why, he's a great man! You know, the other day, he threw me in a corner, and said *I should've been a pair of ragged claws scurrying across floors of silent cheese? Hahaha.*"

Errol Flynn pats the guffawing Lorre on the back, and says: "Nay, pardon my erstwhile Euro-cultured companion. Actually, I heard Witz simply called you—a cockroach?"

"Wait till he finds out I'm a Jew!" laughed Lorre.

Flynn responds, "I think he did," as they bray and haw, holding one another up as they clink and throw back their drinks to exit.

Errol Flynn bids farewell, then turns back 'round and shouts: "Sending me a special delivery?"

Sweets stands at attention, slicks down a patch of out-of-place hair, and dutifully makes the salute of a two fingered Cub Scout.

"Heh, this town is brimming chock-full with fun Assholes," said Sweets. "Too bad too many big Asses run it. But alas poor Yorick—*mine's not to reason why. My lot is to do and die.*"

Later in the office, after the soiree evaporates, Sweets explains how he's schmoozing the military for war film contracts, etc. Apparently, the Cheeze wasn't invited, at least not by Mickey—but showed up anyhow, as is his *raison d'etre* to muscle his way into the limelight.

"Well," grumbled Sweets, "We're really gonna have to resolve this Frankie Witz issue."

"And Dandy Ratshaw," said Satch. "He cursed us with devil's horns—"

"Yeah. And that Dastardly Ratshaw," Sweets' iron fist slammed his desk like a bomb going off, and hollers something incoherent. Then he downed his whiskey: "In the meantime, what else is on your mind? I can't think straight about Frankie Witz until I hear from my people. Maybe I could still help? You said you have a screenplay? One good script can buy back some redemption from this mess—otherwise you have yourself one hell of an enemy to stab at you from every corner."

"Well, damn," said Duke, "I'm a big shot myself. It's like a tornado in a hurricane. Gimme a sec," as he worked on another Martini. "Well. Let me see. One idea I've had is a film about the life of Hypatia. She taught philosophy in ancient Alexandria, Egypt. Invented the astrolabe prototype, which of course opened the means for ships to navigate the oceans, triangulating coordinates by the stars. But the Christians accused her of paganism, assaulted her, smashed her skull, and scraped the flesh from her bones—"

"Nawp. Won't do," quipped Sweets. "Won't get past the censors."

"Right. I do have a screen adaptation of Flannery O'Connor's *Wise Blood*. Brilliant how she originally translates her influences of Conrad, Dostoyevsky, T.S. Eliot, into contemporary deep South America. At first I considered Ed Norton for the lead, but then there's Crispin Glover—either one is born to play the role of Hazel Motes. And Owen Wilson, if not Glover, could just as well make an outstanding Enoch Emery—kind of a foil to the Motes character. Great comic parts as Enoch is a museum guard who likes to stalk a woman after work at a pool, watching her from the park bushes; believes he has wise blood which tells him what to do; he converses with a deer in a painting; and finally gets stuck in a gorilla outfit."

"Ha! That's killer," responded Sweets. "But who the hell are Cristin Glovebox and Opie Wilson? Unknowns? Never mind. Less expensive to sell to the bigwigs at the studios. What's it about?"

"Right, I suppose those guys won't be available anyhow. It starts with Hazel Motes on a train. He's just returning from France and the horrors of World War I."

"Hold it, what do you mean: World War *One*?"

"Ah. I mean, The Great War! The *war to end all wars*. To be original we could add exposition that's not in the novel—adapted for cinema. There's numerous doorways to open space for creative play. For example: Hazel has a nightmare flashback of his platoon gasping from a nerve gas assault. He's the only one in the foxhole trench with a gas-mask. His comrades start asphyxiating from the chemicals. They claw at him for help, as blistering yellow pus and blood disintegrate their skin. They grasp and paw desperately at him. Hazel pushes them off as they convulse with shocking death. Then he wakes in the passenger car on his way home to Tennessee. Hazel looks tense as thin steel in a bell factory—enough to want to jump out the car—pull his skin off.

"Countryside and farmland zoom by the windows. The sun's drenched blood red behind a horizon of trees. Well darn, it'll probably be in black-and-white, so, maybe an inverted negative shot of a shining corona black sun.

"Hazel notices a large, flowery woman next to him who's been trying to share a conversation. Hazel is deaf in one ear. Speaks in a terse raw diction. He strains to listen to the annoying lady, uninterested, and simply responds in a scratchy drawn-out, cold, Southern drawl accent: *"I reckon you think you been redeemed?"* Which is a line he asks whomever he meets throughout the story.

"He's clothed in a black, wide-brim hat popular with preachers. A stone tie, and an odd blue suit, like Adam Sandler in *Punch Drunk Love*, or Jack at the beginning of the show *Lost*. Well, you wouldn't have seen that, but there's likely aspects of Nathaniel Hawthorne's *Young Goodman Brown* in all this to play up since Haze, like Brown, is directly challenged by the desperate existential questions of faith, religion, and evil confronting us every moment, as life flies by.

"Hazel Motes, like Brown, never smiles till the end of his days."

"Heavy," Mickey gruffed, pouring another glass of whiskey.

"So Haze begins his post-war journey of a new life by going to the pits of the city depicted as a wasteland: there's a bathroom stall with the mark of a serpent and the address of a whore (who he looks up)—there's a saturation of macabre representations: asking the price of a car and being told it's "Jesus nailed, " then driving down *Route 666* . . . There's a legion of swine in the road. Then, driving, he runs over his doppelganger double. He's in a small city surrounded by people described as: sour, frog-like, dogs, bats, and cadaverous, and their smiles like the blade of the grim reaper."

"The South sure sounds like Hollywood's America," quipped Sweets.

"Hazel has a vision: he perceives in the back of his mind an almost Gothic Jesus, following him in the woods, leaping above through the gnarled limbs from tree to tree ' . . . a wild and ragged figure motioning him to come into the dark . . .' —much like Kazantzakis, whose Christ describes God as an 'Abyss' who wants to push him over the edge.

"When Haze tries to escape to another town, he's stopped, as if there is no other town in the whole world. Trapped in a twilight zone limbo: maybe he really died in the war? Is he an example of post-war trauma? Condemned to a living circle of hell? A repeating cycle of Purgatory?

"Is Haze's tendency to constantly perceive sin, doubt, and evil among signs and folk around him, instead of goodness and redemption, part of his problem? Although *sin, doubt, unkind discourtesy, and evil* do gravitate to him in post-war America. In the bigger picture: is this becoming America's problem overall?

"Since Haze is hell-bent to find God by denying God, he creates a penance for his sins by placing crushed glass in his shoes. He only relates by identifying with darkness and suffering. Is it similar to the Hindu idea of the Left-hand path?—that the saint achieves God after seven reincarnations, but the sinner in only three since he is always *'thinking'* about God—exponentially confronted with consequences of his bad karma and sin—creating the suffering and friction that burns him quicker towards wisdom, and the need of redemption through the world of unquenchable desire and consequent pain? Whereas Sabbatai Zevi preached that only by committing copious sins and blasphemy would God be forced to return."

"Hell," responded Sweets, "where'd you find this kid Satch?"

"Another world."

"No doubt," agreed Sweets. "Son, at first, I didn't expect much from you, but you're Satch's friend, and you never know with you artist types—you're all a bit—inexplicable—out there. Eccentric."

"Certainly eccentric," Armstrong fondly and sternly responds.

"It's a bit deep for me," continued O'Donnely, "but I see where you're going with the script; it needs a nifty dash of editing. Jazz up the horror aspects of the conflict? Hey, make it during Halloween so you can have folks creeping about masked like frogs, devils and bats, as you say."

"Keen."

"Marketing! That's key. This is Holy Wood, not Paris. I'd recommend Paris, *but with those Nazi's mucking up Europe right now—it's not the safest of times* . . . Throw in some romance, tone down the abstracted symbolism—make it accessible—could be a decent flick. Maybe even a hit with the right director, crew, cast and backing. I'll chat up some of the producers around town and let you guys know."

"Wow. Thanks Sweets, you're something else," said Satch.

"Thank you Mr. O'Donnelly," said Duke. "Honestly, I—."

"You're welcome. Alright guys. I'm having hearses deliver some of these coffins," said Sweets. "T'will be a delivery job like no other. With some special surprises inside, as we speak. Ha. There'll be chocolates. Champagne. Lingerie. And someone wickedly sweet keeping those outfits warm. Won't our high-up military brass just love it? Hell, you can put all that in the flick too! Ho ho ho!"

Sweets, strikes a match, lights a cigar, and triumphantly watches the smoke fill the air.

Episode 7

Forking River

What is Africa to Me:

Copper sun or scarlet sea,

Jungle star or jungle track,

Strong bronzed men or regal black

Women from whose loins I sprang

When the birds of Eden sang?

One three centuries removed

From the scenes his father loved,

Spicy grove, cinnamon tree

—*What is Africa to me?* Countee Cullen

The silk steam of mist fogs across the river swamp.

Another time, a different world.

A teenage delinquent is solemnly rowed across, heading towards a hidden thatched hovel along a savannah that tributes out like a brackish tidal lagoon to the Mississippi Delta before ending in the Gulf of Mexico.

The teen clutches a wrapped object closer as the creeping tendrils of this night imprints and crowds into his ghostly imaginings of over-saturated and over stimulating perception.

Seamless, the boat drifts nearer. Old stumps spike up from the shallows. Duckweed and sawgrass clump through the marsh with Lizard Tail leaf in the silt.

Chimes haunt the air, and fill the space with vibrating waves. A Jew's Harp tangs and hums. A discordant rhythm of a Berimbau string twinge. Tambourines.

Pipes. The blur of a rusty harmonica bends and growls saws by. A slow drum: dropping beats from low, to high—to quiet. Then rising again. *Boop Bop bop bop bop-ah shhh. Boop bop bop bop bop-ah shhh.*

A chorus singing moans distant at their pyre. Frogs, crickets and owls drone among the mud and weeds, or perched on the hickory.

Spanish moss proliferates and hangs off limbs of tall cypress. Dank algae climb up the trunks. Muscadine entwines Myrtle.

The overgrowth of trees harkens back to DNA's scorched memory—spanning the Mesozoic and Eocene—burying sediment strata of fossilized fauna and bone from when the gargantuan reptiles roamed Earth.

One of their gnarled, scaly, green descendants floats by, as if out of the Cretaceous Era, startling the young man—who jumps and rocks the boat with a spasmed jolt—see-sawing from port-side to starboard—left to right, from the disturbance.

"Hey!"

His rowing companion giggles nervously, and immediately regrets having expressed any profane blasphemy after just stating: "The great hag will know. This Voodoo shit is real man."

How easily the circus of civilization recedes in this jungle devouring time. How does one reckon the incalculable age of millions of years? Even while entering the mysteries of the sorceress?

Long snout of teeth like a Basilosaurus skims by the river surface, and re-submerges.

"Careful! Ha, don't let these alligators spook you, Satchel," spoke the wiry rower, hefting the oars. "The queen—she will have a message for you. You can feel the emanation of her potent magic, like an ascending totem to be feared with veneration."

"Hope you're right, Miguel. Right now, I'd prefer downtown Battlefield New Orleans at midnight, or even the Lafayette Cemetery to this slither and snarl Hoodoo scene. You know—it's not too late to return. I think I hear my Mama callin' me back with a sixth sense of worry."

"Aw, c'mon, Satchel. We've come too far. This is too important not to miss. You're at a terrible juncture. The spirits would not be happy," as the growing dread in Miguel's face betrays his words.

"Well I don't know what to think. I'm even missing the Colored Waifs Home for juveniles they sent me after I got caught shooting pop's gun in the air for New Year's. Regrettably, I was a bit lit when I let you talk me into this shadowy witch-country trip, man. My spine is tingling with fierce heebie-jeebies, even if the spirits—*are* happy."

The crackling of the land seems to ask, as they glide the current, in this fertile spawning ground of evolution: Is each life a unique soul? A sparking neuron atom in the constelled buzzing mind of the god? An amalgamation of coded cells. Billions of souls in a galaxy of connections? So many, uncountably cascade, to populate the cosmos. Surely we are recycled in an economy of the second law of thermodynamics, to newly experience these myths of suffering, and the painful grace of brief joy before the stark chasm of amnesia engulfs us? The realized moment of no return. Death does not dissolve our bonds to all things, however powerful and inevitable the crushing jaw of darkness.

Hard to imagine a trillion disembodied souls sailing in orbit around a hollow empyrean throne, singing holy holy holy—Forever.

But anything is possible. No one has all the facts.

Knock!

The ferried craft bounces unbalanced with the uneven water flow. Knocks loudly reverb when the boat clawks against the staggered pier. The hollow clunking against wood girders—knocking for entry to the Stygian shore of the desolate night.

Twin pillars greet them at the dock crowned with painted skulls and talisman beads, candlelight flickers peeking out through their cavernous skull eyes.

A howling group crow and cry into the night, further off along the haunting woods, where participants ceremoniously shout entranced around ritual bonfires.

Groaning dirge and revel. Piercing flute of pipes. A stark refuge, summoning ancestors—far from legendary Timbuktu, far from the Sahara, Kilimanjaro or Serengeti.

"Bonsoir. Mise en garde! Alla prudence. Allez allez. Throw me the rope—s'il vous plaît mon ami," called out a haggard raspy man to them from the platform, staring bloodshot and animated from the landing. "Rapidement! *Le risque*"

The boat is tied and docked. A steel hand from the jutting promontory pulls them up, and warns: "Silence—she awaits you."

Pungency and sweetness sours their cautious inhalations. Hogs, steer, roosters, and goats roam the embankment.

A commanding voice beckons from inside: "Kristoff, let them come in."

Entering the temple hovel, Satchel meets the ominous personage of the Queen Mother Marguerite . . . She is burning brimstone to cleanse and purify their aether.

Austere and regal, her silken headdress wrap adorns her with wide loops of gold earrings.

Incense. Altars. Strings of tin and bells. Holy water. An azure statue of the Virgin Mary. Red and white candles. Spears. Dolls. Horns. Skeletons. Ivory. Ginger. Oil. Wine. Onion. Garlic. Cloves. Thyme.

A wise cat observes behind veils and feathers . . . Tribal figurines gnash and cry with loud quiet—gargoyle faces from Ghana, Senegal, Haiti, and Dahomey.

The Sorceress queen mixes Jimson weed, sulfur, and honey for a concoction boiling in her cauldron to extract under the auspicious conjunction of the full moon, Mars and Saturn.

Queen Mother Marguerite conjures the great Presence of Blackhawk: the warrior spirit who reigns across the heartland . . .

The sorceress slowly judges this young man. She rolls her eyes in trance and channeling. Serpent round her neck hisses cradled in her hand as its tail is twined round her phallic staff. She circles the man hypnotically to the beats pounding out the truths from the ancient earth.

The ritual outside grows louder. Wild lamentations split and cut into the wilderness. Cackled flecks of cinders popping up the belching flame.

The priestess Marguerite dances around her tall staff, spreading a white powder on her face for the possession of the dead.

Swaying, she blows the ash of powdered bone at Satchel. He is blinded a moment—brave but terrified—she continues her vulturing circulation with long strides and rhythmic steps. Breathing dragon-smoke through him, then spitting out rum in shooting sprays of releasing energy, placating the deities. A primal pantomime, a violent invocation.

The congas speed up, turbulently—more madly.

"Louie. I know you. I know you, Louie," she called out. "Your dream-self will be transmogrified. Just as evil is fought in the physical world, so evil is also opposed in the meta-physical realms merging invisibly about us. As above—so below. As within—as without.

"Clashes of unseen spirits, angels and demons inhabit astral planes which intersect layers of what we can and cannot perceive. Breaking through into communication and possession. Manifestations. Kula se ma mah'," breathing and exhaling more smoke into his aura.

Spellbound, knotting stomach, Satchel averts his frozen gaze from her piercing glare.

"Louie, you already possess a profound nurturing talent. Unfolding great destiny. You do not need charms and talismans from me. You! You are the living Tal-lis-man. You are blessed. You'll invoke the charm to enchant when you're truly born, and the time arrives. Kulu se' ma mah.

"However, I will bathe and anoint your instrument as an empowered amulet."

Marguerite takes the brass cornet Satchel is grasping from his chest.

"The potion will resonate from it into your dream-self. It will vibrate again through all your instruments. Your horn will help hold back the demonic titans from smashing this planet of lost Eden, at its verge and brink of doomsday. Many the world over will love your music. Few can ever comprehend its secret significance.

"You will sing to the Loa spirit to protect those who truly hear, as well as the innocent, and the guilty who need to be redeemed, or punished. It's channeling resonance will communicate its manifestations—an object of power to access and aid up the spiraling realms, and ages—its frequency will pitch and penetrate the higher and lower octaves of Being we do not hear, nor see—as a stranger one day will pass through a blast in an opened gateway. Your other self will help him, as he will help you.

"But, I must bless your dreams. As you will be a messenger of light to the world in the day. At night, the light will fight the darkening. There your soul and psyche will summon to combat these evils . . . As the portals will open . . . Kulu se' ma mah. Jah suis petit dei marquis."

Screaming. Conjuring. Tongues. Queen Marguerite unleashes in her revelatory chaos of ecstasy, raises a curved dagger. Speaks above her, then rips it down like a scythe across the throat of a black pig.

She slaps the blood of the fresh carcass across Louis' face: "Shindo la magie Loa maquita lalindo zalin malai malito, budei una goh spiritu nooma. Zha zind a vous zackra la clair la chantes esclavage liberte! Liberte esclavage afriqca amerika voo zha dei melodie. Hopita!"

Louis grimaces, eyes concentrate wider, and warms into the terror of the transcendent.

Marguerite works herself in a last ritual frenzy. Satchel discerns an ectoplasm of gods and goddesses dancing with her? A wrestling translucency. Merging. Building. Climaxing.

"Hecate glorio selah, hopita! Ibo! Mandingo! Invocarus hiiiigh hiiiiigh kristalgoslia remediah incantario Kalahari hiiiigh loa luminare!"

She grabs Louis by the shoulder and a severe pain shocks through him. He cries out and stares back with horror and wisdom, as if questioning this seeming cruel torrent.

"This is where the wound is! Diss is where she stabbed you! Marguerite and the Loas know."

Loosened and petrified, he's alerted to the wound where his abusive prostitute girl recently knifed him—his avenging mother had rushed out and almost choked the bitch to death. How close did the hand of wickedness strike forth—almost snuffing out the seed and treasure of his purpose?

"It will not be only your demise if you ignore your talent and slum it up in The Battlefield, pimping and scamming till it lowers you beyond redemption, once that levee protecting you breaks, but the whole world would suffer.

"Do you see? The devil wants you! He rages, a devouring beast for you. Wants your soul—and what a strong valuable soul it is. The Crossroad tests you. Be bold. Be brave!"

The holy smoke and transubstantiated liquor spays, smudges and tremors to the core of his awareness.

"Cells and molecules will never be the same," said the queen. "A shining light already exists and permeates, growing from you—which cannot be heard, but will ever bridge and transmit the radiance, to *exorcize* whatever shades of venomous hate and infections of bad juju that plague the world it chances to heal—however, I have opened the portal that frees this strength to elevate in mazes of astral dimensions.

"Prayers and acts of saints, shamans and songs of the chosen, hold back the catastrophes which would cannibalize all things if the deadly *Will* was not thwarted from an apocalypse of world-annihilating zombification."

The queen firmly twirls and spins him. Hitting his wound with her staff, spraying rum and smoke. The blood boils. The old cut burns, almost nerving a sharp thread to sting and strangle his heart. Then she points her staff and draws out a fire of pain, a gravity of hurt magnetized, drawing out the hideous clawing poison.

She swipes with fury at the noxious residue vaporing the air, to slash it to the ground—smashing this toxic entity, crushing it with her raging feet and staff.

A fever releases from Louis, he almost falls, and lands on a humbled knee. The insanity slows. A storm has passed.

Episode 8

Castled

There's an old saying . . . that says:

Fool me once, shame on —shame on you.

Fool me —you can't get fooled again.

—President George W. Bush

Frankie Witz, home, at *The Castle*.

There's a moat, rumored to be stocked with alligators. Highly illegal, though Witz pays the building inspector off.

Towers. Walls. A drawbridge over the moat. Witz bought up all the props from the last King Arthur and Robin Hood movies, besides enlisting his gangster pals to obtain extra building materials at cut-throat prices . . .

"Maury. Hold my calls."

"Yes, Mr. Witz."

"Unless it's William Randolph Hearst, or Herr Goebbles. Or a hot buxom blonde."

"Yes, Mr. Witz. Oh. A—uh, I did that thing you asked me."

"Excellent. Do you have the updated Friends List?

"Yes sir."

"I don't think you do, Maury. Don't think you do."

"Huh."

"Why'd I receive a call from the Lebrewski's? They're on the enemies list."

"Pardon me, sir. They were asking for Amanda Hugginkiss. Wasn't she here last week?"

"Jesus, Maury. You already know where all the bodies are kept. Do you want to be one of them?"

"Apologies, Mr. Witz."

"Sharpen-up, Maury. Prescott Bush?"

"On the Friends List."

"John Foster Dulles?"

"Friends List."

"Henry Ford? Joan Crawford? John Wayne? Eddie Mannix? The Schicklgrubers?"

"All on the Friends List."

"Ahhh, the Schicklgrubers always gave me the best apple strudel. The best. Globs of cinnamon. Mountains of glazed sugar. Doughy and gooey, such delights.

"How about Trumbo? Mankiewicz? Henry Wallace? The Lebrewskis?"

"Enemies List!"

"Outstanding! Be off now. I need my afternoon sunshine nap. And tell Consuela to stop putting out scented soap. I require unscented soap. And my hand towels rolled, not folded . . . otherwise, her and her whole illegal, sweaty brood will be sent back to the barrio gutters of Mexico City."

"Very good, Mr. Witz."

"Is that Suitor schmuck who bumped into and soiled me added on the Enemies List? Is my guy following up?"

"Of course, Mr. Witz."

"Didja get the papers? Anything good? Huh? Look at this crap. Who pays these people to write this impertinent trash? What do they teach them in these colleges?"

"Don't know at all, sir."

"All time high 'epidemic' of unemployment. Why can't these people find jobs? Make a business? Get a loan? And they want me to pay more taxes to solve it? Lazy bums. They should work as hard as I do . . . They'd cry if they knew how hard I work for my riches. Look at my wealth; why, I'm a job creator. That's my job. My brain is too damn big. Need lots of energy and fuel. Money helps. Whereas the bums are born to lose. I come from winners, not losers. Daddy scored a fortune on war bonds. He was like a prince. Now look at my own empire. That makes me an emperor. Maury. Did you know I'm an emperor?"

"Yes, Emperor Frankowitz. A great emperor. The biggest."

"Ha, I like that. Emperor Frankowitz. I'm so big they should be filming me all the time. I'm so amazing I should have my own show. My super wits—crowning this body—of an Adonis? C'mon. My own daily movie. The Big Me Show. No no, that sounds terrible. Too pompous. I'm not pompous. I'm great. The greatest. The Emperor Show. Yeah that's right. Hey. Let's get our pay-rolled news-guy, Chazz Mullroony, to spin me as emperor of Hollywood in the tabloids. We'll have a coronation ceremony at the big soiree. I'm already in a freakin' castle. And a king. Maury, what's bigger than a king?"

"An emperor."

"That's right. Look at the brain on Maury. My wits are rubbing off. There's hope for you. Yes. It will be a Roman theme. We can get D.W. Griffith to break out all that biblical paraphernalia from the studios. Gonna be huge. Speaking of huge, get me on the line with that fake millionaire getting less huge."

"Who?"

"C'mon. Roll with me here. Howard Hughes."

"Right. I get it now. That's why they call you the Wiz."

"Damn straight. Nothing crooked here. One dame said otherwise, and you know what happened to her? Now get that show-boating bandstander fuckler on the phone."

Maury dials up Howard on the telephone and hands it to Witz.

"Howie? Hi Howie. Do you know who this is?"

"You're kidding me," barked Howard. "How the hell did you get this number? Do you know how much I'm worth—by the minute? What momentous inspiration has prompted you to pontificate to me on this historic occasion?"

"Don't use your big words on me, Howard. My name is bigger than those ten-cent words. Gotta make yourself important, huh, tough guy?"

"Huh??"

"I saw that article you wrote about me."

"What article? I didn't write one. I've got more important things to do than examine and publish your . . . *accomplishments*," said Hughes.

"You published under a pseudonym. *Amonymously*," said Frankie Witz.

"*A- mon- y- mous- ly?* Yeah okay. Really now?" said Howard.

"It was unflattering. I'm profoundly unflattered. I know how jealous you are."

"Jealous?" said Mr. Hughes. "Heh. Is this where you micturate in my face and tell me it's raining?"

"Micta-what?"

"Piss."

"Ahhh, big Texas talk," scoffed Witz.

"Jesus, Witz—Jealous of what? You moronic Neanderthal. I'm the center stage of your nightly wet dreams. You wish you were me."

"Duh duh duh duh. You're so smug and stupid. But I've got your number, pal. Micta-rate huh? I don't micta-rate in anyone's face."

"Crankowitz. You over-sized child, I've heard otherwise. Especially if she's a brunette, hahahaha."

"Why you—fink. I'll have you finked so hard you'll be micta-rating in bottles. This must be about Hedy. You've seen me out and in the press with the most beautiful woman in the world. The MOST beautiful—"

"She's not that into you, Frankie boy. You promised to produce for her a real theatrical role for a change. Or is it blackmail? I know your secret, you Franken-penis."

"Yeah, what's that? You shmucking putz? You schtick fiddler."

"And I know where you came from," said Howard.

"From Germany. Proudly."

"From Poland. Poorly."

"How dare you. I'll sue for slander."

"You're a Kowsky, not a Wittenberger."

"Prove it," said Witz. "You're going down, like that Alamo from that ugly Texas of yours. You know what happened to the Alamo, Howie?"

"Well, aren't you one hyperbolic fatuous anus of historic proportions."

"Don't get all fancy and foreign on me," said Witz. "I may have gone to the best schools, but I didn't waste my time learning effete French, or how to speak like dead Romans. But I kick ass like Romans do."

"And party like one, you flatulent maroon. Do you have an encyclopedia?"

"Yeah, I have gold-leafed encyclopedias."

"Well, leaf through with your golden Midas little-fingered pages and look under: idiot. There's a huge picture of you. Period."

Witz's voice becomes low and flinty, like whispering gravel, at a cemetery trying to spark a campfire: "I'm going to take a giant dump on your grave. A huge steaming shit. The biggest turd ever. Right on your grave."

"Brilliant. Take a dump on me? Now you've truly out-under-classed your-self. You have a below zero threshold of honor, sir. The bank called and said your honor is depleted, Crankywitz ol'boy."

"My honor is bona fide."

"Bona fide as a queer steer. *You know I fly?* I've got a squadron of planes. I'm gonna bomb and dump fertilizer all over that nouveau riche fake castle of yours."

"Go ahead, I dare ya. I've got a 50 caliber machine gun, and a team of dirty Jew lawyers who say you don't have the sand to do it."

"Sure, sure. I know all about your . . . origins, and your parents. Your fa-ther laid a twisted dildo on an operating table, and then tied electrodes to lightning rods. The lightning sent a mild current of electricity into that dildo, and behold: you were created."

"I'll tell you what," said Witz. "I know what you do. You eat cocks. Cocks! And dicks! You muck fuckster."

"Bye bye, cranky Frankie boy. Tell your mashugana lawyers: flugal moy gushbloygen, you sonofabitch big man-baby. Adios. A DIOS A-MIGO, as we say in Texas."

"I'm calling my lawyers. I'll sue for a hundred million. You'll have zilch to squat on. You won't have a pot to pee in. I'll savage you. I'm a savage. I'm TarZan dammit. I'm frickin TARZAN. Do ya hear me Howie?" Witz screamed, turning red to green.

"Howie? Do you hear me? You hang up on me? Or run away? No one hangs me up. You chicken. Brock brock brock. That's what a Howie chicken cock a doodle-doos like. No one hangs up on me. That makes you: No One, you pam-pered egomaniac."

Emperor Frankowitz throws the phone across the room. Ka-clank. Thunk thud-ring—ka tink.

"Well, that was a pleasant exchange. Phew. The nerve of that guy. The gall stones! I'm so steamed I could— Geez I'm pissed. Piss in *his face* and tell him it's raining? He thinks I'd like that? That fuck-ling. It's sad. Ugly fuckling. I'm mad as hell, but—I ain't gonna be sad like that *preverted* abortion. I'm so furious I could— Watch this."

Frankie grabs a wad of paper and starts chewing it. He shapes a wet pellet, grabs a straw, and walks to the balcony. He leans over the railing to survey the gar-den. He sees Manuelo gardening below.

"Watch this." Witz expertly missiles a spit ball right on Manuel's neck.

Manuel shouts "Ay Carumba."

Maury titters, then shrugs his shoulders.

Frankie Witz wheezes and chortles with glee.

"I was a champion spit baller in school. Champion! I was so good they had to ship me to military school. Well that, and when I kicked that smartass bitch teacher in her gonads. She went to Princeton. She thought she was smart! Soooo smart. Ha. I was better off in military school . . . and did I look good in that uniform! Dolls loved it. But boy did they kick my ass there. Made a man of me. That's where I get my discipline from. Remember Maury, I'm nobody's fool."

"Nobody's fool! People are foolish to fool with you Mr. Witz."

"Oh, and tell Lizaveta—the new Mrs. Witz, that is, that I'm not cheap, but—5,000 roses will be far too many for the soiree. A thousand should be plenty. We'll need at least two hundred pies though: apple pie, blueberry pie, peach, and especially cherry and Boston Cream. Nobody goes pie-less at my party. Best pie in town."

Then Witz slams shut his gold-trim office door.

Maury scurries off to see what books he could cook while organizing the most recent materials, photos, documents, etc. from their thuggery of Private Eyes, to swindle and blackmail their way to their next contracts. Primarily, Maury's most important protocol is to lock any specialized papers up in the vault.

Unfortunately, after securing the safe, Maury left the key on Witz's counter.

Episode 9

High Marks

From the necessity of the divine nature must follow an infinite number of things in infinite ways—that is, all things which can fall within the sphere of infinite intellect . . . Hence it follows that God is the efficient cause of all that can fall within the sphere of an infinite intellect.

—*Proposition XVI* Spinoza

Duke wanders the neighborhoods of L.A.

Mind like a grinding wheel to grist through the chaos he's swept into—questioning his sanity, yet feeling rational and functional— though tortured by anxiety.

But it's more than anxiety. Something isn't right. As is if flesh is dissolving. The angst that this impossible chasm is devolving his soul spins him dizzy with terror until he grabs a stop sign and feels grounded again.

Then he's further torn by the sense of awe and wonder, crouching now at a hot curbstone, to rest before moving on.

He passes a bookstore; even this curiosity of detail mesmerizes him. Along the shelves, there are new author copies of Huxley, Joyce, Djuna Barnes, Tolkien. He can't resist snagging a stack.

From the window Duke spots a raggedy black top-hat over reddish goldilocks bop by the outside rack and snatch a comic book with a flash into his raincoat.

Duke quickly drops his stack of finds at the cashier's counter, without any dough, and shoots off zooming in to stalk and surveil the elusive Harpo Marx unnoticed.

Harpo antics and ambles along the street. He glides onto a tricycle laughing like it's a skateboard and honks his own horn.

A trolley bus trundles near. Harpo jumps on its runner. Duke trails behind on the other side of the car. Then Harpo leaps right into a hopscotch game, as girls swing a wide jump-rope. He lassos in and out. Flips through their roping—then tumble flops into a game of marbles.

He pulls out his prize Aggie marble. Licks his thumb to measure the breeze. Squints his eye, aims, and flick! Wins the bout, and takes the winnings like they're casino chips.

He greets a gang of rascals along the way.

Then whips out a flute. Starts fluttering some notes. The kids smarten up and give a cheer. He pulls chimes out of his trench coat and hands 'em out. There are finger cymbals and maracas. Opening his shirt he reveals a washboard, which he hands to a punk named Spanky wearing a propeller beanie hat, and gives the propeller a spin. Petey the dog communicates an approving yelp.

Harpo digs for a small xylophone and hands that to Stymie who's feeling sharp in a bowler derby and vest. Buckwheat, in a corn cob hat, gets a triangle. Alfalfa, wearing a starched shirt and bow-tie, and Violet in a flowery dress, get kazoos. Etc.

Harpo leads 'em off like a pied piper parade through sidewalks and back alleys before they embark into trails skirting the foothills that weave in between ghettos and mansions, kazooing and singing along.

"Holy smokes," Duke muttered, as he spotted Laurel and Hardy strolling from the other direction. Ollie starts to juke and jive and twirl Stan around, mixing up some Foxtrotting and dosey-doe square dancing, while they pass parallel with the jolly procession.

Reaching past the marchers' end, Stan turns and spins back in reverse to follow along with the inviting piping procession, trying to get an instrument to play. Suddenly Stan gets walloped from behind by Ollie:

"Hey, will you quit it? Honestly. Do you want to be late, again?"

Stan shrugs and scratches his wispy hair, and thereby resumes their original destination.

Sirens treble off in the distance.

Incredible. Duke is almost tempted to follow them instead, but he's already mesmerized on a mission to stick with the harping caravan.

This goes on merrily for a while. Harpo plays through John Phillip Sousa marches. Nursery rhyme tunes, sea shanties, classical ditties, changing up from *Yankee Doodle Went to Town* into *I'm a Yankee Doodle Dandy*, shifting themes sharply into Ukrainian folk-songs to *Ein Feisty Burg*. Finally revving up a crescendo of accompanying cacophony of swingin' bluesy pop tune melodies, whistling and piping *Flying Home*, *Honeysuckle Rose*, *Rhapsody in Blue*, and *Sweet Georgia Brown*.

Duke's astonished. He can't believe anything that's happening, but it's happening.

This is wild. He couldn't turn back if he tried. His suede shoes are getting scuffed and muddy, but just doesn't care.

They trudge and trudge, like some kind of quixotic trekking Canterbury pilgrimage on a children's crusade. Geez. Where's Harpo taking these kids?

Sloping down the geography of Hollywood hills into vistas of Los Angeles. He heard rumors about moguls abducting children for satanic ritualistic cannibalism, but, surely, this wasn't it?

The manicured lawns and the Archimedean terraces of sculptured horticulture, the quasi classical gardens. The Euro-villas and chalets, the ribbed masonry. The faux-Egyptian symmetry and obelisks and Tudor-angled roofing. The Art Deco facades. Terracotta tile. Rococo glass. Japanese pagodas and Arabian Orientalism down to the Samoan huts, past squatters and bums, and dust bowl Okies, and bungalows—the endless tall rows of sparse palm trees under undying sunny skies.

Eucalyptus and pepper trees line the roads. Spires. Canopies. Shiny automobiles. Ersatz nouveau-riche ornamented ostentation of contemporary pavilions, soon to be warmed up for the next party to spill out on hot pages of tomorrow's tabloids and riotous press scandals.

They trundle another rocky hill.

Finally, they come down to a clearing.

Chico looks up from a sprawling overgrown yard by a duck pond, "Heya, boss. Here he comes. Here. He. Comes! And guess who he brought along to dinner? Again!"

"Crackers almighty," exclaimed Groucho. "Why me, Lord? Why'd I have to be related to the biggest clown in town?"

"You could say that again boss."

"Aye, carumba."

"Biggest clown—in town?" sardonically asked Chico.

"You're not wrong—the nation," replied Groucho, then hollering out: "Harpo! What's wrong with you? We can't feed all these kids, however noble. We're trying to lay low. This is our hideout. That means we're supposed to be hiding. Not showing."

Harpo beckons, his hand motioning as to an unjust offense, and for Groucho to shoo and scurry off with his faithless condemnation. Harpo reaches into his coat and pulls out a loaf of stale bread. But wait, here's a loaf of less stale bread, and another loaf of fresh bread. Then he empties out strings of sausages, a roll of provolone cheese, tins of sardines, and anchovies.

"Hey gimme one," yelped Chico. "Always a barrel of happy surprises."

Harpo pulls up a fishing pole, miming that they'll also catch some fish to feed the lot for a feast, like out of some storybook scripture, then signals the kids inside to relax and have a game of cards.

Duke had been lingering behind. Groucho spots him.

"You? Ya finally found us. It's about time. What are we gonna do next? Boy was that Bette and her poolside harem furious. It's been a challenge to land work since. Why, do you know, she's had the audacious temerity to defame us across town? Even deriding us as Marxists! Can you believe that? What would give her that idea? Scurrilous. Geez. It's tough enough being impoverished and eccentric."

Chico adds: "And Jewish."

"What do you expect from a town founded on the honorable and virtuous pursuits of Real Estate, Railroads and Oil? Now, cinema," lamented Groucho. "Inoculated with a whiskey vat of cynicism . . . Look at California: stolen from Mexico . . . Have you heard the story of Queen Califia? No? Neither have I. Apparently she led an army of black amazon women warriors . . . fascinating. The Spanish named California after her, once they brought enough disease to kill the locals who'd been here for a thousand years.

"The biggest cities still sing with the named tongue of conquistadors and Sancho Panzas: San Diego, San Francisco, Los Angeles—a far cry from John Wayne Winthrop, and the Smiths and Joneses. I'll tell ya. But who am I to judge? The Spaniards stole it from the Natives, then the Mexicans claimed it, and America stole it from the Mexicans. You gotta be a professor, or a nut, to keep score. Isn't comedy more fun? Do you think God gave up some time ago?"

Chico sings out: "He's making a list. Checking it twice. Gonna find out who's naughty and nice . . ."

"When I read my first history books," said Groucho, "Yeah, I can read—it struck me stupid that this is just a record of who robbed what from whom. Then who gets killed or ripped-off from getting a good idea. And I thought growing up on 93rd Street New York was nuts. The mayhem has been snowballing for ages.

"And the one big book everyone professes, throws at ya, and preaches—the one with THOU SHALT NOT STEAL or KILL —no one listens to, yet swears by. Yet they beat you up for not believing it. Even killing each other over not following what they never follow which commands them *not to kill*. I can't get over it. Steal a country: rape and murder! Then throw this book at them, teaching not to rape and kill. Brother, it's too much for me. Well, you know what they say.

"Sometimes I'd sit in Central Park as a kid, and picture it, oh 300 years ago, playing cowboys and Indians. (Though, it was usually real live German bohunks chasing Hebrews.) I marveled how the 'White Man' bought that whole island of Manhattan for twenty-five dollars. Maybe they threw in some Rosary beads and a barrel of Bourbon. What a steal.

"Then there's Hollywood. What a joint. Another good name could've been Rainbow's End."

"Hey boss, that makes a great movie title. Even a song to go with it," said Chico.

"We shall. Shan't we? You know, we're just a block down from a cascade of mansions."

"Speaking of Hollywood," said Duke, "didn't the film industry begin with companies fleeing New Jersey since Thomas Edison owned the film patents, so he was reeling in all the kickbacks? Besides the fact he stole lots of patents from everyone else."

"That's what I'm talking about. Did you know they make magic wands out of holly wood trees?" said Chico. "Makes ya wonder." Sings: "Wonder and wand-er. Wand-er and wonder . . ."

"It's a freaky town," said Duke. "Magic is afoot."

"Here's an abandoned estate," said Groucho. "Moss and vine-covered, with a roomy enough guest house to crash in. Our hideout, as it were. Who could afford rent? Let alone settling for one of those overcrowded flats with no hot water, or any water for that matter. Insufferable. New York City was a battleground; it's war all over. At least it's warmer here. Poverty is bad enough, but this Depression is killing me.

"It's depressing," commented Chico, throwing down a second Ace of Spades, playing cards with Harpo and the Rascals.

"Yeah that's right, this depression is sour pits. That's why we joke all the time. If we didn't, can you imagine how goddamn miserable we'd be?"

Groucho leans forward to convey: "To be honest, half the time we're just plain silly. I can't figure out what's just silly funny, or silly stupid, from the comedy anymore. Lost track. It's a blur, in a blurry world. Even staying blurry gets expensive, especially with my friend Harvey."

"Harvey who?" said Duke.

"Wallbanger."

"Ahhh. Write it down," said Chico.

"So, we're covered by enough trees and sloping brush to shield us from being seen, but this sun is too much," said Groucho. "Do come inside? Shall we?"

Indoors there are Currier and Ives wallpaper prints. Calico upholstery on old couches. Some rocking chairs. A couple of tables.

"It's cool," said Duke, "like some secret rogue club for refugees of American pain, on the lam, yet drab and ghostly. Good enough."

"Take a gander around town," said Groucho. "Look in between the lines, behold this exodus desert of humanity. They're living in *abjectional* poverty."

"Don't you mean objectionable?"

"Well, that too," replied Groucho. "These narrow garrets. Soggy Bottomsville. Piss poor bungalows. Not a pot to piss in. Which is why I guess they call 'em piss poor."

"Is that where the name porridge comes in?" interjected Chico,

"Huh?"

"The food of the poor is the slop of *poorage*?" Chico said.

"Get outta here," barked Groucho, taking Duke by the sleeve: "Eh. All the jokes can't be good. Ya gotta expect that once in a while. Well, I'm no *entomologist*, but you may have a point there. Indeed. It's a Balkanized lot. Dens of vice and iniquity. And simple pauperism. Their crime? They lack pockets full of pennies from heaven. What a line, what a phrase, eh? Pennies from heaven? Only if there was such a thing?"

"Heaven is quite the pie in the sky," said Duke.

"No, I mean pockets full of pennies that came from heaven. Like Manna: bread that big-daddy Yahweh rained down to the wandering Israelites, which was white like Coriander seed, and tasted like a wafer made with honey. So they say. After Holy Moses split the Red Sea leaving Pharaoh and his chariot-racing thugs behind once the Hebrews made it across and the sea collapsed back, smashing and swallowing pharaoh up.

"He Brews a mighty sea," retorted Chico. "That's a why they calls it the Red Sea. From all the blood."

"Give that man a cigar."

Harpo leans over and grabs Groucho's cigar and hands it to Chico, maintaining his dexterous concentration on the game.

"No! Not my cigar," yelled Groucho, snagging his cigar back out of Chico's mouth. "These, guys, I tell ya. Never a dull second. It's exhausting. Anyways. I used to query Grandpa: Papa, *once the water was swept away, wasn't it muddy? How'd thousands of hobbling old and young slaves, and wagons get through all that mud?* I'd picture it. *Were there fish flopping around? Did they swipe 'em up and make leavened bagels and lox?* Boy he would swop me.

"Well, at least we didn't have anything to do with the Black Sea. Boy those Africans must've been upset," said Chico.

"Don't mind him, he was dropped on his head as a small child. We sometimes cut his fingernails off and smoke them. Me? I was dropped on my head—as a big child. No wonder you gentiles need Jesus. Look what Jehovah did to us? The chosen people! Chosen? We were made slaves to Egypt. Then the Assyrians. Then to Babylon. The Greeks. Then the Romans took over, desecrated the Temple, which was the beginning of the long exile and exodus throughout the world. Murderous pogroms in Russia and Germany for hundreds of years. Whereas, few realize, Christian kings were forbidden from lending money at interest, so they would coerce their Jewish subjects to do so, that's how we got a bad rap for usury. Then, when Jews were owed for their services, or if there was a disaster, it became convenient for the monarchs, sometimes having an itch or greed, would accuse Jews of corruption and evil, thus the king would steal our earnings or unleash a killing spree in the village. Now these Nazis? The tragic legacy of the Lord's chosen people. How much better is it for the unchosen?

"Grandpa used to joke how crude the Torah and Talmud were, in his emphatic Yiddish cadence: 'Julius! Jules, my boy. You think the Torah's bad? You-should see- what's in the Talmud!' Then he'd repeat it in a more rhythmic and faster higher register of additional emphasis: *'You should see what's in the Talmud!'* The unfunny part about that commanding exhortation was that he meant—*I shouldn't see what's in the Talmud.* Found that out the hard way."

"How so?" said Duke.

"I looked into the Talmud."

"What happened?"

"Grandpa almost knocked my block off. *You're not old enough* he chastised. I said you're cajoling and coaxing me to see the Talmud—then knocking me sideways for viewing what you told me to see?—when I go to see it? No wonder Jews are so commonly associated with that popular pathology of neurosis."

"You take the old roses, I'll give 'er the new roses," quipped Chico.

"Well, it's a human dilemma. That was my earliest education into the dizziness known as religion, metaphor, sarcasm, and irony—which multiplies up to cynicism.

"Heavens, I thought: Don't I have something to look forward to? Once I can get my hands on that darn Talmud. Boy oh boy. These adults, I thought, they're really something. I have to become one, one day? Good luck. They didn't make any sense. Heck, they still don't make any sense. And look at me. I'm supposed to be an adult? I hardly make sense to myself, or to anyone else for that matter—besides the fact of being stuck with these guys all day.

"Religion! So. Here's something that's revered with the most sanctified reverence, pomp, and profundity, of our traditions, culture, Civilization! Then it's treated like some kind of forbidden pornography."

"Or the way people treat Marxism," said Duke.

"You can say that again. Ain't that a kick in the ass? *Hey, watch it.* Ain't it though? No wonder all unpersuaded denominations are so mixed up. When Grandpa really got on a roll he'd talk about Chapter 38 in the Book of Genesis. Sometimes when us kids would get riled up, which was daily, he'd kvetch and holler: *Oy vey iz mir. You should all get Onanized!* We never knew what that meant. Mama Minnie, I'd ask, what's papa mean? By *Onan-ized?* She'd get frantic and roll her eyes, and cross herself." Well, let's just say ix nay on the ox nay has to do with spilling seed.

"Hold on. She was Catholic?"

"She *wasn't* Catholic. That's how bad getting Onanized was!" as Groucho motions the sign of the cross backwards. "Well, what do you expect from a story that begins with Adam & Eve naked in a garden with a serpent and an apple? Well, I'd tell you about Onan and Chapter 38, but, there's kids present. Remind me another time.

"Nevertheless, it gets better. Can you imagine being a child and hearing the story of Abraham and Isaac? The fiery lord of brimstone Jehovah orders Abraham to the mountain to sacrifice his only son—and get this—Abraham is 90 years old. His wife Sarah was barren her whole life, and now she's a ripe 80 or so? So he's 'commanded' to fornicate and copulate with their young, vivacious bond-slave Hagar, whose progeny starts the Canaanites or Arabs . . . Arabs and Jews have had no end of conflict since. But the kid went wild. Sarah was jealous; it just didn't work out too well.

"You'd think God Almighty, with his foresight and omnipotence, would say: *Hey, Abe, don't do that! Bad idea. People are messed up as it is. I already murdered everyone on earth, except Noah, with the flood, and I'll burn everyone else at the end, before they burn in hell. Though I truly love my creation.* But I'm getting ahead of myself here. What's prophecy for? *Let's avoid thousands of years of this trouble in the future. Hey, that's why they call me God. Take my advice, please! I'm the Supreme Master of the Universe . . .* Right? We would think. Anyhow, God says: *I'm gonna give you guys a child, though you're old enough for great great grandkids.*"

Chico looks above and motions for everyone to move the table further away.

"Hey, where you goin'?" asked Groucho.

"To avoid the lightning," responded Chico, then crossed himself.

"My God, I thought: I'm the chosen one? Terrific! So were all those other crazy characters in the Bible. And look what happened to them? Abel? The first chosen one—murdered. Samson, blinded. Joseph—thrown into a well by his dear brothers, Daniel and the lions. And how about Lot fleeing Sodom and Gomorrah? That's a hell of a story. The Jewish tribes were ever in bondage and persecution throughout history . . . Don't even get me started on the Book of Job—we'll be here all night. Even Christ, whom they claim as Hebrew (at least on his mother's side), and look how things turned out for him? Besides the tribulations of our 'chosen' tribe in bondage and persecution, especially since they crucified that poor innocent Jesus? He only wanted to help people, as far as I can tell.

"Maybe, deep inside, people sense and resent that we 'invented' this complicated ambiguous Bible to make their lives miserable? Ever see a happy bachelor? A married couple ribs him that he needs a bride—'bachelorhood, it's not for you!' Why? So he also can experience the unhappy sanctification of matrimony just as they are too.

"Religious wars, inquisitions, persecutions. All the guilt, murder, and misery, etc. Then they're mad 'we' killed the messiah, or so they think and blame us. The Romans did the crucifying, and they became the church! Talk about obfuscating the blame. Then they're mad we didn't become Christians. What's the fuss, Gus? It's too much for me. Where's Harvey?"

"But if Jesus wasn't killed, how could he have died for our sins, conquered death to redeem the world? So they say," asked Duke.

"Exactly! Thank you Judas! You need a Wallbanger too. It's a mindbender. Logic. Unless you teach kids something like, I don't know, basic Aristotle, Plato and especially Wittgenstein — we're done for. Despite the silliness, I'm not trying to make light of the subject."

Thunder crackles above. Chico looks at Groucho.

"Don't say it," said Groucho. "Anyhow, back to the trip to the rock with Grandpa Abe and myself as the chosen one? It clearly reminded me of the Abraham and Isaac story. So it hit me like a shekel ton of bricks. Just us, hiking up to the park on the rock cliff, the chosen one? With Abe? I've been chosen! I'm Isaac!

"Grandpa was always ruminating about the need to make sacrifices. Well? It occurred to me, I was it! I was terrified. I ran and hid. He chased me all over the tenement. Then all around the park. He gripped me like iron. I thought I was a goner for sure every time we had to go somewhere."

"True or not, as I got older, I realized, Christ! I love my family, but these Jews are crazy! And I gotta be one? Proud, but skeptical. Now I thought I knew why the neighborhood beat us up: *Hey! Look!* Here comes one of those nutty Jew bastards. The chosen people. Get 'em! But *if everyone got what they deserved—who'd escape whipping?* It's hypocrisy all around. Confusion versus confusion. Who can win?"

"I'm rather perplexed that more Jews aren't great athletes," said Chico.

"How so?"

"Since we gotta run away from getting beat up, hunted or thrown out of countries all the time," said Chico, raising a glass to cheers: l'chaim.

"That's why we got to be doctors, professors and lawyers. Someone has to heal these beaten-up Jews and defend them in court. Look at poor Adolph," said Groucho

"Adolph?"

"Harpo, I mean. Good thing we changed that name. Well. When he was in Second Grade he used to get thrown out of school all the time."

"Why, he was a troublemaker?"

Harpo looks up to make a face, snubbing his nose and puffing out his cheeks, tongue, and other obscene gestures.

"No no no. Literally. Because he was a scrawny Jew runt. When the teacher turned her back, two big Irisher kids would grab him, then toss him out the window."

"Holy shit."

"And how, that's some shit that's holy. Good thing the ground floor wasn't too high off the ground. He'd dust himself off and creep back in. The teacher thought he always had to go to the bathroom. He didn't want to squeal and get beaten-up worse. So. One day they tossed him out after Ma knit him a new red turtleneck. They pulled it over his head and snagged the yearn as he fell out. Half the sweater was gone by the time he got to the door as the string trailed behind him. He said that's it. That was the end of the second grade, and his education in life began. And what an education. He had quite a childhood, but didn't really get to be a child, so, look at him now.

"But he got tougher. Klutzing and kibitzing his way through the neighborhood. Losing one, or two jobs at a time. The only job he got fired from that wasn't his fault, was when his boss was drunk and informed him he had to challenge the office next door to a kicking contest."

"What?"

"Yeah, whoever kicked the highest wouldn't have to pay the rent. Harpo, at five foot two at the time, you can conjugate what happened. Bunch of Shylock meshuggeners everywhere you go, and boy were we Shylocked."

"Hey, that gives me an idea," said Duke.

"Terrific, just be careful: if you give Chico an idea he'll steal it. If you give Harpo an idea he'll run away with it."

"Isn't that stealing?"

"No, he'll play with it for awhile, but he'll return it to ya later."

"Well, what if I wrote a script for you guys? We'll call it the story of *Shylock* Holmes?"

"I like it. I like it, tell me more. I see the possibilities. A whole playground of contexts."

"You'll be the Jewish Sherlock Holmes. Except half your sleuthing will be a cover front for a Shylock business: lending and loan-sharking money at excessive rates of interest. The problem is: you really want to help people, so you're losing more money than making it."

"Hot damn, that's grand," said Groucho. "I can see where you're going with this."

Chico perks up and says, "Deal me in . . . "

"Chico will be Watson. Or Witzon, no. Wattzowitz."

"Wattzowitz, that works. Perfect. What about Harpo here?"

Harpo takes off his top hat and imploringly projects a sad grin.

"Harpo will be—your other brother Wattzowitz."

"Capital! The sleuthing office of Shylock, Wattzowitz & Wattzowitz."

"Hey," said Chico, "you lose'ah your money, and come to us, and we'll help ya lose more of your money. Heck, we should be doing that now. Ain't that right, Taco?"

Harpo winks and chortles back.

"Maybe you're right, sonny, maybe you're right. Well, we'd only be scamming on the crooks. But they'd find out and want to kill us!"

"Exactly."

"Who ya callin' 'sonny'?" said Chico.

"Pardon moi, si vous plait, you are correct sir. Age before beauty. You wouldn't think so, but I'm the youngest. Though the most mature."

"Heh."

"Well, ya gotta grow up fast in this family," said Groucho. "What would you nutty pikers do without me? Ya'd be schlepping your asses around then plotzing all over the place."

"Heya, you do your own share of plotzing."

"You mind your own business and leave my plotzing out of this," said Groucho. "Alright, you know how it is. Hey, how can you tell a schlemiel from a shlimazel and a schmendrick? They all go for a ride: the schmendrick crashes the shlimazel's car, and the schlemiel apologizes."

"Sounds like a few guys I know. You're a real shagatz," said Chico.

"Shagging this, shagging that," said Groucho, "You don't even know which way you're shagging or shugging? Eyn umglik iz far im veynik. *One misfortune is far too few for him.*"

"Lakhn zoler mit yashtherkes. *He should laugh with lizards,*" said Chico.

"What the hell does that even mean?" asked Duke.

"Funny," said Groucho, "that's what I always say. But I like it. Who makes this stuff up? Jews do. Just like the Bible. Freudianism, Swingism with Benny Goodman, Marxism—thank you, and that quantum relativity cosmic jargonography with Einstein—"

"You mean Jargonology," said Chico.

"Right. Whatever," said Groucho, "And don't forget that wisenheimer Spinoza."

"Don't be spinning your nose at me," said Chico.

"Is any of it real? It's pretty hifalutin stuff. Nobody knows."

"That's right, Pops, nobody knows, round and round she goes. Wherever she stops, ya get a wallop with a rubber hose," said Chico.

"Yep, he does laugh with lizards, and he should," said Groucho. "What would the world do without us? But hey, nifty script idea, but ironic as it is, the Jews who run Hollywood wouldn't go for it. It's too ethnic. Even as it plays to a stereotype, which we'd try to play off and tear up. In the early days of film they'd screen lots of unflattering bigoted portrayals. Hypocrites. Maybe there's hope for the future?"

"It's a damn shame," said Duke.

"Another kick in the ass."

"You know what's crazier than what Jews make up?" joked Duke. "The stuff people make up about the Jews."

"Ha, you should read *The Protocols of the Elders of Zion* sometime," said Groucho, " Though it sounds like you may already have. I mean, you shouldn't, but you know what they say."

"Well, I gotta run, guys. It's been swell. If I find some first-rate work that needs to go sideways—I'll definitely give a call."

Episode 10

Tea Palace

Find meat on bones that soon have none
And drink in the two milked crags
The merriest marrow and the dregs
Before the ladies breasts are hags
And the limbs are torn . . .
when the ladies are cold as stone . . .

Rebel against the binding moon
And the parliament . . . autocracy
 of night and day,
Dictatorship of sun . . .
Rebel against the flesh and bone . . .
And the maggot no man can slay.

—Dylan Thomas

Young Hedy had been quite cushioned with her new husband's estate in Austria, several years back.

For all this elaborate opulence, bathing in the night and day glow of wealth and elegance—she felt cheated.

Life is pulsing by in a brave new world of technology, culture, theater, youth, and cinema—while she lingers, sidelined; an exotic prize in the ostensible prison of a magnificent dollhouse. And so young.

Fritz's castle, her home, Schloss Schwarzenau, resides in the woods and hills of the outer Niederosterreich in Lower Austria. Surely, inexperience didn't prepare her judgment for this state of affairs. A caged bird in a paradise, and only at the mature age of eighteen!

Hedy yearned to return to acting. She loved it. And she could be great. Not rather stuck here in an almost real life role as Henrik Ibsen's *Hedda Gabler*, a sleeping beauty in this grand glass mausoleum.

The Prince Charming, Freidrich Fritz Mandl, found that the slipper fit, after his earnest pursuit and courting—but not the heart, mind nor soul.

She'd performed under Reinhardt and Granovsky, but had quite a break when discovered by Gustav Machaty to take the lead role in a Czech film *Ekstase*—filled with its Freudian symbolism of acts of desire, then censored from their actual portrayal, although the shortening of skirts was in vogue.

In fact, despite being a minor at the time, Hedy's movie spot was the earliest first feature film to reveal the glory of naked breasts.

Fritz could never seem to get over this, not the breasts, but that his wife's are nakedly flaunted on celluloid for millions to see—and he, a powerful man!

Fritz's armament factories were vast, from Hirtenberg, Ronsdorf, Weimar, Meiningen, Wiener Neustadt, to the Wollersdorfer cartridge factory . . . he manufactured Mauser Rifles and bullets for the Austrian fascist Heimwehr, as well as helping to rearm Adolf Hitler's Germany . . .

As the new sense of romantic freedom spread with social change, even the prevalence of prostitution declined as an outlet. Couples of the new youth culture generation gained more access to admire and play with one another. The receding pall of Victorianism and the cumbersome buffers of repressive tradition dispersed with the past, launching into the motorcar cigarette speeding future, and the harbinger of radio spirit frequencies blasting the airwaves like magic.

Fritz was actually the third richest man in Austria as a prominent arms dealer: factories all over Europe, and lucrative international contracts, the aristocratic elites of generals and state ministers knew him well. What could such a powerful man of influence desire? Why nothing less than the most beautiful woman in the world, (and her tits strictly for himself).

For many who've asked, what did the face look like of Helen who launched a thousand ships to Troy—it would be Hedy's.

Fritz wooed her, and made her his.

After all of his dashing overtures of strength and gentlemanly intelligence—once in his matrimonial household—Hedy was forbidden to enjoy her career. He perceives her as being raised up into the solid heights of a fairy tale; contrarily, she's fretting over what good is all the money in the world, if—?

Hedy notices Fritz haggling on the phone again.

"Gustav, listen to me!" commanded Fritz. "If they have a cache of copies of Hedy's film, then buy them. I know I've spent millions already. What's the point of investing all that if there are still copies of her lush naked supple young mammaries for thousands of salivating men to see and lust over? Intolerable. Mein Gott! Macht schnell!"

Fritz slams the phone.

"Honestly, Fritz," said Hedy, and saunters away.

Palaces, yachts, jewels, furs—a silver-plated dream that bred unhappiness. *What's the cost of such things*, she contemplated. And what's the moral source of such riches, at its core? Warehouses filled with weapons shipped to armies . . . Who did it all affect and harm?

Even while she perches, herself, a pet on a diamond leash, tighter and tighter.

Those large classical eyes peering through a living Greek statue's porcelain skin. Breathtaking glimmer of vision illuminates when entering a room. Blithe, glamorous, milky silk, and a wickedly brilliant mind for the sciences, mechanics and for invention . . .

Hedy speaks to herself in the gold embroidered mirror: "My beauty brought me here," she pondered. "Now I'm bought; I'm unable to leave. Look what beauty does? It's a commodity. I'm an object. A gilded smiling mannequin awash in gauzy hair and flowing gowns and ornaments. God, I'm sick of it. Some fairy-tale."

Though the dense legacy of Grimm's fables creeps amid the surrounding forests of wolves, dwarves, ovens, and children devoured by witches presages a more accurate life of drama and imperfection than does the Disneyfied Cinderella. The original, unfiltered fairy tales certainly did not always have happy endings.

Now, after two delirious decades of peace, and rapid social/technological developments, few imagine how horrible the next European political war storm brewing will leave a tornado of graveyards across the sleepy bourgeois world, between peasant and aristocrat. Everything is speeding up, including Werner von Braun's blueprints for a new pilotless rocket to blow up enemy factories, churches, schools, hospitals, and homes.

Grimm's nightmares . . . Hedy's intuitive drive to escape is viscerally palpable.

"Oh darling," reminded Fritz, from down the hall, "Remember, Benito Mussolini is coming to dinner."

"Schisser."

All day she paced and mulled over her ugly dilemma.

"Whether I'm a star, a princess or a laundress, no sane, decent person should share a table with that demented pig and murderous bully. Mussolini. This blowhard Nero-Nimrod. This parading clown. He's a butcher. Here? How grotesque.

"How do I look into his snide face and not splash a pot of hot coffee all over his pompous ostrich feathered uniform? And curse him for murdering how many Ethiopian children and families? For his new Roman Empire? A sick joke. And Fritz, my own husband, invites this monster into our home? It's disgusting. Unbearable. The Rubicon of my heart's patience has long crossed and passed. I've got to get out. This is it."

She adorned herself in all the jewelry she could wear. A good excuse to say she's showing off "how much her husband loves her. " She stashes the rest of her valuables in one of their maid's uniforms that's just the right fit.

Hedy stares in the mirror. She knows this is a grand performance. The most important one in all her life. She can pull it off. These damned clowns.

It's time to head down to dinner. Before dessert, and lots of good wine and cognac have been served, she'll excuse herself due to illness, then make a quick change of clothing, and skip out to the train station . . .

Episode 11

Bone's Alley

I've known rivers ancient as the world and older than the

flow of human blood in human veins . . .

I bathed in the Euphrates when dawns were young.

I built my hut near the Congo and it lulled me to sleep.

I looked upon the Nile and raised the pyramids above it.

I heard the singing of the Mississippi when Abe Lincoln

went down to New Orleans, and I've seen its muddy

bosom turns all golden in the sunset . . .

My soul has grown deep like the rivers.

—Langston Hughes[2]

"I'm not fond of the idea of being visited with a baseball bat as an emblem of negotiation? And persuasion? Mr. Mugsby," grumbled an indignant Satch.

"Listen, Armstrong," grated back the flinty baritone, "You're on a contract and I'm here as the muscle to see that you follow through," said the pugnacious thug, in a fat overcoat which cloaked other weapons to be sure.

The narrow dressing room grows claustrophobic. He can smell the killer's mix of sweat and aftershave. He calls him Mugsby in jest, but knows the notorious knave he's dealing with.

A loose bulb *zitts* on and off, like his flickering heartbeat caught ambushed in this turmoil of danger and outrage from Dandy Ratshaw, in the not-too-distant past.

---

[2] The Negro Speaks of Rivers

"Louie, as I possess a signed copy of the document, you are clearly committed to fulfilling your obligations. Otherwise, unsavory repercussions shalt follow. Do you know what that pertains to? In English?"

"Yes, I may be black, but I'm familiar with the language."

"Then, if you'd prefer not to be black and blue—on your way into the red, I'd heed this succinct communication translated into business terms as: Very. Bad. Things. To punctuate it, bluntly."

Doubtless, not a dint or dime of placation will ameliorate this beast hawking him.

Satch has an obtuse thought about Al Capone, who dug Satch's show at Chicago's South Side Savoy Club, where he blasted through 30 choruses of *West End Blues*. Capone would rock to shreds these other mobster upstarts who spin through a revolving door like clockwork, lining up to compete as next in a jostling-line to hassle him. But quickly dismisses the fantasy, since he would thereby forever be beholden to an uncompromising criminal Titan top-dog like Capone.

From frying pan to fire. Nevertheless, Ratshaw is more than just the typical gangster knucklehead.

Seems one has to sell one's soul once cornered into the spotlight, and coerced into a prop golden idol instead of a happy and free ambassador of entertainment.

As the Karnofskys used to say, he felt like he was going to Kvetch, as he caressed the Star of David on his lapel, which he kept in memory of their kind support from when he was an impoverished child. They hired and fed him—gifted him his first trumpet, *"Dear Jesus and Jehovah dancing on the mountaintop."*

God bless the Karnofskys.

He wanted to finish practicing through some Mozart and Beethoven, then having fun with the gang, getting drinks, some smoke and Chop Suey.

"This is America, damnit," he thought to himself. "But I know far too well the true history. If it isn't the British Empire, slavery, the taxmen, divorce, Jim Crowe, or the Ku Klux Klan—it's the mob and managers—life is tragic enough without having to contend with a cold shakedown between every corner.

"Throw forth your hard-wrought crafted pearls of talent to glow on stage, and the swine hound your treasure right out from under you.

"God Almighty, I'm not some snot-nosed punk trippin' over his shoelaces. These transgressions are downright humiliating."

The greatest musician, among the most significant innovators and fount of influence, of all modern music—echoing through records, radios, films and performances—affecting all of civilization and consciousness . . . And he has to swallow whatever gumption he can muster to capitulate, and pray to higher powers above for safe passage through this dirty maelstrom and gauntlet of hustling blackmail.

"The world is one hell of an amusement ride. After artfully dodging the snares and pitfalls of impoverished streets and cannibal blades . . . ain't this a shame? Husked and shirked like a two-bit mutt. Mercy must get us through.

"The big money world of bright lights, tuxedos, gloss, glitz, and plasticity just has bigger cannibals of havoc—they're just more well-dressed. From the penthouse to the White House. Ain't that some shit."

"You're knee deep, Louie. A wrong step further and its neck deep in a sinking precipice."

"Son of a bitch," Louis sighed.

Episode 11 B

Foxtrotsky Red Slips For Pinkos

I see Red. And it hurts my head.
Guess it must be something that I read . . .

Thinking about the overhead. The underfed.
Couldn't we talk about something else instead?
We've got Mars on the horizon ... A pair of dancing shoes.
The Soviets are the blues.

The Reds. Under your bed. Lying in the darkness.

Dead ahead.

—*Red Lenses* Rush[3]

Duke maneuvers into the backroom of Musso's Bar on the boulevard, sleuthing about to get a pulse on things.

The whole miasma of legal artillery feints and battles had been heating up between the SWG Screen Writers' Guild and the Hollywood moguls who owned the studios and their hierarchy of producers, directors, managers, lawyers, investors, and politicians. All lined up, like an army, to crush the unionizing efforts for a fair distribution of the titanic wealth that cashed into their coffers for all who labored at the studios, besides the ring-leading writers who went with it, embittered to be wrung by the nose.

Through the static, a radio station tunes in at the bar . . . "Ladies and gentlemen, welcome to *The Paul Revere Hour* with Normal Rockwell. Thank you for so duteously tuning in, my ever-gracious stalwart citizens. My dear, fellow Americans.

"As our great nation tries to rise from the swamps of depression, we are darkly besieged and attacked from within. How can we overcome our venial sins when we are burdened by a generation gone wild? They're infected and poisoned

---

[3] Grace Under Pressure. Lee, Geddy. Lifeson, Alex. Peart, Neal. LP. Polydor Records. 1984.

by a plague. An epidemic that will slide and slither down an ever perilous slope. This epidemic? The jazz craze. The jazz generation, all jazzed up like Hottentots. Haughty and naughty. Loose and floozy. It's a disgrace.

"A flaunting disgrace. A generation of '*cooool*'—headed straight for the gutters of hell. How cool will it be there then?"

Normal Rockwell cavorts unseen, but imagined, behind his gilded microphone in his sweater, bowtie, suspenders, and bifocals. He fights back his rabid vitriol, which his audience cannot see, but are made to feel and sympathize with his patriotic fervor and alarm.

"A new hero is arising to save us. His name? Franklin Witz. His ever perspicacious quiddity projects an honest audacity almost never seen before. Only comparable to the raw populist grit of the Know-Nothing Party. Or the staunch anti-elitism of our beloved and legendary Andrew Jackson.

"We need a strong man. Of superior genes and breeding to preserve our sacred and inviolable institutions. America is built on strength, not on weakness, cowardice or by the bookish conceit of Eggheads who think they're smarter than the rest of us. You know what I'm talking about, my fellow concerned citizens, during these dark days.

"Someone to save us from F.D.R.'s red tides of socialism. He will sink us. But the U.S.S. Liberty must never falter.

"Mr. Witz. A longing nation calls on thee. Become our leader. Make us proud. Restore confidence in our business moguls to navigate us back to success. Not immigrants, know-it-alls, heathens, radicals, and the shiftless poor. Where would we be if the radicals had their way? What would Thomas Paine say? Would he not cry out: *Where is our common sense?*"

"No he wouldn't," commented a hissing listener at the bar. "He'd—"

"Shhh!"

Rockwell's monologue continues: "This depression, both financial and moral, has been hard for many who wish to work. But our Captains of industry, our Brahmins of Wall Street, will steer our ship of state certifiably docked back to a safe berth. Freedom is not excess, or a *free for all* party. Give us liberty or death. Liberty! Are we not free?

"Hoppin' mad jungle bunnies. Jiving slang. The ruination of good English, and our King James Bible—"

"James was a sissy fairy," chortled an English listener. "Like a Parisian and an ex-pat Brit being best friends. Gay as a picnic basket."

"Hey!"

"The court used to say, Elizabeth was king, then James was Queen."

"This program blows."

" . . . the devil made jazz. And socialism, in his charcoaled image. The beasts and hyenas. Herding into dens of vice and depravity. Booze. Marijuana. Jitterbugging. Doing The Funky-Butt!—instead of proper dancing. Pre-marital sex. Drumming the morality and brains right out of them. The savagery. They call, in their slang, drums: 'skins.' There's insight there. It's skinning them alive. Music that will cannibalize you! Like Indians scalping you right off. It's a cultural revolution. The socialists want to eat your children up! The Decline and Fall of the United States of America, ladies and gentlemen. Once their parties peak, they'll ceremoniously devour your babies. America, I weep for thee, under the drumming cacophony of this long heart of darkness—black night of our souls.

"And where do drums originate? Yes, that's right: Africa . . . It's regressive and primitive shadows.

"They can't keep still. Jukin' and swingin' like a bunch of monkeys and Tarzans. They should be swinging —from a tree . . ."

"Alright, that's enough. Switch that the hell off," yelled one of the group so they could commence their meeting.

Only a limited circle of the best screenwriters were fairly well paid, but they rarely received copyrights or recognition for their scripts or scenario contributions for the motion pictures.

But the guild also fought censorship, the manufacturing of deluded illusions, the lack of creative cooperation against the mass-produced, commercialized, lowbrow schmalz they were made to hack out. And rather fight for a progressive idealism to be expressed in their films, inspired for a hungry and embittered young nation in need of hope. To envision a better world. More just, more questioning of authority and the seats of power, more inclusive and creative . . .

No fucking way.

The struggle for unionization is the subtext and subterfuge for the war of American eyesight and psyche. The moneyed bigotry of subliminal sublimation—conditioning all that you're paid, pay for, and perceive. It is part of the history of American labor. It's not merely about the vast chasm of material disparity separating the worker from the owner class, but the power and control of which that wealth maintains and fiercely lords above us.

The radicals and golden goose writers brace under these conflicts and lucrative thumbs of producers, owners and moguls. The barometer fluctuates between spying and pressuring the "malcontents".

The chaos of the whole coliseum fumes with cigars, cigarettes, whiskey-soaked satin shirts, dancers, and new cadillacs.

In the aural montage of the highway traffic jams conversing between Herman J. Mankiewicz, Dorothy Parker, Lillian Hellman, Ogden Nash, Frances Goodrich, Dalton Trumbo, John Howard Lawson . . . Duke is in over his head, and just hangs out, an inconspicuous observer.

This is a condensed abstract convex approximation of the arguments, points and jesting of what he hears:

Amendments and negotiations. Bylaws and amalgamations. Penalties and statutes. Caucuses and conferences. Reps, reprimands, ARTICLES and constitutions. Codices and codecs. Blocs, members, and signatures. Capitulations. Overtures. Small print. Fine details made finer. But not fine.

Press, slanders, journalists, and campaigns. Solidarity and schisms. Contracting and disputations. Thrills, skills, and craft. Idealisms and idolatry. Rights, and Copyrights!

This is what you want? This is what you get!

Pandering and hysterics. Objections. Demands. ACTS and actors. Regulations and status. Inquisitions and indoctrinations versus solidarity and consolidation. Tables and ameliorations. Drafts and charters. Management and solvency. Dissidents and controversy. Prosperity and disparity. Manipulation and domination.

Too risqué, but not sinful enough.

Coercive bargaining. Facts and factotums. Maligned contingents and contingency.

Beware! Beware! The red menace of the swamp monsters will steal the pavilions, columns, and decor of your summer homes.

Collectivity and execs. Freedoms and tethers. Creativity and crapaganda. Sallies, assaults, foils, maneuvers, tactics, and strategy. Muzzles and modifications. Labels and suspicions.

The shade of backdoor dealing. The hyper parade of patriotism and patronizing.

Shhhh, not a word about anti-Semitism, even though Ukranian Polish Jews own the biggest studios whilst the red, white and black banners and flags of Nazism are flying higher, smashing in glass and faces. The mass crunch of boots spreads across Europe. Not a peep about it! In the fire with that script.

Burn that witch.

Autonomy and cooperation. The autocracy of "democracy." Precarious emoluments. Liberations and Fronts. What could've been. What could be. What is!

Charlie Chaplin got away with one, but not the next round.

Catch phrases to latch and snatch your trusting amazement. The butterfly netting of innocence. The Jesus you see doesn't pass the audition. The crucifixion of humanism. Crosses of morality and the smiling epic of sin. Red taping the first amendment. Censorship and cynicism. The gagging of satire for the syrupy gags of meaningless silly.

Magazine cover gloss. The new stained glass.

The snarky gravitas and conglomeration of irresistible "hip. " Mirth of damnation. The urgent convulsive tempo of criss-crossing double indemnities. The insolence of persuasion.

Gotta have a song and dance routine. Gotta be in 4/4 time, and gotta rhyme. Maintain the fake clichéd propriety, while purveying all the sin they can get away with.

Selling the dream. They sold the unreal. The schadenfreude joy in other people's suffering. Of BIG screen to big news-reeling. Reeling you in:

Hey, nobody has it better than us.

Bombs away, but we're okay. Stars and stripes forever with armies of angel warriors. March and salute to that swingin' beat! Or be beaten in the backroom to the dumpster.

Breadlines and coffee dimes. From Bethlehem to Frankenstein. Birth of a nation! Gizzards of Oz, D.C. and Disneyland. (D-Day and Hiroshima hover on the near horizon to make it safe for the Mickey Mouse Clubs.)

Cops and robbers! Guys and dolls! Patriots and Reds. Cowboys and Indians!

The languid lingo industry of pomposity and advertising tease of heroic bombast and pure American heraldry. The exponential promulgation of the haus-frau kulture of kitsch. How nice. How lovely. How marvelously convenient. And everyone fits so neatly in their places.

Reins and velvety blinders of sugar cube mediocrity of schmalz. The long roller-coasting death of adulthood. The embalming of childhood kindergarten and the marketing of toys and accessories. The ecstasy of sell, sell, heaven, and sell. The ersatz fakery of imaging over the montage of fake imaginings. Pass the fizzing soda and the buttered snap crack jacked salted popcorn.

Ideology.

Duke takes it in like a puzzled sponge, but didn't understand half of the legalese he heard, though he gets the content and implications as the rocket's red glare flames in the crossfire of parrying repartee of the hardest-drinking, mercuri-al, keenest wits and twits in towns across the nation.

A couple of broad shoulder thugs with crooked noses and sharp hats poke in the bar to do a reconnaissance. They were on the hunt for Frankie Witz's public enemy #23, which placed Duke pretty high up on an unhealthy list.

Duke is taking notes when he spots these pinstripe bruisers ogling in his direction.

"Hell no."

They smile, and grit their teeth, ready to bite.

It's time to fly.

He shoots through the backdoor and leaps up the nearest fire escape, just as the alley door slams back open and the thugs run down the narrow corridor to thrash him.

Might be time for an out-of-town retreat.

Episode 12

Deadwoods

> There's something solid forming in the air,
> The wall of death is lowered in Times Square.
> No-one seems to care,
> They carry on as if nothing was there.
>
> The wind is blowing harder now,
> Blowing dust into my eyes.
> The dust settles on my skin,
> Making a crust I cannot move in
> And I'm hovering like a fly,
> waiting for the windshield on the freeway.

—Fly On a Windshield, Genesis

Afraid of mobsters. Mad avenging starlets. Lurking henchmen of Frankie Witz. Ex-wives. And Imperial Japanese bombers rumbling in the distance—Satch & The Suit had to escape Hollywood—and hide out at a lake-house cabin in Northern California. Especially as people they knew started to disappear.

The Pacific hovers over the ridge, along the rock-carved coast, as the roaring great ocean, mother of earth, surges under sunrise and sunset.

Nebulas of fog cascade the slow time of air. Pines stretch gigantic. DNA seed and code of ancient redwoods around Big Sur.

All trees in time are melded to their collective Mind and hive psyche of the One Nordic Yggdrasil Tree: like a giant brain-star entity . . . A billion branches rooted to memories of Antediluvian ages.

As the Age ends, the world serpent is breaking out to decimate the Tree . . .

Duke has been drinking more resiliently, as reality continues to shift. The ground he treads on isn't solid.

Slowly Duke begins to feel he's turning upside down, glued in a roller-coaster ride. His body begins to disappear. He can't breathe. Hyperventilating, his heart pounds into a fit of epilepsy. Like some metaphysical attack of delirium tremens. Migraines spike and knife into his pressurized skull. Even his past weighs as a blocked enigma receding behind him. He passes out.

Duke wakes in this cabin, and stares out onto the water.

The threat of falling bombs is bad enough, as the Empire of Japan is conquering the Far East, a sprawling octopus into the Pacific. And now, something bubbles in the lake. It seems to rise from the Unconscious. It wants to burst to the surface.

Fog drifts thick off the frosty, near Pacific.

Far away, a train engines and whistles, howling the night sky. Its horns sound like dissonant angels trumpeting the impending Judgment Day, or some seaweed drenched Satyr blowing on a titan's conch.

The lake itself is too quiet. It strangles the heart.

Duke shivers with fright. Feels like he's ten years old. It's ugly. Wants to shake off the trauma. Where's his bravery? What's to fear?

They can hide here. How long?

But something searches for them. How will it find them? Does it smell fear in the soul? The silence is all. The long, quiet, dark matter submerges a saturation into everything. Every cell, every sinew, every atom—which he imagines in drowning detail . . . He tries to shake off this wave of angst-pounding schizophrenia.

The phone rings!

Satch's face lights with dread.

Ring ring ring.

"Dear lord, don't answer that! Take the cord out! Christ that's loud. It'll wake up every cannibal troll in the valley."

RING RING RING.

"Huh?" Duke never heard Satch sound so angry.

"Get that phone out of here! Pull the damned cord out the wall socket!"

RING! RING! RING!

Frantic, they try to trace the wires behind the furniture. Scurrying to where the phone's tangled up, under the green sofa, though it looks gray to Duke.

Ring ring rang.

The brittling, loud tin bell of the telephone is hideous, like a signal tolling towards carnage and hell. Enough to wake the undead. It's usually annoying and disruptive, but now its shrill hag of Harpy noise ghostly accentuates a macabre monstrosity to pop from the basement and throttle them.

A viscous malady. An alarming mockery.

RING RING RING!

"Turn it the fuck off! They'll find us! *Turn it off!"*

It stabs out to break the distance between safety and whatever seeks to gnaw-out their eyes.

Finally they find the socket to yank the phone. It won't come out. They both grasp it, sweating with their might. It breaks free. Thank god.

But then it keeps ringing.

Madness.

They freeze. They hear gurgling. Their legs turn to gauzy rubber. They sneak a peek through the front blinds.

The lake is bubbling. Dear god. It churns frothy at the center. Something rises from this hazy foam. It towers up in the darkness.

A Sea dragon serpent emerges from the water?

"Dear Christ Almighty!" said Armstrong.

"No!" barely rasped the Suit.

Pristine ancient grandeur and vitality. Indigo bird-like feathers jut from scales and its gnarled face and weathered reptile elasticity.

Impossible Intelligence radiates from its stern and imperious figure.

A Lord of Time and the abyss. A Great Diabolic-Wise King of the earth towers above the dock to the cabin. Aristocratic warrior with demon slit eyes that pierce their vulnerable walls. Even into the thin walls of their pulsing brains, and desires.

A young blonde girl from the other cabin steps out to the dock, dressed like some Heidi sheep herder from the Alps. The beast austerely glances down on the girl, almost as if to smile. She's mesmerized by his gaze.

She pees herself. The Beast, with a superior grin, lunges forward. Teeth slicing through flesh, and simply eats her. Muffled screams swallowed by licking forked tongue lips.

Satch and The Suit scream themselves, like shrill girls. Freezing sweat breaks out in trembling fever.

Is that evil eye hex of Dandy Ratshaw and his ritual come to fruition?

Ratshaw, Imperial Japanese, vengeful ex-wives and heartless mobsters are all only the plaguing minions of this soul-eating entity—this hydra, this ink blotting flood into their heads. They are Legion.

The towering serpent dragon turns its attention to peer its slit pupils through the blinds into the cabin. Closer. Sulfuric fog drifts inside. Purple, emerald, and silver erupt into Duke's black and white vision. The power of this color invades his brain. And spin.

Duke swoons into darkness and ice.

Thirteen

Yes, he's here again
Can't you see he's fooled you all?
Share his peace, sign the lease
He's a supersonic scientist
He's the guaranteed eternal sanctuary man.

Look, look into my mouth he cries
And all the children lost down many paths
I bet my life you'll walk inside
Hand in hand. Gland in gland.
With a spoonful of miracle . . .

—*Supper's Ready* Genesis

Duke revives from the blank and black coma, slouched in the dark. Film glitters on a screen in a movie theater. Is it some bizarre version of *Nosferatu*? *The Cabinet of Doctor Caligari*?

Satch is next to him, laughing, with a big box of popcorn spilling all around. Duke wipes off some of the kernels tossed about.

A group of Japanese high school girls lean over, from behind, one says, "Hello Mister. We think you are very handsome. Tee-hee-hee."

The Well-Dressed Man is thrown off guard. Slowly he turns around, begins to smile, and wham, one of the girls swiftly karate smacks him.

"Tee-hee-hee," they giggled, and Satch guffaws.

Duke replies, "Yeahhh, you think this is funny? But tell me, why is there sticky blood under our shoes? How'd we get here? I feel like hell."

Armstrong whispers under the projector's unreeling clack, "You've forgotten what happened? You blacked-out, man. The Serpent devoured that girl and sank back into the water."

"What?"

"You swooned and I caught you. They made a phony newsreel about it. It's big news. It was just on. You've been in a catatonic fever. We're trying to get you some oxygen. It's air conditioned here."

"Yeah like a freezing meat-locker. But why's there blood everywhere?"

Lifting up his suede shoes, he feels the ugly tack of gluey smeared red. He begins to fear the dragon is actually still around.

They're under its spell?

Is it on the other side of the screen?

Everyone in the theater had been invited there on the pretense of a University of Berkeley Science Professor who had a Halloween gingerbread party. The refreshments are laced with intoxicants, maybe to hypnotize while everyone dies laughing?

Silver Teeth carved delicacies, one by one. No meat tastes sweeter than laughing meat. Fear kills the dish every time.

"Ha ha ha haw haw," bellowed Satch.

Or is it Old Scratch?

Duke worries at the sinister carnage menacing it all—*hey, can Satch hear my thoughts?*

He's getting paranoid, more paranoid, and distrustful even of his friend? How could he? A lurid phosphorescence stains his trust. Was Satch really Mephistopheles? Surely the sound of Armstrong's trumpet would exorcize any demon? Or is Lucifer that powerful? That deceitful?

A chorus of show girls come out—and dance, like the Andrew Sisters. Wait. It's actually the gals from Sweets' coffins? They sing:

The smoking signs are on. Arriving at your departure . . . Your Thoughts, thunder thick-wrought chasms, like drowning days. Slog and shagger. A sinking island. Sunken ships aflame—your hungry-eyes salivate with a lust-funk gaze.

Drink deep the crimson wave.

Snatch a vine,

blood of red wine—under a twisted stairwell's's cosmic maze.

Dionysian Bacchantes tear & torn

Surging horses gallop over the sails summoning a sign

Savored lust & glaze in your nightmares

as I'll be in yours, if you'll be in mine. And survive on the ocean of Being?

Look to the sky, crave a ray that carries bloody time in

Thoughts wandering mad & dazed.

Sucked into the blaze of gravity's vortex.

Prayers scarcely lift the changing gray

Of low-hung-clouds & gloom, searching for those semi-divine Eyes,

(savored most—for their lustful graze and phase of frictioning choreography)

Treasure scorned and found in loss of thy lovelorn play. Holy ghosts

Swallow in a tarn of brackish burnt mind. Soul scorched in its furnace of forged Being and pain.

Thoughts plunder the ugly muck of crazy days.

Shower eyes most with their lust-fucking haze.

Ushers, as in church, pass around baskets. The audience somnolently dig into their pockets and deposit all they have: wallets, cash, jewelry, watches—even taking out their gold teeth—while others line up, one by one, in the aisles, to walk to the front, and behind the screen.

Who's in the projector room?

The thumping agitation builds. Duke's leg cannot stop shaking. The over-startled Suit bolts and runs as he hears shrieks behind the movie screen. He runs up. Runs down the bloodied aisles, slipping among the laughing crowd into the lobby, slowing in motion as he tries to leap for speed.

Some mysterious aura, magic ember, enshrouds his negative perceptions like a weapon of glue and amber. As the lobby doors swing open he walks onto a purple gold oriental carpet that bleeds fiercely breaking into his black white vision.

Friederich Nietzsche, the philosopher, appears to be banging on a piano: he looks up. Eyes completely two black hole pupils.

Are people being taken out in body bags?

Greta sees Duke and glances at him like a steel dart. She's in an other-worldly occult outfit of sable leather and silver, like some Babylonian/ Egyptian goddess ready to welcome home daemonic aliens.

Are they coming through the Hadron Collider's portal? Why would he even think that?

Eyes in a trance. Duke freezes in a violent fever of tremors—trying to keep his nerves together. To spark embers of warmth and courage from this fury of shuddering.

"How do I explain?" Greta slowly muttered, but words tumbled out with increasing rapidity. "This is the Factory. And the temple. A razor edge of paradox. Where all things possible contrive whilst the current god Pan observes and passes, then vapors into ether and foggy woods, and wonder what magic whispering incantations to learn in the sweep and gush of Aeolus's breath.

"The mind, a loud tangle of chimes. A spectrum of chakras from toes to top. Ramm to crown. Aum to micro-cosmological orbits home and back again, to this far away dreaming world cascade. The Graveyard haze sifts through future headstones. Marble polish gleam hints of secret infinities. Froth of tomb's resurrection reincarnate ghosts sustained in the curve of sustenance, from sources of light strained through stained glass windows."

"Greta, stop fucking with me."

The words seem to slip out as ciphers that morph into numbers and equations.

Greta's not sure why he's not hearing her: "Don't surround yourself with yourself. Diagonal Bishops intersect with Rooks and Knights in the garden. Queens and trauma Pawns play closeted in the day. Delve the pneumatic flex of the crypt. Monks boozed in the cellars. Hopscotch sorties of the melee. Stellar doorways. Send an instant karma to out-swirl the checkmate maneuver with the King's levitation. A freeze and seizure of fright cold radiance, to exorcize and excoriate the possession. Bidding the invisible melt the veils in a Phoenix on fire. A cauldron living force of sentient ritual whose clandestine conjugations you pray release from the always, ever-receding secrets just evasively held out of sight.

"That's incredible," said Duke. "Nor do I exactly understand, but half-meanings and connotations. By the way, I'm having a nervous breakdown—"

"I'm sorry. You must come with me," she takes his hand, leading him back into the theater.

"Christ, Greta, if that's how it is—why not bring Kierkegaard and G.K. Chesterton into it? They say *Reality* is so incomparably strange that we look to a crucified paradox of unified opposites for a transubstantiated divine messiah as One mysterious truth we *transcend* with!

"*You Lost me . . .*" she replied.

He's losing track of who said what to whom.

"That's how fast time acts, and words play in a field—of meaning—by an imperfect sayer in the crunch of wayward revelation," said Duke.

"Doubt and specialized science hover as gravestones under a cemetery mockery, of the absurdity of it all. I'm straining blurry to know what hides on the other side of the screen. The smashing now, of epiphanies onward.

"Lower your voice dammit," scolded Greta.

Light-headed and giddy, bordering on visionary convulsions, Duke continues arguing to explicate the codes she triggers in the churning mosaic of his subconscious: "Though the Brain seizes in a thunder-clutch of electrocution-shocking *antidote*, a Pharmakos/remedy is needed to release the decaying meat of us, the seeming virus of Life—infected by banks, and generals, dictators, demagogues, and demi-urges—giving a polarized shift elevated in Neo-Platonic architecture of form, as Plotinus or Iamblichus would conceive," but he has no time for that.

The terrors of eternity await at the end of a line—like a meat-grinding machine, bewildering his field of vision. Cosmic radiation explodes behind his bubble of eye-sight.

Some achieve realizations. This was Existentialism. Every moment throttles importance. Questions bash his face with urgency. Messengers of the Fates smacking him with significance.

Life, a sphere surrounded by dying, every pulse of him, and of us. Before and after. His shadow turns to flame and its dry ash of shade disintegrates. Walking out of this abyss into the current fire of the self, re-creating memory, sustained by the rising inhalation.

The stage curtains unveiling while concealing.

Every encounter, choice and questioning—a challenge by a devouring Sphinx and a supernatural anesthetist. Catatonic hypnosis. Catatonic awakenings. Atomic conjunctions. Solve the initiated equation, or morph further into molecules and cells infused in a web of consciousness? The gravity of fractal whirlpools at the end of the rainbow. Every second along the spectrum—the black hole ahead, the black hole behind.

The next life calls, to merge in Oceanic stardust? To do so—aswirl with oblivion and Sentience? Timeless simultaneity of possible happenings. Boiling in the warping cyclotronic cauldron pot of the Multiverse.

Vishnu dreams splintered in diamond prisms, of us. Holy Ghosts grin to host concerted concentrations of accumulated Light, a cognitive concerto—condense in Chakras and Deoxyribonucleic Acid—uncoil and ascend, from source and destination, to ascertain in a dual rising Caduceus—Hermetically aflame above entrapped circles of Karma. Interface, the ongoing original Mother/Father Face of All. The original conception. The original moment. The only moment.

That, that is. The It. Even where the spirit seeking warrior, Arjuna, has to turn away from the blinding exponential blaze of Brahman Krishna, the shadow of Jehovah's Lord, Abraxas, and Void, the over-inundation of incomprehensible infinity—unmitigated bliss and wrath of the tornado cosmos, as *Job* cries before the imaginary Whirlwind—like Lilliputians tossed in a hurricane sea of multiplying Leviathans, desperately stretching to deliriously grasp for Jacob's ladder, the fabled portals of Enoch—a relief, if to bask, under blue sapphire fearsome reach for Grace. Swept up suddenly and vanished into the speed of light.

An unfathomable nirvana recedes, just out of reach. An unattainable cosmos away. A Ka-trillion neurons trail behind and return from the future. Just follow the new key masters to step six feet under.

Words for the impossible gods and forces hurtling us at warped velocity, watched by those who stand still at the speed of light.

Duke spies someone distantly familiar, unlock a door and duck in. He runs off to follow and enters a darkened claustrophobic dense cluttered office. He hears the click and clacking of a film reel. He's in the Projector Room.

"Who's there?" Duke asked, with impatient trepidation.

"Aloha. Some would call me—the Projectionist. Hey, where's that Dioxin adhesive?"

"What?"

"Pass it over here please. Everything is connected. This is where the magic exists. As is the God Shiva's painted death-face of galactic destruction and reformation. If only to find an eternal smile behind the unbuffered mask of complete emptiness. But infinity can't stop. The eternal all encompassing voice simply and mysteriously gives birth to form. The end and beginning of time do not exist. Creation and destruction is occurring right now, every moment. Everything in the Multiverse is happening simultaneously. Therefore I need to splice in a non-linear secret. You know, there is so much hidden wisdom in the random information of the architecture found at centers of power. Do you realize that the Defense Department is scheduled to build The Pentagon on September 11, 1941? The floor area will be 6,636,360 feet. Fascinating."

The shadowy figure is feverishly at work as he converses with his back to Duke.

"Did you also know that *Snow White & the Seven Dwarfs* was released on December 21st, 1937? On the pagan winter solstice holiday of Alban Arthan. The location of release was the Fox Carthay Theater which is built as a perfect circle extended into a cylinder set inside a square. Similar to this theater, which also possesses a quadrilateral double isotoxal rhombic dodecahedron. This kind of radical edge transitive construction exudes the impression of a rotating construct. Who would imagine the kind of transdimensional tesseract conductivity that can be initiated through the vehicle of such precise geometric math?

The strange technician leans over a sewing machine type mechanism with a strip of film reel clamped down, cutting it, then adding pieces joined together by an acetone solvent to dissolve and fuse the superimposed overlap of new joints of film, capturing the light of the moment re-presented . . .

"Want to take a scene out? Place in a new one?"

"What are you talking about? There's no time."

"Au contraire. All the time in the world. How about we splice in a few frames of a Coke, an ice cream cone, a naked Snow White, a Rooster, a caduceus yantra, the Virgin Mary and some cigarettes? Why, just manipulating the exact coded coordinates and we can transport an audience into a year of Atlantis, Shangri La or Timbuktu. *Zappa-Ra-Cadabra*! Punch out the perforations—and that should get 'em! Eh?"

The figure stamps it, then feeds it back in the reel.

"Voila!"

Duke sees himself on film, laughing with his ex-fiance? Then the gauzy stark pale eyes of Bela Lugosi's Dracula appear—to hypnotize . . . The Projectionist reverses the film. The couple on screen start going backwards, engaging in a kiss, then waving goodbye into the past absorbed into a nuclear explosion?

Uncontrollably Duke finds his body and mind also rewiring its gears into an altered inverted glue of backwardness, reversing his steps, irresistibly, trying to hold on to the moment as it seems to unstoppably disintegrate."

".ohalA."

"?ereht s'ohW"

Duke's outside the door.

"What happened? How?" Oblivious, clutched in anomalous confusion. "There's something in this room?"

He proceeds to turn the knob. It's locked.

"What the—?"

"Hey. There you are," said Greta. " You disappeared. C'mon!"

Against his rebellious uncooperative will, dragging his feet, Duke follows Greta, arguing the whole metaphysical conundrum in hypnotic reluctance. Hammering drums of mental wavelength vibrations of focus.

How long has he been thinking these thoughts? Oh my God. Are they true? Has he been speaking all this time? Or talking with himself? Can she read my mind? Is It reading my mind? Scanning me? Testing? Preparing?

Duke turns around several times to go. But Greta's grip, cold steel tight. He notices her gold necklace has a crab with a symbol on it.

She leads him down the thick sticky crimson of the aisles. As inevitable as birth and dying. Through shrieks and laughter . . . The most unimaginable moment, however, Duke feels he's been here before. Primal.

"Is it the dragon?" More alive and conscious than any human or animal known. Imperious and wise, a demi-god. The Universe?

They're behind the screen, as the line progresses and screams cinder into illumination.

Yes. Duke looks up to behold: *A* gold and black eye: a porthole through the cosmos. Its indigo-emerald scaled feather wet head leans toward the Well Dressed Man.

Dragon leathered nostrils sniff loud. Speaks? Telepathy . . . Opens its mouth wide. Sweet exhalation, like fantastic spice vaporizes Duke's mind. Has been subliminally communicating with him this entire time?

Greta turns to him, and says, "Trust me."

They walk inside . . . Fantastic light and spectral tunnels, like the neural flickering of a strobe, blaze into his brain. He sees flashes of his past. Then he's shot into hyper-space . . .

Episode 14

Horizons

I know in what human way they imagine the Madonna, and I think
of young Titians through whom God walks burning.
Yet no matter how deeply I go down into myself my God is dark, and like a web-
bing made of a hundred roots, that drink in silence. I know that my trunk rose
from his warmth, but that's all . . .
I love the dark hours of my being in which my senses drop into the deep and become wide and powerful now like legends.
Then I know there is room in me for a second huge and timeless life.

—Rainer Maria Rilke[4]

Traveling in the angst of stealth, immersed and swallowed into endless night. Morning would not come.

Through breathless corridors of agitation: impatience clawing in the back of a curtained hearse. Speeding to the wharf at land's end—a sabled claustrophobia hunts after them with invisible teeth snapping for their necks.

Greta and Duke flee through their peril—he wonders what happened to Satch? What happened to them in the theater? And beyond the compacting sky and walls closing in. Crushing.

The jaws at land's end. Engulfed in a crest and trough of harrowing amnesia, as if blanked out of life then violently reposited.

He suffers in a smothering comatose purgatory, losing vast blocks of time. Another personality or mind who also inhabited this soul, now eclipsed behind another? No tangible connections between here and there.

Duke blacked-out earlier. These deathly episodes are increasing. The dragon's gravity had him: being launched into something which keeps getting deferred, yet imminent. A metaphysical bill to be paid. The momentum continues winding

[4] *A Book for the Hours of Prayer*. Selected Poems of Rainer Maria Rilke. Translated by Robert Bly. Perennial Library. NY NY 1981.

him tight, to be released. Kinetic. Launched by the banking centrifugal forces, to rocket his psyche to teleport into a catastrophic revelation.

The sun is blocked. Blackened. Beaten back. Turning day to endless night, an ashen mass of heavy cloud fuels a brewing storm. Shadows tremble with reaching fingers: tantalizing, violent, creeping.

Cold rain drapes down in waves and torrents.

The ground teeters in vertigo that conceals the unreality of what's hiding and holding down the world as a substantial and knowable entity.

Time and the road was quicksand. Where can they be heading?

They reach a dank, fog-drowned port of salt-eaten decrepitude, far, *far* from Los Angeles.San Francisco? Swiftly they get out and ascend the planks of the gangway into the air, to embark on a departing ocean liner.

Steps creak with shrill echo, nails in coffin, the cracks up the vine to alert the Giant . . . Immediately muffled by some sinking presence that eats sound—engulfs their vibrations. Elusive with gathering momentum.

Greta and The Suit ascend the rickety gangway as they cling to the railing.

The foghorn bellows, loud and distant at the same time, gurgling with an archetypal turbulence, a monstrous Wagnerian horn to cross the River Styx.

It shakes Duke so belligerently that his knees buckle and give way from an insomnia of bedlam.

Greta grabs him from keeling over. In that clasping instant he feels a surge of unknown strength return.

Her Nordic eyes speak intensity. Unromantic. Unsentimental. A Valkyrie? A thick skin and skein of Being who shields a volcano of emotions.

She senses his communication of relief, awareness and awe, then proceeds to search for a cigarette along the ship's top railing.

Lighting up with a slow, long drag, as if inhaling all the world: alchemized, and exudes the smoke of a burnt offering, an unholy expiation from an impossible gravity of lips. Then tosses it to the sea.

Greta's cool dark tone, Nordic—almost Slavic, smooth and intelligent, languid and charcoaled, straightens his spine.

She says: "Nothing will ever be the same. They know who you are. For now I can protect you, but we must get you to *the Cathedral of Roses* and the catacombs of our Order, where we house our Emerald Tablets, and the secret codes of Plato from the Mystery Schools . . . leave America."

"But what about—?"

"We've been mining a tunnel to break into the hidden library beneath the Vatican. Keep your mind clear and brave. Fear is their poison and sight. They feed on fear. Only your commitment, and the Supreme Being can save you now . . . A history of demonic war and cruelty has infected Mother Earth's nurturing body and allows them to feed on her axis, and disrupt the magnetic poles. The animal bodies we inhabit still crave a heredity of primitive blood.

"The polar axis is shifting. Even as the balance of consciousness is shifting. But they are Asuras, Rakshasas, Archons, spirits, and species lost in a gnostic flux; agents of providential—multi-directional cause and effect—to bring about a great polarized realignment of knowing. A new golden Dawn—or, an apocalypse. But nothing will stop the change.

"Time has unglued. Being is unhinging. Everything that has ever happened is still in our atoms and cells. The more we realize this, the more is mind over matter, even into the unknowns of Heraclitian flux evolving through the friction struggle and survival—the discovery of fire! And the world and universe responds in kind.

"The psychic dam that the ancient, over-lording hierarchy impugned and stamped upon our earlier species trapped and conditioned them into an inferior ego identity. For thousands of years. Deep Aeons and cycles. Although the compartmentalizing of these transitions of ego is part of the evolution in a world of forms.

"The Superego is unraveling; the Id is unleashed and the Unconscious is unlocking and flooding the world all at the same time . . . our heritage and inheritance. Forces meant to remain dormant are bubbling to the surface by ancient cast spells of regressive myths of repressive illusion. The destructive greed of power from the primitive past, as the Philosopher's Stone draws near.

"The rich, the occultists, scientists—conjunct with the demi-gods: have always colluded to go too far. Tapping into fragments of occluded knowledge. The fruition of magic with technology. How can one imagine the power? The initiation? The consequences? Metamorphosis? But the politician, king and populist are just as dangerous as they become entangled. The ego. The pain. You must remember; but you know too much already, and as a defense mechanism you've been psycho-somatically stricken with idiocy."

Duke guffaws in a swamp of ecstatic curiosity and lacerating infatuation. Then feels indignant, self-conscious, seriously and deprecatingly reflective, as he squints his eyes uncomfortably to the distance.

Has a more brilliant facet of himself been hidden? Set a maze in his bilateral cortex? Laughing in some distant tower, throwing away the key? To put him up to this? All in all, to shield him from—insanity? A challenge? From being overwhelmed? Discovered? To protect? To incubate? To uncover a mandelic talisman? Or a ruse just to find her? All the above?

And yet, something further sinister to be manipulated?—something painfully unseen? A vortex of paradigms. Many dimensions. Motioning between two mirrors. Infinite vision of the one. The all-seeing Eye?

The foghorn bellows, like Siegfried's dirge, in its far away summons—a strange comforting.

Announcement. Passage. Destination.

Signaling into the hypnosis of the remote, toward an epic conjuring. Losing the moment, diving into a Gothic womb, or Taoist wellspring. The endless rapture of a Bach organ.

The crossing. The liminal confusion. Truth approaches.

Art cannot explain it, but its urgency expresses it.

Hear them calling from across the great river. The quest ignites the spirit on fire. You become one with the flame, or burn. Lost in its displaced Tibetan trumpeting, primordial, grand canyons of universal void and relative time.

Duke whispers: "To be conscious is not to be in time. But only in time can the moment in the Rose garden, the moment in the arbor where the rain beat, the moment in the draughty church at smoke fall, be remembered . . . only through time is time conquered."[5]

Greta's melting coal dark eyes turn to the passing horizon.

Had she saved him? Or is she a trap? A distraction? From what? The truth? *What is the truth worth in the face of distraction?* Extinction? Survival? Her face? A diversion from what? Beatitude? Satori? Sainthood? Nirvana? A safe trip? *Godhood?* Ahhh, Goddesshood! Was he supposed to be Christ? *Or the fool?* Human, all too human.

Do we all lay down the cross? And run to something . . . more bloody? Keep missing the light? Sophia?

Is desire also a poison? A mythology of suffering? The road to salvation? A non-Platonic Beatrice to sink into the material world of generation, in the land of Beaulah? The sloth and carnage of burning flesh? Everything aflame. Her every allure, a conflagration. Eden a glorious inferno. Paradise on fire—he thinks *Paradise Fire* would make a good film title, and vaguely regrets reading all those books on Gnosticism—this terrifying confusion between who is God and Lucifer—which one is which? But his nightmares haunted him with visions of this world before he

---

[5] T. S. Eliot The Four Quartets: Burnt Norton

read a page, seemingly justifying his insanity while balancing the razor edge that this madness is a reality . . . Maybe the Buddhists are right . . .

Surely desire and temptation is the greatest fire in the universe. Desire, the seed, promulgates existing. The big bang.

Aren't there greater heavens? A more lasting paradise? Or just gateways? Doors within doors. Always throwing our bliss to the horizon. Stages, scenes, veils, connections through the wormholes of the Divine?

Mystery and awe. There's a door he's trying to get to. It eludes and allures. It awaits him back on the other side—of time?

She knows this. The door is here. He must travel to the limits. Push the boundaries of this realm to get through the portal.

Why this temporary entanglement of need and madness? Of possessive attachment and electric neurosis? Is there no way out? From the dragon to the devouring woman? Born from the tomb of Woman to the womb of Death? Does the womb of death give a radical new birth? Should he trust religion to take him through? How? Which one? Cryptic paradigms have gained firm hold on his racing brain.

Death is a word. A word most impossible to define and perfectly incomplete, whose defining moment is inescapable and seemingly unreturnable. Perfectly natural. Shared by all. Into the All.

Words, words, words. The anti-nominalist theologians were onto something.

Death—a word, like Bachelard's psychoanalysis of *fire*, like *love's body*—communicating endless evocative streams to pivot a spiral of binding meaning between subject and object, and get lost in, as the plurality of truths are uncovered in the exploring karma of lostness . . . A fantastic allure to embrace, until embraced into the approaching moment of nothingness. Creating a synthesis of something bonded and new. The chemical reaction. The reactor's alchemy. Then we pass. The Dimethyltryptamine launches the soul.

Receding from the motley recrudescence and luminosity of cities and cloud, the sky unveils layers of holy diamonds. Ablaze in blackness.

Leaving behind the faint splash of rude pastel and sparse scintillation of modern sky, in a seeming flat two-dimensional canopy, slowly gives way to depth and curvature. A geometric skein and lattice-work of constellation and spiral galactic density.

They look up, and behold a galaxy.

The breeze howls and Greta curls into her fur. Duke notices and nuzzles close to her. They feel warmer.

The night of civilization is dark, but night is not black. Not a second-hand patching of poor stage-work lit by phosphorescent plasticity, as the city blocks off the cosmos for its own usurping deification of microcosm worlds within worlds. The idolatry of flesh—of movie stars and starlets.

We are surrounded by awe. Children immersed in the phantasm. We are its pulse and breath, the very bodies of its Thought. Desperately tossed into an immense velocity: an inverted Tabernacle of tangled astrological cosmology. We are its eyes. Atomic particles and stardust comet spires, of which we are made, vanish in a flash.

Greta commented, "Do you believe it's all fate?"

Duke, gazing above said: "This cosmos—swimming planets and galaxies of unseen color—stirs, some captive radiance of light inside. The elements we're made of. What we live in. Paracelsus, the Renaissance alchemist who innovated modern chemistry, taught something of our equivalence to the stars in the great chain of being. That the stars are our twin-sisters. Not our fates. As two twins that look alike, which has the likeness of the other?

"A dual mirror. The planets do not command our destinies, but map where we are in the seeming chaotic synchronicity. Nicholas of Cusa says—'God is a sphere whose circumference is nowhere and whose center is everywhere.'"

"Hermes originally said that," responded Greta.

"Hmm?"

"Hermes Trismegistus: author of the *Corpus Hermetica*—attributed as a god of writing and interpretation, somewhat like the mystical exegesis of hermeneutics. Plato refers to such things in the Timaeus and Critias concerning the secret texts of the Egyptians, and the sacred geometry applied to build the pyramids, the Temple of Solomon, the Gothic arching cathedrals . . . As above, so below. Jakob Boehme's cones of the symbiotic intersecting of light and darkness, such as the polar balance between Yin and Yang. All esoteric interpretation takes on a momentum and cascades in emanations to an initiated fulcrum of meaning. A simultaneity of the real and the symbolic. Always projecting a vehicle beyond itself. Metaphors unconcealing what we truly are, right now, galvanizing this necessity of deconstructing the compendious abstractions. The Kabbalistic tree's Ein Sof of the Infinite—the foundational program and paradigm of all things. The mysteries of the Shekhinah, the divine feminine . . . The All One. We are originally One. Form naturally begets polarity."

Duke's hands become heavy. As if by magnetism he reaches to touch Greta's arm, ever so invisibly. Her skin, like light upon water.

Luminosity of flesh and Artemis, air gliding upon the impassioned sail of wind.

"Why can't we drink the moon? Why is there no vessel to contain it?" whispered Duke.

He caresses her with fingertips. Every minute hair and cell accentuated melting sparks of chimes tingle up the spine as waves of electricity pulsate the released endorphins in their bodies.

She throws defiant eyes at him and draws away. A ghosting residue of power lingers in the space she stood. Her scent trails through vast chasms of his brain. A gateway to the primal interface of Creation.

He follows.

Episode 15

Subterfuge

What is a poet? An unhappy man . . . whose lips are so fashioned that the moans and cries which pass over them are transformed into ravishing music. His fate is like that of the unfortunate victims whom the tyrant Phalaris imprisoned in a brazen bull, and slowly tortured over a steady fire; their cries could not reach the tyrant's ears . . . they sounded like sweet music. And men crowd around the poet and say to him, "Sing for us soon again"—which is as much as to say: May new sufferings torment your soul, but may your lips be fashioned as before; for the cries would only distress us, but the music . . . is delightful."

—*Either/Or* Soren Kierkegaard

That night, in the dining hall, Greta flirted with their waitress . . . She brought her back to their room. Greta tied Duke to the bed while they danced the tango.

He thought they went to Yellowstone National Park for a hike, since Daria, their waitress, had enough of serving on the high seas, the wild ports and sporting travelers, and is moving out there to become a Park Ranger, so they watch hot geysers, as earthquakes keep going off.

Greta found a white horse to ride. She drew a sword. *Must be a dream?* She drew close, and held up a crystal ball, like a snow globe, which grew larger as he saw the snow was the swirling galaxy. She throws it at him as the ground gives way. His heart turns into a metal hammering pendulum. He's swallowed beneath into a gigantic blanket that covers a bottomless lake, and he's then spit out as a jetting spring—into the mountains?

He becomes the geyser. Exploding into nothingness, or somethingness.

Duke wakes with a start. Still loosely knotted—and discovers he's alone.

"What the hell? Where is she?"

He feels sickly. Maybe nausea from sea sickness. But he's starved nonetheless. Coffee? A buttered bagel? Smoked salmon and omelets? Honey and locusts?

Sluggish, he pushes himself to roll out of bed. Splash cold water on his face, and stroll out for a bite.

Last night the ship whispered and creaked eerily. Ghostly. Few passengers. The enormity of the hull groaned like a leviathan.

In the overcast daylight it still appears eerie, but even more quiet. Ominous foreboding preys on his spine.

Down the hall and into the smoky light. The raw fragrance of salt and spray blast the air. The song of surf cuts through the rumble of prow and sea. But he does not hear the turbine of the ship's engine.

The gray of morning is solemn. He stands along the rails to soak in a moment to clear his head and prepare for what's next.

Damn, the sea's pretty rough today.

The ship is pitching up uneasily. Waves crash into the prow a bit high. The wind is kicking up.

We're not heading into a damned squall are we? Who's the Captain? Is that an iceberg?

Curiously, he walks through the decks more aware that no one is around. At all.

No crew. No porters. Maids. Millionaires. Or society ladies with wide hats discussing horticulture.

Top deck, around the pool, there is a faux Tiki Bar with a pedestal in the center. It had two poles from which dangle a pair of ropes. Was this for a magic show? To tie some maiden up for sacrifice? For King Kong? Is that what happened? Yeah, he was the tied-up maiden. Too many Martinis? Did Greta give him something—?

"Who's driving this ship, eh? Is my soul fading? Am I actually dead or something?"

There's a bell ringing. Was it from the wind? He hears a bleary "Baaaaal."

Around a corner he finds someone.

A goat?

"Holy creepers. Did you eat everyone on board, or what?"

The goat yelps "Baaaal." It disdainfully rears its horns and trots off.

"Jeepers. What the—?"

Then he notices a cat. Splotched gray and white.

"Gandalfo?"

It solemnly stares up at him, and closes and opens its eyes, as if to consciously blink at him. Looks like his recently deceased cat.

He takes a step and falls. He's confused. He didn't trip on anything? Looking around he sees nothing to trip over. He gets up and falls again. As if his strength is giving way, dissipating. Or is it—orientation? He feels thin, as if evaporating.

Must be extremely starved? His hand trembles. Looking at it—it seems to flicker in a transparent flux. Momentarily his hand vanishes. Then comes back into view.

"Lord. What now?"

He's torn between this immersive anomaly, and this nowhere place—jolted by rejuvenating adrenalin spikes to keep "living. " To Survive. To exist. To be alive. *It's the goddamn spasm attacks from being in this—*

There's something moving around the corner. He's about to holler out when he sees a large black shape trumble along.

"Christ Almighty! Is that a bear? Did the whole crew stop at Circe's island and turn to swine and animals?

"Most likely, that traveling circus on board got loose and everyone is hiding? Or abandoned ship?"

Running aside the railings, he doesn't see the lifeboats.

"Damn."

He hears a grunt. The rotund black shape is drawing closer. He gasps, unable to breathe. But he can't breathe loud so as not to alert the—gorilla? An effing gorilla?"

Indeed, an ape is waddling along the deck. Sniffing about. Hungry? Does he catch his scent? He shouldn't have put that cologne on, damnit.

It stops, suddenly aware of someone crouching behind a lounge chair. It grunts and growls, then pounds his chest to alert him he's seen.

Duke slowly gets up and backs away. The gorilla shows his teeth.

"Easy fella."

The gorilla leaps towards him, and they're off.

"Got to make it to an open door."

He reaches into his pocket and finds a leftover sandwich. He tosses it behind him. The gorilla, ready to pounce on him, stops to smell it.

Duke runs. Grabbing at doors that won't open. He heads into the ballroom. Door swings ajar. Thank God he's in.

He bends over huffing and panting, supporting his hands over his knees to catch his breath.

Gazing about, darting back and forth—no one to be seen!

"*What on earth?*"

In the meantime, the gorilla is pawing outside. Duke's famished. He spots a silver tray of leftover hors d'oeuvres. He scoffs some down. "Where's the kitchen?"

Slam. Doors swing open. The gorilla's inside.

Gulp.

It's turning over plates and sniffing.

"Dammit."

He gasps his drying throat. *That brute will throttle me.* A bead of sweat glistens down his cold forehead.

Frozen. Still as congealing cement. A hungry ape. *And horny too?* His heart pounds in his ears.

The gorilla pops in its mouth the last of the hors d'oeuvres, snarls, spots him crouching, and lunges towards him.

0210102030405060607080000102020030040050060070080009080907090600900509004
09003090020090020008001010919283736564738392010299385980807996885798794912687768683767365263542551434342516627356477990010100393857924875194604263982478673658913751602290090901920190193829883775656574747309840933408746027777777777777-094097483888819737268731-249-37585388647983840000000000000000000000000000000000-012908638848480574078934829309018769528394024897831698940289546974895724934210-48972805684502834-1209902-947895784731984-2489048750943-=34-34023931777-54923939047835694348249382-98873811386778789^&*%&*&*)&&1111111111111111%%5587979219727943442546667879009877*((*)()()(*)(((*()^^^^^$&**%*%7777777777*%**^*8##@#@#!@3@#34
%6787*(7879)(90(*&*&(*&*(&*(&%^&(*&^^%**&&%^$$@#$$&&%WEETUI(&%
*ZZZZZZZZZZZZZZZZZZZZZZZZZZZZZZZZZZZZZZZZZ%^&&*UPIHG*&**)PLKH*
)&^*(OJUU(O*&(IOIYp9fjihq0rfkoir9d89uy7HUYFR&*OIotg9dkkwifn98u(PKJUYG
&^&U*Ojiuh7ty789rwgw978uuGFRWRYUIMJ*HUYBIPJIJGYg6hh8jfir9g8wtjgig9i7
24hhwuwiuqqppwoowiieuuryythhgjjfkkdlls;lammzmnxnnbcbvsxzzzqaswxwseedrfvrgtbg
njymhiko,poqazwsxedcrfvtgbhnujmuk,il.o;qazwsxedcrfvtgbyhnujmik,ol.p;.,.,popplmokn
ojbihvugfttyfdxrdesszwawqwdfvhoppl,okmijnuhbygtfdxesz3aqqpl,okmijnuhbygvtfcrdxes
zwaqwaqwaqwaqeseszeszessseszesezrdrxrdrxdrdxtftfctftftcftcygygvygygyvgvhuhuhb777
uuhuhbiiijniijnokokmkokomlplplpmplpnlpllpbllplpvplplcpllplpxplplzokokokokojkokoho
kokogkokofkokodkkokoskokoakokijijijiujiijijhijijyijigjijitjijifjijrijijdijieijijsijjiwiijiajijqijq
qwawqesedqrd5qfftf6gqyuuhqijiokopzplplzokkokzijijzuhuhzyzztgtfzzrdrdzesewawqzlkz
kzjn777zhbzgvzfczdsxzzlzkmzjnzhbzgvzfczzokzijzuhzygztftfaswsaeddraftfatgaygyggayh
auuahhuiajiiajardrdraftftagygyauuhuajaijiaokokaoplpaazsaxdacafavgaabhanajamka,alalpa
oaiau3ahyagtafaradrsdtquhujxixjxokxplxygxtfrdxrdsdxxvxcxxhbxjnnjnxxmkmxxnjnxxuji
jxuh7777uhxgygxxtftfxxrdrdxxesexwxrdrftxyyhxuhujxxxo0o0x9i9i9x8u8u8x7y7y7x6t6t
x5r5rx4e4x7773w3wx22qx1q1xw2wx3e3ex4xxr4rxx5t5tx6y6yxx7u7uxx8i8x9o9o9xx0p
0x9o9ox8i8x8x7u7777x6y6x55tx4r4x3exwxw2wx2wx4xe4xeeedxtfgxygygyxhuuxjijixk
koxkokxox50403029786439200988777777786378857893996717839999945784254\]\][]
[]{}{}[]||[__{{{-[-[-[_{_” '-'-'-'_”7777777777777777777777777777777””-_> > >__>>-.-
._>_<-,-,-,_<_,-._-._-_>-.._,-__--,,--<-,-__--0_0-)_9--0-0_9-0_)_)(()))_0---07777777-99_99---
)_p---{[[_{-
[=]]=]=}|\\\\\\\\\\\]|\\\\]|}[][][][]{}{}{}{}{}}]|\\\\\\]}[}[}[}[}[]|\\\\]\{}{}{}{}{}}]\|\\
]\|\][][][][]{}{}{}[][]\}[}\\\\]|}[}[}[}[][]]]+[-[_[-[_[-
[_=[=[[;[;{[[“]”}”}”]T]T]”{:{:{:[[.000[.[.[}}?]/]/}?}{>[.[.{?}?]/>{p>{.[>{[,{:,;<:;;:<:>”'
{;Pp;P:P:[;[;{;[;[{“”{:[;[Plp{.000L<.,.?//,/./>//,/.?,/,.'.~`[--
p11111!1!`1`1{[;{;[;[“]]”}']]”}”}”}TT||\\|\\]}[]\\]\|}}|\}]][[;':'?>/?000??/>>???////?////////>
>;;:.””:';'}”]}”}}}”T{:[;[;[;{:{:{:[;[;[;[:>:>:.,;;,;,:000>:>:>:<:<><><>,.<><>
,.<>><.,,>>.,,.<><<,>>><';'><><.';'>><><”;'<><><<.,.<0000><.,,.,,.<><<>,>”“;;::”:
[;[::{:{:{:{??>::>:>;.;:”?:>;[.[>>>>>>>>>>>>>.000.........>........>{?//////////??????>;.[

:{"}}"""""""""""""""""""""""000}"}"}"{:P:;}"}}""}"}"}"}"}}""}"}'}TTTTTTT"}"}"}"}"}'}TTTT]
'T"{:{:{:{:{:[;[;[["{ "{ "{ "{T'[000'["{ "{{ "{{{{{{{{{{{{{{{{{{{{{{{{ "''''''':::::::::::::,;;;;;[;
:_--------- _p_P_Pp-P_p-P-p_P000-p_p-p_p-p_p-PP_P_P-p-p-PP__P-p-p-p_PP_P_P_p-
p-p-P_P_P_P_-o-o-o_OO_O_O_O-o000-o-o__OO__l-l-L__L_L_L_L_l-m-m_m-m-k-
MM--K_K-k-K-k-k-k----o_O_O_-i_J-j_000JJ_J-j-i_I_I-i-N-n{n- yyzyx--b-bb-n_--
jGgNnjIHuH^^^^6t6t6rRdde#3dFvgvouey000uijuwrhhfuruw8uiuedudivbvncmxklalpqpq
owieueyrttlaksjdhfgmznxbcbvncmxzallakkajj000ahhaggsggdffqooqppwooeiiruutyyruuei
qqyqwueepeooriituuyjjhjjgkkflldllsmmnnnzbcnhci000udsbyfwriwbcui::::::::::::::::::..............
........00000000010000100010001100010001000100010011010101001010010100100101 0
010090190901909109019090101070170701707017070170801090109090107010901709
010917010701001010990190010010100111111111111111111111111111111111111111111
1 1 1 1 1 1 1 1 1 1 1 1 1 1 1 1 1 1 1 1 1 1 1 1 1 1 1 1 1 1 1 1 1 1 1 1 1 1 1 1 1 1 1 1 1 1 1 1 1 1 1 1 1 1 1 1 1 1 1 1 1 1 1 1 1 1 1 1 1 1 1 1 1 1 1 1 1 1 1 1 1 1 1 1 1 1
1 1 1 1 1 1 1 1 1 1 1 1 1 1 1 1 1 1 1 1 1 1 1 1 1 1 1 1 1 1 1 1 1 1 1 1 1 1 1 1 1 1 1 1 1 1 1 1 1 1 1 1 1 1 1 1 1 1 1 1 1 1 1 1 1 1 1 1 1 1 1 1 1 1 1 1 1 1 1 1 1 1 1 1 1 1
1 1 1 1 1 1 1 1 1 1 1 1 1 1 1 1 1 1 1 1 1 1 1 1 1 1 1 1 1 1 1 1 1 1 1 1 1 1 1 1 1 1 1 1 1 1 1 1 1 1 1 1 1 1 1 1 1 1 1 1 1 1 1 1 1 1 1 1 1 1 1 1 1 1 1 1 1 1 1 1 1 1 1 1 1 1
1 1 1 1 1 1 1 1 1 1 1 1 1 1 1 1 1 1 1 1 1 1 1 1 1 1 1 1 1 1 1 1 1 1 1 1 1 1 1 1 1 1 1 1 1 1 1 1 1 1 1 1 1 1 1 1 1 1 1 1 1 1 1 1 1 1 1 1 1 1 1 1 1 1 1 1 1 1 1 1 1 1 1 1 1 1
1 1 1 1 1 1 1 1 1 1 1 1 1 1 1 1 1 1 1 1 1 1 1 1 1 1 1 1 1 1 1 1 1 1 1 1 1 1 1 1 1 1 1 1 1 1 1 1 1 1 1 1 1 1 1 1 1 1 1 1 1 1 1 1 1 1 1 1 1 1 1 1 1 1 1 1 1 1 1 1 1 1 1 1 1 1
1 1 1 1 1 1 1 1 1 1 1 1 1 1 1 1 1 1 1 1 1 1 1 1 1 1 1 1 1 1 1 1 1 1 1 1 1 1 1 1 1 1 1 1 1 1 1 1 1 1 1 1 1 1 1 1 1 1 1 1 1 1 1 1 1 1 1 1 1 1 1 1 1 1 1 1 1 1 1 1 1 1 1 1 1 1
1 1 1 1 1 1 1 1 1 1 1 1 1 1 1 1 1 1 1 1 1 1 1 1 1 1 1 1 1 1 1 1 1 1 1 1 1 1 1 1 1 1 1 1 1 1 1 1 1 1 1 1 1 1 1 1 1 1 1 1 1 1 1 1 1 1 1 1 1 1 1 1 1 1 1 1 1 1 1 1 1 1 1 1 1 1
1 1 1 1 1 1 1 1 1 1 1 1 1 1 1 1 1 1 1 1 1 1 1 1 1 1 1 1 1 1 1 1 1 1 1 1 1 1 1 1 1 1 1 1 1 1 1 1 1 1 1 1 1 1 1 1 1 1 1 1 1 1 1 1 1 1 1 1 1 1 1 1 1 1 1 1 1 1 1 1 1 1 1 1 1 1
1 1 1 1 1 1 1 1 1 1 1 1 1 1 1 1 1 1 1 1 1 1 1 1 1 1 1 1 1 1 1 1 1 1 1 1 1 1 1 1 1 1 1 1 1 1 1 1 1 1 1 1 1 1 1 1 1 1 1 1 1 1 1 1 1 1 1 1 1 1 1 1 1 1 1 1 1 1 1 1 1 1 1 1 1 1
1 1 1 1 1 1 1 1 1 1 1 1 1 1 1 1 1 1 1 1 1 1 1 1 1 1 1 1 1 1 1 1 1 1 1 1 1 1 1 1 1 1 1 1 1 1 1 1 1 1 1 1 1 1 1 1 1 1 1 1 1 1 1 1 1 1 1 1 1 1 1 1 1 1 1 1 1 1 1 1 1 1 1 1 1 1
1 1 1 1 1 1 1 1 1 1 1 1 1 1 1 1 1 1 1 1 1 1 1 1 1 1 1 1 1 1 1 1 1 1 1 1 1 1 1 1 1 1 1 1 1 1 1 1 1 1 1 1 1 1 1 1 1 1 1 1 1 1 1 1 1 1 1 1 1 1 1 1 1 1 1 1 1 1 1 1 1 1 1 1 1 1
1 1 1 1 1 1 1 1 1 1 1 1 1 1 1 1 1 1 1 1 1 1 1 1 1 1 1 1 1 1 1 1 1 1 1 1 1 1 1 1 1 01000010 01101001 01101110
01100001 01110010 01111001 00100000 01001110 01110101 01101101 01100010
01100101 01110010 01110011 }}:{;[[[,[{>000{>{.[:>;;'/'}'9999999999999 99999
100100
1999999999999999999999999999999999999:[;::;,,<LPLAO000KOKAIJJIJAUHUHAY
GYGATFTFARDRDAESEAALPPAKOOAAJIAHUUAAHUGAYTFAARDAEASAW
ASAEDAXASZAFAXAFACAGAVAHABAJANAKAMALAOALAIKAUJAOZOXO
COVOBONOMOLOKOJOHOGOFODOSOAOQOWOEOROTOYOUOIKOOILPLPLP
UKOKOTIJIJTHUHUHYGYGETFWFRFWDQESQDADSZSCSFCFCDGVVGVFHB
HBHGJNJNJHMKKMJL,L,L,KLPLPLKPP,P,KOKOKOJOMOMOJJIIJIUNINIUNINU
HUYHUHHTBHBTHBGVGVRGVGRTFTDFTCEFCFCDDXDXDXXXRSRDASEQ
WSQWAQSESEQSSQDXDXQCFFWFCFCATTGGVGRYYDHXHHGYHUBBHBFH
BUHUHURHUHUTJIJGJNJNJHNKKYKOOOKOKOKOMGMIJIBJIJUFURUHRHY
GDUHKSKHDJHAHFKHCHBHVBKHIOJIIHFROOBDUFUWRUWYRQRUVJWNI
URIHWUYICJNVBYEHVHWNNCUKANXMZINRYUHXGFBXJISUBUUBVYRGE
FWIDJIMCInuvlisrvvcm;ojcouhodijdclifvahaidkuajks,fjcuterkhfideotryeuwigfdhsjka000
00000000000000000000000000000000000000000000000000000000000000000000&&&&&
<<<<<<<<<<<<<<<<<<<<<<<<<<<<<<<><>>>>>>>>>777777777777777777
mok0kohiokoujoaijisijruirhvbvhgughuuhbplmokmijnuhbygvtfcrdxeszwaqQ

Episode   16

Centrifugal

I could be bounded in a nutshell and count myself a king of infinite
space—were it not that I have bad dreams.

—*Hamlet II.ii. 254* Shakespeare

Never in one's meditations could being dismembered by an ape be an imagined end. Duke, perspiring and frantic, is shocked to see what appears to be a friend through a round glass window in the kitchen door.

"Is that—? Can it be?"

This is it. He sprints across the ballroom. An alerted grunt snarls to launch after him. He feels the heat of flaring nostrils. The impending pounce of massive power crushing bones. There's a swipe of a leathery palm to grab him backwards into devolving animality.

He leaps to the door.

Slamming through the kitchen. His ears pop. He's soaked as if plunged through a drowning pool while being shot like a cannonball. He's gasping for air. Heart wildly pumping to implode.

Shot through a cannon tunnel. A cascade of hieroglyphs in a latticed skein of layered contours and the convex Fibonacci of a vortex of every number, letter, symbol that is the code of all things. Was he seeing the hieroglyphs? Or is he experiencing hieroglyphs as if becoming the hieroglyphics themselves? The LIFE-FORCE disintegrates into the fractalism circuits of INFINITY:

. . . a breakdown to primordial elements manifested in the vacuity of air, water, fire, earth. Separate and mixing, condensed and mineralizing, vegetative, animality—sub branching into reptilian, amphibian, insectoid, mammalian, astral, pentagonal, ether dimensions.

96

0210102030405060607080000102020030040050060070080090809070906009005090004
0900309002009002000800101091928373656473839201029938598080799688579879499
1268776868376736526354255143434251662735647799001010039385792487519460 42
6398247867365891375160229009090192019019382988377565657474730984093-
34087460277777777777-094097483888819737 26873-249-
375853886479838400000000000000000000000000000000000-
012908638848480574078934829309018769528394024897831698940289546974895724
934210-48972805684502834-1209902-947895784731984-2489048750943-=34-
34023931777-54923939047835694348249382-
98873811386778789^&*%&*&*)&&111111111111111%%558797921972794 34425466
6787900987*((*)()O(*)((()*O^^^^$&**%*%7777777777*%**^*8##@#@#!@3@#34
%6787*(7879)(90(*&*&(*&*(&*(&%^&(*&^^%**&&%^$$@#$$&&%WEETUI(&%
ZZZZZZZZZZZZZZZZZZZZZZZZZZZZZZZZZZZZZZZZZZZ%^&&*UPIHG*&**)PLKH*
)&^*(OJUU(O*&(IOIYp9fjihq0rfkoir9d89uy7HUYFR&*OIotg9dkkwifn98u(PKJUYG
&^&U*Ojiuh7ty789rwgw978uuGFRWRYUIMJ*HUYBIPJIJGYg6hh8jfir9g8wtjgig9i7
24hhwuwiuqqppwoowiieuuryythhgjjfkkdlls;lammzmnxnnbcbvsxzzzqaswxwseedrfvrgtbg
njymhiko,poqazwsxedcrfvtgbhnujmuk,il.o;qazwsxedcrfvtgbyhnujmik,ol.p;.,.,popplmokn
ojbihvugfttyfdxrdesszwawqwdfvhoppl,okmijnuhbygtfdxesz3aqqpl,okmijnuhbygvtfcrdxes
zwaqwaqwaqwaqeseszeszessessezsesezrdrxrdrxdrdxtftfctftftcftcygygvygygyvgvhuhuhb777
uuhuhbiiijniijnokokmkokomlplplpmplpnlpllpbllplpvplplcpllplpxplplzokokokokojkokoho
kokogkokofkokodkkokoskokoakokijijijiujiijijhijijyijigjijitjijifjijrijijdijieijijsijjiwiijiajijqijq
qwawqesedqrd5qfftf6gqyuuhqijiokopzplplzokkokzijijzuhuhzyzztgtfzzrdrdzesewawqzlkz
kzjn777zhbzgvzfczdsxzzlzkmzjnzhbzgvzfczzokzijzuhzygztftfaswsaeddraftfatgaygyggayh
auuahhuiajiiajardrdraftftagygyauuhuajaijiaokokaoplpaazsaxdacafavgaabhanajamka,alalpa
oaiau3ahyagtafaradrsdtquhujxixjxokxplxygxtfrdxrdsdxxvxcxxhbxjnnjnxxmkmxxnjnxxuji
jxuh7777uhxgygxxtftfxxrdrdxxesexwxrdrftxyyhxuhujxxxo0o0x9i9i9x8u8u8x7y7y7x6t6t
x5r5rx4e4x7773w3wx22qx1q1xw2wx3e3ex4xxr4rxx5t5tx6y6yxx7u7uxx8i8x9o9o9xx0p
0x9o9ox8i8x8x7u7777x6y6x55tx4r4x3exwxw2wx2wx4xe4xeeedxtfgxygygyxhuuxjijixk
koxkokxox50403029786439200988777777786378857893996717839999945784254\]\][]
[}{}{}|3|||_{{{-[-[-L_{__"_'-'-'_"7777777777777777777777777777777777""-_>_>__>>-.-
._>_<-,-,-_<_,-._-._>-..._,-_--,,--<-,-_--0_0-)_9--0-0_9-0_)_)())))_0---07777777-99_99---
)_p---{[[_{-
[=]]=]=}|\|\|\[\|]|\|\|]|\}[][][][]{}{}{}{}{}}|3|\|\|\|\}{3|3|3|3|\|\|\|\]|\}{}{}{}{}{}{}}|\|\
]\|\|[][][][]{}{}{}[][|\|3|\|\|\|]}{3}{3}[][][]||+[-L_[-L_[-
L_=[=[[;[;{['["]"}"}"]T]T]T"{:{:{:[[.000[.[.[}}?]/]/}?}{>[.[.{?}?]/>{p>{.[>{[,{.;;<;,;;:<:>"'
{;Pp;P:P:[;[;{;[;[{""{:[;[Plp{.000L<.,.?//,/./>//,/.?,/,'.~`[--
p11111!1!`1`1{[;{;[;["]]"}']}"}"}"}"]T]]||\|\|3||3\|\|3|\}]][[;':'?>/?000??/>>???////?////////>
>;::.""";;"}"]}"}}}"T{:{;[;[;{:{:{:{;[;[;[:>:>:.,;;,;;.:000>:>:>:<:◇◇◇◇◇<◇,.◇◇
,.◇><,.,>>,.,.◇<<,>>><';'>◇◇.';>>◇<";'◇◇◇◇<.,.<0000><..,,.,,.<◇<◇.>"";..":
[;[::{:{:{:{??>::>:>;,.;."?:>;[.[>>>>>>>>>>>>>>.000........>........>{?//////////?????>;.[

:{"}}"""""""""""""""""""000}"}"}"{:P:;}"}}""}"}"}"}"}}"}"}'TTTTTT'}"}"}"}"}"}'TTTT'
'}"{:{:{:{:{:{:[;[;[["{"{"{'[T'[000'["{"{{"{{{{{{{{{{{{{{{{{{{{{{{"""""""::::::::::::::;;;;;[;
:_---------_p_P_Pp-P_p-P-p_P000-p_p-p_p-p_p-PP_P_P-p-p-PP__P-p-p-p_PP_P_P_p-
p-p-P_P_P_P_-o-o-o_OO_O_O_O-o000-o-o__OO__l-l-L__L_L_L_L_l-m-m_m-m-k-
MM--K_K-k-K-k-k-k----o_O_O_-i_J-j_000JJ_J-j-i_I_I-i-N-n{n- yyzyx--b-bb-n_--
jGgNnjIHuH^^^^6t6t6rRdde#3dFvgvouey000uijuwrhhfuruw8uiuedudivbvncmxklalpqpq
owieueyrttlaksjdhfgmznxbcbvncmxzallakkajj000ahhaggsggdffqooqppwooeiiruutyyruuei
qqyqwueepeooriituuyjjhjjgkkflldllsmmnnzbcnhci000udsbyfwriwbcui::::::::::::::::...............
........0000000001000010001000110001000100010001001101010100101001010010010
010090190901909109019090101070170701707017070170801090109090107010901709
010917010701001010990190010010100111111111111111111111111111111111111111
1111111111111111111111111111111111111111111111111111111111111111111111111111
11111111111111111111111111111111111111111111111111111111111111111111111111111
1111111111111111111111111111111111111111111111111111111111111111111111111111
11111111111111111111111111111111111111111111111111111111111111111111111111111
1111111111111111111111111111111111111111111111111111111111111111111111111111
1111111111111111111111111111111111111111111111111111111111111111111111111111
11111111111111111111111111111111111111111111111111111111111111111111111111111
1111111111111111111111111111111111111111111111111111111111111111111111111111
11111111111111111111111111111111111111111 01000010 01101001 01101110
01100001 01110010 01111001 00100000 01001110 01110101 01101101 01100010
01100101 01110010 01110011 }}:{;[[[,[{>000{>{.[:>;;'/'}'9999999999999 99999
100100
199999999999999999999999999999999999:[;::;,,<LPLAOOOOKOKAIJJIJAUHUHAY
GYGATFTFARDRDAESEAALPPAKOOAAJIAHUUAAHUGAYTFAARDAEASAW
ASAEDAXASZAFAXAFACAGAVAHABAJANAKAMALAOALAIKAUJAOZOXO
COVOBONOMOLOKOJOHOGOFODOSOAOQOWOEOROTOYOUOIKOOILPLPLP
UKOKOTIJIJTHUHUHYGYGETFWFRFWDQESQDADSZSCSFCFCDGVVGVFHB
HBHGJNJNJHMKKMJL,L,L,KLPLPLKPP,P,KOKOKOJOMOMOJJIIJIUNINIUNINU
HUYHUHHTBHBTHBGVGVRGVGRTFTDFTCEFCFCDDXDXDXXXRSRDASEQ
WSQWAQSESEQSSQDXDXQCFFWFCFCATTGGVGRYYDHXHHGYHUBBHBFH
BUHUHURHUHUTJIJGJNJNJHNKKYKOOOKOKOKOMGMIJIBJIJUFURUHRHY
GDUHKSKHDJHAHFKHCHBHVBKHIOJIIHFROOBDUFUWRUWYRQRUVJWNI
URIHWUYICJNVBYEHVHWNNCUKANXMZINRYUHXGFBXJISUBUUBVYRGE
FWIDJIMCInuvlisrvvcm;ojcouhodijdclifvahaidkuajks,fjcuterkhfideotryeuwigfdhsjka000
000000000000000000000000000000000000000000000000000000000000000000&&&&&
<<<<<<<<<<<<<<<<<<<<<<<<<<<◇>>>>>>>>7777777777777777777
mok0kohiokoujoaijisijruirhvbvhgughuuhbplmokmijnuhbygvtfcrdxeszwaqQ

Solomon & Pythagoras?—unlock the checkerboard staircase of pyrami-
dal escalation (immanentizing the eschaton) as a rise of wings expanding wide
as streaking solar flares show existence is the question mark as existing seeks the
answer to fill in the blanks or remain blank as the question mark asks one to make
a mark. Marked to remark, or be remarkable.

The MIND craves the ANSWER. Regardless of the possible immortality
as the speeding fuse of one's sand is sucked and drained into the next hourglass, the
mind starves and screams for God, for BEING, to answer, to perceive the prolific
billion years and billion worlds of the complete Cosmos—as we can only catch a
moment of infinity.

Duke, a quadratic equation, a constant: reconfiguring through the molecular data between dimensions—unless becoming as One with EVERYTHING—
one becomes Nothingness to access the ALL.

The molecular flux of deconstructive molecularization, from the sub-atom-
ic to cellular dualities of flesh; an imprisoned individuated ego chasm and flesh as
a medium, a means, a vehicle of knowing. No-ing. It is not that. It is not this. It IS.
Thus. And Now. That is. Isness. Istigkeit. The finger pointing to the moon is not
the moon.

An organic quadrant orbiting an organizing spark in multilinear circumference spherical convergence and unlapping Geometry.

He's triangulated to coordinates of compass points in Maya's illusory
realm of Pleroma & the Fulcrum Interface of a divine supreme Brahman Abraxas—in between big-bangs?

Present. Now. Presence curve of space-time. Beyond time. The circle of
life folds in on itself. Always existing. A memory fibrillating in the Omega Akashic
databanks of stellar astral heavens of pellucid crystalline liquid protoplasm flesh
of ichor.

This unfolding and fulfilling of the expanding collective human psyche begins understanding the energies which brought it here. The magic and technology
which unlock promethean fire of the gods. To know God? To create God? Become
God? Words evaporate like mere poetry under the exploding weight of math and
music of the secrets which scream at us.

A fate. A seed. A vessel container vestibule, for his soul to circle in a momentum that births into a spiral into the same life on another octave from 1 2 3 4 5
6 7 to Zero to 1 2 3 4 5 6 7 !, from primal tones implied in all number notes of C D
E F G A B back to C but vibrating at its higher frequency pitch. The soul forever in
flesh and not flesh? The vessel is emptied to receive the next soul in the great chain
of Being. Then nothing. The seed.

$$\psi_{n+1}(\vec{r},t) = \int K(\vec{r}-\vec{r}',t)f[\psi_n(\vec{r}',t)]d\vec{r}' \quad dE + \delta w_u \leq 0$$

$$\delta w \leq -dU + T_R dS + \sum \mu_{iR} dN_i \qquad -\Delta S + \int \frac{\delta Q}{T} = \oint \frac{\delta Q}{T} < 0 \qquad G_{\mu\nu} = R_{\mu\nu} - \tfrac{1}{2}Rg_{\mu\nu},$$

$$\kappa = \frac{8\pi G}{c^4} \approx 2.077 \times 10^{-43} N^{-1}, \qquad\qquad R_{\mu\nu} - \tfrac{1}{2}Rg_{\mu\nu} + \Lambda g_{\mu\nu} = \kappa T_{\mu\nu}.$$

$$g_{\mu\nu} = [S1] \times \mathrm{diag}(-1,+1,+1,+1)$$

$$R^{\mu}{}_{\alpha\beta\gamma} = [S2] \times \left(\Gamma^{\mu}_{\alpha\gamma,\beta} - \Gamma^{\mu}_{\alpha\beta,\gamma} + \Gamma^{\mu}_{\sigma\beta}\Gamma^{\sigma}_{\gamma\alpha} - \Gamma^{\mu}_{\sigma\gamma}\Gamma^{\sigma}_{\beta\alpha}\right)$$

$$G_{\mu\nu} = [S3] \times \kappa T_{\mu\nu} \qquad\qquad \textbf{6430 Å = 6430 x 10}^{\textbf{-10}}\textbf{ m = 6.430 x 10}^{\textbf{-7}}\textbf{ m}$$

c = λ f **f f = c/λ** **f = 3 x 10^8/(6.430 x 10^{-7}) = 4.67 x 10^{14}** **c = λ f**

λ = c/f **λ = 3 x 10^8/ 10^6 = 300 m.** $\quad ds^2 = -\left(\alpha^2 - \beta_i\beta^i\right)dt^2 + 2\beta_i\,dx^i\,dt + \gamma_{ij}\,dx^i\,dx^j,$

$$v_s(t) = \frac{dx_s(t)}{dt},$$

$$\alpha = 1,$$
$$\beta^x = -v_s(t)f(r_s(t)), \qquad r_s(t) = \sqrt{(x-x_s(t))^2 + y^2 + z^2},$$
$$\beta^y = \beta^z = 0,$$
$$\gamma_{ij} = \delta_{ij}, \qquad f(r_s) = \frac{\tanh(\sigma(r_s+R)) - \tanh(\sigma(r_s-R))}{2\tanh(\sigma R)},$$

$$ds^2 = \left(v_s(t)^2 f(r_s(t))^2 - 1\right)dt^2 - 2v_s(t)f(r_s(t))\,dx\,dt + dx^2 + dy^2 + dz^2.$$

$$-\frac{c^4}{8\pi G}\frac{v_s^2(y^2+z^2)}{4g^2 r_s^2}\left(\frac{df}{dr_s}\right)^2, \qquad i\hbar\frac{\partial}{\partial t}\Psi(x,t) = \left[-\frac{\hbar^2}{2m}\frac{\partial^2}{\partial x^2} + V(x,t)\right]\Psi(x,t).$$

$$\Psi(x,t) = \sum_n A_n \psi_{E_n}(x)e^{-iE_n t/\hbar}.$$

$$\psi_{n\ell m}(r,\theta,\varphi) = \sqrt{\left(\frac{2}{na_0}\right)^3 \frac{(n-\ell-1)!}{2n[(n+\ell)!]}}\, e^{-r/na_0}\left(\frac{2r}{na_0}\right)^\ell L_{n-\ell-1}^{2\ell+1}\left(\frac{2r}{na_0}\right)\cdot Y_\ell^m(\theta,\varphi)$$

$$|\delta\mathbf{Z}(t)| \approx e^{\lambda t}|\delta\mathbf{Z}_0|, \qquad\qquad \psi_{n+1}(\vec{r},t) = \int K(\vec{r}-\vec{r}',t)f[\psi_n(\vec{r}',t)]d\vec{r}'$$

$$K(\vec{r}-\vec{r}',L) = \frac{ik\exp[ikL]}{2\pi L}\exp\left[\frac{ik|\vec{r}-\vec{r}'|^2}{2L}\right] \qquad x_{n+1} = rx_n(1-x_n), \quad r \in [1,4].$$

$$\int_{-\infty}^{\infty}\exp(ax^4 + bx^3 + cx^2 + dx + f)\,dx = e^f \sum_{n,m,p=0}^{\infty}\frac{b^{4n}}{(4n)!}\frac{c^{2m}}{(2m)!}\frac{d^{4p}}{(4p)!}\frac{\Gamma(3n+m+p+\tfrac{1}{4})}{a^{3n+m-p-\frac{1}{4}}}$$

$$c_{\frac{p}{q}} = \frac{e^{2\pi i\frac{p}{q}}}{2}\left(1 - \frac{e^{2\pi i\frac{p}{q}}}{2}\right)\cdot z = r\left(\frac{1}{2}-x\right), \quad c = \frac{r}{2}\left(1-\frac{r}{2}\right).$$

Reverse. Repeat. Cascade of the non-linear. Eko Eko Azarak. Eko Eko Zomelak. Eko Eko Aradia. Ego consecro et benedico istum circulum per nomine Dei Altissimi ut sit mihi et omnibus Elohim invictus . . . YOLCAM LONSHI PIR. YOLCAM IALPRG IAIDA. BYNEPOR OD BUTMONO. BNAPSEN OD BRALGES. YOLCAM LONSHI TOX. ZACARE CA OD ZAMRAN, ODO CICLE QAA, ZORGE, LAP ZIRDO NOCO MAD, HOATH IAIDA.

Aum Namo Shivaya. ADRPAN COMSELAH MADRIAX. While All is in The All, it is equally true that The All is in All . . . PaVeh GedGalOrUnGraphTal Gon.MaUrMalsGorDruxPalMed DonCeph Van Fam Gisg Aum Vajrasatva Hung Aum mani padme hum Aummmmmmmmmmmmmmmmmmmmmmm
mmmmmmmmmmmmmmmmmmmmmmmmmmmmmmmmmmmmmmmmmmmmmm
mmmmmmmmmmmmmmmmmmmmmmmmmmmmmmmmmmmmmmmmmmmmmm
mmmmmmmmmmmmmmmmmmmmmmmmmmmmmmmmmmmmmmmmmmmmmm
mmmmmmmmmmmmmmmmmmmmmmmmmmmmmmmmmmmmmmmmmmmmmm
mmmmmmmmmmmmmmmmmmmmmmmmmmmmmmmmmmmmmmmmmmmmmm
mmmmmmmmmmmmmmmmmmmmmmmmmmmmmmmmmmmmmmmmmmmmmm
mmmmmmmmmmmmmmmmmmmmmmmmmmmmmmmmmmmmmmmmmmmmmm
mmmmmmmmmmmmmmmmmmmmmmmmmmmmmmmmmmmmmmmmmmmmmm
mmmmmmmmmmmmmmmmmmmmmmmmmmmmmmmmmmmmmmmmmmmmmm
mmmmmmmmmmmmmmmmmmmmmmmmmmmmmmmmmmmmmmmmmmmmmm
mmmmmmmmmmmmmmmmmmmmmmmmmmmmmmmmmmmmmmmmmmmmmm
mmmmmmmmmmmmmmmmmmmmmmmmmmmmmmmmmmmmmmmmmmmmmm
mmmmmmmmmmmmmmmmmmmmmmmmmmmmmmmmmmmmmmmmmmmmmm
mmmmmmmmmmmmmmmmmmmmmmmmmmmmmmmmmmmmmmmmmmmmmm
mmmmmmmmmmmmmmmmmmmmmmmmmmmmmmmmmmmmmmmmmmmmmm
mmmmmmmmmmmmmmmmmmmmmmmmmmmmmmmmmmmmmmmmmmmmmm
mmmmmmmmmmmmmmmmmmmmmmmmmmmmmmmmmmmmmmmmmmmmmm
mmmmmmm

The Jewel is in the Lotus. Amen the thunderbolt in the VOIDDDDDDDDDDDD DDDDDDDDDDDDDDDDDDDDDDDDDDDD
DDDDDDDDDDDDDDDDDDDDDDDDDDDDDDDDDDDDDDDDDDDDDDDD
DDDDDDDDDDDDDDDDDDDDDDDDDDDDDDDDDDDDDDDDDDDDDDDD
DDDDDDDDDDDDDDDDDDDDDDDDDDDDDDDDDDDDDDDDDDDDDDDD
DDDDDDDDDDDDDDDDDDDDDDDDDDDDDDDDDDDDDDDDDDDDDDDD
DDDDDDDDDDDDDDDDDDDDDDDDDDDDDDDDDDDDDDDDDDDDDDDD
DDDDDDDDDDDDDDDDDDDDDDDDDDDDDDDDDDDDDDDDDDDDDDDD
DDDDDDDDDDDDDDDDDDDDDDDDDDDDDDDDDDDDDDDDDDDDDDDD
DDDDDDDDDDDDDDDDDDDDDDDDDDDDDDDDDDDDDDDDDDDDDDDD
DDDDDDDDDDDDDDDDDDDDDDDDDDDDDDDDDDDDDDDDDDDDDDDD
DDDDDDDDDDDDDDDDDDDDDDDDDDDDDDDDDDDDDDDDDDDDDDDD

DDDDDDDDDDDDDDDDDDDDDDDDDDDDDDDDDDDDDDDDDDDDD
DDDDDDDDDDDDDDDDDDDDDDDDDDDDDDDDDDDDDDDDDDDDDDD
DDDDDDDDDDDDDDDDDDDDDDDDDDDDDDDDDDDDDDDDDDDDDDD
DDDDDDDDDDDDDDDDDDDDDDDDDDDDDDDDDDDDDDDDDDDDDDD
DDDDDDDDDDDDDDDDDDDDDDDDDDDDDDDDDDDDDDDDDDDDDDD
DDDDDDDDDDDDDDDDDDDDDDDDDDDDDDDDDDDDDDDDDDDDDDD
DDDDDDDDDDDDDDDDDDDDDDDDDDDDDDDDDDDDDDDDDDDDDDD
DDDDDDDDDDDDDDDDDDDDDDDDDDDDDDDDDDDDDDDDDDDDDDD
DDDDDDDDDDDDDDDDDDDDDDDDDDDDDDDDDDDDDDDDDDDDDDD
DDDDDDDDDDDDDDDDDDDDDDDDDDDDDDDDDDDDDDDDDDDDDDD
DDDDDDDDDDDDDDDDDDDDDDDDDDDDDDDDDDDDDDDDDDDDDDD
DDDDDDDDDDDDDDDDDDDDDDDDDDDDDDDDDDDDDDDDDDDDDDD
DDDDDDDDDDDDDDDDDDDDDDDDDDDDDDDDDDDDDDDDDDDDDDD
DDDDDDDDDDDDDDDDDDDDDDDDDDDDDDDDDDDDDDDDDDDDDDD
DDDDDDDDDDDDDDDDDDDDDDDDDDDDDDDDDDDDDDDDDDDDDDD
DDDDDDDDDDDDDDDDDDDDDDDDDDDDDDDDDDDDDDDDDDDDDDD
DDDDDDDDDDDDDDDDDDDDDDDDDDDDDDDDDDDDDDDDDDDDDDD
DDDDDDDDDDDDDDDDDDDDDDDDDDDDDDDDDDDDDDDDDDDDDDD
DDDDDDDDDDDDDDDDDDDDDDDDDDDDDDDDDDDDDDDDDDDDDDD
DDDDDDDDDDDDDDDDDDDDDDDDDDDDDDDDDDDDDDDDDDDDDDD
DDDDDDDDDDDDDDDDDDDDDDDDDDDDDDDDDDDDDDDDDDDDDDD
DDDDDDDDDDDDDDDDDDDDDDDDDDDDDDDDDDDDDDDDDDDDDDD
DDDDDDDDDDDDDDDDDDDDDDDDDDDDDDDDDDDDDDDDDDDDDDD
DDDDDDDDDDDDDDDDDDDDDDDDDDDDDDDDDDDDDDDDDDDDDDD
DDDDDDDDDDDDDDDDDDDDDDDDDDDDDDDDDDDDDDDDDDDDDDD
DDDDDDDDDDDDDDDDDDDDDDDDDDDDDDDDDDDDDDDDDDDDDDD
DDDDDDDDDDDDDDDDDDDDDDDDDDDDDDDDDDDDDDDDDDDDDDD
DDDDDDDDDDDDDDDDDDDDDDDDDDDDDDDDDDDDDDDDDDDDDDD
DDDDDDDDDDDDDDDDDDDDDDDDDDDDDDDDDDDDDDDDDDDDDDD
DDDDDDDDDDDDDDDDDDDDDDDDDDDDDDDDDDDDDDDDDDDDDDD
DDDDDDDDDDDDDDDDDDDDDDDDDDDDDDDDDDDDDDDDDDDDDDD
DDDDDDDDDDDDDDDDDDDDDDDDDDDDDDDDDDDDDDDDDDDDDDD
DDDDDDDDDDDDDDDDDDDDDDDDDDDDDDDDDDDDDDDDDDDDDDD
DDDDDDDDDDDDDDDDDDDDDDDDDDDDDDDDDDDDDDDDDDDDDDD
DDDDDDDDDDDDDDDDDDDDDDDDDDDDDDDDDDDDDDDDDDDDDDD
DDDDDDDDDDDDDDDDDDDDDDDDDDDDDDDDDDDDDDDDDDDDDDD
DDDDDDDDDDDDDDDDDDDDDDDDDDDDDDDDDDDDDDDDDDDDDDD
DDD

Spiral ethereal DNA, ascending a wizard's lighthouse, attains its blazing revolution . . . the wordlessly miraculous transpires. He beholds the illumination. A density has been transmitting with him, interfacing in this transference. This transportation. Locating and redirecting his signal, his genetic signature and consciousness.

Even above the already intricate conduction of information codifying through a visionary aura—insofar as a point within the celestial geometry of things can access the nodal fundament of illuminating all-encompassing truth—the incendiary bliss-filled integrating of the All-Answering Question, its epic fulfillment, at the end of all dreams, at the keyhole of our *raison d'etre*, our reason to be, stamping us with a gigantic question mark when we come to birth—in the limbo space of absorbing awe warps an evolutionary physical ego sentience—invisible force vacuums the Answer, backwards out of Duke's knowing—losing all memory of its stellar nirvanic realization, and is shot back into the tunneling portals of kaleidoscopic, strobing color.

"Suitor! What the fuck? Are you alright?"

A hand grasps to steady him up. Duke collapses into a familiar face, clasping and embracing, as if he's escaped being a marooned hostage on Pluto.

"Geez. Doug, where have you been?"

"Tom?"

It's his pal—Thomas Cochrane.

Duke falls to the floor, hugging it, and just lays awhile. Back from a rollercoaster while receiving electric shock treatment and raped by aliens. From world to world. How does he still have a body? A mind?

He's in a kitchen, but no longer on the ship . . . back to where the party had been—the one he left before getting warped to Hollywood. Seems years since he's been here.

Episode 17

Windows

It does no good to ask the weakling's pointless question, "Is America a fascist state?" We must ask instead, in a major rather than a minor key, "Can we make America the best damned fascist state the world has ever seen?"

—Lewis Lapham *Pretensions to Empire*

Chunks of memory seep into Duke's blanked mind.

"Where in hell did you just come from?" asked Tom.

"I—I don't know how to even answer that question," said Duke.

"Always a freakin' riot, eh?" Thomas responded. "Look, not to be cruel, but you're behaving bizarre."

"Bizarre?"

"More Abby-normal than usual." Cochrane paused, oddly observing him.

"Hey man, did you have any cake?"

"Cake? What? What cake?" said Duke,

"Cake, yeah cake. Not a difficult question. Did you get into this cake? I mixed it up by accident. It's not really meant for consumption."

"How—how's that?"

"Didn't I tell you?" said Cochrane. "I put out a Chocolate cake made with ganja butter—potent stuff. However—I also, accidentally, placed out a different one—an apple carrot cake. Experimental! Verboten. Forbidden as such."

"Wh-what do you mean—fffforbidden? Experimental?"

"Experimental?" cried Thomas. "The fruit of the Tree of Knowledge from Eden is what I'm talking about. We sent drones down to drill into the earth's core to retrieve the Pomegranate seeds from the lost ancient kingdom of Hades in the underworld, where some of the Atlantians absconded to, near Agharta. They had the original. There's an entire goddamned civilization down there under the earth. It will destroy people's minds. We used the mathematical codes in the seed's DNA to create a frequency to apply to the Hadron Collider Atom Smasher to enable us to travel back in time—in conjunction with Stephen Hawking's equations and the Tesla based tech which, even the Germans worked on for their anti-gravity Bell, and—not to get too complicated—we sent our time-bot back in order to peer into what happened at the Dawn of creation . . ."

Duke's finding this as incredible as he imagined.

All that esoterica Greta carried on about seems to make sense. This is IT? He feels caught, a ship at the edge of a whirlpool. A planet passing a black hole's event horizon and—

"Ha, Doug, you know what? I'm surprised you didn't anticipate this. You know me—of course I'm messing with you," slapping him on the back. "But seriously man, you don't look well. Sit down. Here's a glass of water. Seriously. Regardless of all that hooey, there's something at work here.

"This cake I'm talking about is no joke, substantially potent—as its ingredients do possess special properties as it underwent a radical—let's say—revolutionary process. It's meant for lab animals. To be synthesized appropriately once we configure an accessible dosage and chemical schematic analysis. Something we can imbibe before interacting with the atom smasher, to create a synergy . . . If possible. Conceptually along the lines of a Quantum Entanglement."

"Quantum entanglement!?"

"Yes, it's a medium by which when a group of particles are separated by a vast distance, yet function identically, even allowing for telecommunication across light years—"

"I know what the hell it is! What's the context? What in God does it have to do with me?"

"Yeah, sorry Doug. That's the astronomically complicated part. Especially since we've been utilizing the latest prototype of quantum computing Artificial Intelligence. We call it ART. Although it's been integrated into H.E.G.E.L. The point is—I'm thinking, maybe you ingested some? If you did—I'm surprised you're alive. Thank God. It works! Heh."

"What?"

"We may need to rush you to a hospital. You're feverish, and exhibiting symptoms of paranoid schizophrenia . . . It would take a Nobel Prize winner to explain the whole process, over at least a few days. Maybe that'll be me? Eh?"

Cochrane snorts with nervous but giddy laughter and adjusts his glasses.

"However, if we actually pursue this route, well—God knows how the doctors and authorities will react once they sample your blood. There'd be too many questions. This is a rather secret program."

"Obviously it's a goddamned massive secret. Especially to me. Tom, what in the fuck?"

Duke stands up belligerently and Cochrane tries to calm and sit him back down.

"Come on, man, take it easy. Now I know since Jill left, and your cat died, and those government grants didn't go through, you've been struggling through a hell of a time."

"I—I just don't know. What the hell is in it? Really?"

"To be honest, and technical: we worked with the vesicles of Liposomes to experiment with their spherical-shaped membranes of phospholipid bilayers as the best delivery system of the most cutting edge medicines utilizing nanoparticles . . .

"Nanotech? Christ!" grunted Duke.

"Extensive testing of reducing toxicity with endosomal/endosomatic synthetic and nutraceutical biocompatibility. Originally, some of its recipient ingredients included the synthetic soy protein to cure world hunger, known as Nutragood, but it was taken off production due to its as yet debugged negative side-effects.

"The inherent random vibration in particles must exceed the counteractive forces of gravity for optimum uploading and delivery. Amplified sonication extrusions would stimulate models for best kinetic absorption. Reduced tension with mono-layered surfactants whose stability maintains even when smaller than wavelengths of visible light.

"As we progressed with applying cyclotronic accelerators while emitting waves of radiation of high-speed ions and protons within magnetic fields of atomic nuclei, these pharmacological gradients of positronic radionuclides inevitably steered us towards transposing this approach on a quantum level with the most powerful accelerator on the planet, i.e. the CERN Hadron Collider . . .

"Thus, enabling us to bond relevant isotopes with multi-lamellar mononuclear phagocytes. A complete morphology of biometric range was analyzed, of course, with a dynamic photon correlation spectrometry. Once we reduced sedimentation of insolubles within the micronized intracellular radius, we solidified uninhibited uptake.

"Through these tempered aggregations we achieved enhanced immunogenic schemata of regeneration!"

"My God!"

"Full synergizing of homogenous cohesion of pharma-kinetics. The next marvel was how this delivery system synchronized its isohexyllic vehicle into tessellated honeycombs. It was this extraordinary endocytosis, thus, through vagination forming a vacuole of the cyto-plasmic enclosure of the cell of the nano-dot-particles—like a eukaryotic enzyme . . .

"Now you're losing me."

"Well, you know me. At this juncture, I thought, why don't we apply these bio-nano-organic/Nano-emulsive media into Dimethyltryptamine as a conduit? It can be charged and laminated by the Hadron, while being tracked by nanotech through the A.I. (hence, the quantum entanglement)—Thank you H.E.G.E.L. So, if we charged it through the Lightspeed cycles of the atom smasher—how would this alchemized medicine interact with a biological subject?"

"No."

Cochrane steel-eyed Suitor, impassively nodding his head.

Duke's hands shake with both fear and rage. He leaps to grab and throttle him.

"Tommy, you're not fucking with me? These postulates sound a bit too goddamn real. I didn't sign up to be a cosmonaut. What's going to happen to me?"

"Hang on Doug," as Tom fished for something off a silver tray. Finding the right Syringe, he slammed it into Duke's arm.

"Ow," yelped Duke.

"Well, that should sharpen you up. Man, we had some radical chemists on staff theorizing possible effects of psychotropic drugs put through these processes of bio-chemical physics, and what effects that will have on their properties, and thereby for a subject inducing them as theoretically utilized equations and conditions to open a small black hole, or wormhole—teleport the subject through, then back: traveling near the speed of light, while magnetizing and maintaining the quantum entanglement neural link/nanotech factors as we track it and communicate where it goes—spatially, or inter-dimensionally speaking, because of the entanglement."

"Jesus."

"Yeah. So we made a compound synthesis of Lysergic Acid, Mushrooms, Peyote & D.M.T. synergized with a nano-molecule—radiated by the energy generated by the Hadron Collider, which itself is trying to simulate the energy created during the original big bang. The scientific implications are—limitless."

Duke feels his gorge rising—vomit. *Did he actually partake of this? While interacting with his TV? It would inexplicably explain . . .*

"Thus, with access to the Hadron Collider, we shot particles through the cake batter verging at the speed of light to affect the ingredients and test if there's any, say—quantum alchemized, or cosmic effects. Like turning lead to gold, which the collider has been able to achieve, physically, in trace amounts. Now, to immerse the genetic structure of these other cells and atoms blasted with such velocity and energetic conditions, passing through their physical composition, unlocking exponential speed, while irradiated, entering a hyper-space opening singularity—the possibility of warping, its effects on matter . . . Low 'appropriate' levels of radioactivity to stimulate and mutate the cells towards metamorphosis: extracting a synthesis of this process as 'safe' enough for a bio-genetic agent to consume—The Cake. Apparently, you ate some?"

"I—maybe. I did? Tommy. So, you've used this massive device as a billion dollar decarboxylating oven?"

"Well—"

"This is so fucked. Cochrane—I've been trapped in the 1930s."

"What!?"

"I've had amnesia about my identity and past—which really may be my future. But how possibly in a film? Because I'm not actually traveling time into a real past."

"This may prove the most fascinating of crossing boundaries in human history," said Cochrane. "The other day our lead scientist, Dr. Verlock said: '. . . with the medicine of immortality by the All-Master. Be unseen . . . by all those wandering the wastelands of life. Be hidden, until an older heaven births human beings worthy of wisdom . . .' Actually, he was quoting the last known words of Hermes Trismegistus."

"Trismegistus again, huh? He wasn't a physicist. It's all that occult madness you geeks are obsessed with. Is that why there's that statue of Shiva outside the facility?"

"Doesn't matter. We're talking the end of Homo Sapiens—at a crossroads, towards—what? But, wait, what do you mean? Traveling time in a film?"

"I've been trapped in a black and white film. There's Louis Armstrong. The Marx Brothers. And fascists are trying to engineer a coup within the government. I may be in love with Greta Garbo. And Heddy Lamar. I don't know man. They're both phenomenal. What the hell are they talking to me for? Makes no sense. I'm truly scared out of my gourd."

"Rightfully so, Doug. Rightfully so. Holy mother of calamity. What kind of plasma vortex matrix Narnia/Disneyland have you been transformed into? Maybe we could market it?"

"What!?"

"I'm half-tempted to try it myself. Well, exaggerated emphasis on half. Still—"

"Are you saying this process has transposed me into an—Imagination Land?"

"Yes! Wait, what?" replied Cochrane.

"You know," said Duke. "Imagination Land. That episode from South Park where science uncovers a dimensional portal to a living collective universal psyche where Santa Claus, Luke Skywalker, fairy tales, myths, superheroes and gods, etc. actually exist."

"Wow, you're really out there on that. Really frickin' out. You've read a bit too much Carl Jung maybe? But, you know, you might have a point. In some parallel way, but we don't have a language to describe this unknown territory. You've done it, Doug. You're like Neil Armstrong. But you've landed on the *Dark Side* of a Moon no one knew existed. A metaphorical moon that's literal. It could radicalize society. Transgress and multiply the paths of evolutionary consciousness. We could have some serious marketing potential here, besides a complete breakthrough for the species and our relationship to all matter, even as we are making machines conscious. Seriously! Maybe it's a reverse invasion of body snatchers from the TV. Possession and or integration. Their spirits become tangled with their shadows in the Ethernet, or their actual particles are transmitted in these waveforms, and like the entanglement, using such unbelievable force and energy from a nuclear reactor, unless, this whole process also has something to do with the interfacing with the Artificial Intelligence?"

"What? How so? My worst nightmare would be being trapped in a computer-generated virtual reality."

"No, this is way deeper and more advanced than that."

"That's a relief."

"Man. We need to get you to the labs immediately. We'll run some tests and uh—"

"No no no. No tests. No labs. I've been through enough. I'm not a Guinea Pig. At least, not in this facility. Now that you mention it, I'm remembering Jill leaving. It was after that last miscarriage. And everything else that's happened."

"Jill's doing fine."

"What do you mean? You've seen her?"

"Yeah, we just had lunch. She needs consolation, since your disappearance."

"You bastard. You always had a thing for her. Hey, did you set me up for this whole scenario? Knock me out of the picture? You know I like cake."

"Pal, come on. That's just—crazy talk."

"Crazy talk?"

"You know I wouldn't—"

"You would! You sleazy rat. I could strangle you. Right now. But I don't want to be thrown in jail, or a lab. Or hell. I'm already in a hell. Look, you wonky sonofabitch. I'm not coming back. I miss Satch. He needs my help. I have to save Hedy. I have to save that world. This one is already fracked. Maybe it's all related."

"Dear lord, Suitor, c'mon. How are you not dead?" Cochrane grabs Duke to get him to the labs, and lunges for another syringe.

"Maybe I am? Is this the Tibetan Bardo ghost world?"

Suitor pushes back at Cochrane.

They struggle. Wrestling and choking at each other's throats. Cochrane's grasping for the needle to sedate him.

Suitor relaxes and shouts: "Okay. Okay! Stop! We need to find out what's happened to me. I surrender. Peace." Duke makes the peace sign with his two fingers.

Cochrane smiles relieved, until Duke takes his two peace fingers and fiercely pokes him in the eyes. Cochrane yelps. Duke grabs the cake. He takes a bite. And jumps back through the door he came in. *The hell with the gorilla.*

His ears pop. He feels flushed down a toilet worm hole tube—spiraling at hyper velocity.

He crashes through a door and lands on a carpet.

"Heyyyy, Pops, another unbelievably bad day?" giggled a familiar voice, and put a trumpet down.

Duke looks up to see Satchmo. "Thank God it's you."

"Who else? I was just practicing some Stravinsky and Robert Johnson. Where've you've been? Worried sick about ya," said Satch, as he pulls him up.

"Holy smoking Jesus. Where'd—," suddenly Duke feels his guts spilling out. He explodes with vomit.

"Shit. What kind of trouble you in now?"

"Where'd the ship go? We were in a theater smeared with blood while a dragon devoured sacrificial victims. I escaped with Greta to an ocean liner headed to Europe to be initiated into the ancient catacombs as we face some kind of cosmic Gnostic Apocalypse . . . Then everyone vanished off the boat. A gorilla chased me and I ended up back where I came. I was told I ingested something that transported me here. But all the details are fuzzy."

"Dang son. You sure are trippin'. Fuzzy ain't the word. Sounds like you've had one hell of a dream. Or vision, more like. I'd say you're in the right business. Although, knowing you, half of it might be true. What it means, no idea. Though Margueritte warned me something cataclysmic of this nature was destined . . ."

"A dream within a dream? It's even more than that. What does it mean?" asked a perplexed Duke.

"Man. It means there's more things to heaven and earth than dreamt of in your philosophy, Horatio—*and,* you're out of your mind. Madness or not, still doesn't mean something significant isn't transpiring. Years ago, the voodoo priestess told me this would happen . . ."

"I'm really frightened, brother, life, body—and soul."

"Well, breathe deep. You know, in-hale. Ex-hale. Everything seems okay?" Satch pats Duke's back as he hands him a watery ice bucket and a towel.

"Yeah, thanks."

"That's the best we got. Reminds me of a time this Jamaican gave me this monster reefer, and man—I didn't know what planet I was on. So no judgments. Not that you're hittin' any hardcore dope, or are you? So the divine must have one heck of a plan for you."

"Maybe I am. But one heck of a plan indeed," said Duke.

Satch lights up a joint.

"Now what, Satch?"

Satchmo takes a long slow drag, "Now?" exhaling: "We bait the Cheeze."

Episode 17 B

Zing & Zebra Odds on Zero

Artistic creation is a "deflection, " a changing and transformation of reality . . . that art involves a "making strange" of experience, modifies any simple notion of art as a reflection . . . the effect of literature is to deform rather than imitate. If the image corresponds wholly to reality (as in a mirror), it becomes identical to it and ceases to be an image at all.

—*The Writer and Commitment* [6] Terry Eagleton

The Suit heads out to get some milk, then finds it's been delivered at the door. Satch has a gig to play, so he decides he'd like a drink anyhow to clear his head, work out the next move.

He's certainly rattled by the series of phantasmagorical nightmares, or whatever revelatory psycho-trauma-entangled trials or teleportations to land him back . . . How is it possible? But if he ingested a cake composed of psychoactive components, refined in an atom smasher, while channeling radio waves from the electromagnetic spectrum to transpose him to another dimension, then—anything is fracking possible.

On the street, audacious Fords, Chryslers, Chevys, Packards, and Buicks scoot by. Horns blare. Pedestrians mill and criss cross streets. He notices Alfred Hitchcock?—anonymously strolling—observing the world, somewhat rotund and enigmatic. Hitch realizes he's recognized and looks back, touches his nose, points to the sky, then walks on.

Duke races after him, trying to get through the crowd when someone shouts "Boss!" and grabs hold of his sleeve.

"Boss! How've ya been? We missed you at the rendezvous. I'm still sorry

------

[6] Marxism and Literary Criticism. p.50. University of California Press. Berkley and Los Angeles. 1976.

how that job went south. I know you and Satch are heavy hitters with big ideas and connections. What could go wrong from here? The land of opportunity! Where is it? Please give us another chance. I promise, we won't let you down. Well, I won't let you down.

"The boys and I have been trying to land a part in a film and we're barely living on animal crackers. There's gotta be another job for us. How can we make it up to ya?" pleaded the insistent Groucho Marx.

Duke is reluctant, and torn to chase after Hitchcock and the weight of impending options and doom . . . But now that it sinks in, he's mildly glad over Grouho's enthusiasm. More so. As Groucho pleads for an opportunity to do something—an idea strikes Duke like a diamond bullet to the Third-Eye—twang-zing zap! He smiles wide.

"Yes. There's something you can do my friend."

"Wonderful. Anything."

"Are you familiar with The Cheeze?"

"The Cheeze?" said Groucho, alarmed. "Frankie Witz? Who isn't? Not that I'm acquainted with him personally but—"

"Excellent," said Duke. "Well, Frankie's got a big soiree coming up and we've heard he's overdue to have some painting done at his mansion up on Mulholland Drive."

"Splendid, splendid. *By Jove*. Thank the gods. And Zeus too."

Then it occurs inside the vast M.C. Escher scheming of Groucho's cunning brain—where one idea gets lost and ends up chasing another—until there's a brawl: "Hot damn. Eureka. This could be our big break. We'll introduce ourselves to Witz and reveal how talented we are. Golly. Can't wait to tell the guys. We'll be stars. No more soggy mush and soup lines. It'll be fresh sardines, caviar, fine wines and the finest broads to fan and tickle us with feathers. Whatever kind of ticklish situations we'd like. Have to get ready." Then he says aloud:

"Thanks, Duke. This is the best decision you've ever made. You won't regret it."

Groucho zooms off.

The Suit thinks, "Indeed," as the idea is knocking about and growing like a Kansas tornado in a bully bull's China Shop that, "the boys will wreak havoc against The Cheeze and create the distraction and opportunity we need."

Episode 18

Interregnum

I was cruisin on the Mayflower, where we sought to snag some land.
I holler up to Captain Ahab, "Hey Bob, let's rob a song & scam a band!"
He's sunning on deck & said don't forget, we're a Mighty White Whale—
Into the fried dyed blue yonder: Cut & bait the bottom line, & charge
high Interest rates—to tip the scales . . .
Think we'll name it Amerika! They proclaimed! As we dropped anchor
On dry sand. We'll funk it up! & Make it great again? So
I took a deep hit. Fell down & could not say—Amen!
Officer Ahab starts gerry-mandering properties, & whiting out some
Deeds. By decree, he said, let's erect a fortress & start stealing the place
with Whiskey, & Rosary beads.

Dylan Bob's June 19th Dream

Duke, metabolizing and impossibly digesting this traumatized frictioning dissociation of worlds and questioned sanity, of unrelieved angst, remains fevered with a biting crave for distraction, inspiration, or any available moonshine, and heads into a below-ground bar. It's dark and woody like a former Speak-Easy. There's a cavernous quality.

He has a flash of wind, as if whistling from the Aegean Sea as a raving John of Patmos is transported from there to an ethereal ocean of Carnelian and Jasper glass at the empyrean throne of Yahweh, about to reveal the scroll and seven seals and trumpets of the Apocalypse leading to the last judgment, "*Behold, watch this . . .*"

"Bartender, a double Martini please."

In the corner there's a smoky cloud circulating an aura larger than life. A voice bellows within. A bard, rumbling atop Mount Sinai out of thunder and a burning bush. A familiar compelling cadence booms the voice: "We have heard the chimes at midnight."[7]

An irrepressible persona sits alone but full of characters out of this nebulous mist reveling in an illimitable grandeur of underdog pomp with wry urbane

---

[7] Shakespeare, William. Henry IV

charm.

Duke, by gravity, draws near.

"Sit my curious friend," he said invitingly.

"Sir, may I offer you a bottle?" asked Duke.

"However cordial, call me not sir, nor fool, *till heaven hath sent me fortune.* Nor Mr. Welles neither—Much like Shakespeare's Duke Orsino: *If music be the fruit of love—play on.*"

Orson. Holding court amidst an array of empty wine and cognac bottles, chomping cigars: "I am besieged by the lurking enigmas, these slang arrows of personal and worldly discouragements. The elusiveness of success and art, even as the earth withers to withstand an epic epochal storm against freedoms. Freedom of thought. Freedom to create. Freedom to fuck, bwhahaha.

"We laugh, so as not to cry and immerse ourselves in suicidal ideations. However, it is no laughing matter," paused to down a cognac, and inhaled, slowly upon his smoldering cigar.

"Freedom of expression. And to live while under the coercive force and juggernaut fueled penny-pinching horde of gold misers of funding! *How* is fun even rooted in that word—fun-ding? Gross etymology of my silly analogy—nonetheless. Producers, lawyers, sycophants, hacks and backers—*bah!* And—among the least imaginable of all species—the businessman. Whose one pointed focus of di-abolique devilry outsources and outsmarts the ethical and intelligent . . . No baser form of least imagination (its chief hijacker and plagiarist) exists to propagate the conjugations of our purgatorial rounds of churning money-mills. Politicians all, *in crossways and floods where they should have burial,* as they mire and entrap us in our own foul sins of human nature, which look to summits of vertiginous heights to climb out to the air and light. The gift and determination not to bury our talents, or have them swindled by the ever-roaming, devouring adversary—as doth the parables say.

"Surely we all wish to live it up and receive high rewards for great deeds, however too many suffocate under the grime of insufferable poverty—trash, ped-dled to them as ideals of culture. An ignominious travesty I earnestly reject.

"*Type of the antique Rome. Rich reliquary of lofty contemplation to time eaten towers wrought* [8] . . .

"We are at this crossroad, even before the rot of a rising empire has set in, with its gravity of superfluous decadence. Their procrustean system of sanctimo-nious tooling condescension.

"Spellbound in this half-world. Drawing us, like insane moths to a lumi-nous center of coruscating momentum—the circuit of perpetual motion, a prime

____

[8] Edgar Allan Poe. *The Coliseum.*

mover of sustained consciousness—dynamic sunfire piercing the pupils of optic glint and spark. Survey the eye's glancing sensuality of her alabaster skin. Milk of flesh and joy, Xanadu voice, or Abyssinian maiden's silken grace of inspiration— pushes one to fight for these ideals to live! Fight these beasts and jingoists of fascism, even as the moguls engorge in greed which play to the simplified conditioning of our vulnerable gullibility. As we suffer to relinquish our shared poverty to feed in the milk and mead of earthly nourishment of our own imperfect sins. Drink! Cheers! Ah *Sir?*"

"Duke."

"Sir Duke? Another duke, as Duke Signior exiled in the forests of Arden and Jaques playing the Fool, as you like."

"Duke—Suitor."

"A suitable name . . . Do you know the splendor? Of having played for the working class public theater?"

"*The Cradle Will Rock*," interjected Duke.

"Certainly, my dear Duke. We produced that play with the irrepressible John Houseman with FDR's funding for the arts, until such Republicans and milquetoast representatives canned it. *Swine*. That 'fun' word again . . . Are you an artist, then? Of course. I see the searching madness, bleak and terrible, tormenting in your eyes. Have you also found your life to be Quixotically Kafkaesque?"

"Indeed," replied a transfixed Duke.

"Yes. You've been to the other side—finding the opposites to be one inexplicable paradox of a conundrum, and back. And I alone have escaped to tell thee."

"You understand."

"*Pardon*," Welles called the waiter, "*Garçon. Plus de vino s'il vous plaît*," ordering more wine while exhaling another exuberant mountain of Cuban cigar smoke. The fog of scorching spleen, a burning Prometheus scathing the oblique heights of unforgiving Parnassus.

"We thread up the rocky paths and thorns. What cauldrons bubble with possible tragedies and the evaporating triumph of our fates as we grapple to the unforgiving summits to attain greatness! We consume and imbibe the dragon's fire, for tomorrow—we may die," and cavalierly swigged another glass.

"Can you hear the fleeting applause of the much-too-many dissipate? We perform and portray for the masses. To elevate. Not for the elite in vaulted encrusted heights tinkling flatulence among the porcelain doll pantomime of mannequin tea cups. Kill the real world and you defang the frictions of the existential crisis which make us human, a saccharine malaise, like a synthesized sugar."

"Until the mad disciples of Dostoyevsky leap out of his prophecies and set it all afire."

"You've been through the night sea journey. Fellow traveler. *Fellow kinsman, kindred brother mine.* This fulcrum point of kinetic physics of felicitous energy to smash the ennui, the haggerty of boredom—summons a nemesis to bash us to a cindering Icarus for our pride. We, like D.H. Lawrence's initiate in his last work *Apocalypse*, stand on this new threshold of war and revolutionary upheaval, towards an ultimate denouement—best represented, in zodiacal symbolism of the ancient stargazer cults, Chaldeans and Mayans, who charted and defined the skies, defying rational explanation, along such amorphous agnostic borders of the supernatural mysteries—though not beyond Reason.

"Thus, we have the arts. Emblematic of a mystical liberation of the self. To more than sublimate the conflicting friction of paradigms battling in our individual and collective psyches, and attain these disintegrating minutes, aspiring to the peaks . . . of the sublime.

"It's all apocalypse. Every turn of the clock. God's last but never-ending farce of a play. We live, fight, die, and fleetingly immortalize in this unfathomable process of alchemy—simultaneously, all at the same time. *As flies to wanton boys are we to the gods; they kill us for their sport.'*

"Think of the billions of souls in our world's history sharing this multifaceted exponential experience at once."

Another cloud exhales into a Fibonnaci solar system.

"Boggles the mind . . . The master playwright, summoning this clay to life and drama. Science and religion must again find their unity in the marriage of heaven and hell. Even as the Four Horsemen spread across global action in the outer macrocosm, triggering metamorphosis, the catalyst to enact drama of evolutionary catharsis up the spire to the cerebellum and third eye of enlightenment and transformation . . . hogwash some say—but I can tell, you know there is something to it all.

"Behold, the cascading carnival parade, as the supreme jester's bells jangle and clang from resounding churches, laugh at the comedy of our gifted pulsations and breaths. I Am Absurd—therefore, I Exist. To uncover and reveal the absurd is attaining the core source of wisdom. What is more explosively dense with the absurd than—Infinity?

"Even as the imperfections of these churches fill with simple people, tortured with passionate yearning souls, nonetheless—reach earnestly into the nether depths and ether above for aid and betterment. To be in the best of possible worlds, with their sacrifices, for ourselves and the next generation, through the flux of becoming. We're all family and brethren. From the first ape battles to Cain and Abel, Judas and Jesus.

"The Sirens deafen and deceive. Irresistible seduction of ravaging temptation and ecstasy—torn out of oneself. Through the sloth and muck of Puckering disdain—the mundane of ordinary every day, every moment details. Purpose and commitment to the presence of Now. The pyre of the Phoenix. Visionary derangement of the senses. The unconventional odyssey. The inconvenient epic. The unsolicited connection? The irrepressible indefinable consummating quality of the *je ne sais quoi!* The surprise decisive thrill of an enigmatic Satori, bhwhahaha," downing another transubstantiating crimson draught of the blood.

"*Salut, mon frère!*"

"*Salute!*" clinking glasses.

"To leave a monument of living work aspiring high as a pharaoh's pyramid. Thrust and parry to cast out the demon swine of capitalizing piracy, of swill merchants. A heaping shit on their kulture of kitsch."

"They steal the E out of e-schatology," said Duke. "Mass producing a propagandizing scatology of crapagation. The Holo-topia. Forget Ontology. Throw out Philology. They reduce understanding to a patented cinema proctology of the crapacious. Which actually creates the conditions for an eschatological armageddon."

"That's a way of saying it. A cesspool, where we navigate this maelstrom of ever-shifting malevolence of crapitalism, though the Behemoth of communism may not be the opposite cure to our neurotic and selfish complexities . . . The artist fights just to create an enema to clean the bowels of such scat nonsense. You bastards!"

Orson stirs louder, almost rising out of his seat with irrepressible ebullience to toss the tables aside with boundless exuberant frustration at projected enemies, made tangible with imagination's inebriated passion.

"Orson, I share in your enthusiasm and doubt not your veracity, but do not let it disturb you so."

"Disturbed? We need to be more disturbed. More disturbing. Art is a disturbance . . . to deflate the larceny of the pricks who steal, pocket and profit on our dreams. Our role is to disturb—the complacent mind and psyche—saturated with the strings and chains of their codes."

"Inflame the downtrodden and neglected," said Duke. "Ignite a fire under the asses of higher ups, the languid cradles of our overlords, rock them into consciousness or unseat them."

"Indeed. Signal the immolation of our unholy golden calf images, lighting the alarms of unguided perplexity. The multi-directional unity of dissonant harmony. Build chords, melody and cacophony in the fibrillating rhythms whose—no matter how scattered shreds of shuffled beats in polyphony—always land and return to one, on the One. As we are One.

"Pardon my overzealous flights and ramblings, my good sir. So tell me. Are you also troubled, and disturbed?"

"To be honest," said Duke, "I've been overwhelmed by the inconceivable. Impossible to explain. Meanwhile, I've been searching for someone to produce one of my scripts, however, it's been disastrous while dealing with the conniving antagonisms of Frankie Witz—"

"Witz? You say? That bastard, mongrel rat-beast of an aborted Chimera. Why, he's the epitome of all these hollow scoundrels who tread down upon us. Our lickspittle media and propagandized fools fawn over him. That Cerberus of many heads, and no brains, nor personality in any of them.

"Yes, he's a bastard of mythological proportions."

"You may be intrigued to know, recently I rescued a secretary of his whom he so callously assaulted . . . He premeditatedly bought the deed to her parents' mortgage, and holds it over her head so she won't press charges."

"Motherfucker."

"A creeping Uriah Heep of damnation and ugliest calumny deserving of the most severe floggings. She may be able to provide some private insights into dealing with him and his network, and would be much relieved and comforted by some justice and safety from his monstrosity. I'll put her in touch with you."

"That would be something."

"It's encouraging to think so. But conjuring his name is giving me indigestion . . . You said you had a script? Send it to me. I'll see what I can drum up."

"You're too kind, Mr. Welles," said Duke.

"Remember. Dispel the doubt of existential commitment. Do not mire in any moment wallowing in the cowardice and unworthiness of lukewarm waste. Seize hold of the grip and grit of determination. Grind the marble grist of your destiny. Catch the wave and tide out of the shallows of neurotic serfdom and self-absorbed mediocrity we are birthed into. Love is the key. For those about to be born—we salute you! Even as the minions of hell marshal their forces and doomed legions against us . . . Kick his depraved ass and surmount the fertile pastures of higher grounds. *Adieu mon ami. Adieu.*"

Episode 19

Eureka

It's on America's tortured brow that Mickey Mouse has grown up a cow.
Now the workers have struck for fame, 'Cause *Lenin's* on sale again.
See the mice in their million hordes, From Ibeza to the Norfolk Broads . . .
To my mother, my dog, and clowns—

But the film is a saddening bore 'Cause I wrote it ten times or more.

It's about to be writ again as I ask you to focus on
Sailors—Fighting in the dance hall. Oh man!
Look at those cavemen go . . . He's in the best-selling show . . .

—*Is There Life on Mars?*[9] David Bowie

The Marx Brothers unload at Frankie Witz's castle. Phase One is in action. Cadbury the butler greets them.

"Hello, my good man. We're here to paint. Here's our papers," ruffled Groucho quickly, handing him a stack of newspapers with a doctored work permit while they proceed to walk in with paints and ladders . . .

As they're setting up, they wander upstairs and find Witz's office. Groucho puts his feet up on the desk and pretends he's the big cheeze:

"Yes, for Mr. Witz: *Room service, Room service!* We'd like roast duck. Mushroom soup. Two hard boiled eggs. A rib eye steak. A porterhouse steak. Two more hard boiled eggs. Six dozen oysters. A dozen lobsters, and—what's that Harpo? Oh, a tub of pudding. *What? Anchovies?* Alright. And pies. Lots of lemon-meringue, Key Lime and chocolate cream. Extra whip cream of course. Oh and 100 shares

---

[9] <u>Hunky Dory</u>. Bowie, David. RCA.1971. LP.

120

of stock in Ford Motor company—no! Screw Ford, make that Chrysler. A hundred shares in Metro-Goldwyn-Meyer, and a $1000 on *Kalamazoo Jo* to place, and *Sucking Lemons* to win.

There's a gold-plated radio. Chicko turns it on: "Attention, attention. S.O.S., Mr. and Mrs. America, and all ships at sea: This is your duteous voice, Normal Rockwell. Thank you, Mr. Limburgher. Welcome to the most important hour in the world. The Paul Revere Hour with your humble servant, Normal Rockwell. Presented to you by General Electric, and good ol' wholesome Ovaltine.

"Yes, ladies and gentlemen. The hour is late. I hear the boots marching. They're coming for your white picket fences. Hold on to your Bibles. Are you holding them? They are your shields, Christian soldiers. Hold tighter. And your bank accounts. The Harlot of Babylon is upon us. Forget about those fireside chats. The insidious epidemic of sin! And socialism! Is creeping, and spreading, and infecting our great nation my friends. Are you ready? Are you with me? You can bet your bottom dollar, I and Sister Mary Agony are! Are you armed and prepared for what we have to do? Our duty as god fearing patriotic moral Americans . . ."

"Turn that off! Yikes. The radio used to be such a happy place," said Groucho.

Chico and Groucho jostle around Witz's drawers.

Harpo discovers a key on the mantle. He glances around. Stands in front of a mirror, making faces. Mimes to himself: *Yes Mr. Marx. Whatever you please. That looks wonderful, Mr. Marx. Ha ha haha. Yes, you have the key.* Hmmm.

Meanwhile, he wonders to himself, *where's the lock that goes to this key? If I were Witz, where would I place something of great value? Ah, eureka!*

He then removes the mirror to find the safe. Takes out the key.

Voila.

"No Harpo, don't do it," cried Groucho. "Though curiosity overwhelms me. There may be treasure? But it's not ours. Remember: never going back to jail. There's no place like home. No place like home."

"Hey, we do need some treasure," said Chico. "Besides, Duke said we should ferret out whatever info that can be useful against Witz. This is why we're here!"

Harpo cuts in, speedily engaging in ornate choreography, sketching that there may also be writing that a monocled director will use to film them, as he cranks a camera, pretending they're using a script that may be in the vault they can study, so they'll be guaranteed to receive the part.

"Ah, so you think there may be a script in there," responded Groucho, "to help us pass auditions and get into the pictures? Alright, alright. Have at it, boys. Let's take a peak."

And? They find the mother lode of documents: stocks, bonds, investments, blackmail, whitemail, pornography . . . this includes Frankie Witz's true family lineage.

Harpo stashes the pornography.

"This is one hell of a story, gents," said an excited Groucho. "It's the Family History of the Chizz—? The Chizlow—? Hmm. How do you say? The Chizlow-witz-kowsky's?

"That's one heck of a bold name. You'd have to be bold to carry that one around. This story isn't *The Brothers Karamazov*, but—who knows. Read on . . .

"It looks like for generations they were the Witzkowskys. From a country suburb of Krakow, Poland. But they were never the brightest lamps in their village, so they became the Lowitzkowskys.

"Then, they developed a chain of hotels where some specialized in brothels. It turns out they always skimmed profits off the top from their investors and pocketed the embezzlement. Nice people, doing nice things.

"Besides ripping customers off. Look at this: Newspaper clippings. Court summaries. Lawsuits . . . Scant dinner portions. Watered-down wine and whiskey. Unpaid bills, etc. Always cheated on taxes. Escaped military services, etc. So they became known as Chizzlers. Hence the name, the Chizlowitzkowsky's [Chizz-low-witz-kow-sky's]. The Polish courts forced them to change their name legally, so that innocent citizens would never trust a Chizlowitzkowsky . . . Gosh, that's harsh. What a bunch of clowns. No wonder they fled to Amerika . . .

"Hey. Look at this article. Apparently there was a longtime feud between the Chizlowitzkowskys and the Zulawski family . . . In the early 1900s, the philosopher Jerzy Zulawski wrote a science-fiction moon trilogy called *On the Silver Globe*, a pessimistic and philosophically drenched drama concerning a crashed expedition to the moon where humanity attempts to build utopias and religions conflicted by a savior complex . . .

"Recently, there was a large contract being groomed to turn the story into the greatest sci-fi epic film ever produced. A popular artist, Stanislaw Szulkalski, agreed to do mythical costume and set designs . . . like nothing ever seen before. Fritz Lang is considered as director. Soundtrack composed by Igor Stravinsky, and George Antheil from the Bloomsbury avant-garde who synchronizes concertos with mechanical pianos . . .

"Witz, meddling through lawyers, copyrights, charges of radicalism and bribery, blocked the deal going through, thereby denying the Zulawski family the prestige and profits from Jerzy Zulawski's lunar trilogy. Wow, this scallywag just doesn't let a grudge go. If we get on this tyrant's bad side, we're burnt toast. What to do?"

"We may have no other recourse," said Chico, "but to do something we've never quite done before."

"Do tell," said Groucho.

"Thoroughly think it all through. Very carefully."

Episode 20

Shuffle

You can fool some of the people all of the time, and those are the ones you want to concentrate on.

—George W. Bush

Greta settles in at a small round table with Duke. She's regaled as a high priestess gypsy. Her glazed eyes pierce impenetrable like a sphinx. Candles flick shadows about her. Incense drifts heavily. She thumbs an ashen paste onto her forehead, then Duke's.

"A metallic crow and lark's mocking tongues haunt the chasms of my nightmares, overlapping in layers of confusion—just out of grasp . . ." revealed Duke.

"We must map out, repulse and neutralize this invasive sorcery encompassing and closing in . . ."

She hands him a bottle.

"What is it?"

She stares coldly.

"What is this?"

She pushes it closer against his reluctance.

"Drink!"

He imbibes. Bam! A bomb sets off in his shaken brain. Eyes pop their sockets.

She consumes a drink of the potent liquor and lets out a howl. Suddenly a curdling wail erupts from beneath the shuddering draped table.

Duke leaps in terror. "What the f—?"

The table begins to rise and levitate.

Greta's eyes stretch open alarmed. Daunted by this unexpected explosion of occult magic, she crosses herself and chants forcefully:

Exsúrgat Deus et dissipéntur inimíci ejus:

et fúgiant qui odérunt eum a fácie ejus.
Sicut déficit fumus deficiant; sicut fluit cera a fácie ígnis,

sic péreant peccatóres a fácie Dei.

Duke is tense on his feet with fearful paranormal disbelief. The draped table hovers just above the ground—it begins to shake and wobble unevenly.

Greta pauses, grimacing with furrowed concentration, then carefully lifts the table cloth to peer below.

"Whhhhat? You devil! *Din Javla Faaaan! Helvete skit as fitta kuk zucker fyyy!* Get out! Get the fuck out you hobgoblin sprite of a Puck. Now!"

Harpo pops out grinning.

"What's wrong with you?"

She grabs his hair to boot him off. "I'll deal with you later!"

However, when the ritualized electrical nouminous magic of Greta's fingers seizes Harpo—suddenly he's thrust into far away Long Island, where a stunningly tall woman, with her straitened and tidy in a Gertrude bun, throttles him down into another direction to throw him back onto a piano he's supposed to be playing in Freeport.

"Du fluchen arschloch. Halt verdammt der mist donnerwetter!" scolded a six foot three Mrs. Schanger, fuming on a cigar and downing straight gin.

Harpo finds himself dazed, dizzy and nauseous, sweating and chilled with a severe fever . . . And zits? He's 16 years old!? What?

He's trying to stay awake and conscious through the bifurcations of his dis-jointed mind, to keep playing: A Myrtle of Venus with Bacchus Vine!

"Das ist ja eine schisser. Adolph! I don't care how sick you are ya little Jew! You're paid eight dollars a month, ya runt, +plus room and board to play. Hor auf so Depp zu sein! Don't stop!"

There's a raucous poker game getting heated as four tawdry gals appear to be soliciting the customers, flaunting raw cleavage and making eyes . . .

"Look lively! This isn't the melancholia saloon on the moon. It's The Happy Times Tavern! Happy times! Make happy happy. We're in America now, verdammt!"

A brawl breaks out between Fitzgerald and Miller over whose turn it is with one of the girls. Schanger grips them both by the scruff of their collars and tosses them out like mannaquins.

The room is turning in circles. The piano seems to be levitating up and down.

Harpo jumps up confused, like a harlequin Jack-in-the-box—he just wants to crash and sleep in a bottomless well.

Home. Home. Take me back home!

Mrs. Shanger slams Harpo back on the piano stool. He fears she broke his ass. He has to bang loud on the Francis Scott keys to appease the roadhouse. An exhausted pall and torpor turns his white face pale, along with his draining strength. He slides off the piano.

The whores take pity on the kid and drag him upstairs. A doctor checks him out: measles!

Schanger screams, get this sick useless Jew out of here.

Chattering and barley conscious Harpo is brought to the train station by the prostitutes. They chip in to see him safely back home to East 93rd Manhattan.

"Lil' Adolph, you're the cutest, with those curls. Love how you played Waltz Me Round Again Willie! And Love Me and the World is Yours. We know you came here to work and earn something, but you don't belong here, and don't know how blessed you are to be outta this dive shack from hell. We'll miss you!"

The blurry ringing begins to recede. Harpo is slowly returning to Hollywood from whatever occultic transposition that fracked him into his past. He now recalls through the haze—as the drumming in his ears subsides—an article came out that revealed Mrs. Schanger and her son were part of a notorious gang, robbing houses throughout Nassau County, and were convicted and found guilty by a jury shortly after Harpo's povedential departure. One night, he recalls, Alma Schanger, hair unusually frazzled from her Gertrude bun, and armed with a pistol, had Harpo drive their buggy to the nearby Pot O' Gold Saloon. Schanger bluntly told Harpo she was out to murder one of their conspirators.

They sat at The Pot O' Gold as Alma slammed gin.

Harpo incessantly asked when someone strolled inside, "Is that him? That's him? That guy, it's him!" Boy, I want to see this gun go off.

Pow!

She kicks him. "Shut your mouth! I'm going to kill this rat cock sucker."

Fortunately for the excitable young Harpo, the intended victim, Hans Niederdorf, never showed. He's the one who turned in the whole gang.

Who knows what could've been the consequence if not for some angelic grace to keep lil Adolph safe?

Even Max, their bartender, disappeared one night—never to return.

Turns out Chico revealed that he himself was the former piano player at The Happy Times Tavern. Schanger thought Harpo was Chico when she hired him at a Bowery gig for their Friendly Inn On The Road Show.

Luckily, Chico was also fired, for finagalling with the girls.

Honks trail off in the distance.

Duke sighs relieved. "Holy shit! That guy!"

"He's a lecherous knave—blessed by God," she said and crossed herself.

"To think *what kind of god* would create such a creature?

"He's the reincarnation of Wolfgang Amadeus Mozart!"

"Dear Lord, that would explain a lot. God *must* be absurd—therefore—She may exist."

"Honestly now, " said Greta, "sit back down."

She unfolds from a silk cloth a deck of Tarot cards, takes another shot of the liquor and howls. Speaks strange tongues of incantation. Goes into a trance. Conjures a state of ecstasy and speaks channeling from far away:

"Vinyan'na Zed Mar'lova—Zarn harrah mateel Zohd telarr A Lava Zufaahus

Suplor videl krador unsheel—Baqueros farin holoria zail Gal Un Ceph

Pularros delekion—Guhn-dyardik spieyontos—maderia zeldekios valandyroh.

Solpeth Monons Manin Jaida Iad. Jaida El Ohim

"Anchorites of door guardian sentinels beckon a coruscating code and communion, to the key masters. Riddle and rhythm—unlock the sculpturing vibration, to challenge the Castle keeper. Unlock the gates. Brighten and untangle the beacon of illumination. The feast of abundance—sing with every touch, step and glow. A feast of lights. Through the pillars. The ten Sefiroth. Ein Sof. From the all One Monad bliss giving Cosmos.

"Spirits hear us! Jachin and Boaz. To inscribe these lines rhyme, warm with the cold pages of time, yielding open the holy Cosmic ocean. To be named? Wisdom of Solomon. Unleash the invocations, release of unreal burning skies afire of knowledge.

"Spirits hear us! And come to our aid.

"Horizons of disaster swallow the advancing entrance. Carving hallowed caverns in hollows of existence. Captured and congealed ice of space cuts a transforming essence. Matter and manifestation. Theurgical thermatology. The hidden dreams trapped in the unconscious astral plane of chaos to carry streams of resonance—to alchemized fruition.

"Spirits heed us and come now to our aid!

"Tongues ignite in signs of seraphic lit expression of light out of darkness."

Greta's voice rises, reverbing like melting brass, with invocation's suppliant commands.

"Birds of kingfisher fire swing with wings unable to remain out of the darkness. Breeze through the fang and bruise of your reflections to free the frozen beauty of their pain—[louder] out of the darkness—come to our aid.

"Born to rule, a strange and theater'd role, unveil these stages and worlds: to sing and throng with souls who hear—and are come to our aid."

Self-hypnotized, Greta, shuffling the Tarot, the entranced whites of her possessed eyes flutter manic, she commands Duke also shuffle the deck, and cut it using his left hand.

She then picks up and places upside down the first card: The Hanged Man.

"Of course," Duke murmured with a grimace.

"Shh! Silence."

Covering the first card she places The Tower, across the Hanged Man, horizontal. Duke marvels at these first components, as if they're the first puzzle pieces to unlock this mandalic vision of an occult communication device. Could they possibly reveal more than some carnival hocus pocus? Duke stares at the engraved lightning bolt that strikes The Tower. It triggers some secret hiding pocket within the tachyon particles of his cellular neurons. He reaches to touch it. Startled, a jolt surges through him.

"Don't make contact with the conduit of the table!" scolded the entranced Greta.

Left of The Hanged Man she parallels The Fool! The fourth, lands to the right, the numbered 1 card of the deck, after the Zero which is the The Fool: it's The Magician. Mercurial, with the sciences and skills, manipulations and thrills. Healing and mystic arts of orbital sun, the stars, the moon, he seals. Like a twin binary star system, or proton and electron, simulacra and simulacrum, these two archetypes, zero and one, Yin and Yang, past and future, dance around the crucified

Hanged Man, like a Janus faced Trickster of the inescapable epic depths of matter webbed illusions, mirrors and trajectories, spun before us, like the adornments of sabled domes burning with diamond dust from light years, observed through carbon and flesh, the elements of the dichotimous Void, manifest the destined gates and bookends of sunrise and graveyard.

Fifth, above the first two is placed, grinning: Death. Below these, enshrouded with a lantern, the sixth card has a number is identified with a number 9, as the shape of its figure depicts, the most esoteric of these sets: The Hermit.

Seventh, fitted along the bottom right side to the center pile: The Knight of Cups. Next: The Black Magician/ The Devil. Then: The 9 of Swonds. Finally, ten: The Judgment Aeon, completing the pattern of a Celtic Cross.

"With a portentous reading such as this, I like to pull an eleventh card, a magic card, to show what alternate force may be oscillating behind it all . . . eleven is: The Hierophant.

"Extremely odd to see so many of the Trump cards! Pertaining of the Major Arcana—the ruling archetypes of the great secret . . . This unravels an auspiciously uncanny reading, of critical metaphysical transecting circumstances.

"The synchronicity principle of the cards uses a numerology as a type of code based on the 22 major arcana found within the 78 of the complete deck, which correlate to the 22 letters of the Hebrew alphabet and Egyptian numerical system. Whereas the 22 numbers included the zero.

"Do you realize how cumbersome it is to do complex math, whether for business, architecture, equations or science—using Roman numerals? Without a zero? The Arabs passed this on, through shunyatta, from India— to the primitive ancient West.

"These numbers have their symbolism and correlation with the archetypes of the collective psyche, the idealized perfected forms which are the Platonic templates and architecture to all things. But these forms, planets, gods, as related to their astrological correlary—also receive our projections—therefore the most popular gods receive the most projected mental spirit energy which builds in a vortex like a residual accumulation—a banked cache of ether. To form a complete holistic science.

"The synchronicity of these symbols (as with the I Ching, or the oracles of Delphi and Shamans) operates on the psychic gravity of a magnetic law of attraction, as an acausal connecting principle, interacting as a universal parallelism and integration of mind and matter as one. Locating these symbols depicts the coordinates of these correlations, to map out and discern their conicidental signals and meanings.

"Your Hanged Man, represented by zero, tells us of your past, where you came from. To the West, the cypher zero, is nothing. An empty negation. Esoterically however the zero represents everything. Everything comes out of zero. It's positive openess is the Taoist source by which all forms, the entire universe is born out of.

"The Tarot is significant as the gypsies brought the cards to Europe via Egypt in the 1400's, even as Lorenzo De Medici, patronizing Ficino and Mirandola, had his paid agents recover the lost sacred texts of Plato, thus ending the dark ages dominated by the scholasticism of Aristotle, thereby ushering the age of the Renaissance and modern civilization, to flourish with idealism, dialectic, love, flesh, freed form and geometry; along with the magical emerald tablets of Trismegistus: handed down to Cornelius Agrippa, Michael Maier and John Dee.

"Besides the cosmic significance of zero itself, the discovery of the Rosetta Stone revealed the connection between the cards' symbolic imagery and the source hieroglyphics. Zero is important to this reading since The Fool is numerically the zero. The common poker deck is actually a Tarot deck without the 21 major arcana. The only remnant is The Joker, which in fact is The Fool.

"Notice how it is The Fool who survives? Of course the minor arcana is what remain as the poker deck. The four suits of Swords, Pentacles, Wands and Cups—each suit with a King, Queen and (dropping the Knight) there is the Page, which becomes the Jack Knave. The four suits become Spades, Diamonds, Clubs and Hearts. Esoterically these for suits correlate to the four elements of matter: Air/Swords, Pentacles/Earth, Fire/Wands, Cups-Hearts/Water, as these have their counterpart in the astrological system."

"What is the Zero?" asked Duke.

"Think about its significance. Zero is the void. It is an infinite space from which all numbers can function within and proceed from. The zero can join and become, or imitate any number. Hence, Joker's are wild!

"The Fool plays, thereby he can mimic or challenge all the other cards, which represent archetypes of the gods, planets and personalities which life plays out in these dramas and unfolding scenarios of conflict and union. These codes were understood by the initiates of the Mystery Schools. Be they inherited by the Eleushians or the builders of the pyramids."

"With all our technology, thousands of years later, we still don't know how they were built," said Duke.

"So you can precisely imagine that the architects possessed a magic of mathematical knowledge that was beyond some superstitious mumbo jumbo most people just scoff at, which is rooted in this 22 number system."

Equations with a geometric three dimensional depth of topography cascade through his mind. Like transmissions, bleeding with meanings he cannot reach.

"Jesus Christ," he exclaimed.

"Nooooo. Not Jesus. Whereas, somehow I'm dialing through the static of messages, getting tuned in . . . I'm channeling how the leader in the world you hail from is intrinsically fucked. A true shmuck putz bastard of a jackal. More like a jackass put in power by the Jackals—high and low. He is the fulfillment of culminating arcs and perversions of dark karma. He represents the dark side of The Fool upside down.

"I see red. You have a strange relationship to this representation. Hmmm. Sometimes the cards are more compartmentalized to their category. But this overlay of an inter webbed nexus of cards tells a story, as the initiate begins as a zero and ascends through the challenges of all the archetypes, their challenging gates of testing situations, to then become and transcend their form, until the entire process is complete. Then one ascends, reincarnates, or disintegrates. But there's such a vast mystery to what's concealed, however close we are to this, my vision is blocked from deciphering it clearly.

"I've never encountered anyone so—intrinsically disturbed with the implications of these signs, the warped intuitions of catastrophic clairvoyance.

"This first card, The Hanged Man. This has been your present circumstances. Forces of the world have captured you, hung you on layered dimensions of the cosmological world tree, the Nordics call Yggdrasill—even as King Arthur's lost knights were hung there on their quest for the Grail.

"In a sense, you are dead. Seemingly you are dead to that world. Yet, a part of you is still there. But the man is hung upside down, so your entire world has been inverted, if not perverted. From the Universe to the Inverse."

"I'm not sure I know what you're talking about, although we were discussing it during our—--truncated voyage, which got a little crazy, after that night on the boat. I'm not here to be messed with!"

"Quiet. I don't know what you're talking about. I see into your soul . . . Everything is inside out. But if we reverse the card upside down from hung to upright, you see: he is dancing. This is you in this realm: You must right yourself. Reborn and resurrected from this upside down death and nightmare . . ."

Episode 21

Heavenly Escalator Under the Hill

Happiness involves knowledge . . . with the control of information, with the absorption of individual into mass communication, knowledge is administered and confined. The individual does not really know what is going on; the overpowering machine of education and entertainment unites him with all others in a state of anesthesia . . .

—*Eros and Civilization* Herbert Marcuse[10]

Witz strolls importantly down the curving balustrade from his office.

"Boy I'd like to put in one of those new escalators in here—with marble."

Witz hears piano playing. He jaunts over and sits in a French Divan chair to listen.

The brothers are back mucking around the Witz mansion again. Someone tied up the other regular work crew in order to get the Marx crew back in the door.

Harpo is playing Chopin, and looks up from the piano and smiles. Witz yawns. Harpo frowns. Starts to play Rachmaninoff. Witz grimaces to go.

Harpo closes one eye to think. Then shifts gears and plays *High Diddle E Dee, it's a happy life for me* . . .

Witz pauses and starts to rock to rhythm, and hums along.

Harpo's eyebrows express an "Ah ha." Then he delves and indulges into '*O Susanah,* and *Three Blind Mice* as he jazzes it up.

"Bravo kiddo! Come work for me. You're hired. You can work the party this Saturday. See Maury about the details," then he sauntered off.

---

[10] Marcuse, Herbert. New York. Vintage Press. 1955.

Harpo tips his hat and plunks out *Happy Days Are Here Again* and jams awhile on *Blue Skies*.

Chico is behind the bar in the next room. Notices Frankie Witz and coughs: "Ah, salutations boss. The greatest gentleman the world has ever known and will ever see. Certainly the gentleman with the sharpest eye and mind enjoys cards? Pick any card please," as he dexterously shuffles and launches cards back and forth from left to right hands.

"Really?" replied Witz with skepticism.

"A true gentleman cannot resist a gentleman's game."

Chico lays out several cards.

Witz shrugs and picks one.

"Ah ha," proclaimed Chico. "The King of Hearts. Must be you," he quickly mixes the cards around. "Okay boss, which one is your card?"

Witz grabs the middle card.

"It's the KING OF HEARTS! Again. A winner. Cheers, Mr. Witz. A million dollar pick!"

They do this a few more rounds with Witz winning.

"You're a master at this, sir. Never have I seen a keener wit, if I may say. Hmmm, let's try something harder. What's your favorite card?"

"I don't know. Ace of Diamonds."

"A rich choice sir."

Chico then reshuffles. Has Witz cut. Then opens the deck face up. "Where's the Ace of Diamonds?"

"Wait a second," said Chico. "You're no amateur," then reaches into Witz's sleeve to pick out the Ace. "Whoa ho! How about that? A master!"

Witz chuckles. "Pretty neat, pal. Would be a blast if you could do this in front of our dinner guests on Saturday. Knock their socks off. You're hired. See my accountant about the particulars."

Witz shoots off and Chico pours himself a double Scotch. "*Senior Amici, molto grazie bene*. Salute."

In the dining hall Groucho accosts Witz: "Ah, the grand wizard wazoo of Oz himself!"

"The painter! Great, I'm thinking gold leaf all around."

"Yes, yes. Please be seated. This will only take a moment for the most handsome man on the planet. What am I saying, excuse me, *the Universe*."

"Why thank you but—"

"Ah, there, there—this only will take minutes."

Groucho wears a smock on his overalls, beret cap and a pallet of paints. Stretching his hand out with the brush to eyeball the counterpoint of Witz's face from his easel, then unleashes a fury of lightning strokes on a canvas in front of him.

"Hold on pal," Witz protested. "I mean the walls. No time for this. I have enough portraits. Or do I?"

"Sir, I've been commissioned to make you a magnificent portrait, it'll be featured in *Look Magazine*. For the most magnificent of real genius crowning tycoons of our great America, even greater because of your uncompromising steamrolling industriousness and intolerance for rebellious rabble rousers . . . "

Witz scoffs as he sees Groucho flailing his brush around madly.

"This is insane," as Witz gets up to go.

"Emperor Witz! Behold!" Groucho spins the canvas around and there's a portrait of Napoleon with Witz's face.

"Well I'll be damned!"

"Indeed sir. Indeed."

"This is magnificent. I've never seen a painting done so quickly. I'm amazed. And it takes quite a bit to amaze me, let me tell you!"

"Thank you, thank you," as Groucho clutches his heart with some glee, and bows with humbled modesty. "An amazing painting for an amazing man."

"You're hired, damnit. This will be a blast for my guests. A real firecracker up their asses kinda blast. They'll be quite entertained. Best party in town. Just don't paint anyone as good as me."

"I wouldn't dream of it Mr. Witz. No one is *not* as good as you."

At least that was the way the Marx boys thought it would go down, as it played out in their imaginations—but it quite didn't happen that way.

However, the actual reality still worked to their advantage . . .

Episode 22

Three of an Imperfect Pair

> . . . Take the moral law and make a nave of it
> And from the nave build haunted heaven. Thus,
> The conscience is converted into palms,
> Like windy citherns hankering for hymns . . .
> And from the peristyle project a masque
> Beyond the planets. Thus, our bawdiness,
> Unpurged by epitaph, indulged at last . . .
> Squiggling like saxophones . . .
> Your disaffected flagellants, well-stuffed,
> Smacking their muzzy bellies in parade,
> Proud of such novelties of the sublime,
> Such tink and tank and tunk-a-tunk-tunk,
> May, merely may, madame, whip from themselves
> A jovial hullabaloo among the spheres . . .

—Wallace Stevens[11]

"**O**kay, you fuckheads! This is how it's gonna go down." "Whatta ya gotta be so mean for, Mokowitz?"

"Already you clowns with the whining sissy bitching? You think F.D.R. is gonna save ya with another welfare check? Shut yer yowling trap before I sock ya."

"Yeah, Mo, geez. So, let's get this straight. Does that mean—you're gonna punch us? Or stuff socks in our mouths? I ain't gettin' stuffed with no dirty socks. Say it ain't so, Mo!"

"Both!"

Mo takes his two associates and bangs their skull-popping heads together. "Get to work, ya bastards. Real wise guys. The boss wanted this done a while ago. We're behind as it is since we were mixed up with that Sweets character and got

---

[11] "A High-Toned Old Christian Woman." *The Palm at the End of the Mind*. Random House, Inc. New York. 1967.p.77.

135

railroaded in the slammer for a week. Or we'll end up with permanent socks up all our asses. Andale. Vamonos."

"Alright, alright. Just say please. With sugar on top."

"C'mon."

"Say please!"

"Ain't that cute. Okay, I'm sorry. Wait right there," said Mo, and strolled into the side-door kitchen.

"Hiya Midnite, what's cookin'?" said Mo.

"Yowzah, boss Mo. Looks like they're fixin' to be a big party. Much to do."

"May I trouble you for some sugar?"

"Sho sho, here's a cup full. Plenty for your sweetheart, too."

"Thank you," said Mo and walked out.

"Hey Middleton," said the assistant cook, "what do you have to talk that way for? That's just demeaning."

"Why heck son, that's how these folk think we talk," said Middleton and giggled. "So I ham it up and keep it agreeable. No Shakespeare routine is gonna work with these cats. Keep it Simon Simple and yowzah boss. Stay out of their way, out of their orbit. Or gravity will crash. We've families to feed."

"Ain't that the truth."

"Frankly, to be honest, I've been looking for other work. Maybe those investments we discussed, collect my last couple checks and, sayonara. Man, would I love to have my own restaurant. Believe me, you know I don't put up with bullshit. I've tried. I'm also playing it low-key so I can find opportunities to mess with these clowns. Don't let them think you're so bright, and they won't see you coming or going. Play the fool. Like emperor Claudius. Man. You have no idea what these clowns and this Kingshit Witz are capable of. Just need to get paid and move on. I've seen the proverbial, and literal, shit hit the fan with these motherfuckers, *forgive me Jesus*, like you wouldn't believe."

They laugh.

Mo brings the sugar outside.

"Here's some sugar honey, won't you please forgive me?"

"Aw Mo, ya shouldn't have."

"Oh yes I should," and dumped the sugar on their heads.

They start to mix and tussle. Then a pitcher of water splashes down on them.

They look up, splashed and flustered.

"Hey what's the big idea?"

"Attention you Numb-skulls!" shouted Maury from above. "No big ideas here. Just a little idea. Get to work before Mr. Witz sends Bruno down to knock ya's to smithereens. Scram ya idjits. Why, if ya weren't distant cousins—emphasis on distant—you'd be six feet under pushin' up daisies. Hooligan schmucks! Forget about it," as Maury Chuckowitz slammed the window shut.

"You've done it now, lame-brains. Don't we look like a fine pair of misfit basket cases now!" said Mo.

"Aren't we more like a trio of basket cases?"

"Goddamn ya, Curly rascal. We're still paying for that piano you dropped, and that was two years ago, or I'd wash my filthy hands of ya."

"The piano *I* dropped? Nyuk nyuk."

Mo grabs his ear: "C'mon!"

Episode 23

Carpe Diem

Hebrews born enslaved, to the Pharaoh. Obey his
every command.

Cry in fright . . . Now, let my people free. Sands of Goshen:

Go, I will fly with thee. Bush on fire. Blood, sunning
crimson strong–

Up the Nile. Plague, darkness, three nights long frogs to fire.

Thus, let it be written. Thus, let it be sung. Summoned by
the chosen . . .

—*Sleeping Death* Metallicus[12]

Knock, knock! Who's there, in the other devil's name?

—*Macbeth II. iii.*

Back at the Marx hideout, Satch joins Duke to brainstorm their final mul-tilayered strategies to find out what's happened with Hedy, and deal with Witz, since the brothers infiltrated his operation and uncovered his secret documents. Hedy had been brought to the Witz castle, and Greta lost contact with her, fearing the worst.

Duke got in touch with Witz's former secretary through Orson, so they all pooled their resources. Connecting the dots.

"The big masquerade party at the estate in Laurel Canyon this Saturday will allow Witz to sneak in his cronies and mostly wicked connections, providing them the ideal opportunity to disguise themselves so their covert mission and meeting succeeds. Witz's former secretary said he was receiving calls from Germany. Hedy's former ties to an Austrian arms manufacturer makes her a valuable and vulnerable commodity. A dangerous and desired object to certain sinister parties. Whatever it is, it's some diabolic shit," said Duke.

---

[12] <u>Drive the Lightning</u>. Must Stain In Peace Records. 1934. LP.

"We have our ears to the grind," said Groucho.

"It'll be quite the gutsy caper," said Duke, "with various angled contingencies, in case something goes wrong, some detail always lands sideways. Nothing goes as planned in the elusive spinning world. Some of these foreign documents are in code. Mickey O'Donnelly has his Air Corps buddies looking them over. With the intelligence we've accumulated from our sources, things look far more dangerous than we've imagined. The worst is yet to come. This is what we know so far . . ."

Meanwhile, the Little Rascals are hanging around to play pool, cards, and devour another miscellaneous life-saving feast.

Wrapping up their meeting, they hear a coded knock on the back door. Chico answers, "Ah, thanks for the delivery, Butch. Ya get a game of pool later. C'mon in. Have a sandwich."

Chico glances at the headlines.

"What's in the papers?" asked Groucho.

Chico tosses the newspaper on the table and replies: "Nazis."

Harpo leaps up, slams the paper on the floor and stomps on it.

"They're not inside the paper, you nut," yelped Groucho. "Gimme that!" Swiping it back off the ground.

Satchmo chuckles and lights up a joint, passing it to Harpo.

"Oh I wouldn't do that if I were you," warned Groucho. "He's a big boy, but we'll see. Oh, no thanks. None for me. I'm nit-witty enough."

Looking back at the paper, Groucho snaps and crinkles it to shape: "These damn Nazis. Don't we have enough problems? Looks like they keep clambering to annex more territory where folk speak German. Or they threaten there's going to be war. Whad'ya think will happen when they consolidate all the German people?"

"There'll be war," said Chico.

"Don't they see," said Groucho, "they want all the Germans on one big team first? What are these politicians, stooges?"

"They ain't Marxists," said Chico.

"We may be from New York," said Groucho, "but there were immigrant Krautenheimers bullying us all the time growing up. You know Harpo's been through Germany? Emphasis on through. He won big at roulette once. The happy kook spent it all on a trip to Europe, and brought a harp back."

Harpo choreographs a series of disturbing gestures: harping, hands up, marching, saluting, then punching himself, etc.

"He never was so frightened in his life," said Groucho. "Got out of there fast as a jackrabbit. Hasn't been quite the same since."

Harpo, takes another hit from Satch's smoke and starts hopping around like a bunny, stopping at his harp, which he plays backwards—notes in reverse.

"Ha, I really dig *Mack the Knife* by Kurt Weil and Bertolt Brecht," said Satch. "Can you play that one? Germany is immersed in incredible music. How could such creative people keep starting wars? Practicing Bach and Mozart elevated my playing to another level . . . Nothing brings joy to young and old like tapping your foot to melody and rhythm. Whereas killing joy is a treacherous descent from metaphor to actual killing. Those tight fascist bastards. You know, my music was getting pretty popular over there. But they've banned me, and jazz altogether, as degenerate jungle Negroid-Jew music. Ain't that some evil bullshit? Good times between Blacks, Jews, and everyone in between mixing it up sure freaks folk out."

"Amen brother," said Chico as he slapped hands with Satch, and returned to shuffling and dealing another hand.

Duke, marveling at Harpo's ongoing display, said: "I'm pretty certain we'd kick their ass. But it'll be a catastrophic bloodbath."

"Doesn't sound like fun. Personally," said Groucho, "I'm feeling a carnage of mixed emotions. An anomalous caricature of my own essence. But what an essence! As if things aren't right. Not what they're supposed to be. Obviously, for starters, this poverty sucks, for example. But it's more than that. Something else. Ineffable. Intangible. It's damn weird. Makes my head spin. Something isn't Kosher. Somehow I have this hunch, it's your fault," as he looked up accusingly at Duke, raising his voice in anger: "You have something to do with this, don't you?"

Duke momentarily turns pale, guiltily shaking his head *no*, feigning ignorance.

"Hmmm. Yeah, well, there's something you're not telling us. It's probably better if you don't tell me. I've a stark intuition I wouldn't believe you anyhow, and wouldn't understand. You don't even understand! Things aren't what they appear, or are supposed to be. Look at us, squatting in a hideout. I feel larger than life—though my rumbling rib-cage would disagree."

"Man, there are mysteries to this existence we'll never know," said Satch. "Worlds within worlds. But if we got soul, we'll make it. Though we're in for quite a ride."

"We were finally livin' high on the hog," continued Groucho, "till the stock market crash wiped me so clean—I'm filthy poor. At least, that's how I remember it. Things took an odd turn. Like there's another life somewhere. Another me. We're destined for greatness. This motley lot of bungling clowns surviving on our wits, talents, and hard at work screwing things up. Then working even harder to screw them up even more. And we're Nowhere."

"That's right, boss. Nobody outclasses us as screw-ups. We're the best," said Chico.

Harpo clasps his hands and raises them in victorious postures and continues jamming, deconstructing melodies backward and forwards.

"'If the fool persists in his folly, he shall become wise.' William Blake said that," remarked Groucho. "Eh, it's all so Quixotic. If life is crazy, and we're crazy, are we not the moving target and epicenter essence of it all? The model epitome of life itself? The big philosophical questions: solved! Therefore, the only remaining question worth our while is: How crazy can we get?"

"You said it. And we live it. To the max!" agreed Chico.

"It's a Quixotic Odyssey."

"Don't know what that means, boss, but it sounds like another good film title."

"More of a subtitle, with none other than Luis Bunuel and Salvador Dali directing and writing, but who'd buy it? *Chasing Windmills* would be more like a working title. Though I feel we've mounted the assault on the windmills already, thinking it a projected dragon. We've clambered and hacked upon it, but it's spinning us around dizzy. The great Dharma Wheel of Fortune. We're now totally disoriented from the world. At its magic center: it's spun us so fast, maybe it's a way into another world, like Shangri La. Maybe it spun us into this other realm? I was speaking metaphorically, but now I'm literally talking crazy. 'At the still point of the turning world. Neither flesh nor fleshless; Neither from nor towards . . . there the dance is . . . Where past and future are gathered . . . I can only say, *there* we have been: but I cannot say where. And I cannot say, how long, for that, is to place it in time.[13]'"

"That's fucked up, man," said Satch. "Heavy, and sharply articulated, but you're freaking me out."

"I hear ya!"

"There's your film," said Duke. "You could intersect the poetry of T.S. Eliot and Baudelaire as absurdist/philosophic dialogue, interspersed with slapstick gags in a surrealist context, building a plot confronting the magic powers of the cosmos, while being challenged by it. You could start out as a vaudeville troupe of magicians, who get caught up in the conspiratorial initiations of real esoteric magicians when you discover the most secret books of the Kabbalah, thereby justifying the use of pyro-technical special effects and free-play of dazzling actions, which have a purposeful context, both aesthetically and conceptually, while affecting the consciousness of the audience. Adventuring—through a dream, fighting the sys-

---

[13] .S. Eliot. Burnt Norton.

tem. What if in the magicians underworld you meet a secret agent who's trying to stop the dissemination of *The Protocols of Zion*? The Czar's Okhrana secret service created the protocols as a means to divide Germany during The Great War to divide while fostering its elements of rabid anti-Semitism with lying propaganda that Jewish bankers are funding the antichrist beast from The Book of Revelations to rule the world, while cannibalizing Christian children. Even as they call Hollywood the Dream Factory, make it so. You'll be transported into the astral Unconscious. Battling good and evil on all levels, fighting off the wicked with magical slapstick. Think of it!"

"Stupendous," riled Chico. "But this kid is a dreamer. Sounds expensive."

"True, it would sound incoherently stupid to the Hollywood moguls," remarked Groucho. "Shoot it down like a flaming lead zeppelin. They'd flatulate and grimace and deride it as expensive art, not entertainment. Too esoteric. Too controversial. Too much substance. Although we'd make it entertaining."

"The dream factory builds illusions of reality," said Chico. "Not illusions that un-dilute: that there isn't such a thing as deluded reality, or realities that are different from theirs, or from the realities they want you to see."

"Alas, poor Yorick," said Groucho. "Thus is the Quixotic project intrinsically too Quixotic itself to see the light of day in a darkened theater. Slings and arrows! Rest in peace—*the Quixotic Movement*. Next! Don't be disappointed, kid. Keep laughing, as the world keeps laughing at you. Didn't take me for a bookworming philosopher, eh?"

"If only Socrates, Voltaire, Swift, and Rabelais were here," commented Duke.

"Heh, this guy," laughed Chico. "We once chipped in for a Model-T Ford. Grouchy Julius here brought it in for service. He was so into his book that he finished it in the driver seat, still elevated up on the mechanic's lift."

"I'm no professor, but I could play one on stage," said Groucho.

"That's right: Professor Wagstaff," riffed Chico. "And Harpo here would make quite the symphonic conductor: Maestro Zeronkovich of the Zeroist Dada Orchestra . . ."

"Wagstaff. Heh, that's good. I like stories. What they mean. How they end. How's this one gonna end bub? It better be good!" Groucho wagged his finger at Duke. "It's no fun being beaten. Ending a washed-out loser. All your dreams mocked and mucked up. Slings and arrows, my friend. Slings and arrows. We still have a few tricks up his sleeve."

Chico picks up a queen of swords for his poker hand.

Someone knocks at the door.

"Hold it," warned Chico. "Nobody knocks on the front door. This is a hideout. Quiet, get down."

There's a tense moment of jittering stillness. Harpo covers his mouth. Frowns, then covers his eyes. They icily stare back at one another. Duke hears their hearts pounding. They stare at one another, wide-eyed. The silence is creepy. But nothing happens.

Should they get up?

A barrage of cannon thunder explodes. A hail of bullets blisters through the walls. Everyone ducks further. Tables are overturned. It's a desperate calamity.

But Harpo can't refrain from laughing. Duke yanks him down to the floor. Harpo pops back up. A bullet zings through his hat. He laughs harder.

With Harpo off his rocker, Groucho turns to Satch to comment as they're crouched behind a sofa: "See what happens? Say, I could use some of that smoke now, brother."

Chicken feathers spew forth from the shot-up pillows. Kids are screaming.

"We've been set up. Hoppo stay down you lunatic," yelled Chico.

"Dear Lord," moaned Satch, "it must be Dandy Ratshaw."

Harpo leaps through the fusillade of hot gunfire and grabs pots and pans to put over his head and body for armor, then swings the iron plating around like a whirling dervish to repel the bouncing shrapnel.

One bullet ricochets back and nails one of the marauders outside who yells, "Sonofabitch I'm hit. They're firing back."

Another round bursts through. A bullet zings Harpo's ass—still laughing.

Chico finds his .38 caliber and shoots back. Satch and the others grab what kids they could to provide shelter.

But then Petey the dog is hit and howls. Spanky hollers in despair.

Stymie crawls out to save him but he's shot in the shoulder and wails in pain.

Glass, plaster, and wood are splintering and crashing all over. It's a war. Who the hell? It's a din of madness. They can't hear each other.

The guys shout and signal to make some kind of retreat with the wounded and shelter the kids.

Alfalfa jumps up with a heroic spurt of courage to snag Stymie.

"No!"

"Hey kid, stay down!"

He's about to drag him to safety when a bullet pierces Alfalfa straight between the eyes. Shrieks tear the room.

Alfalfa drops to the floor.

"Is he dead?"

"Holy shit!"

"Oh my God."

"Christ Almighty. They got Alfalfa."

Groucho vomits amid the murderous hysteria.

"Times like these," said Groucho, spitting up, "It's hard to be an atheist."

They hear sirens roar, growing closer. The shadowy gangsters yell: *Hey, time to scram.*

Dust and debris settle, as if in slow motion.

Is it safe?

A ringing drum drones the ears. The taste of sour copper clogs their throats.

The battles over? Adrenaline still hammers like a dying racehorse. Thank God the police are here.

The cops storm in: "Everyone out with your hands up."

"We've got wounded," the gang shouted back.

Harpo sees that Alfalfa is dead? He finally stops laughing, then starts to slobber with the rest of the shell-shocked kids.

"Sarge, I'll call an ambulance. Looks like a massacre."

Satch goes to help Buckwheat when an officer whacks him with a club: "Are you responsible for this mess? Huh, Spearchucker?"

"Lord Almighty," growled Satch. "Whose payroll are you on? Just get this poor kid to a hospital, then worry about me."

The cops harass the group, which they call a bunch of kikes, ragamuffins, spooks, and a faggot.

"Hold on, hold on," demanded Groucho, who's now raving, shaken and unhinged: "We're innocent. Until proven crazy. We've been sieged by a squad of Neanderthal psychos—and I get the impression you're not distant cousins. But for the legal record, by your logic, mind you: I'm a Kike, my brother's a Kike—"

"Heyyy, watch what you're saying," yelled a red-eyed Chico.

"Respectfully, albeit contextually," replied Groucho, twitching with eyes rolling and pupils dilating—giddy with defensive laughter. "But these other guys? Which one is a—?"

"Alright, alright. C'mon, buddy," sneered an officer. "It's all over now."

The police search Satch. Finding his marijuana, they grin, and put the cuffs on him.

"Goddamn L.A.P.D.," grumbled Satch. "A judge would look more kindly on me if I shot a Negro in the ass, than be brought in for Mary Jane. Hey, someone please call my lawyer."

"Well, well, we got an uppity King Sambo here. Looks like our royalty gets a chauffeured ride downtown, with lots of explaining to do, after a few cozy days to cool off. Damn shame punks, but ya shouldn't be here. Let's go! The rest of ya bums are all under citation for trespassing. Move it!"

Episode 24

Masquerade

If George Washington were alive today, what a shining mark he would be for . . . . professional patriots! . . . the richest man in the United States, a promoter of stock companies, a land-grabber. . . a bitter opponent of foreign entanglements . . . He had a liking for all forthright and pugnacious men, and a contempt for lawyers, schoolmasters and all other such obscurantists. He was not pious. . . . He knew far more profanity than Scripture . . . He had no belief in the infallible wisdom of the common people, but regarded them as inflammatory dolts . . . today, George would be ineligible for any office . . . on trial in all the yellow journals for belonging to the Invisible Government, the Hell Hounds of Plutocracy, the Money Power, the [special] Interests . . . under indictment by every grand jury . . . a recruiting officer for insane asylums, a poisoner of the home. The suffragettes would be on his trail, with sentinels posted all along the Accotink. *Damn! A Book of Calumny*

—H.L. Mencken

The silver reflections off the sea of chrome bumpers in the parking lot of the Witz' estate unhinged Duke's thoughts. It's bad enough Satch is still in jail. But they had to move ahead with their plans.

Instead of a static pattern—there's an amorphous flow: inundation of over-exposure. Uncontrollable forces.

The hammering angst of what he is about to do—terrorizes him. Even as the ground beneath begins to disappear, once again. The vertigo dementia of his insubstantial stability in this world.

An abyss widens to swallow into a vast arena of interiorized hollow landscape, an overlapping paradox of a labyrinthine topography of psyche, as if no longer his own. The uncanny realism gnaws and challenges the all-encompassing impossibility smashing Duke's head in this teleported phantasm. His untenable and precarious substance.

It stabs his brain. Schizophrenic tremors wash him in a terrifying worm-hole. Engulfing him out of time. Cells and atoms fibrillate with a teetering insanity towards a slow, gravitational pull of frictional negation into the cosmic dragon.

His heart tightens. The feverish skin seems to liquefy. Sirens boom in his eardrums. Sound is mesmerizing, a monotonous drone of cyclic revving troughs and crests of menacing waves of vibration.

Some gripping hand of power and gravity wants to tear him out of the universe. He bends over to vomit, but only wretches with unrelieved dry heaves. Choking for a breath and stability, Duke grabs the side mirror of a gleaming Chrysler to hold himself up, inhale, and stop the spinning until the ground rematerializes.

One of the parking lot attendants sees him, and despite Duke's well-dressed attire (albeit in 16th-century refinery as Othello), angrily yells with ugly electricity: "*Hey nigger!* Get the hell away from that vehicle . . . "

The irate valet rushes over and brandishes a black-jack from his pocket: "Hey you sonofa—"

But when Duke looks up, the valet fueled with rage raises his weapon—about to follow-through, but suddenly apologizes: "Oh! Sorry, sir! Pardon me. Didn't realize you were in costume."

"You better be sorry, punk! Mr. Witz wouldn't take kindly to his guests being harassed."

"Please sir, it's dark; you must understand. We wouldn't want any perceived undesirables—messing with what they shouldn't."

Duke wants to pop him but knows he has to keep his cool and not blow his cover. Maybe later.

He shakes himself loose, and proceeds to the castle.

Outdoors there's an array of Chinese lamps and Tiki torches. Tables decked with ice carvings keep the rows of oysters, truffles, sorbet and sherbet chilled, for the cool and sultry. Faux yellow brick roads wind through the property that lead to contingents of hired munchkins dancing, singing, or engaged in acrobatics. Duke steers clear of the pool.

Despite the danger, he surprisingly giggles. There are even Punch & Judy shows in mini-theater tents, where dwarves are the live-action Punch & Judys pummeling each other. However, he feels a twinge of guilt as he realizes how these little folk are being exploited.

But then Duke hears women screaming. Apparently, a number of the "munchkins" are sneaking under women's skirts. Over to the side, he notices midgets are holding down the even smaller and more vulnerable dwarfs to force alcohol down their gullets.

"Christ on a Christmas tree! It's human nature, in miniature. No escape from the beast who shadows us."

Duke hands over his doctored invitation at the door and enters the castle through the foyer and its long mirrored alcove. Suddenly seeing himself: Black! The alien beauty of black skin—reflecting, alienating— staring back at him.

He's quickly confronted with how swift his disguised perception, to those around him, can cruelly transform impressions and reactions so out of context: the ugly social impositions, the moral history, and crimes of bigotry. The terrible shock of discomfort for those who can't wash this "make-up" off, and don't bloody need to, but made to feel so.

Like a wall.

An enemies barricade, surrounding one right where you live, everywhere you go. Cutting you off. Haunting. Stalking them—within a prison. Not of their making.

To then wear a different type of make-up. To wear a mask. Subjugated. Undermined. An inferiorized role. The sobering realization of walking in another's shoes. Even as Duke tumbles in this warped dimension of a world upside down. Revolving with unstoppable turmoil.

The grinding international slaughter proceeds apace. An expanding worldwide torture chamber. This very moment. No words possible for those being starved, burned and bayoneted in Manchuria. The cold-blooded steel knife in the heart, spilling the hot blood of innocence . . . For what?

Delusions of an individual's empowerment by raising a murderous flag. The noose choking neck. Mass genocide. Shallow graves.

Millions to be slaughtered from China to Poland, Armenia and Kiev, while nooses still rise from Oklahoma and Jacksonville, from Mississippi to Alabama, for the unwelcome beautiful masks they're born with—judged and executed to the cloning molds of death, even while defending their nation.

Now this—jovial facade.

Duke walks, tottering, with platform boots, onto the parquetry and mahogany flooring of the mock medieval mansion's ballroom under crystal chandeliers.

A carnival of champagne-popping illusion. How lucky they dance over the strata of bones, while the tormented fall beneath the earth to harrowing rapes and extermination, at the far side of the planet, or down the road, at the bottom of the hills. How lucky we are, who're still free, and loose in this lawless asylum. We who still have faces . . .

A variety of stars, gossip columnists, agents, designers, stylists, politicians, and bankrollers of the industry are schmoozing amuck the happy ruckus, along with the actors, directors and writers—some willing or otherwise.

It's a party. They seem suited to the grotesquery of masks and outfits, as much of what they do in fact involves so much masquerading.

Mingling aloof a moment, Duke looks above to witness Frankie Witz descend the stairwell of grand polished marble and gold gilded balustrade, costumed as the most famous General—George Washington. He's accompanied by the beaming doll of Mrs. Witz, lavishly decked out as the irrepressible Marie Antoinette. Sparkling with jewels, towering wig, and reflections of powdery face cream and rouge.

The party crowd applauds their entrance. The band strikes up a mock jazzy: *Here Comes the Chief*. Groucho is also decked as a junior Revolutionary War officer, and turns to Chico and Harpo: "Ain't this swank."

Chico, in uniform, is dressed sharp and austere with slicked-back hair and martial beret as Mussolini; toasts and clinks champagne with Harpo dressed as the opera clown Pagliacci, and washes it down. They're keeping a lookout for Duke, and nerve-wrackingly anticipate the next cunning phase of the unfolding drama.

A Lionel model train circulates the halls with freight carrying fresh bubbling glasses, besides the numerous waiters offering drinks, paté or appetizers of caviar and clams-casino. The Marx Brothers like the train.

Cigars, cigarettes, and cheroots fume through the drift and layer of haze amidst the animated choreography of glinting earrings, necklaces, and watches; losing time with the cackling and hoots of the guzzling night.

Duke still sees black-and-white, yet the overload of pressure and stimulation seems to push multitudinous hints and flashes of orange, purple, green and magenta that scintillate and burn through, making him a slight delirious, as he doubles his resolve to focus.

Duke makes his way across the crowd of Sherlocks, Tarzans, Cleopatras, Gunga Dins, cowboys, impersonators, fairy tales, myths, musketeers, devils, Nerfertitis, Romans, vampires, pirates, Buck Rogers, Robin Hoods, and royalty.

He overhears the cross-fire snatches of conversation:

"So then we invited the entire chorus-line to the pool party . . ."

"He said. Then she said, then she said that he said that she . . ."

"Cheeky."

"Do I look horrid?'

"I feel ravishing."

"I'd like to ravish you."

"Fritz, that was mesmerizing."

"I thought his name was Harry."

"I'd like to have you for dinner. Then for breakfast. How well do you cook?"

"'*Fool! Don't you see I could've poisoned you a thousand times had I been able to live without you.*'"

"Fiendish."

"Well, if you're going through hell—keep going."

"They should free a madman, and lock *you* up!"

"Feast your eyes on that."

"Razzamatazz, and all that jazz."

"Just don't end up jailed in Alcatraz."

"Oh that reminds me . . ."

"I'm not in the least surprised."

"Yes dear, you've most certainly earned your PhD.—in bullshit."

"How now, brown cow?"

"What the frick does that even mean?"

"What's so bad about fascism anyhow?"

"I was her in a past life. What did I do to deserve this one?"

"Indeed, even fools are right sometimes."

"It's in all the papers."

"Honey, tabloids aren't really newspapers."

"It's just pulp with print which palpitates the exaggerated heroism and scandalous exploits of our sold-out silhouettes."

"We're mimicking shadows of ourselves—projected on the mass public imagination—of what they dream . . ."

"And what they should dream!"

"You mean what *They* think the masses should dream . . ."

"Manufacturing an escape from a harsh reality with so much distraction that they'll never be able to escape the harsh realities."

"Ha. That's why they pay us. To put their hands up our ass."

"Figuratively, and literally."

"What did you hear?"

"Preposterous."

"These are the hollow papier-maché mogul Mephistopheles of movie industry machinery to perpetuate the complacent vulgarism of debasing women in the assumed classiest ways possible."

"Are these commies Reds or Pinks? Which color? I don't get it."

"Rewrite it with more sex."

"I'll bet you a thousand dollars . . ."

"Well, I'll pay you two thousand if . . ."

"Democracy is the worst form of government . . ."

" . . . Yeah, except for all the others."

"She's from Nebraska."

"Thought you said Alaska."

"Same thing."

"I meant Kansas."

"The assonance of your . . ."

"Well, screw you too."

"I was really drunk at the time."

"When are you not?"

"He tried to direct a film where the Indians win. No one has seen or heard from him since."

"We only think we exist in this dream of nothingness. As soon as the brain is dead we simply cease *to think* we exist."

"Ah, but do we continue to dream?"

"That's what I mean."

"Is it?"

Episode 25

Masque

Circus, *n.* A place where horses, ponies and elephants are
permitted to see men, women and children acting the fool.

—*The Devil's Dictionary* Ambrose Bierce

Duke is side-stepping and dodging his way through the spectral collage of characters.

"No way!"

He's headed right for Joan Crawford and Bette Davis from the pool.

"Christ."

He makes a swift turn to avoid them, and runs into a tall woman wearing a white Guy Fawkes mask with its upturned smile and 17th century costume.

"Ow! Pardon me!" she screeched loud and startled. An inordinate voltage of electric shock jolts and frictioned between them. They both almost swoon into one another.

"Excuse me, and mind your boots sir. Wait! Were we hit by lightning? Did you feel that? Chills. Like deja vu. What on earth? A serendipitous omen? A portentous harbinger? Oh! Hmm, how odd. Don't you look familiar, mister!" said Ms. Fawkes.

He sees a furrowing brow and narrowed eyes as hot coals in her mask's eye slits. Duke turns aside, bleary and disconcerted from the uncanny collision, to persevere.

"Oh no. You won't escape from me so easily," as she zeroed in on him.

"Possess or pretend to have the manly courage to face me when I address you," she said.

A bead of sweat falls to the frills of his tightening neck collar.

152

She steps back and *flaunces* her cape to make room to draw out her sharp rapier from its sheath.

Duke gulps, and she pronounces:

"For *that I did love the Moor to live with him, my downright violence and storm of fortunes may trumpet to the world: . . . I saw Othello's visage in his mind, and to his honor and his valiant parts did I my soul and fortunes consecrate.*"[14]

Speechless, but Duke is momentarily at ease with relief, while she beams back at him with a devious glare.

A turbulent silence passes awkward amid the sea of frivolity. She raises a stern, impatient eye. Then he unsheathes a Spanish sword to match hers, and keenly responds:

"*Let her have your voices. Vouch with me, heaven, I therefore beg it not, to please the palate of my appetite. . . and proper satisfaction. But to be free and bounteous to her mind . . .*"[15]

"It's *beg*—not plead, and rather, *palate*—not taste. But well-replied *extempore*. Good effort. Bravo, Sir Othello! Clever accouterments. *You're a well-dressed man.* You must have friends at the studio wardrobe? Nice to see some thespian persona in this kitschy palatial den of malaise."

"La ringrazio mille, " said Duke.

"Bring class to a classless society, I always say, ha ha ha ha ha," she retorted. "Between you and I, isn't this ghastly? Quite the pompous spectacle. Look around. Behold a paean to luxury and status. An audacious epitome of a Scott Fitzgerald novel fashioned to a lively facsimile, and without an ounce of irony. "Bold" wouldn't be a sardonic enough term. *King Midas Frankie* out-hollied Hollywood with this grotesque display of Louis XIV post-Baroque opulent poor taste in decor of decadence, if I've ever seen. And I've seen it. Granted—besides a flaunting Dark Ages moated exterior, erected by an overgrown bratty spoiled school boy, and his fantasy of feudal knights, queens, and wenches of perverse medievalism. Rather a disreputable clown clueless to real history, though barbarically appropriate. *Where's the rack and Iron Maiden?* In the dungeon basement with Boris Karloff and Bela Lugosi, I gather? Golly, I'd rather fly this scene presently and not find out.

She flaunts her hair, which reddeningly bleeds through the gauze of his vision.

"Don'tcha think? What's your opinion? A fool's ball? Or a ball of fools?" She raised her mask. It's Katherine Hepburn.

Holy heck.

[14] Shakespeare, William. Othello. Act 1.
[15] ibid.

"What's the matter? A tongue-hungry cat? Please don't tell me you're star-struck? We should go to an observatory for that. Dazzled? By my beauty then, are you? *Really?*"

Duke smiles inside, some unplaceable connection . . . but the palpable phantom of expediency is stalking at his throat as he spots Witz. His brain stuck in a revolving door.

"This posh soiree should be fun, shouldn't it? Although I'd prefer a cozy cafe. But the *Cheeze* makes my skin crawl, as these sycophants fawn and prostrate to his moldy eminence. And to think last year he was Julius Caesar?"

"Where's Brutus?" replied Duke.

"Indeed," as she rolled out a high-pitched laugh. "So what in blazes am I doing here, you're wondering? Well, you can bet I was roped in. And by the looks of this place, m'Lord Witz would love to have me roped in. And I do mean tied up," Hepburn said, and shivered as though sharp icicles ran down her spine.

"Have you seen *Twelfth Night? King Lear?* Well? Of course you have. Look at you. You're not some troglodyte? Are you? You're here by yourself? Your cultured girlfriend didn't put you up to this? No? Your wife? Instead of allowing you to come as Superman, Babe Ruth or Flash Gordon? Did she?"

"Why, no."

"No matter. It'd take a modicum of effort to know those lines, if not an implicit knowledge to the initiated. The studios are just raving with pioneer Western flicks lately. Dreadful. Nevertheless, it is quite a different view of America from the West Coast, isn't it?

"Sorry, didn't catch your name, my dashing Moor."

"You may call me—Duke Orsino."

"My my. Of course you are. Right out of the Bard's Illyria. Too coy you are, sir. Can you believe it's going to be April? Spring! Hard to tell in sunny California. It's not Cape Cod. The poetry of the seasons. The joy of anonymity. A place without autumn hardly has a soul. I have to smile so much, in bright light—both day and night—with those hideous flash bulbs popping off, that my face is cracking. The publicity machine. But there's worse off with far larger problems in the world.

"Quite the relief, wearing a mask. I'm here at request, to butter some executives, take some photos, then I'm off."

Groucho strolls by and gives Duke a wink. Chico and Harpo signal behind with rude gestures. Duke makes a cutting motion at his neck for them to quit.

"Is there something wrong with your throat?"

"I'm fine, thanks."

"Well. This Roman debauchery goes with the territory. Pageants of the enslaved. Feeding Christians to the Christians. Orgies after midnight. Will America ever recover? This Babylonian avalanche is what you get when cash rules, not culture or universities. The Moguls, God bless them, escaped the starvation of the European ghettos and Jewish pogroms in Russia for a better life, and to Americanize. Now they're absotively afraid of appearing to be not American enough! Can you imagine? Lost their perspective. Breaks my heart. They have mansions bigger than this one. But that's how the game puts us through the looking glass.

"Oh, they're not all evil; but the illusions and momentum of forces beyond their control have conspired to control them. Despite the enormous influence they wield, and think they wield. What do you call it when good men turn away and do nothing in the face of widespread hypocrisy and injustice?"

With Hepburn speedily versing, Duke repeatedly attempts to get a word in. But it's better this way, best not to say too much, as he spies the whereabouts of his objective, and may need to cut the conversation short, if permissible.

What to do? He imagined some hand of God bringing him into this world . . . And here she is. Inexplicable. It all can't be in his head? Unless, still debating the providential vehicle whether some Tibetan, Gnostic, Cartesian schizophrenic, psychedelic, or Quantum-entangled mad scientist unknown way.

"Why it wasn't long ago," continued Hepburn, "this was all onion fields, poinsettia farms and avocado groves. Have you had an avocado? Aren't they grand?"

Errol Flynn strolls by as Zorro, and Peter Lorre as a cockroach, amidst flirty pouts and wolfish prowling. Hepburn momentarily pulls her mask down as they pass.

"Ha! What a banal composition of joy, apathy, and decadent condescension. Castle Witz. Quite the capitol to the necropolis. This Imperial self-aggrandizing royalty is endemic to the whole shebang. The roaring Twenties all over again, la-dee-da. However, we're now through the boring Thirties; the rich are still vultures high on the hog, treading the grapes of wrath. Glory glory hallelujah. Buy, sell and swindle. Owners and chattel.

"I do enjoy people watching, but look at these headless Arthurs, Sir Galahads and the Lancelots of our time in this pseudo-Xanadu—all sauced-up in the celebration of ego rooster poncing about. I could spit. Wouldn't that be unladylike?"

"Ms. Hepburn, you could never be unladylike."

"Merci beaucoup, monsieur," smiled and warmed Hepburn. "Ah. This cavalcade of foolery, stealing and appropriating Jungian archetypes to condition the nation, and the world, into being fools. Strike that. Into being more foolish than we already are. What a fine example to set. They should rename movie theaters as Plato's Caves. Odd analogy that one. Once the slaves are liberated from the projector's illusions on the wall, who's behind it all? Who holds the truest truth? It's calcified vulgarism of the worst exploitation of delusional exhibitionism. Just an occasional ray of magic talents through.

"I'm not innocent, mind you. Certainly not naive to the beleaguered marginalization. Cinematic triumphs of mesmerizing pervasiveness. Forgive me, but living at a heady pace of years spinning in high-speed merry-go-rounds of cynicism, well, frankly, it makes me batty. Dust one off, powder up, and keep smiling."

Duke nods understandingly, but, *are those the Three Stooges? Wearing overalls and burglar masks? Peeking from the foyer?*

"All I ever wanted to do was act. On stage and theater. Ibsen. Pirandello. Chekhov. Shaw."

"Aristophanes?" said Duke.

"Now you're talking. Not this barbarism hyped as sleek shiny modernity. Technology, state of the art, the most revolutionary fascinating inventions after thousands of years . . . the marvels we can accomplish . . . and it's just goofy with canned lampoonery, buffoonery, overgrown boys with cap guns, and the romanticized glamour glitz of movie stardom. Showbiz."

"A show of business. A gilded age and cage?" said Duke.

"Yes, young naïve me assumed it would get better," said Hepburn as she briefly grab Duke. "Give me a script with lines. Dialogue. A redeeming moral dilemma. Art! Sure, an occasional comic farce and caper is fun for all, but now I just don't know. These bloody studio contracts. The moguls, the money, directors, the republicans and the industry. It's worsening, getting so entrenched itself, as so—conservative!

"Not this dilettante trapezing of marionette dollhouse fussing we're condemned to be puppeted by. Reducing film, this revolutionary artform, to steamroller commercialism. Even while we're tethered to our signatures stamped on legalese. Boy would I like to work with a Hitchcock, or Fritz Lang."

"How about a lead role in a new sound and color version of Metropolis?" said Duke. "An original new script and plot. Relevant to today's angst of working class automatons and the dehumanizing issues?"

"That'd be marvelous. I'd say start right now. But good luck getting a backer. *Metropolis?* The future? Why, we'll all be enlightened, as robots do everything; popping super-pills, in a brave new world, won't we? Ha ha ha ha."

"That's exactly what's going to happen."

"Synthesized mescaline. Benzedrine. Phenobarbital barbiturates. Cocaine. Opiated dope. As if booze isn't enough? I'm sure these miracle cure pills will only improve, at least in potency. Pillage the brain. Make bigger fools of us. Especially these bamboozling diet pills. Why the other day I saw poor Judy Garland. She seemed like she didn't know if she was coming or going. I said hello, and her agent just dragged her away. *C'mon doll.*

"I do my best with the iambic punctuation of syllables in what they toss me. These scripts? All this silly Plautus rip-off melodrama, and frolic pandering farce, of who's marrying whom and who's Modern Roman slave or maid is in on the caper, of mixed-up identities and motives. It's juvenile. Been done before. People deserve better. Cinema mirrors the lies we're sold for the lives we live.

"Selling just enough 'sex,' if you can call it that, to be spicy and risqué, but keeping it safely on edge to meet the 'family friendly' standards of the censors. From D.C. to your scarlet lettering righteous ministers popping out of cotton and cornfields like scarecrows.

"Keep it family friendly? Well, if they want to keep things family friendly there shouldn't be kids going hungry from Harlem to Appalachia. Nope. Just shut up, here's your check, doll. I'm not ungrateful. But, *keep smiling. Keep it up—the sharks are circling to write you off, or take your place. Look sharp. Keep it rolling. Action: take two.*

"Makes me so hot my incendiary hair'll catch fire if you don't watch out. Why I'm dangerous. Hang out with me long enough, get too close, you're likely to explode."

"Doubtless," concurred Duke. He was feeling a bit warm, wasn't he? Burn wasn't in her name for nothing.

"Evolution, it's become a victorious survival of the un-fittest. This charade of a chameleon's paradise. Glossy magazines and snazzy motorcars, bland Glen Miller orchestras, ugh . . . Disneyland, cigarettes and ice cream . . .

"Their smug coquettishness. Meowing and 'pewling' coterie of *bombasticating* ballet of bullies. Obnoxious swindlers in a heist of dream factories on how to be a tramp, as they hustle bright-eyed damosels in an apoplexy of hysterics. Cooing and wooing. Herded to a claustrophobia of leering wolves in agent's clothing to a howling audience. This pied piping of manipulation of desire and repression. Don't even get me started on Sigmund Freud . . ."

Duke is about to bring up Frued's nephew, Edward Bernys, who's been teaching Wall Street how to propagandize and manipulate the public into mastering advertising sales techniques—triggering a mass hypnosis, even worse as these techniques transfer over to selling political campaigns, which the Germans have picked up in spades—but a group of hooded figures walk in.

"Holy smokes," said Hepburn. "Dearth of a nation. Surely a sick joke? Talk about a costume party—Well I'll be. Speaking of the devils."

Two dozen white-sheeted Ku Klux Klan file along the back; a mumbling stir among the attendees.

"You know, I must warn you, Ms. Hepburn. I don't know how to tell you this but, if you're really so keen to make your appearances and vamoose out of here, I'd advise you to do so. And I don't mean that as a blow-off, as it's been a sincere pleasure. You must trust and know, I have it on good authority that some of Witz's worst cronies and gangsters will be here. Since some of these underground characters don't get along, all hell's going to break loose.

"Truly? At this juncture, I'm fairly convinced. But, how'd you know that?"

"It's classified."

"Oh, a spy novelist wiseguy? Worse than this? Well, sounds like a sight to behold, but better safe than sorry."

Duke spots an entourage approaching nearby who surround Witz, cajoling him with obsequious word wagging prostrations, or venturing to tease with familiarity, at their peril. Duke slyly edges nearer to overhear.

"General" Witz stands austere, not giving a shit, with his pale, bloodless lips.

"He has a complex," someone joked about Witz.

"I have the greatest complex of all time," responded Witz.

"Eh. Well there's nothing complex about him," replied Mrs. Witz.

"How is it no one has produced a complete epic of Dante's Inferno?"

"Capital idea."

"Smashing."

"Ha, we all could be in it."

"She means that literally, *and* literally."

"We already are."

"You're on fire tonight, darling."

"I already signed that contract."

"Didn't we all?"

"It's where the lot of us are headed."

"Most of us, anyhow. Speak for yourselves."

"With the Nazi's, Soviets and the Empire of Japan fumbling amok, it'll be here soon enough."

"What a cruel god. What happened to the likes of Dionysius?"

"You mean you don't know?"

"Hocus pocus, meant to scare us. Opium of the people."

"Hopefully God has a mercifully infinite sense of humor."

"Obviously. Take a look around."

"It all gives me the Willies."

Groucho steps in: "The Willies? That sounds like a hillbilly venereal disease."

Duke eyes someone in the wings signaling to Witz that it's time. Franky begins pardoning himself to his guests before he steps out: "Excuse me ladies and gentleman, some important matters to attend to. So nice of you to come. Do enjoy yourselves. Tell everyone you've been to the greatest home and party ever seen. There'll be some fireworks . . ."

Duke raises his sword high to also signal the guys that the plan is afoot.

"Miss Hepburn, I'm cordially delighted to have made your acquaintance, but must regrettably tear myself away from your magnetic company in order to save the world, or something like it."

"Herumph. Golly."

Duke is about to weave closer to Witz, then thinks twice and spins back to Hepburn.

"Or?" Duke said, "You know, you could do something to help. Quickly. I need to infiltrate Witz's 'good' graces for this rather specialized espionage and sabotage mission for—*the Writer's Guild.*"

"The SWG! The writer's union guild?"

"Shhhhh!"

He leans in and whispers in her ear. She nods. Then steps back.

"Why, how dare you!" she thundered, and Hepburn delivers him one hell of a slap. Out of the ballpark. And storms off

She smacks him so hard he feels knocked into an electric chair as a Chinese gong goes off in his head. Gong! Gong!

He's delirious. The clanging ring is so loud and real—trying to shake it off. The metaphysical angst of it. *What does it mean?* Gong! Gong! Like the bells of Notre-dame. Quasimodo is in his brain.

Duke turns around, and an imperial Fu Manchu costumed Chinese with a mallet is banging a huge gong right behind, hung high on a string, laughing at him: "Ha, aren't you a fool! She slapped you to Shanghai."

Someone warmly places a cold firm assuring hand on his back, and tells Duke over his shoulder:

"Boy, I bet you told her! These silly broads. Who do they think they are? Chicks! I should bring you to *Sugarbush Island* sometime. All they want is a bigger dollhouse. And they want equal rights? That'll be the day. Damn 19th Amendment. If they're equal, well then, you should be able to pop her right back. Pow. *Shut up bitch*. That'd make a killer movie line! There's no questioning a man's dominance. She's nothing but an actress, anyhow."

My God, Duke realizes the ploy worked, and it's General Washington Witz, and *he doesn't recognize me*.

Painfully smiling back, Duke nervously giggles and finds the courage to concur in an English accent: "These wanking Hollywood elites. They all think they're bloody well better than us. What a flogging I'd like to give them."

"Damn straight. Well I'm going to make sure things are going to change. I'm about to see some important people about it. The best. Only superior genes can solve these problems, and lead us patriots with pride."

"Smashing."

"You should join me. You're welcome here anytime. Oh, I like the ironic outfit. Ha, a black Shakespeare. Genius," said Witz, and walked off.

"Holy hell!"

Witz exits to chambers below. Duke cautiously follows after nudging to his conspirators that it's begun.

Episode 26

Corridor Labyrinth

> The rusted chains of prison moons
> Are shattered by the sun
> I walk a road horizons change
> The tournament's begun
> The purple piper plays his tune
> The choir softly sing
> Three lullabies in an ancient tongue
> For the court of the Crimson King.
>
> —King Crimson[16]

Torches light the way of sulfurous incandescence descending into the cellars below, following behind Witz. There is a maze of mirrors. Corrosive opulence.

A surging pit of nausea plummets Duke's stomach. A smashing sense of smothering infernal claustrophobia.

This abomination of a cadaverous crypt galvanized with demonic life. Through the vaulted corridor he enters a chamber. Witz waves him in. Amid the swirl of ornate and macabre outfitted men of power and dereliction, he sees her.

It's Hedy! But she's gagged like a mummy at the side of a platform. Nothing he can do.

Duke gulps, and anonymously makes his way to the back of the underground chamber.

Esteemed guests mill about in their sacramental robes: Charles Lindburgh. Virgil Effinger. Dudley Pelley. Father Coughlin. Robert Henry Best. Prescott Bush. Charles E Wilson. Lyndon LaRouche. Herman Perry. Normal Rockingwell. William Randolph Hearst. Young Ronald Reagan. Seward Collins.

---

[16] *"In the Court of the Crimson King."* In the Court of the Crimson King . Mcdonald, Ian. Sinfield, Peter. Island Atlantic E.G. 1969. LP.

161

"Is that Allen Dulles in the back?"

With elevating rancor and shadowy exuberance, Werner Naumann, an S.S. member, functioning as a secret visiting envoy secretary of Herr Joseph Goebbels's Ministry of Propaganda—addresses the group, and delivers, with a thick accent but in good English, an overture of inspired animosity:

"Revered and nobly bred gentleman. I implore thee to the higher community of our quality. Unlock the Sarcophagus. Renovate the sepulcher of slaughterous thoughts dashed upon the succor of the wasted, thirsty suppliants who claw for our strength. As our Wolfgang von Goethe said: *Let everyone sweep in front of his own door, and the whole world will be clean.*

"Uncork the World Serpent for Ragnarok. We *are* the wheel of time. Our arms sinew and warp into all worlds. Perish the diminishing idealist . . . dim the sun sinks pending unheard prayers to a chalice of our power. Trolls and Jews look above in dismay from mines and caverns, hoarding dusty jewels miserly with greed under the houses of gashing cats. Carousing and plotting below the sludge of prostituting usury and sewerage.

"Supper is ready. We will expand in our Lebensraum. Thirteen seats at the grand banquet's table. Gush and glut of fiddled bats' wings—scoffing at a president, who does not exist—Only on film reels and scratchy radio broadcasts—or slowly giving out ice cream cones, behind a blitzkrieg of cyclones. Will, Blood, And Soil!"

Blut und Boden. Intoned the group.

Hedy burns observing with a seething mature intelligence.

"In a crush of dust. An angle of rejuvenating vision. The survey of carnage. Survivors of the Flood. Extracting poison and medicine from the carcass. The national cadaver. Pharaohs and Sphinxes. Wielders of scepters. Staff and serpents. Sphincters of popes, we genuflect to flatulent adulation."

They humorously grunt. Duke firmly squints to prevent his eyes from widening, from both shock and perplexity.

"We are the advent of the coming Race. The ascending power. The evolved inheritance. White is the power of your great whale, as the sun at its hottest peaks blazes white in its soaring energy of power, as do all the stars that illuminate the desolate blackness.

"The grid of secrets. Plans within plans; within feints and pantomimes. Banks and contracts. Corporate federations. Union of cartels. Clandestine destinies. Unmanifest to most. Theosophy and incense of our holy ghost. And our imperturbable host," beckoning to Witz, to a chorus of hardy laughter.

"Secrets hiding screens of distraction to launch seeds of puzzle's secreted pieces. Sacred whispers codifying etherized oracles of the New Law of the most ancient anagram.

"Vaporized cells within the grist of cellars: compartments stocked with Arks, Relics and Archaic codes.

"Our agents and supporters infiltrate and collaborate from Wall Street to the corridors of Washington. The coup is upon them. The Blitzkrieg is coming.

"The Machiavellian confetti and calculus: Stockings and laces. Whispered translucent under veils of cloaks. And the supreme maker of invisible eyes and gold watches. We now will own the time, and the clock of the cosmos. The new Immanuel Kants and Hegels. Haggling bog-binders. Towering candles. Harrowing innuendos.

"Choirs and incantations. Of secrecy sworn and swearing—a curse of royal satanic verses among our catechisms of ostensibly Christian brethren. Incorporated bankers bow in obeisance. Submit to the way of masters.

"Grails so buried that their meanings are concealed from what's forgotten to the unwashed sheep and herds. But we will have the Grail. We are the grail! We are the holy blood!"

Here here!

"Inconceivable—the exponential catalysts converge. Encoded Judas of the scriptures. Hail and shallows. Halls and hollow thralldom. Crucified beggars and silk of thieving ministers.

"Where is Indra? Zeus? Jehovah? Bacchus? Tiamat? Astarte? Ishtar? Ahriman? Azrael? Lucifer? The inner light?

"Illumination. Thrones and gallows. Vestments, and the hallowed be thy names?

"Unsheathe in cryptic shelter. For we have Odin. And Thor's hammer. Sacrifice and rites. Drunk womb, and monumental tomb. To talk to God. To slay God. To become gods. We do not inherit the earth with the meek. Who are the meek but the weaklings sanctioned by the fabled Jew-god? Slaves. We take the earth because it is ours. Worthy. To the strong. *Ubermensch.*

"Pages. Parchments. Sacraments. Scriptures. Cacophony of the degenerate races we cast into the grand furnace which fuels our ascending glory and history. A new era.

"Ink dye dust of papyrus. Wells and cisterns of blood. Encryptions. Memory and archetypes. Fountains and baptism. Tablets and tables. Drops and elixirs. Distillations and vapors. Mazes. Laboratories and labyrinths. All evolving or discarded into our convergence and attainment.

"Eleusinian Walls. Links. Connections. Periodic elements. Treasures. Taboos. Vats and vineyards. Riddles and parables. Symbols and metaphors. Gilded figures of speech.

"Thus Sprachen zie Deutsch of our great Zarathustra. Rise and ascension. Assassins and Templars. Ancient contracts in the desert. The books of life and Doomsday on altars, garland and sword. Swarm of Royal honey. Coil and tongue. Sting and hive. Torn stained mantles whispering. Knots and thorns. Stung Vestments. Crest and shield. Goblets and gowns. Rings and crowns.

"We stand firm. Booted on the threshold of a new age. We must amputate these inferior limbs of leprosy—of Jews, Negroes, intellectuals, homosexuals, free thinkers, women's suffrage, the Freemasons, the weak, the sick, the mentally retarded, the liberals, the socialists and communists with their whining tirades of worker's rights for the low insignificant echelons of labor who are ours to command, empowering the worthy—versus this savage colored leprosy of Jazz, a sub-culture of sub-humans: twill be eradicated, and thus make way for the New Order."

Duke squirms in his seat, trying to disappear into the wall. He's never felt so non-existent. Claustrophobic in the viper's den.

"Spartan education emboldens us. Unstoppable potency. Our seed's fruition—forever. Not these burdensome academics and philosophers who implicitly subvert what the Party stands for, and the vitality of the race to be free of their obtuse nonsense of over-constellated syllogisms, their perverse abstractions of wordplay and perverted conceptuality, and adulterous idealisms, such as their—Existential, *gestalten*—angst. Their phenomenological Weirding- warped-fluxegesis."

The hall laughs.

"Their twisted Meta-teleological-ontologies. Enough! Nauseating smug tarts and swine!

"We possess Thor's might reborn! Raise the hammer!

"We can make Amerika great. The greatest ally and rebirthing ground of the master race. The Vrill of it all."

Enthralled, the throng of hyenas cackles with sharp teeth.

"Resourceful. Disciplined. Uncontaminated. Obedient. Unquestioning the wisdom of our dear leader, Der Fuhrer, who loves our people. Loves our nation more than . . ."

Secretary Werner Naumann, in a paroxysm of spirited heights, much like his beloved Fuhrer, so consumed with hateful love, is overcome by excitement, and momentarily squeaks, and loses himself in a loss of words. Recovering after a glass of milk, he proceeds to climax in a jaundiced catharsis:

"Pollinate the world, and the galaxy's future, with our potent fertility of evolving species, supreme. Wagner and Beethoven shall radiate and echo through the arms of the Milky Way. Can you envision the legions of storm troopers which shall marshal our eagles and swastikas planted firmly across the many worlds? Werner Von Braun unleashes our pathway of rockets to conquer the stars. All shall tremble and worship our empire forever. We are the gods.

"Our great Whiteness shall tower and shine over the fools of the earth, stairwells to the heavens, and illuminate the black depths as our own! Zeig Heil. Zeig Heil. Zeig Heil. Die Fahne hoch! Die Reihen fest geschlossen! Jews will not replace us."

Fanatically the enclave release emphatic responses of: *"Zeig Heil! Zeig heil! Jews will not replace us. Jews will not replace us. Jews will not replace us."*

Episode 27

Carnage

Rory end of the regginbrow. Ringsome upon the aquaface.

—*Finnegan's Wake* James Joyce[17]

Muffled screams.

A rumpus shakes within the grand bedroom upstairs.

"You beast! Get out!" scolded a flounced Marie Antoinette, barefoot and sprawled on a magnificent bed. "If you tell anyone, whomsoever, you were up here with Mrs. Witz, I swear upon the Hex and Furies' Evil Eye, I'll put your balls in a vice!"

A giddy Pagliacci clown wearily opens the door on his way out, then assents and gestures with frightful shock in response:

Absolutely not!

Harpo then closes the door and guiltily tiptoes downstairs.

Meanwhile, the party is swingin'.

Chico, feeling still more imperious in his Il Duce uniform, scoops a cupful from the crystal punch bowl, though he shouldn't, since they're on duty as there's a plan in effect: "Eh, not strong enough. I shouldn't drink more, but this crowd needs to be sauced, " he said to himself, and walked off.

Curly Stooge, in a robber's mask, walks over to sample a cup. "Huh, someone should put some punch in this Punch. Since I've been usin' my noggin, my wits are sharp as nails tonight, and my foresight warned me to be prepared. I've just the thing. Boy oh boy. Rahrw!"

So he pulls out a jug of vodka he snagged from the pantry, and: glug glug glug glug, dumps it all in. Then. Fills a glass to sample. Chugs a swig, "Nyuk nyuk nyuk. Ruff! Ruff!"

---

[17] "Regginbrow." : See endnote –

Curly fills another cup and saunters off.

Chico returns, glances left and right, and pours in a jug of Gin swiped from behind the bar.

"Now we're cookin'."

He partakes of a shot. "Bam! That's spiked," he wheezed heartily. "Peasy weasy. The guys deserve a rocketjuice taste of this." Chico wanders back in search of the brothers.

From another angle Harpo skips over with a big pitcher of crushed lemons, limes and ginger roots, giggling as he dumps the tangy mixture into the spiking punch.

Captain Groucho steps up. "Okay, okay, enough of that. Check the kitchen and foyer and keep an eye out for those Stooges. They found out we've been workin' their gig, and boy are they steamed."

"Wait a second," Groucho sniffed about and detected perfume.

"I smell a French whore."

Harpo shakes his head in doubt.

"Not you. An expensive whore nonetheless. Say. Weren't you with Mrs. Witz?"

Harpo vigorously shakes his head: *no no no*.

Groucho starts to tickle Harpo. Harpo starts squirming uncontrollably and shakes his head: *yes yes yes*.

"I thought so. Only Jean Patou's finest for Lady Witz. Did you know they have to stuff in 10,000 Jasmine flowers and 28 dozen roses to make a bottle? How does it all fit? It's as bizarre as finding an elephant in my pajamas. So. You were tickling her feet, weren't you?"

Reluctantly nods yes.

"You beast. You should be ashamed of yourself. On second thought, it makes sense. I hear Mr. Witz, besides his reluctance to shake hands, abhors feet. Even his own. Won't go near them. But you will."

Harpo nods furiously, and trots off.

"Marvelous."

While I'm here, Groucho says to himself, *someone handed me this bottle of Absinthe? They called it the devilish green fairy.*

Let's see.

Groucho pulls the absinthe out of his jacket and pours it in, then scoops up a cup. But sees Curly coming back so he hides behind the drapes.

Curly, mingles about, a bit disoriented, and downs a fresh mug of the uranium punch—Pow! Making some indecipherable sound effects: forgetting why he's here (as they're looking to confront the Marx Brothers for shanking their Witz contract).

Curly bumps into someone. But there's no one there, and lets out a high-pitched squeal of frustration: "*Mmmmmmmmmm,*" and did a double-take gazing into his almost empty punch mug.

He feels a tug below. So he looks down.

"Gosh, look at all these little people," said Curly.

"Magnanimous Sir, pardon our humble appearance, but we're not little people. We're Leprechauns."

"Leprechauns? I'll be damned. Hey! I thought your kind is only found in Ireland?"

"Aye, well, that's astute of ye. No fooling you! Correct, more like the Emerald Isles of Erin, as we call her. However, it's a wee bit of a story. But me throat's hankerin' mighty dry from the journey."

"So you kids are Irish? You must be thirsty!"

"By the frosty long beard of King Fergus, must be. That there punch bowl is nearest, but a shillalagh stick too high for our kind to obtain, if you catch my meaning."

"Well come along, I'll ladle out cups for all, nyuk nyuk."

"Splendid, kind and venerable sir. I'm Darby. Darby O'Gill. At your service," said Darby, taking off his buckled green hat and bowing.

"Pleased to meet ya."

"The pleasure is mine. And allow me to introduce Mugsby O'Halloran. Stitches O'Connelly. Eugene Pug McMurphy. Kitty McMouser. Gretel Pixie Crumbdrubin. And Bunky McCorker."

Hello hello hello hello.

"Greetings and Erin go' braless." Curly ladled out cups: "Everyone has some?"

"To your health. Slainte! *Better to be quarreling than lonesome.*"

The leprechauns and Curly drink up their toast. They all wheeze and hack. Darby pats their backs.

"Breathe, Bunky, breathe," said Darby, his voice a chalky hot whisper on fire: "By the full moon of the Druid's circle, that's fierce liquor."

"So how'd ya get to Californee? What brings ya to Hollywood?" said Curly.

"Why, this is the end of the rainbow," cordially continued Darby.

"No kiddin'?"

"Fer shorn, good sir. We followed the rainbow bridge here, using our lucky charms of magic shamrocks from the Hibernian Isles. In today's busy world of scientific invention, smoke stacks, nylon stockings, motorcars, and mathematical facts —few believe in us anymore. Gold's become scarce, and we have no use for cash, as the big folk call it. So we put our shamrocks together to find the biggest rainbow, on quest for the last great pot o' gold. And since we've heard Hollywood is a magic land of dreams and fortunes, it brought us here."

"Wow, that just sounds wonderful. Boy. I'd love to have a bit of that gold. Man am I tired of gettin' bossed around by the ear and the nose."

"Indeed, laddy. Why, now that you've seen us, and shown us a dear kindness—plying us with a distillation of your most potent elixir brew of frightful alchemy—we're obliged to let you in on the spoils for the quest of the rainbow's gold. Though we are ancient and magical, we need a sharp, strong, strappin', big-hearted, brawny poker like yourself, to aid in our valorous endeavor."

"Shucks, soy-tin-lee! I'll be happy to help. Hot damn."

Kitty sidles up and gives Curly an obscene handshake from below. "Well hello there big boy. Pleased to meet ya. Do ya have a lollipop for me?"

"Woo woo woo woooo. Woof woof!"

"Take it easy there Kitty. She's taken' a shine to ya. There's nothing like the enchanted glamour and favor of a faerie whore on this whole earth."

"Ya don't say?!"

"That's right my good man," said Darby. "The love of a Lady Leprechaun is the glitter of legend. You're one of us now. The time strikes to complete our quest, now that we've landed at the rainbow's end to the glitz of the Hollywood hills. Our last task is to contact the gatekeepers of the hidden treasure. How much money do you have on hand, good sir Curly?"

"Hey, I thought you claimed you had no use for cash?"

"We don't. But the keepers of the treasure gate, the gnomes, do! To be precise, rather, they must be bribed with shiny things. Only cash, in this part of the world, will allow us to procure as such. Anything stolen won't do. It'll ruin the moral of the magic. And thus, we may unlock the path to fabulous riches."

"Well, we're in luck."

"The luck of the Irish," said Darby, whose eyes brightened.

"It just so happens I ran into Maury who handed off our back pay for me, Mo, and Larry. Gee, won't they be surprised when I turn up with suits, cigars and a bag of gold."

"They will indeed laddy, they will most assuredly indeed."

Meanwhile, Midnight, the chef, has been keenly observing, and motions over Clydesdale to listen in, who started to guffaw but Midnight signaled him to keep quiet.

Curly dips into his pocket, and yanks out a wad of cash which he eagerly hands off to the happy Darby and his tittering puckish compatriots.

Darby and his lollipop gang stuff their wee pockets with the dough, and pronounce: "Upon the enchanted glamor of *all* the faerie folk! May your spirit cross into the pearly gates of heaven an hour before that scoundrel of a Devil knows ye are dead."

"Damn straight. You bet. Let's grab that gold."

"Indeed. Now you wait here, as you surely realize you're far too large to fit into the cavern door, invisible to human eyes, that enters into the hall of the gnomes who inhabit these hills. We shall snag the treasure, and be back in thirty shakes of a lamb's tail, as the cock crows over the moon."

"Swell."

Curly giddily helps himself to another well-earned serving of the Punch Pow Punch.

Mo turns up with his perpetual frown.

"Hey Cueball. Maury said he handed off our pay. Let's have at it."

"Pay? Mo, even better! You won't believe what just happened."

Curly explains . . .

Mo's eyes steadily darken. Eyebrows twist. Invisible steam vapors from his ears.

"You palooka putz son of a fuckballs bastard cock sucking cocksucker. Why I'll murder ya. Those weren't Leprechauns. They were these blasted munchkins of Oz extras, tarted up as Leprechauns for the masquerade ball, whom you can plainly see gagging about and slapping you in the face with a bunch of blarney moonshine, ya idjit mongrel—"

Mo, is turning red and blue; his cursing devolves into incoherent growling, and grabs Curly by the throat to strangle him.

"B-b-b—Mo! Gah. Guh! But Mo—!"

Larry frantically grips and tussles with Mo using all his might to extract him off Curly.

"Mo!" pleaded Larry. "Get off him. We'll murder Curly later. We've got to find those midgets!"

Mo's eyes are popping out, as his hands are glued tighter and tighter around Curly's throat.

Close by, Midnight is laughing with tears in his eyes turning to Clydesdale to say, "Ain't this some shit? What did I tell you?"

Mo finally lets go. Curly falls down gagging for air.

"Do you see what happens, Larry?" said Mo. "Do you see what happens? But, you're right, damnit. Where'd those mother-funking Munchkins get to?"

Midnight opportunely steps over to tell, "Munchkins? Yowzah, boss. They went that way!"

The Stooges look up through the French Doors to see the green garmented midgets gaffing about as they make their jaunty exit off the patio.

Mo snarls and orders: "Sick 'em boys!"

And they're off.

As the erstwhile Leprechauns stroll and loll in their glee and gaggle about the "Knucklehead at the end of the rainbow," Darby notices a bowl-cut madman racing towards them.

Darby's corncob pipe falls from his mouth and he shouts:

"Run for your lives!"

Darby, Mugsby, Stitches, Murphy, Kitty, Gretel, and Bunky McCorker all scatter in every direction of the four winds like their feet are on hot coals. Every trundling and tumbling step, hardly touching the ground, until some dive into bushes, under tables, under gowns, as Darby rockets across the lawn with Mo huffing crazed behind: knocking over waiters and dancers, shoving a Peter Pan, tripping up an Alice in Wonderland, running over a Snow White and a Dracula knocked aside. One by one, as they scramble in a blurry rage.

Bunky leaps passed the little rascals with Larry just behind. Larry mistakes Spanky for Bunky and grabs him up.

"I got you now you little runt," said Larry.

Spanky yells, "Heyyyy, what's the big idea?" and starts pulling Larry's hair.

"Owwww. Stop it! Let go. Stop."

The Marx Brothers had also perked-up hearing the friction in motion. Chico runs over and pops Larry in the nose.

"Ow!"

"Drop the kid, ya mongrel," yelled Chico.

"This Leprechaun stole our dough," cried Larry.

"What are you talkin' about?"

Curly is racing behind Stitches and Mugsby. He bumps into a clown as a honk goes off. Harpo Pagliacci pops back up and yanks Curly back down by his pants. Curly grunts and barks.

Harpo grabs a clown button off his costume and hands it to Curly, who throws it aside and tries to stand back up. Harpo pulls off another fluffy button and hands it to Curly, who throws it aside. Then another. Then another. Then one into Curly's mouth. Then one into his own mouth, giving Curly a handful of spoons. Then a teapot. Forks and butter knives. Then a fish.

Curly yelps helplessly and starts smacking himself in the face.

Groucho, as well as Maury and a bodyguard, jot over. Chico is dragging Larry by his scraggly hair.

"What's with all the hubbub, you wise cracking bastards? This is it! It's curtains and the zoo for you," said Maury.

Mickey Sweets O'Donnelly arrives and is also closing in on the scene, as they all huddle up, in the middle of a party chain reaction growing riotous.

"The Leprechauns stole our pay," squealed Curly.

"What the fuck are you fucks fucking up this time?" cursed Maury.

Midnight steps in. "Pardon me, gentleman. This is none of my business, but please try not to knock over Mr. Witz's *dessert* table."

Midnight artfully and purposefully placing the emphasis on the word *dessert*.

Harpo and Groucho glance at the long table.

Covered with pies.

They look back at each other. Wink. And nod. They grab pies with both hands each.

And smash!

Smashed pies into the faces of Maury, the bodyguard, Larry and Curly.

Mickey punches the bodyguard as his fist lands into a mush of pie.

Mickey licks his fingers. "Mmmm, lemon meringue." He proceeds kicking ass as the pie-faced punks try to go for Harpo and Groucho, but they're already ahead working their way down the table, launching pies through the air in a frenzied juggler's pace.

"Who wants chocolate cream?" shouted Groucho. "There goes a Cherry. Key Lime. Bam! I see Uncle Sam. Here's an apple pie! Stars and Rhubarb for you. Here's a banana cream."

"It's a banana split now," said Chico.

A few little rascals are helping as they also smash pies into their own faces and lick their lips.

Harpo tosses Spanky some fireworks. In a moment. Roman candles start to spume. Someone circling high up in the far distance notices the signal.

All this time Mickey had been busy orchestrating behind the scenes. A huge stack of speakers has been set up for the stage. And a microphone. A man with a larger-than-life persona approaches the platform to grin and greet, and lets out a wail of voodoo-charged trumpet which blasts loud, even louder through the amplified speakers . . .

The Masquerade turns into a combustion of Attila and the Huns sacking Rome with trumpeting reverie at the masque of the cherry pie death.

Mo and Darby, the Marx Brothers, and Stooges are all igniting a wildfire trail of chaos, like tumbling dominos.

The brawl spreads. Pies fly, flinging and launching like catapulting UFO saucers.

The party roars. People don't know what to do amidst the cacophonous screams and laughter. They hacked and blistered. Tripped and buffeted. Ripped and elbowed. They hatched and pawed. Parried and thrust. Slugged and forearmed. Slaps abound. Heaving chests. Panting. Bruised and black-eyed.

Some munchkins regroup and hop on poor Curly. Kitty palmed the sexy peach fuzz of his bald scalp, licking the cream off his ear.

At this point, the crowd is more than intoxicated. Especially those who partook of the now emptied punch. A midget dove into the last of it. He's still pretending he's a swimming goldfish at the bottom.

Curly, boiling in frustrated rage, tosses off the hoppin' Leprechauns. Tottering about blearily, he runs into Chico who delivers a kick right into poor Curly's stomach. Upon receiving this decisive and discourteous reception, Curly responds with a shoot of vomit on one of the green, now greener munchkins, while simultaneously defecating in his pants.

Most foul.

Things couldn't be more topsy-turvy in the hurly-burly California night.

Another table gets knocked over. Screams. Couples are naked underneath, covered with cake.

Battered and frazzled guests exasperate aghast as they dodge pies and wipe off cream, pudding, and fruit. Those having the most fun are just eating dessert off of each other.

Fuck it.

Ain't this a blast?

Wait til' this gets into the papers.

Where the fuck is Witz?

I can't wait to see his face.

I can't wait to throw a pie in his face!

Where's Mrs. Witz? Hahahahaha.

I'm calling Mr. Normal Mr. Rockingwell!

What's next?

I'm coming back next year . . .

But then, the sultry sweet drift of musk in the night gives way to the buzz of engines above: zeroing in.

Something falls from the dark sky.

Their nostrils are assailed and grilled: assaulted with the acrid pitch and stench of brimstone. A fury of fungoid hay and sulfur, and it wasn't Curly.

Mud plops violently into the faces of Mo and other guests. As if, from above. They realize, too late, to their horror, it isn't mud, or fudge, as they lick their lips, expecting chocolate.

Howard Hughes, and several planes from his private squadron, dive bomb the party to gift a payload of fertilizer from Hughes' backlot stables.

"Where are ya, Witz? You shitbag upstart? HAHAHAHAHA!" bellowed and howled Hughes raving from the clouds. "Here comes Texas!"

Mickey let Howard in on the Air Force contract. Those happy Air Corps generals made a deal to turn a blind eye to their *Witzkrieg* operation, especially when they were shown the evidence the Marx Brothers snagged from the vaults that Witz escaped military service because his doctor diagnosed a bad "Achilles heel." Besides his Nazi affiliations . . .

"Holy shit! They're bombing us with shit!"

"Who the hell is that?!"

Slash. Swat. Slap. Dash. Doosh! Slop. Poop! Plop! Plotzed!

Pummeled and minced. Dented in the fray of violent valedictions. The crowd push and shove in the turbulence outside. Pies still flying! The Marx Brothers pull out their stashed raincoats.

Witz loves pie. He always orders extra. But *someone* called in ten times as many.

Harpo is launching pies like a whirling dervish machine.

The whine of engines begins to louden and speed in their diving approach.

"Here they come again."

"Is it the Japanese?"

"Take cover!"

As the planes make another run towards the party sprawled on the great lawn, the corralled gang of revelers begin to understand what's happening and stampede frantically toward the other direction, not realizing in the confusion of their headlong escaping momentum, with nowhere else to go, thudding pell-mell, they're are herding themselves right into the long pool behind them.

Howling, splashing and hooting.

Crying and screaming.

Manic laughing and wicked spells of cursing.

The horror of jeweled and costumed ladies wail and ring across the valley, the blood escaping from their pale draining faces, covered with pie and manure. They're further startled when they meet the burning coal-sparked eyes of Errol Flynn, who's hypnotized in an ecstasy and thrill of adrenalin he's rarely experienced, but bleeds for, in his excessive debaucheries and thrills between dredging through the dulling seconds of daily life.

Catching his breath, Flynn soaks in the broad montage of his vision, beholds a sweeping animated picture, like a live Michelangelo, Da Vinci, and Picasso simultaneously reveling and wrestling into one, four-dimensional mosaic. Spread in a grandeur of post-Western carnage.

"My God!" Flynn whispered giddily to himself, after downing a last glass of rocket juice punch, and slamming another of Witz's thugs with the blunt ka-thunk of a silver serving tray, while preserving its last frail martini.

"God damnnnnn glorious!"

Peter Lorre sidles back to his mate, gasping in pain and laughter.

Errol feels Peter's tug at his trousers. "Eh?"

Peter tries to pull Errol down.

Errol pulls Peter back up unsteadily.

Peter is gasping and choking.

"What?"

Cough. Choke. Gasp. "I—"

"What is it man?"

"I— I— Can't . . . breathe, bwahahaha," sputtered Peter.

Like an unwinding top, spinning, Peter knocks a table over.

Errol picks him back up.

"Did you swallow that last crab claw filled with cocaine?" asked Errol.

"Noooo. Hahaha. Mayyyybe? Bwahahaha. Help— I— can't— stop— stop— laughing, heh heh heh. Ahhhhhhhhhh," Lorre wheezed through the un-stoppable giggles. "I can't breathe."

Errol slaps Peter's back.

Peter spits up some pie, wiping more of it out of his eyes.

"Flynn," Peter rasps in his flinty, weaseling voice. "Make it stop. Make— it— stopppppp." Cough. Hack. Gasp. "I'm going to die laughing. HAHAHA. Ah-hhhhhhhhhh! Bwahahahaha . . ."

The delirious hilarity is contagious as Errol cackles madly with him, bay-ing at the moon.

Snot shoots from Peter's nostrils. Snorting and sneezing back out mucus, pie, and cocaine?

Errol douses Peter with a pitcher of ice water.

"Maybe we should get you outta here, Peter, Peter pumpkin pie eater!"

"Nooooooo! Bwahahaha," guffawed drunk, crazed Lorrie.

"Well, either way, I'm staying till the end."

Mickey Sweets O'Donnelly looks up to the roof and locates his cameraman, making certain he's filming it *all*. Sweets signals him his stern Boy Scout's salute, a duteous thumbs up. Then immediately launches into a stiff football lineman's crouch, to face a speeding berserker coming at him with a pewter vase aimed for his head.

Sweets sidesteps him like an erudite matador; then, utilizing the jiu jitsu-judo force of his attacker's committed momentum, Sweets throws him into the pool, laughing maniacally.

The Marx Brothers, their uniform costumes in tatters; scuffed, banged, creamy, and bandaged, extricate themselves from the exhausted mangled mosh.

Harpo's eyes reflect an unknown-before level of ecstatic lunacy from this dizzying delirium. They all are feeling an adrenal release of euphoria, especially after the trauma of gunfire at their hideout.

Euphoria, like the most evil of all drugs: *War*.

"My God, boys," exclaimed Groucho. "This evening proved quite the unimagined success. Hip hip."

"Hurrah Boss."

"Honk honk!"

"We shall remember this day," said Groucho, "for all time. With rabid solemnity of festive commemoration. We shall call this day—Well, what will we call it?"

"Fool's Day," casually replied Chico, nodding with an approvingly Mussolini *mannerismed* frown.

"Fool's Day!"

Harpo, giddy and grinning, pulls out a flute, and slaps their chests for attention, and starts playing a patriotic medley.

They begin marching in place, surrounded by the rocket red glare of cries and shouts upon an estate ruined, turned battlefield.

Chico pretends he's drumming.

Groucho, in his disheveled general's garments, grabs one of the many pie-stained tattered flags that decorated the event, and begins to sing:

Goddddd bless A-mer-icaaaaaa.

Laaaand that I love.

Bump, bump, bomp, bommmmmmb!

Stand beside herrrrr, and guide herrrrr.

From the light up? Up? Up? From abovvvvvvve.

Dum dum dummmmmb.

(Some of the munchkins join in.)

From the fountains. To the fairies.

To the oceans.

White with foammmmmmmm.

Dum! Dum-dum-dum dummb dumb! Dumb!- dum-dum-dumb! dumb! dummmb!

Goddddddddd bless A-mer-icaaaaa.

Bump bump bump bump bump bump bump! Bump! Bump!

(They harmonize in barbershop quartet fashion, Groucho bends a knee and kneels with imploring open arms)

Myyyyyyyyy

    Hooooooooommmmmme

        Sweeeeeeeeeeeeeet

           Hooooooommmmmmme!

Episode 28

Katakombs

Since then I have pretended ease,
loved with the trickeries of need . . .
I drink the five o'clock martinis
and poke at this dry page like a rough
goat. Fool! I fumble my lost childhood
for a mother and lounge in sad stuff
with love to catch as catch can.

And Christ still waits. I have tried to exorcize
the memory of each event . . . Sweet witch,
you are my worried guide.
Such dangerous angels walk through Lent.
Their walls creak Anne! Convert! Convert!
My desk moves. Its cave murmurs Boo
And I'm taken and beguiled.

—The Division of Parts Anne Sexton[18]

During the brawl upstairs, the KKK descended into the castle's lower chambers toward the clandestine congregation. Through a corridor adorned with armored knights. They pound at the door at the end of the hall.

The hooded luminescence of white shrouded Ku Klux Klan stands at attention. Waiting. Quiet. Some marvel at the metallic reflections of suits, weapons, shields, helmets . . . Their dark eyes haunt and mirror back to them from the silver sheen of polished steel.

The heavy door creaks open.

"Brothers!"

---

[18] *The Complete Poems of Anne Sexton.* P.44. Houghton Mifflin, NY. 1981.(1960.)

"Brothers, you're welcome all! Please come in," said Werner Naumann. "The shock troops of America's last great burden of hope . . . "

Applause greets this troop of white knights.

Meanwhile, Duke Othello is working his way towards captive Hedy. She's to be a gift for the Nazi's to take back to Germany, to punish this runaway Jewess for helping the U.S. military with knowledge of her former husband's German armament manufacturing, as she's working out secret blueprints for a radio-guided torpedo that can oscillate, or hop its frequency so it can't be jammed, in between her busy film schedule.

The Grand Vizzard, dressed in purple, steps out from his white hooded robed regiment brethren and replies: "*Sic semper tyrannis*. Hail the hallowed pillars of wisdom from ancient Egypt, built with its obelisks, pyramids and sphinx, of hieroglyphic secrets of the sacred. The cornerstone of our civilization, order and Africa. As we salute our brothers of Antifa, and the Bavarian Illuminati in Europe."

The self-satisfied congregation of Witz's assemblage, incensed with promising power, looked confused.

The purple Grand Vizzard grabs two Nazi heads, and bashes them together.

"What?"

Then two more.

"Halt. Stop! What is the—"

The rest of the KKK proceed to do the same.

"It's an ambush!"

The American fascists are hemmed in a trap by KKK shock troops alright.

"Mach schnell! Schisser. Aud der auffgerder hordler!"

Werner Naumann wrestles with the vizzard. The vizzard's purple hood comes off.

Naumann turned pale and gasped: "Negroids!"

The black Vizzard is actually from Satch's Prince Hall Lodge of Freemasons and pops the stunned leader pow with a bloody nose, a chipped tooth, then a black eye. Horror sweeps the cursing ruckus of the cellar catacomb.

In the turmoil of the riotous combat, Duke unties Hedy and rushes for an exit.

There's a corridor of mirrors. A convexed maze of themselves in multiplying angles and turns.

"These monsters had their paws all over me," said Hedy. "If this is an escape, thank you, truly. I'm impressed, for now. Let's see how far you get."

"Wait a second," said Duke, "I thought this was the way out."

Each turn brings them nowhere.

Hedy stops, pulls a thread from her garments, and ties it to a candle holder. Then they rush off and track where they're at.

Witz enters the hall and grabs an iron mace off one of the mannequin knights.

"You sonofabitch!" he hollered. "I knew something wasn't right about you."

Turning the corner he sees them. "There you are!"

Witz bends his knees to swing the momentum of the heavy mass down on them.

Ka-crash. Smash. A thousand shards of mirror splinter off.

"Fucks!"

"Here we are!"

Witz turns, then with all his might yanks the mace down behind him.

Ka-zing ka-tash. More shards break off like shattered diamond ice.

"That's it," said Hedy. Through the broken mirrors, they spot the way clear and zip out.

Leaping up the stairs, they enter the ballroom to an array of scattered debris, dishes, food, torn curtains, overturned furniture, folks passed out, bruised, wounded, delirious . . .

Munchkins snoozing inside the piano . . .

Some few straggler folks are still partying!

"Holy Christmas! Like a hurricane."

They make it out across the patio. A hell of a lot more carnage outside. Most of the party has fled.

The grand yard is smeared in manure and trampled pie.

"Groucho! Chico! Harpo! You did it! I knew I could count on you. Excellent. This is Hedy. Let's get the smack out of here."

"Ain't it a sight to behold?" said Groucho, as he inhaled his best cigar.

"Absofuckingtively! Let's roll! Come on!"

"So what kinda loot are we lookin' at boss?"

"Loot? There's no loot! Come on, hurry! You fools!"

"He's calling *us* fools," said Groucho.

Harpo pulls out flowers and hands them to Hedy.

"Arsch mit ohren," uttered Hedy.

Harpo cast his eyes down at the unkind dig of an *Ass with ears*.

"You're supposed to have the car ready for the getaway," yelled Duke. "We're dead."

"Is this the cavalry you promised?" sneered Hedy.

"Waiiiiiiiit!" screeched a blood curdling command from the huffing and puffing Frankie Witz. "What in hell did you do to my place? I'll kill the lot of ya. Slaughter your families. Cats and dogs!"

The Marx Brothers grab Duke.

"What in god's hell on earth are you clowns doing?

"Hold'em tight," shouted Witz. "I'm going to give you such a piece of my mind that it will break your mind into pieces."

Words echo out in the vast hollows of Witz's head as if a divine powerful king is decreeing, as he imagines himself high up from a towering throne, and a tall crown. These words originate from some far place he can no longer see clearly, driving and decreeing his actions further. But if he were to see clearly upon a closer examination, he'd find a small child atop the tower, who was never good enough, never allowed to show feelings, have a say, recognize doing any wrong—only groomed for greatness and absolute privilege. An aristocratic slave to power.

Witz exhaustedly lurches up to Duke, steaming red, and smacks him.

Duke, draws a breath, looks around, and begins to laugh hysterically.

"What's so funny, punk?" Witz slaps him again.

Duke still laughing.

Witz looks over at Chico Mussolini. Chico, austere, martial, and cruel marches over and reaches into Harpo's trench coat pockets, and pulls out a dildo. Chico drops it. Reaches in again, this time wielding a blackjack weapon. Weighs it, then slams the back of Duke's head.

The lights go out.

Fade to black.

Episode Zero

There's a lot of money to pay for this war . . . the oil revenues of that country could bring between $50 and $100 billion over the course of the next two or three years . . . We're dealing with a country that can really finance its own reconstruction, and relatively soon.

—Paul Wolfo'witz

"Achtung. Angetreten. Lass das Sein! Halten Sie!" commanded a German officer casually inspecting the premises. "Was ist los? Stillgestanden! Steht Noch. Schnell! Weltparasit Ruhig! *Zagan facalor*. Weitermachen. Abschaum saugham damon holler!"

A searchlight panning from outside blinds Duke while it flashes the room, scanning across the yards. He's tied up to a table he's laid out upon. In panic Duke looks through a barred window. Watch-towers. Barbed wire fencing. Guards strapped with sub-machine guns. Barking dogs devour the night.

Duke hears symphonies, effusive with white noise through a record's scratchy Victrola needle ripping its sonic vibration, a metallic thorn slicing through his tissues and bone, a polar axis needle ripping time and flesh away.

A doctor orders a nurse to administer more Pentylenetetrazol.

"Ah, zee Duke of Holly Wood," said the strolling officer, now leering above. "Auftragstaktik? Quite the Zeit-volk-weltengeist we have here, no? Alles in ordnung. Alles in ordnung.

"I am Captain Sigurd Oberalberich. My, my, has the Ouroboros turned for you? We've made you an honorary star, mister Holly Wood. How do you like it? Why, did you know, holly is what the best magic wands are made of? Makes one wonder, eh? Holly can summon and control its spirit entities, or banish. Excellent for material gains, beauty, even revenge, and the evocation of dream magic. For ceremonies of death and rebirth it burns hot. Very hot, indeed. Faszinierend. Fascinating. Ya? Well then. Es ist zeit. You didn't think we were going to sing: *Haben sie Gehort das Deutsche Band?* Eh? Mit a boom. Mit a bing. Mit a bing bang-bang boom boom.

"Herr Doktor? Shall we surgically operate into where this wonder stems from? Die fröhliche wissenschaft? Ha ha. Once dissected, I hear the pituitary gland goes rather well with a tankard of ale, some jagermeister, and a side of beef. Let's see what's in your brain? Ya? Jetzt. Sofort!"

One hundred volts rip a surge through Duke's insides.

Episode 29

Sanitarium

First Clown . . . Every fool can tell that: it was the very day that young Hamlet was born; he that is mad, and sent into
England.

HAMLET Ay, marry, why was he sent into England?

First Clown Why, because he was mad: he shall recover his wits there; or, if he do not, it's no great matter there.

HAMLET Why?

First Clown 'Twill, a not be seen in him there; there the men are as mad as he.

—Hamlet V.i. 149 – 57

Duke wakes surrounded by white. Amorphous presence of mind immersed in a saturation of cotton. Disembodied. Hollowed out.

There's a somnolent buzz in his Being. Time has slowed—or ceased to exist. *The wall clock looks backwards.* Did he? *Is he? Dead?* Finally. After this epic ordeal. A post-mortem Bardo dream state before dissolution into a forever of Nothingness, Nirvana, or rebirth? Though Nirvana is for the enlightened liberated soul, and he feels far from . . .

Duke always anticipated once the Dimethyltryptamine at death is released in your brain, kaleidoscopes explode in the retreating psyche before entering the light? *Where's your Plato and Bach now?* The celestial mathematics and metamorphosed blood and equations of Pythagoras?

Will it last a moment? Or to infinity?

Is it all one?

Why's heaven associated with white? The projected purity? He finds it horrific. That blankness. Devoid and cleansed of all color. More like purgatory, or limbo!—or worse. Oblivion of the white whale.

Difficult to move in this pool of sedation. *It's probably worse.*

His brain holds a dull, diluting ache soaked in a margarine amber. If he still has a brain, as thoughts wretchedly form out words in backward phrases. If it only could dissolve into a dew, absorbed into the ecstasy of a melting Aum: Vishnu's happy lobotomy. Getting through Shiva's episodic role is the traumatic part. Essentially he's clawing up from a dungeon, for what everyone wants—a better life. An impossible redo.

"Who said: 'if' is the middle word in life? Much wisdom in if?"

The blurriness of cloud-vision sifts into focus. He's in a bed. A hospital?

"Hell the how? Dead not I am? Frrruck!"

There's a curtained partition. Odd noise stirs from the other side.

No more, no more. Make it stop.

There seemed a burst of commotion earlier from that region before waking, as if heard from underwater.

Resurrection of the comatose.

Memory floats in waves of fog. One swashes by—he was at the bottom of a pool with a piano. Trying to play *Stars and Stripes Forever* out of a coffin. Mermaids sped round him. He innocently smiled up at one who giggled in a moment of innocent hilarity, then she wopped him with her tail.

Pulling at the piano, he can't bring it to the top, he's stuck—thuds of books bomb the water with sinking concussions. Then he resurfaces to stark brightness.

In and out of consciousness.

He overhears a woman say from behind the partition: "He's like a brand new baby boy," then shrieked, "Stop that!"

The woman walks over, also dressed—in white.

A nurse? It is a hospital.

His body is shot, and wrangled. Delirious, but nothing appears cut or broken, though he's severely bruised, moving painfully.

"Hello there Mr. Doe," she chirped. "Feeling better? Welcome back. Let me take your blood pressure. Have some fresh water. You've been terribly dehydrated. Take your pill."

"Wha—wait."

"Take your pill. Be a good boy. Bottoms up. Yum yum."

Gulp.

"There you go. The doctor should be in soon to check on you."

"Nurse?—*Nurse!*" He called out hoarse and strained, barely able to make words. "What, here am I for? What's with me, wrong? Ugh. Why am I in, strapped? Wha-what's happened? Ah. Am I where?"

"Mr. Doe, relax. You're in the mental ward of Our Lady's Triple Saint's John."

"Dear God."

"Patience. We cater to all kinds of Hollywood types. The doctor will take good care. He comes highly recommended," she exited curtly.

More rustling behind that curtain to his left. It gets kicked open. There's an occupant on the other side.

"What? Harpo? In a straitjacket?"

Harpo's eyes widened.

"Holy smokes. How am I surprised?"

Harpo cavortingly laughs and chuckles.

"Surprised to see you, not the location. How'd you get here? Damn. That's almost a rhetorical question."

Harpo blows up his cheeks, then pops out the air.

"Yeah, a bit difficult to explain at the moment, eh?" Less groggy, Duke gradually feels more coherent.

Harpo raises his eyebrows, after shaking about in the white sack of buckles he's strapped in.

"Wow, we're so mother-fucked! Well, I've no idea what happened. It's been stark raving mad. Everything is a haze. I'm freaking out. It's all so improbable. Maybe amnesia isn't so bad? Obviously—I must be insane."

Harpo shakes his head in dissent, then vigorously switches to a happy affirmative.

"Yeah, yeah, you're not wrong. Hey. How the heck do you still have your Top Hat?"

Harpo gives a sly look of pompous confidence and unsuccessfully communicates how indeed, then winks that he'll explicitly answer such inquiries shortly.

The nurse pops back and says to Duke, "Oh Mr. Doe, you've met our Mr. Anonymous Arthur? He's quite the handful," she turned to admonish Mr. Arthur Anonymous—with a flirt of dominance before leaving: "Behave now!"

Harpo displays an embarrassing grimace as a rude protuberance rises under the middle of his sheets.

"Oh, naughty naughty. *And Mr. Arthur*, don't you dare poop yourself again! I'll have to clean you *alllll* up."

Harpo makes an *Oh* face, then looks over and shrugs his shoulders.

"You're a real sick sick fuck, huh?" said Duke.

Harpo smiles.

"What did you guys do? What happened? There were thorny hedges? Was it a birthday party? Was it the birth of Jesus? Or a crucifixion? It's starting to come back to me . . ."

The Nurse shoots back in.

"Well, Doctor Hackenbush has arrived to evaluate you now," said the Nurse.

"That's Doctor F. *Quackenbush*, Nurse," chimed the doctor. "Doctor Hackenbush is on another job."

"What does the F stand for?" replied the Nurse.

"Wouldn't you like to know. Ring me up when you get off and I'll show ya."

She responds with a playful slap.

"Ow," Quackenbush gives a growling meow. "Faust. Doctor *Faust* Quackenbush, from Wittenberg University. Those were the days. Ah, the fun of doctoring. "

"Groucho?" Duke shouted hoarsely.

"Ah, ah ha. Feeling grouchy are you? *Shhhh, the name's Quakenbush.*" Groucho then raised his voice: "Let's see how we can perk you up son."

"Quackenbush, eh? Son? You son of a bitch. Something went terribly wrong. My head's killing me. What've you done?" Duke lunged to throttle Groucho's throat, but slumped over weakly under restraints.

"My poor boy, let's not get lost in re-projected transferences already—or any unnecessary Freudian slips—God forbid. By the way, speaking of Salvador Dali—how'd you like to give her the Freudian slip?"

"Groucho you mongrel fffff—"

"I know I know." Groucho lowered his voice aside in confidence. "Listen boss, I'm truly sorry. Save that for Franky Witz."

"Who?"

"Hmm. Yes, I'm a scoundrel. Poverty to power went straight to my head."

Groucho gestured over to Harpo—"Except in his case, it went straight to a jacket."

Harpo jerks and shimmies in response.

Groucho replies: "Feeling comfortable?"

Harpo licks his lips.

"Hang in there—yes, I'll get you more whiskey-soaked ice cream post haste immediately."

"Quackenbush!" gasped Duke.

Groucho starts placing his stethoscope on Duke's head.

"Hey that's not how that works! Leave me alone."

In a fast quiet tone Groucho replies: "I'm a brain doctor. Work with me here. They think I'm a real doctor. I'm here to help." Louder: "*Ah yes son I have an unorthodox methodology*. Take one of these."

"No, wait," gulp.

Lowering his voice again: "Hey! Listen kid, forgive me."

"For what?"

"I had a revelation. In the midst of festive celebrities and celebration—I was getting more tipsy than I've ever been—tipsy? More like tipping the iceberg and sinking straight to the sky. So much so—I tipped off the edge of the world. Who knew the world was square? Anyhow, so I took something," said Groucho, glancing paranoid over his shoulder.

"Something? I took everything. It was a buffet served up by every rich fiend libertine in the Holly Hills. Joy of joys. I don't know what I was on. Far far far away from any Moonshine Bourbon back on the vaudeville circuit in Kansas. Pills, powders, concoctions—then they presented me with the absinthe! Have you tried this? Elixir of Olympus. *Feed me more!* I said. Well guess what? Had a monster bash powwow with Bela Lugosi, Boris Karloff and the Wolfman, boy were they hooked up: obliged with a special brew. After the absinthe, they laid me out on a Dr. Frankenstein table. Karloff the Frankenstein placed an oxygen mask on me. Dracula Lugosi turned up the tank and juiced me full of ether. The Wolfman howled. That's when I fell off the edge. Well—the first time! There's many edges, and falls. Off the edge? At one point I fell so long that—I fell *into the edge*.

"A green abyss.

"How does one say? I ended up in the book of Ezekiel—I was in the lion's den, no, that's Daniel; but these wheels within electric wheels manifested in the air. Then it was the Book of Job. Christ, *thank God it wasn't Leviticus*. But my face melted off into my hand. I turned it around to face me, deliriously I said: *Fancy melting you here*.

"The face replied back: 'You should see what I'm seeing.' Horrible." Groucho shuddered.

"Then it morphed into a whole library. Never did so much reading in my life. It was like—I was trapped in these books—as if, alive! Living them out—So to speak."

"Funny, I kinda know what you mean," said Duke, suspicious, confused, and intrigued.

"Nightmares, visions, revelations, more nightmares. Then, I met an apparition called the Ancient Mariner. Instead of an albatross he said I had a dead duck on my neck. It was awful. I couldn't pull it off. I was thinking—*if only I could get this heavy penance off my neck, then—hey its barbecue, and absolution!* Then this smoky cloud of lightning and thunder appears."

"Where?"

"Where? At that goddamned Witz castle. Until it turned into Babylonia Transylvania! It went on for days. After you left."

"Days? What do you mean: after I left? I've a splitting migraine . . ."

"Well, more like you were escorted off the premises. It went from the best of everything to the worst frickin' party in history. Geez. Just when Sodom and Gomorrah were starting up in the next ballroom. That's one book I didn't want to miss. And that's where and when the cloud spoke to me."

Groucho grabs Duke and clamors, "Don't ya hear what I'm tellin' ya? The cloud spoke to me! It was—sentient. It rumbled and said: *Where were you when I laid the foundations and made the world?*

"I was speechless. I cowered and replied: I don't know. *I don't know.* Foundation of the world? I didn't know it was flat? I didn't even make it to my first Bar Mitzvah. The second one was pretty fun though . . . Just please don't rain on me. It's already been a rough week, and this tux is a brand new rental."

"Always with the jokes, eh?" said Duke.

"Well you know what they say. Smile and the whole world laughs at you, or slaps you. Just keep smiling. If you get them to smile—you can slap them back. But there was no smiling from this ominous cloud of all consuming Providence and power.

"The cloud boomed. Do you know what happened next?"

"It rained on you?" said Duke.

"Rained? Was a goddamned monsoon. Torrents. Floods. Hurricanes. I held up my melted face, still in my hands. I pointed and said: *He did it! Mercy. Grace. Adonai.* I couldn't stand beside myself any longer. Must've been a supernatural metaphor.

"Then it occurred to me. Like a triple shot of absinthe straight between the eyes. How could I succeed and revel with such scandalous debauchery, among so many cretinous and sexy debauchees, while treating my friends so poorly? These high-falutin' snobs were everything I wanted to be—until I became one. I discovered I had what they call: a soul? Brutal realization. Must make a fortune some other way, or no fortune at all.

"My God, some of these folks sold their souls to the devil in giant circles with pentagrams with crosses using Wall Street contracts. Some were in cahoots with Nazis! I looked in the mirror—and saw The Cheeze! Witz! Franken-Witz. As he really is . . . So that's what's under my face? This is what happens. Like that Dorian Green story. I was repulsed. I'm him! Or turned into him? A bit of him is in all of us I tell ya, it's true! Aw, the humanity."

Duke swipes at Groucho, but falls short.

"Thank you. Actually, turned out it wasn't a mirror, it was a window, with Frankie Witz on the other side. You get the idea, but that's besides the point. I got the message.

"What I'm trying to say is—I'm here to bust you out."

Episode 30

Dreadwoods

My first anxiety attack occurred during a Louis Armstrong concert . . . Armstrong was going to improvise . . . to build a whole composition in which each note would be important and would contain within itself the essence of the whole . . . The scaffolding and flying buttresses of the jazz instruments supported Armstrong's trumpet, creating spaces which were adequate enough for it to climb higher . . . fusing a new musical base, a sort of matrix . . . tracing a sound whose path was almost painful, so absolutely necessary had its equilibrium and duration; it tore at the nerves of those who followed it.

My heart began to accelerate . . . shaking the bars of my ribcage, compressing my lungs so the air could no longer enter them. Gripped by panic at the idea of dying . . . stomping feet, and the crowd howling, I ran into the street like someone possessed.

—*Playing in the Dark* Marie Cardinale
(quoted by Toni Morrison)[19]

Doctor Quackenbush calls Chico in, his disorderly orderly, and they roll Duke and Harpo out downstairs in wheelchairs.

Twin angry lights of a lime green vehicle pull up, revving the engine, screeching to a halt right to the curb. A voice from the car growls: "Get in!" Greta had been waiting outside in this long dusty green Duesenberg Tourster.

They cram in and shoot off, heading north along the coast. The salt air is refreshing, now outside of the antiseptic institution, cruising the dry breath of night. From madness to the overarching sickle of death.

Duke feels California may split in half at any moment from under them. A crevasse tears through. Canyons of crumbling disintegration yanking them under fires of hell.

---

[19] Morrison, Toni. <u>Playing in the Dark: *Whiteness and the Literary Imagination*</u>. p.vii. Vintage Books. NY. 1993.

"We found out," said Groucho, "Witz is taking Hedy to a big ceremony in a place called Bohemian Grotto. Sounds fun."

"Grove," corrected Greta, who stared coldly at the road, gripping the wheel with her black leather gloves.

"Bohemian Grove?" exclaimed Duke. "Oh no, you can't be serious."

"You've heard of it?"

"Yes, it's a private retreat club for elites deep in the Redwoods. There's a giant owl statue, reportedly a representation of Moloch, though claimed as Minerva's symbol of wisdom."

"That must be where they're holding the ceremony," said Groucho. "Likely a human sacrifice."

"Groucho, you filthy bastard. What's going on?"

"Well Duke, that's what I last garnered, whilst schmoozing on the inside."

"Schmoozing?" Duke elbowed Groucho in the head which knocked the other brother's heads like slammed dominos as they're all scrunched tight together in the back.

"Ow! Hey Chico, back off. We deserve that. Just everyone calm down."

Greta slammed on the brakes so hard the guys in the back almost popped into the front seats. She cursed incoherently in Swedish for a while, then they moved on.

"Goddamn it Groucho. You betrayed us!"

"You said it. What could I say? Witz offered us jobs. Movie contracts! Appointed me high up in the loop with the run of things. Swank pay and amenities. Told us how great we were. Dined on caviar and barbequed oysters. The dames. The glamour. The drugs. The dames. *The drugs*. We were hooked. But it just wasn't right. We're only human."

"How long was this going on?"

"The kicker was, he threatened our mother. I like our sweet mother. She's the only one we have."

"Mother," lamented Chico.

"*Honk-onk.*"

"Jesus," said Duke. "You're serious?"

"Once I set Mom up on a cruise around the world, and secured her on the boat, I got in touch with Satch about busting you out."

"Otherwise I would've trumpet blasted you into a deaf kingdom come," interjected Satch from the front seat. "Don't get me started. As soon as I got out of jail and made it to the party, I was amazed to see the orchestrated chaos of things run so smoothly, so to speak. I left once you said *it's all taken care of*. Big mistake. Pull that again and you guys are getting blasted into the next dimension. Man, I'd like to . . ."

"I know, I know," said Groucho. "Once I got wind of it, I knew it was time to end the fun and games. And just get on with the games. So we put together this plan to recover ya, Duke ol' boy. Everyone. We're frightfully sorry."

"Yeah, that's the truth boss," said Chico, remorseful and glum.

"HONK H O N N N N N N N N N N K K K K K k k k k k k k k k k k k k."

"Man, you guys are just effing unbelievable. The frustration is beyond words." Duke fights off the rising vitriol and invectives, realizing he must get on with the task at hand, and shake off the anger and grogginess. "Well, thank you anyhow, you incorrigible bastards. I'm surprised I'm still alive. Whatever this world is."

"Exactly," replied Groucho. "We owe you, immensely. As per Witz's orders, he planted me as a doctor at that mental ward, through some pull at the sanitarium. I was supposed to be poisoning you. Shooting you up with crazy drugs to make you certifiably insane. They were starting shock treatment as well."

"Is that what that was? It's all a backward kaleidoscope. I thought they had me convicted in court and sentenced to death. I murdered someone named Thomas? He was some kind of life insurance agent?"

"Usually some of the worst people in the world—next to most lawyers, bankers, politicians, cops . . ."

"They gave me the electric chair. I was fucking electrocuted, then it shot me back home. I was going to my old job, getting married, then I was trapped in glass . . . My head throbbed and sunk into a giant spastic sponge."

"That's because I was feeding you the 'good' drugs, to keep you certifiably sedated . . ." said Groucho. "Though I couldn't stop all the shock therapy. Enough to prevent you from being zapped into a lobotomized vegetable."

"My hero. With friends like you . . ."

Traversing hundreds of miles later, they arrive at the tall, antediluvian Sequoia Redwoods around Monte Rio.

The vast arboreal trunks, millenia old, wide like dinosaur legs and bones, soar into the air three-hundred feet, petrified in ghostly stages of time. A topographical forest of giants under the sun. Some of these trees were young when

Julius Caesar ruled Rome. Towering foliage of emerald verdure, a green window ceiling, filtering the sky and its dappled strands of dusking light.

Satch, Duke and Greta cover themselves in camouflage and sneak ahead into the woods leading to the Bohemian Grove Camp to scout out the terrain. The ceremony is supposed to commence before midnight.

They cautiously proceed, following the compass and local map they picked up along the way. Security of the camp's perimeter appears negligent. No one dares to venture through here, or would be expected to. Once they spot the camp, Greta decides to wait while Duke returns to lead the boys back to the Owl Altar to organize the next move.

It's purported that the Grove members put on a morality play.

"Hey, let's throw some costumes together," said Groucho, "and infiltrate the theatricals."

"We don't even know which play they're putting on," protested Duke.

"We could stroll out with Armstrong and start singing, *Me and My Shadow.* It'll be a zinger. Well. Couldn't we ring up Howard Hughes, get an inside line?"

"This is just getting way too ridiculous and complicated," said Duke. "*Ockham's Brontosaurus Razor.* However, if we attempt several distinct tactics at once . . ."

Harpo had disappeared.

After several hours he returned, driving a stolen truckload of cattle off the side of the road where they decamped.

Harpo pops out of the cab with a cowboy hat, clasping his hands like a champion. His big brainstorm is to tie torches to the cattle horns while blowing on conches and trumpets, letting them on the loose to put the fear of God into the camp and nab Hedy during the confusion.

"Brilliant Ace. Holy crap," exclaimed Duke. "You never cease to amaze. However, this is a rather inconvenient felony."

Harpo shrugs.

"Won't they be harmed by torches? We don't even have torches," said Satch.

"I suppose we can tie sticks instead," said Duke, "so we don't turn these guys into barbeque. Although it looks like they were headed to the slaughterhouse anyhow—at least they have a chance now. Whatever we can do to get Hedy. It's not like we can trust the police."

"Howard Hughes, bent on his vendetta, gave us a wad of cash," said Satch. "Someone should get in touch with this truck owner . . . let him know our half-wit cousin mistook his truck for one of our own? We'll return it, plus double what the cattle are worth. You know, so we don't end up with the Highway Patrol up our asses to the Hoosegow when we get out of here."

"Good point," said Duke, "though I believe we'll have the Highway Patrol on our ass either way."

"I'm on it," said Chico, "I'll check the glovebox and take the Tourster to the nearest phone-booth. If anyone can convince him, I can. We'll throw in one of our prize race horses we're breeding. Right? Right."

"What a nightmare," said Groucho, fretting and pacing. "I promised Mom to keep Harpo out of trouble, so, what can you do? Hey, we can use that wad of dough to pay off any pesky patrolmen. High stakes. Ridiculous odds. Either way. What's not to love? Chess, not checkers. We're awfully screwed. But we got you into this mess, we'll do all we can to get you out. Come hell or high water."

"That sounds like a disaster either way," said Duke.

Midnight: they observe the ceremony preparations unfold, spying upon the giant, angular, rock-carved owl as the robed participants assemble. An altar surrounds the domineering statue while canopied under the tallest trees on earth.

Eerie organ music hums and drones with a dissonant choir chanting Latin backward . . .

"All this ensemble needs is a trumpet," whispered Satch. "Man, ever since Ratshaw hexed me with those devil horns, it's been a downhill struggle since. Downhill any farther and I don't want to think about what I can imagine next. Is this what the American elites do on vacation? In secret? No wonder politics and the recording industry is so messed up."

"Nobody knows," said Duke. "Witz is like the biggest pig in the largest shithole puddle conceivable. He's plugged into everything in an American nexus, its veined arteries, right to the main nerve. Somehow his presence on the radio now, through supporting broadcasters like Normal Rockingwell and Father Coughlin, fueling the righteous Baptists and fundamentalists, are tuning in and some hate him, some just love him. Ever since socialism has become popular among apolitical working class Christians as being closest to their gospel values, as opposed to the greedy decadence of the very political upper classes. Regardless, we've struck the nerve epicenter of the USA. From Hollywood, to Nazis, to Devil sacrifice? Surely this is a farce? It's freaking me out. But I'll tell you this, we're one heck of a crew to get this far."

Gnarled and combat experienced, eye to eye: they squarely look at one another with respect and exponential apprehension.

Greta gives Duke a nod, he signals the boys down the line to Harpo, who lights small kindling sticks knotted to the cattle horns, leading them towards the camp. The frantic steer moo and bellow, though unharmed, the fire scares them into a heightening pitch to rampage. As the burning sticks fall off and knock about the brush and bushes—fires spark and spread.

"Jiminy Cricket," muttered Duke. "I just don't know about this. These are some of the most powerful men in America. We don't need to burn the whole forest down."

"Maybe we do, Samson," said Groucho. "Maybe we do."

This time the engineered pandemonium is spreading but isn't panning out as desired. Flames smoke and billow in the darkness; the camp goes wild with confusion in the hurly-burly din of braying mad cattle. The solemn attendants at the altar, covered in Druidical hoods stir and turn to shouts that break out across the camp in alarm. Secret politicians and businessmen run amok in flailing robes . . .

"*Ahhhhhhhhhhhhhhhhhhhhhhhhhhhhh!*"

"Holy shit, that guy is on fire!" cringed Duke.

"Man, this is one botched fuck-show," quipped Satch, shaking his head in disbelief and horror.

"Ain't America something else?" said Groucho. "Marvelous to behold. Marvelous. We may land in prison, but in any other country they'd shoot us. As long as we don't end up getting sacrificed instead? What a way to end it. Not with a whimper, but with a bang and lots of whimpering. It's an adventure of a lifetime, I tell ya. If only Walts Whitman and Disney were here. You know, Walt Disney may actually be here . . . saw his name on Witz's roster. Hope he enjoys this dramatic blaze. Well. Can't expect every plan to pull off. Contingencies. Contingencies," said Groucho.

"Where's Hedy?" shouted Duke amid the hollering and mooing hullabaloo.

"Holy Moses! There's Witz," said Groucho. "He has her and he's stuffing her in his Rolls Royce."

"Shit. They have Greta too. She must've slipped through ahead to try and snag her, probably thinking we're incompetent or something. Damn."

"Where'd she get that idea?" scoffed Satch.

"Hurry, Chico has the car stashed at the entrance," said Groucho. "Witz originally planned to bring her to the Guadalupe Dunes, south of Pismo, near the beach," said Groucho. "Contingencies."

"What's there?" asked Duke.

"Some lost city."

"Lost city? Crazy, let's get the hell out of here."

Groucho places his fingers in his mouth and rips out a piercing whistle: Harpo, riding on the back of a steer waving his cowboy hat, dutifully turns back in response.

On the road, they head south to the Dunes. Along the way they pull over at a phone booth for Satch to make a call to Mickey who tells Satch that Hughes is so steamed with his profane dealings against Witz that he's thrown in to help the gang for: "An ultimate fuck you to that bastard sonofabitch cocksucker . . ." Howard, who knows Witz is the slipperiest of rats, will spare no expense to deal with him appropriately. "Frankie's a goddamn Frankenstein. Like crap, in a shitty society, he keeps floating to the top."

Satch tells Mickey where they're headed, then finds out Hughes has paid off a crew from MGM films to snag truckloads of props from the studio lot to bring to an all-out showdown . . .

As soon as they arrive at Guadalupe-Nipomo, the gang surveys out in different directions. Massive sandbanks cascade their way. Trudging along, the boys sink and slide like drunk sailors on a desolate beach. Marooned in the desert, seeking an oasis, but only finding a mirage.

Making their way around a clearing, there's an ancient Egyptian temple?

"What in God's name is this doing here?"

An obelisk tower. A sphinx. Faint hieroglyphics: Amon-Ra. Anubis. Ptah. Hathor. Ma'at. Nephthys. Ramesses. Akhenaton and Itsacon. All partially buried in the dunes.

"What the heck? This is batshit spooky. It's like we're traveling time."

"Must be the original set from De Mille's *Ten Commandments*," said Satch. "The most expensive and elaborate set ever."

"Far out! Apparently, Americans will spare no expense at representing the evil empires of the Bible. Well, get ready guys. Time is not all we're going to travel," said Duke.

"What do you mean?"

"Hey! There's Witz's car, but they're not here," said Duke.

"Keep looking," said Chico.

"Witz is due to take one of those Pervitin tablets, which I replaced with that cake batter you gave me crushed into pill form," said Groucho. "He's on schedule to take one just about now, and he's a stickler about his medication. From what you tell me, once that kicks in, whammo!"

"Yeah," said Duke, "but we'll all need to take a bit of it ourselves when we see him."

"No way, compadre."

"It's the only way. Therefore we can zoom and gravitate into his head-space, or wherever it takes him. The nanoparticles should magnetize to where it leads them. Just take a pinch as soon as we spot him."

As the boys fan out and quietly sneaky-Pete along the bend of the next temple, they see Witz and some of his entourage, still on a bender.

"Why can't we drink the moon? Why is there no vessel to contain it?" whispered Duke. "Where'd Satch go? Satch?"

Hedy and Greta are tied up together. There are looks of shock, fear and bitter disapproval on their faces. Witz and Dandy Ratshaw are waving and careening their arms in cryptic insane contortions at a bonfire.

"They must've taken the Pervertin."

Frankie Witz vomits.

A centrifugal electrostatic vortex begins mounting around Witz in a slow-motion avalanche. Creeping with menacing vibrations of inconceivable energies: at first gentle, but nauseating, as he dances about, unaware of his actions. The vortex drums and drums. Chemical reactions set in. Witz feels pulled, higher and higher, into a tornado?

Traumatized beyond belief. Soaked in perspiration. Quaking and shuddering uncontrollably by forces that smash and tear atoms into particles of gigantic protons and neutrons. The dull whites of Witz's eyes roll into his head. The vortex swallows him into its funneling jaws of gravity and seething infinitely geometric chaos.

A voice booms which sounds like the foundations of the earth and its core . . . A dark speeding rainbow spins within the tornado that's engulfing Witz who screams and screams.

Chico pops his head into the tidal ascending whirlpool, he appears as a large leprechaun, and hollers through the typhoon of wind and storm: "C'mon boss, I'm the ghost of XXXmas Fool's Present! It's your lucky day! Hang tight! Though you should really get loose and just roll with it. They tell me this is a *cyclonnalism* to metastasize you from Kalevala to Kapilavatsu. Go figure? Well, follow the rainbow!"

A magnetizing takes hold of Witz. Gripping vertigo seizes him, much like when a film camera is pulled backward while the lens is zooming in forwards. This collapsing elastic implosion launches him, a catapulted *Looney Tunes* cartoon character. Zing!

And he's gone.

Ka-zang yang yang. Zipppf. Zap. Poof. Zttttt!

Witz is jettisoned into a warped trajectory, experiencing concussion bombs in his brain. A torpedo into upside-down water, and lands through the spectral porthole into a new land surrounded by saturations of explosively vivid Technicolor.

Inks evaporate from his rematerialized skin, although he still feels like a cartoon.

"Twit twit. Twit tweet." Exotic birds are twittering, out of the edge of woods: Green Flamingos? Pink Blue Jays? Witz stumbles out into a clearing where a bright glaring road leads to a futuristic city? Domed gleaning skyscrapers tower above the horizon. It's composed of glass and steel emerald.

Witz is sopping in sweat and residue, crying: "Am I in? Is this? Can it be? I thought I was damned."

He feels more alive than ever, and leaps up and kicks his heels, "Nobody damns Frankie Witz. *The Yellow Brick Road?* Hot damn. Where's this confounded Wizard?"

Episode 31

Blizzard of Zod

The ascending curve of becoming is bent in the circle which moves in itself; past, present, future are enclosed in the ring.

—*Eros and Civilization* Herbert Marcuse[20]

Witz's immediate impression is that Oz is so wonderful, and the folk so silly, naïve, innocent, and gullible, that he's already deciding to make his mark in a *will to power*.

He sees a sign that states: *Under Construction,* and knocks it down.

"I'm going to decide what gets built around here. How it's built. And who gets contracts to build it," grumbled Witz.

Groucho follows behind out of the clearing in the guise of the Cowardly Lion. Harpo is the Scarecrow. Duke the Tinman. Hedy is Dorothy, and Greta the Wicked Witch of the West.

"Hey, there's Witz!"

Before they can catch up, Witz actually outwits them, giving 'em the slip, as he flips a silver-dollar coin to a passing carriage driver, harnessed with purple horses: "Take me to Oz. Pronto!" And they zoom off.

"You've got to be kidding me," cursed Duke.

"Anyone have a brush?" asked Groucho. "Boy do I need a haircut. This fur is really hot and matted. I'd like to look my best when we stroll down this yellow brick road."

"What yellow road?" said Hedy. "I see nothing. This is madness."

"I could hardly move in this thing," complained Duke in his metal casing.

"Why am I dressed as a Leprechaun?" puzzled Chico.

---

[20] p.102. Vintage Books. New York, NY 1955

"Brother, if you have to ask, that's a rough one," said Groucho.

"This green makeup is kinky, but it's burning my skin," complained Greta. "Get it off!"

Harpo, the Scarecrow, starts a chaotic and lanky dancing jig: he catches Groucho's elbow as they *dosey doe,* spin, and dance towards the emerald horizon.

Witz's coach zooms into the city along the golden sheen of cobbled bricks. At the palace, they leisurely cruise around, looking for a way in. Witz hollers *Stop!* and the clopping comes to a halt.

He spots a contingent of guards armed with piked halberds being drilled by their captain. Witz calls to him with grandiose bombast: "Dear Commander, regal, brave, and sharp as knives. I'm on a secret diplomatic mission of the gravest significance. The fate of Oz hangs in the balance. Only I can save it. And you, courageous sir, are the hero to make it thus."

Witz implies a promotion is possible for the officer and a raise for the men, whatever the army wants—with the provision of his prompt emergency assistance: offering the Captain a gold watch, to prove the wonders of the world Witz comes from, and to grease his palm as it were (as everyone knows, this is how the levers of government operate), so he may be introduced into the ruling wizard's chamber.

Frankie's polished charm and cult of charisma is universally irresistible to the gullible, the neurotically sympathetic, or power hungry, whilst conjunct with an unhealthy dose of bribes, blackmail and fear mongering.

The red-faced, orange mutton-chopped commander, adorned with immense epaulets and medals, doubtfully raises a thick eyebrow, but admires Witz's gung-ho tenacity, besides the quality, foreign workmanship of the diamond-studded piece, so he obliges the request, leading the way into the inner sanctum.

Wide halls of opalescent material glisten past Witz over marble-hewn floors.

"There are great dangers heading straight this way to threaten the Emerald Palace. The wizard will fabulously reward us for this vital intelligence. Things are going to change around here in amazing ways. Oz will never be the same, I assure you."

The Captain of the guard continues to eye Witz with an ambivalent mix of caution and ambition, and then clangs a thick brass knocker at the twenty-foot tall door at the end of the corridor.

Upon opening, steam shoots up from pipes and engines in the back chamber. The captain trembles, and remains at the entrance with bowed head.

Witz brazenly steps into the darkness.

A mechanical organ sets off loud ominous diminished chords of dissonance. Glass globes scintillate with captured electrostatic branching flashes of contained globular lightning that crackle, sizzle, and ztttt.

The wizard's head appears large, massive: a green-shaven alien, luminous and floating above Witz; a pronounced forehead muscled with anger, and booms out deafeningly with grave intimidation: *"Whooooo dares disturb the great and all-powerful Oz?"*

Witz says, *"Yeah yeah yeahhhhh,"* and proceeds to pull the Ox-blood magenta curtains aside. He grabs an old man crouching there absorbed in the act of puppetry, and slaps him. The little obdurate wizard had previously had his back to him, absorbed in the pulling of levers and switches, while attending to his open briefcase which is a portable liquor cabinet.

"What's the meaning of this?" protested the startled man, "How did you?— Don't you know who—"

"Yeah, yeah. Shaddup' ya ol' geezer. I'm Frankie Witz—'The Wiz'. I'm taking over. I've got your number, pal. Listen, you conniving homunculus, you've had a good run. I'll see to it that you're well-supplied with booze and royal accouterments. But now it's my turn. I'm your newly-ordained Chancellor, got it? Good! Call in the royal emerald guards. And I want those damn flying monkeys too!"

Events steamroll very fast. Dominoes zip and cascade into a brushfire of transformation across the land.

Witz holds an emergency election. He becomes King of Oz. *Frankie Ozowitz the Great.* He bribed the Flying Monkeys with endless bananas, plus a village of Munchkins to enslave—to steal the voting ballots, since Lady Ozma actually won . . . Frankie orchestrated massive smear tactics utilizing a dastardly propaganda campaign accusing that his opponent really isn't from Oz, and also eats children.

Needless to say, Glinda, Ozma, and the Witch Nation are extremely pissed. They raved all night after the corrupt election. Screaming. War dancing. Tearing their clothes. Boiling cauldrons to cast spells and conjure the elements to be victorious. Though, he may have actually convinced enough Ozlanders to vote for him, however nefariously.

Witz, adorned with a crown and ermine robes, paces incessantly at his throne. He's obsessed with his disdain for the witch country along the border.

"No one is greater nor wiser than I, the ascended Over-Witz of Oz. I've got this figured out. Ministers and Captains, heed me. Now. By royal proclamation, I decree: the 'Gay Lollipop Village People' of funky little Munchkins are hereby ordered to labor, collect, and hoard all the bricks off the yellow brick roads, so we can build a wall! A huge golden wall to keep out those *Witch bitches* and pesky *gay munchkins* along my empire.

"How can this be called the Wonderful World of Witz," cursed Frankie, "if I'm surrounded by nasty free witches? And lil' bubblegum-haired faggots? How's a man supposed to feel like a man? This will not do! And this idea of a society not having money, and people only having to work half a day, stops now."

Witz's mind is half-stuck in the shadowy criminality of Hollywood, and teeters often in a state of schizophrenic bi-polar megalomania, like Narcissus seeing his own image in the water—but arguing with it. Consumed by flashbacks, paranoid hysterias, and anxiety attacks; compounded with decadent benders mixed with spiteful amusements against any opponents.

Envoys are dispatched to the polyglot groups and species within Oz to meet with their leaders and diplomats. In the process, Witz enlists the aid of the Flutterbudgets, the Hammerheads, Skruzzkies, the Cross-Eyed-Marys, the Loons, the No-Mes, the Wheelers, the Sticks-in-the-Mud, and Rigmaroles.

However, of the myriad species, there are many who refuse. Not every nation or tribe accepts Witz's kingdom or sends aid, although many of them split into factions of chaos and feud, especially after the new distribution of *WM&MW* Witz-Mazonick Magick Mirrors.

These groups included: The Mombis. The Pumpkinheads. Wogglebugs. Quadlings. Langiderians. Scoodlers. Ixians. Nolanders. Nonesticans. Magmalanders. Loggerheads. Proudhounds. Darminfloggers. Bobolinders under the Sugar-Pyramids. The Wokelidytes. The Growleywogs. Hogzinfungers. Phanphasms. Whimsies. Mamgaboos. Garkinyoggs. Burzeekytes. Fauxvillillians. Bunskins of Bunnburia. Gargogilfoyles. Zebracrabopollissians. Bomburian-blarnskies. Gillikins. Wink-wonkers. Macvelters. Mifkits. Phreks of Phreex. Even the Zogs hidden under the sea palaces.

The moral and mental strains have so imbalanced the magic of Oz that there's an increase in earthquakes, tornados, hurricanes and disease . . . Uncanny anomalies have been breaking through the now fragile reality of Oz. Some of the once happiest and most stable citizens are having psychotic breaks, or wander and shout that doomsday is nigh.

"Gold! Don't these people know," raved Witz, "that OZ denotes the common abbreviation for an ounce? Which measures gold?! Therefore, they must send tribute to their lord . . ."

Greta and Hedy make a pact with the witches. They pool their knowledge of the esoteric, and the sciences, while pouring over dusty books of ancient lore and scientific magic long-unused that the witches possess in hidden libraries. They ponder the right combination of spells and chemistry to brew a concoction and strategy to utilize upon the full moon . . .

The Land of Ozowitz's Oz continues devolving into confusion and mounting violence, insurrection, and civil war. Many citizens sadly buy into the propaganda and fear Ozwitz's power, even while feeding into old prejudices, or stirring up new ones between the various species.

Ozowitz uses the same technology as the wizard. He's utilizing stolen blueprints of secret methods to tap into mysterious energy sources while connecting to their new magic mirror. The mirror projects and transmits images into the lucid screens of other mirrors, images such as Ozowitz's intimidating persona—as if hallucinatorilly present, a hypnotic holograph. A staged magic commercial centered at a village or city square, from town to town:

"Maybe we can get one in every home?"

The Magic Mirror, (now trade-marked as **M.M.& F.O.G.** *Magic Mirrors of Franklin Ozowitz the Great*) projects Witz as a hero against women who, he claims, want to establish power for themselves in a feminist dystopia, with aid of the queer whiny Munchkins, who're also castigated, as invading his sacred borders of Oz, in mass gangs, raping and looting, then shoving lollipops up people's butts.

Hysteria spreads, increasing wider like a blind pandemic.

"He's corrosively ubiquitous," said Duke, "as if he's an agency of Fate. He's spread and warped everywhere in this world like a dizzying sensation. It was just ripe and vulnerable for such an undreamt of coup. A gigantic pawn to a cowering ego, who's made himself king to make us all his fawning puppets."

"Norns, Dryads, Valkyries, Ishtar, Venus, Folly, Wisdom, Beatrice, Hypatia, Mary, Sisters, Kalifa, Fates, Gaia, Kali! Hear our suppliant invocation, and come to our aid!" prayed Greta.

"Man, you ain't seen nothing," said Groucho, "until you've witnessed a Mifkit, Wogglebug and Hogzinfunger go at it."

Time passes fast in Ozwitz. Too many details transpire for the gang to keep up with. The speed and over-saturation of true and false information creates an impasse of understanding anything: a post-truth world, as society collapses under a despotic hegemony. No one can agree.

"That's why we need a king!"

"It's because of the fake king! Ahhhhhhhhh!"

Folk descend further into atomistic conditions of insular solipsism. Details and complications compile into blurring paranoid phantasms at an alarming rate of lost logic and reality.

"Whoa whoa whoa, how long has this been happening?" said Duke.

"For weeks?" said Hedy.

"I don't remember . . ." said Greta.

"Witz is triumphing as a jaundiced demagogue," said Hedy. "It's as if he thrives in this world! It feeds on drama, character, and conflict. The sheer inundation is exasperating its capacity to withstand this much pressure. Even as most of its inhabitants are frothing with disfavor or rebellion."

"This project was supposed to screw Witz," said Duke, "without actually having to kill him. But we're all kiboshed now. We've got to get the heck out of here. This is psychotic. How are events unfolding this way, after we haven't even experienced them happening? While we are unaware or unconscious? Within what? Days just vanish without us. How is this construct ongoing?"

"I studied what you gave him under a make-shift microscope lens," said Hedy. "It's rather symmetrical, a spiked radius, but radically kinetic and unstable with a highly advanced anomalous formulation. Whatever it is, the molecules, theoretically, appear to act as a transporting mechanism which then expands into a hyper-dimensionality, opening bubble rifts in the membrane between space-time? If possible. There's something, almost, alive in it."

"The bastard tried to sacrifice me. Let's just execute him and be over it," commented Greta dryly.

"Easier said than done, now that he has an army. But the effects should wear off . . ." said Duke.

"And you know this, how?" asked Hedy.

"An intuitive hunch," smiled Duke painfully, as he realized what originally got him here, all this time, hasn't itself worn off. And *now that he's taken a transporting dose within a dose . . .*

"Sounds rather foolish to me," scolded Hedy. "It's bad enough now we're stuck here with these *swinehundt mashugana* clowns who collaborated in our abduction," said Hedy, as she and Greta, exhausted from stress and strain, start to smack and whack Groucho and Chico mercilessly.

"Hey, stop, ow. Quit it! Though we deserve it," cried Groucho, attempting to shield and brace too many wounds at once. "But hey, it ain't half so bad getting smacked by the most beautiful women in the world."

"Schisser!"

Harpo happily jaunts in with more red roses that he's been gathering lately since they've been here.

"Hey wait. No don't!" shouted Hedy with swift realization. "Those aren't roses! Those are . . ."

"Those are poppies," raved an awakened Hedy. "No wonder we've been unglued in this timeline. Christ. *Der fluch die verwünschung.* Get that Mr. Tik-Tok to dispose of these poisoned poppies."

"What's happened since we've been opiated?" asked Duke. "Hey where the hell did the yellow brick road go? Are those Tesla towers in the distance?"

Witz has been manipulating the technological magic powers of Oz. He's even planning to stage an invasion of Hollywood, then Washington. He gathers a cadre of sorcerers who inform him about the fabled Ruby Slippers. Apparently, for this grand strategy to work, they'll have to discover and craft these ruby slippers for an entire army . . .

Misters Thudd and Blunderbuss, royal advisors, enter the throne room hall that's decked in gold, amethyst, and emerald veined marble.

One could only imagine the noblest of thoughts and language to grace the splendor of this exposition of grandeur. There's a nimbus of trapezoidal shapes of art and fabulous riches: tesselating and flourishing with plumes and cygnets, sashes and banners, saffron and scarlet. Mauve and turquoise. Moonstones, sky blue sapphires, jade, topaz, onyx, beryl, agate, opal. Ermine, minks, jasper, lavender, and jasmine: drizzled with diamond dust.

"You tell those Fucks—" riled Ozowitz.

"Ahem, sir. We do not use that language here," corrected Mr. Thudd.

"What? I'm the great Ozowitz."

"Yes, indeed, grand and great all-powerful magnificent one. However, the harshest of words we may let slip is Zibble! With more abrasive emphasis, it's: Freckzibble."

"Well, you tell those Frecking Zibblers to get on with it. I'm looking over these maps of Oz, but they're not large enough. I require a map as huge as Oz itself so I can see exactly what's in Oz, with constant updates."

"Excuse me your Mightiness, a map as large —as Oz?"

"Yes, Zilbert. A life-sized facsimile. Huge, like the monumental statue of your king we're going to carve into the mountains!"

Thudd turns to Blunderbuss and curses, "Zibble!"

"Megazibble!" retorted Blunderbuss.

Bells and chimes announce visitors to the court.

Chico introduces himself as: "Skeezix McNoonan from Squonk-honk-in-nin New Jerkzkey. At your service."

"And I'm McWarpawich Korkiowsky," said Groucho the Lion. "Say. That's not near Macquankinndlonn, Spoonsburg or Hawk-hawka-puss, is it?"

"Nope. Not Weehawken, nor Ho-boken, Metuchen, Secaucus, nor Ho-ho-kus either," said Chicko.

"Good, especially since those dibblers from Squonkhawkachuck really got it coming to them."

"Oh, I'd stay out of Squonkhawkachuck if I were you."

"Mctushawken is the worst though, I hear."

"What is the meaning of this?" queried Mr. Blunderbuss.

"Pardon us monsieur," said Groucho. "Sire, we are here to grace you with your new harem."

Several of the Amazon Witch Warriors volunteered, with Harpo, and entered the court disguised and veiled as Mata Hari belly dancers.

"Harem scare 'em more like," said Chico.

"Shhh!" said Groucho. "Feast, on the hottest babes of Girland, oh Grand Wazoo."

"What's with you guys?" said Ozowitz. "You seem familiar. But I like these leggy gals. Well, that blonde is intriguing."

"Oh she's rather shy, your Wittiness," said Groucho.

Hedy, after extensive tactical deliberation and organizing, gathered an army of witches and women to protest, and fight, at the gates of Oz, now marshaling and lining up in rows and ranks around the city.

The Marx Brothers have been sent in as high-end courtesan pimps with their most nubile athletes to distract and infiltrate during the attack.

Hedy addresses the crowd:

"Greetings citizens and Sisters of Ozland. We meet, with passion and pain, during extraordinary times; compelled to speak and act upon these tribulations which bond us together, whose toxicity we'd rather not acknowledge, but must—of society, of class, of consciousness, our mental well-being—for an unasked, unprovoked war of inequality, and our actual freedom from the corrosive inveterate corruption now imposed upon these realms.

"Impossible to ignore—as the usurping Ogre-witz has seized our skirts, and forces his impious face unscrupulously to stare back at us, even in our very own mirrors."

Hedy pauses, looking around at the many beautiful faces, now resonating with crazed eyes, hatred, and grim attentiveness. The leaden silence of so many hushed impassioned breaths brews a loud impression.

She shouts through the megaphone: "This upstart demented ogre, who has made himself Queen!"

A wicked derisive cackling erupts into a roar of blood-curdling laughter. Blood curdling to Witz, and the denizens of the palace, looking on.

"Politics: generally a filthy word, but this is beyond the general forms, functions, and diplomatic details of a governing State's machinery, now grinding us like a corn mill. The kingdom shall be restored to its parliamentary balance with a qualified and rightfully elected leader, as under Lady Ozma. Not a despotic ruler, this phantom lord's machinations of putrefied flesh of enthroned tyranny! Always meddling, always insulting, seeking headline attention, and thieving our lives.

"Intolerable."

The army of women cry with banshee-scathing hoots and howls:

Tyranny! Tyranny!   Boooooo!   Let's roast his balls!

"There shall be no congress of sexual copulation with your mates until this molding, rotten, aluminum demigod rusts and withers into the forbidden wastelands unto dust.

Women cheer, hooray! Hear, Hear! Though some of them grumble. Louder groans escape from within the city.

"The prattling sycophants unlocked their harbored prejudice and inferior spite upon us. This bile and bigotry was formerly just hidden seeds in their subconscious; shadows from forgotten frictions of more childish days, when lacking in reason or civilized cooperation. But through the conniving of this disfigured head of state disaster, they are galvanized from invisible bacteria into a full-blown plague of power.

"A tornado of greed and ego-megalomania, destroying our lives and pursuits of happiness. They bow and flatter him, even as they bow above us to make us stoop to their hunchback fecklessness and rank misogyny.

"I say NO! Even as we all say: "

Noooooooooooo! Roared the crowd.

"These parasitic dwarves think so little of us that they dimly believe people can't handle the truth. But we can—it's just that we didn't. It seemed too expensive to pay attention. Too much effort. But we paid a heavy toll. Not anymore.

"We shall invest time to understand the demonized other side. They are not your enemies but rather unfortunate opponents who're now othered to a polarized opposite, under Ozwitz's hypnotizing sway of hyperbolic propaganda, where all our shame and blame is heated up to illusions of hatred. They feel a warm, cozy, fictitious solidarity; a space-cadet glow to cast their own sins and projections, to heap coals on their ritualized barbeque to cannibalize in effigy our imagined conflagrations; of imaginary wrongs.

"The objectless objections of lost objectivity. Their perversity of truth is far too rotten to tolerate longer without action and remedy, even as we must check ourselves, self-reflect, that by facing and dealing with this dragon, we ourselves are not infected in the muck, and degrade into beasts. This is how the disease of fascism wins. But we shall triumph. Our gravest peril is that if, by fighting the dragon, we ourselves become the dragon, which we seek to de-flect, not re-flect in our contaminating contact. As I clearly perceive the understandable hatred scorching in your features, but we are here to heal, not to punish with revenge!

"The eldest patriarchal grand wizards told them to tell White-lies at the foundation of elitist oligarchies in earlier, more barbaric times. And those lies, Witz-reawakened, are still white-washing this overarching visceral shadow, this hierarchy weighing over us.

"The love of power does not thrive without lying. And their realm is now the will to power. Their organized crime world of magic mirrors chips away an illusory matrix of paradise.

"If they tempt towards a modicum of goodness, their strings are jerked back, like the puppets they've been subjugated to. Radioactive *Nervous Systems* irked, and fried. One step forwards (and in the shadows); a thousand steps back. Down, down, the dungeons of bigotry, greed and blame.

"Will the angels' trumpets blow down the walls of the castle? Singing hymns with the fury of locomotive breath and battering rams? Ogrewitz shall be deposed! Goddess be with us."

Deposed! Deposed!

Witz beholds the army of women encompassing his Oz in horror from his tower, screaming, "What is she doing? Stop this! Don't we have a bomb?" He kicks a speechless Mr. Thudd in the groin, then topples a clock made with diamonds.

"In my birth land," said Hedy, "a legendary teacher and visionary turned his cheek against violence, but his teachings were co-opted into religion, and are often ignored, flipped upside down and martial for war instead. As our fabled Troy is deceived. Over and over.

"*Hey, you Assholes!* Hiding behind these yellow brick walls. Stop this dick-tator from sleazily penetrating our Oz. Morphed into an inverted totalitarianism. Let's return to fellowship, and peaceful community, to teach us a priceless lesson, better than before, rather than this useless and destructive violence.

"Aghast, although the hour is rather late, instead, the trolleys and carriages run on time! Everyone fitted into their dollhouse places. Thirteen o'clock. *The hands that threaten doom.* Another round of Victory Gin! Like a boot to the brain.

"Unkind. Uncharitable.

"Damn this scam. History books have been written in the shelves no one goes to, edited and re-re-written in the emerald libraries, laminated with crawling metallic spiders and roaches. All this dearth and pretentious patriotism for a devil blood transfusion? The ministerial financiers, who run our shops, have been boosted to rule us for their own gain, and bank rankers gushing with royal flushes. Richer than ever, as many are left destitute and poor. We will flush them!"

Flush them out! Flush them down!

"Ladies and allies, smile up from the spinning toilets and outhouse dumps, with dignity and composure from out of our humiliation.

"Geniuses across the kingdoms are abducted and lobotomized by the regime's mad-anti-science perversities: *to abuse their technology whilst trashing the knowledge that goes with it.* They sign away their souls on the bottom dotted line. The deep-pocketed coffers spindle strings and scalpels of mind control; commingled to mass-market their patents, toys and ideologies, with carnival barking psychiatrist shamans and charlatan advertisers.

"This surrealistic world of negation is too insane to make sense anymore, the overloaded all-seeing Panopticon's simulacrum. *As the Ungreated Cheeze of Ozowitz steals our eyes, his magic mirrors rape our grating souls. He'll turn us all into himself, if we fail and do nothing.*

"Bridges rusting down. Along with the once-blue sky, as the atmosphere is vaporized with the pollution of overproduction, of goods we do not need, which the magic mirrors trick and hypnotize us to purchase, like hooked opium fiends.

"Smash the mirrors. Kill the virus of bloodsucking vanity. Everything I've studied in chemistry teaches that Love is the antidote. Heal the land. Resurrect the *brain-dead* back to life and humanity again.

"An adversity of the Perverse. Through the eye of the tornado into the Yellow-bricked road now walled in reverse against us. Hear and heed us, Ogrewitz: Thou shalt yield!"

Yield! Yield! Clamored the alliance outside the walls.

Trebuchet catapults bring up the rear, as they're rolled forward. Women wearing protective deep-diving suits load up the payloads.

Hedy gives the signal. Triggers are pulled on the siege engines: axle twang, lashings unleash and whip out with lightning fast cracks. The artillery of catapult arm beams snap and arc upwards with alarming precision, a devastating choreography. The mass barrage is launched, bombarding the city of Oz.

The Emerald Guard huddled along the walls duck for cover.

"Look out! Brace yourselves!" Projectiles soar and cut the air. The concussive reverberation of the missile bombardment echoes through field and city.

Upon impact the barrels break open.

"Take cover!"

The containers splinter and pop, to reveal:

"It's only flowers!" the guards cried out.

They fall beside themselves with giddy laughter. Tears of mirth and infectious giggling spread across the metallic ranks, to their stressed relief, as some mockingly hand these flowers to one another in a wink wink—be my sweetheart sort of way.

"So much for that," said Private Arxifuss along the walls, "eh, Sargent Grunder?"

"Indeed, Lad," said the Sarge, yawning. "Bombing us with flowers. Typical women!"

"Silly girls. Boy, were we worried," said Arxifuss. "Sarge? You alright? You're fainting over? Hey Chippo? Rangopuss? Why are you all. Falling. To. Sleep? ZZZZZZZZZzzzzzzzzzzzzz."

Guards fall down together as dominoes. Some, clump and doze hugging into each other, like the sweethearts they were just goofing to be.

"These aren't flowers," cried the guards, "They're pop-pop- . . ."

"Poppies," said Hedy.

Greta unveils her metal armored tits and squeezes them: "Poppies!"

"Excellent," smirked Hedy. "Now, Phase 2."

Hedy swings her arm, and the women take off their tops to reveal their armored bras with spikes at the end of their nipples.

Any guards left conscious, are momentarily stunned and distracted enough to be overrun and captured as the ladders are tossed up to scale the walls. After all of Hedy's trauma, being the first international woman to reveal her lush breasts on screen, before her ex-husband's censorious obsession, and the obsession of the entire world over these sugary mounds of flesh, and all the trouble and controversy—she utilizes them to her victory.

The shock of these glorious tits in a *Rated-G* puerile land as Oz, despite being taken over by an *X-Rated* madman, sends such stunning convulsions among the enlisted ranks that combat and battle is useless.

"Lay down your arms!" shouted the first wave of Amazon shock troops who speedily overcame the walls, meeting scant resistance from the sleepy, wide-eyed guards.

"Ye-yes mam!"

"Mother frecking zibbler Zonkers," yelled Witz. "I'm at my wit's end. I can't even speak English anymore surrounded by you nitwits. I don't believe it. You sissy-bitch puking tin soldiers. You call yourselves guards?"

Witz slaps guards and counselors who are helpless around him: "These women will impale my balls. I'm outta here, jack!" He opens a secret drawer in his throne which holds the Ruby Slippers.

The Amazon harem pull out their make-up compacts and blow enchanted powders in Witz's direction. Some of it gets on Harpo, who sneezes. They both begin to giggle. Their flesh momentarily bubbles, then zoink! A reverse sucking sound realigns their flesh.

Poof! "What in hell's boudoir," shrilled Witz. He puts on the Ruby Slippers, then sees himself in the grand mirror. *What? Sees: Herself?*

Witzilla freaks, and screams an octave higher: "Ahhhhhh, I'm a Queen!"

Most of the royal entourage flee the room. The tall Amazons titter and mockingly bow down with menace.

Harpo, flummoxed by the transformation, feels his, her? Breasts? She smirks a dissolute grin, and sneaks off into the closet.

"Hey," yelled Groucho, "no time for whatever you're gonna do in there. Now I have a sister? Oh brother. Is this really happening? Were we actually in a sanitarium? I was a doctor? You were an orderly? Or are we still in the looney bin?"

"You ask too many questions doc," said Chico, "but, you may have a point."

Witz achieves a complete mental breakdown in a frenzied, mad-hatter fit. He clicks his Ruby shoes, over and over. Nothing is happening. Actually there's a conflux of static interference: a mass conglomeration of boilers, turbines and steam engines below, including Tesla coils and modified spherical Van Der Graaf Generators joined in a tandem of ionic terminals (which Witz carried blue prints of from his uncle) . . . All to amplify the primary Magick Mirror, torqued for optimal conductivity with an alignment of super-charged capacitors, huge vacuum tubes, tungsten rods, and galvanometers of electromagnetic inductive coupling—angled at a delta-theta torsion-laced circuitry, grounded with rubber insulation, to charge the composed borosilicate glass and alloys of quartz, aluminum oxide and sodium carbonate dielectric coatings, connecting all the receptive Magick Mirrors of Oz—processed radiated strings of electrons.

Ozwitz's Necromancer-technicians built the central mirror upon a sulfuric hexafluoride circle and pentagram between the grand pillars, wiring the mirror with structured occult components implemented by the court alchemists.

The Amazons close in to nab Witz. In a toddlergasmic paroxysm of hysterics, Witz throws the switch to charge the Grand Mirror accelerator's transmission magnitude to a dangerous overload. An ionized corona field glows around the buzzing tall frame. The over-pressurized pipes and valves burst with steam, vibrating and ready to blow.

Witzilla makes a leaping kick, with ruby heels and ruby lips: *"Abra cadabra, adios suckers!"* and crashes through the mirror. Then another. And another mirror. Another . . . "No! Nonononono."

A screeching, vanishing, invisible energy and entelechy smashes Witz's face. Pow! Shards of glass turn to liquid. Time dissolves. This wasn't the reaction he was expecting, through a gauntlet cascade of crashing mirrors. Bashing into one image of himself after another. *He's really got to cut down on the Pervertin!*

Soaked in an implosion of infrared light; swimming through a bloody rage of disentangled particles. Then orange, beaming with a piercing, high-pitch frequency. A blaze of bright yellow mirrors smash and reform into green mirrors. Witz sees endless copies of himself, cursing, conniving, stealing, boiling with pain and anger. Cycling through his buried emotions which surface with his defense mechanisms of hatred and blind Will. Phasing faster into blue, indigo, and an immersion of violet blasting with deafening sound waves . . .

Before Witz impacted across—Hedy, Greta, and Duke entered the chamber to witness his maniacal escape. Duke sprints and jumps into the mirror to tackle Witz, tossing a rope behind him off to Harpo, who smiles to grab the others.

"Witz left a doomsday bomb, why would he do that? Hey, Mr. Tik-Tok?" cried Hedy.

"Don't you worry. I'll disarm it," chimed the vigilant Tik-Tok . . .

Transporting into the mirror portal, Duke is transmitted with a vision of a hundred chess boards. Pieces moving themselves. Each piece is a compacted equation sum of symbols condensed. Every game-board has layered planes of boards above it. Neon lines of geometry intersect the pieces below. There's fractal static of equations in radio waves, dispersing this pellucid broadcast.

Duke, in his unconscious mind, feels he's being scanned.

Puncturing this threshold of protoplasmic liminality. Uncharted, non-linear, non-binary. Transcending good and evil. Beyond duality. There's light, and illumination, but not quite enlightenment. A universal pivot. Skirting the frictions against the central monad of the possible unified field of all knowing, the plurality of holistic polyphonous truth. A mind-quake bending the super-strings between matter and dimensions.

Two massive equations of mathematical fields of data collide into a cloud of thundering electricity. A cascade of cinders sparks his fluctuating synapses of spiking dendrites. A nimbus of trapezoidal convexing and isoscelating expansions and reconfigurations of a multi-dimensional montage fractalizes through the curvature arcs of space-time culminating into a spinning tetrahedron. His mind melts and melds, losing consciousness.

Jolting back, he spots Witz. Diving through this phantasmal space, Duke grabs his ankle as they shoot through the void. Witz flips and grasps for Duke's throat, red-eyed and screaming: "Don't you know who I am, fucker? People crave desire over what they need. The irrational dream, the euphoric illusion. The magician's wand! My big personality and the greatest nation in the world. They want to be me—identify with me. People are stupid. They'll die to find something greater than themselves. To transcend their ignominious insignificance and be a cog awash in the fever vision dedicated to a hero of true power. Children at a theater. A goddamn electric box to tell them what's what and what to be. They don't want the big decisions and responsibilities on their shoulders. I'm their big brother!"

"What hell spawned your disease? What's wrong with you?"

"Have you experienced true power?"

Duke pokes Witz's eyes—they both spin apart.

Episode 32

Paradoxica Dessert

Strange to see meanings that clung together once, floating away in
every direction.
And being dead is hard work and full of retrieval before one can
gradually feel a trace of eternity . . .
Angels (they say) don't know whether it is the living they are moving
among, or the dead. The eternal torrent whirls all ages along in it,
through both realms forever, and their voices are drowned out in its
thunderous roar.

—Duino Elegy Rainer Maria Rilke

Facts are stupid things.

—Ronald Reagan

A final chain reaction sets off. This force detonates into Witz's eyes like the roaring of Niagara Falls with thermonuclear pressure. A concussion of volume dynamites his hearing which vacuums and suctions all sound and reality out of the encompassing world: an army of Gene Krupa's, Buddy Rich's and Chick Webb's on an artillery of drum sets. A walled arsenal of amplifiers powered by an atomic reactor multiplies the bash and crashing cacophony, as the moon collides with the earth.

Witz's seeming cells and molecules begin to evaporate, as if he isn't even real, and realign into a flaming, embryonic comet, landing in an ancient Egyptian Sinai peninsula.

Witz's skin turns a golden orange as he lands into a dump of desert sand. He wearily looks up. A group of tribal shepherds and wanderers approach and gaze on in wonder. He wipes off the amniotic fluid he's soaked in.

The shepherds are in awe, and question if he's a god? Witz, aware of their adulation, immediately seizes it to exploit. They feed him wine from a sack off their camel.

"Who's in charge here?" asked and gulped a crazed Witz.

The shepherds explain how their leader is back on the mountain, turning white, and conversing with the burning bush of their god.

Frankie, an incorrigible hunted weasel, quickly assesses the circumstances. Venting into a long tirade he encourages all to celebrate the worship of Baal and Mammon instead. The beguiled tribe, without their leader, become helplessly enthralled by this miraculous apparition, concede, and therefore, with a heaping bonfire, melt down all their gold into a bull that resembles Witz.

So while the cat's astray, the mice frolic and get carried away into a Saturnalian feast. Rage and riot, howling as a tribe of upstarts: complaining and proclaiming they no longer need their Moses who was their intermediary shepherd.

"Moses, shmozes."

Wine flows, and bells, flutes, gongs and dancers abound.

Suddenly there's a zap and crunch of lightning. Under a bright halo, Moses returns, with whitened wooly hair, a long beard, a gnarled, tall staff, and skin that glows ebony and golden like the sun.

"Ah, look who it is," sneered Witz loudly with the swaying crowd. "Mister high and mighty Moses. The head honcho. The big cheese. Numero Uno! What did GOD tell you to tell us this time? Who the hell does Moses think he is? Bossing us around through the desert like this? For forty years? Where's the Promised Land of milk and honey? C'mon. It's only a few miles east of here dammit. You fools are pathetic. Does he claim to be the only one who can speak to God? What nonsense. Are you going to listen to this—this—African?!"

"Well, we're all African. We're in Africa," murmured a few in the crowd.

"Alright, alright," admitted Witz. "Irregardless. WE want to speak with this, our god! Whom you've been hiding. And see him for ourselves!"

"Yeah! Moses! Stop hiding God from us. We want to see God! Yeah! What's the big idea?"

"Come on Moses," shouted Baal-Witz. "You're making this all up. Otherwise, you've appointed and appropriated the power of God for yourself."

Meanwhile, since the magic mirror portal and the Oz spell has been broken, Duke makes his way to these strange sands to behold:

Satchmoses, who ascends with his staff the highest peak of rock around them. He's about to speak to the unruly mob when he notices an erupting orgy with someone dressed in a ragged top-hat and fig leaves dive into the fleshy congregational mêlée. Satch dexterously uses his staff to part the motion of the sassy flush of bodies to hook and pull out the fallen character, and shoves him on his way.

Harpo sneaks behind him to dive back in but Satchmoses hooks him out once more with his pesky sheep crook staff.

Witz and the intoxicated unruly revelers grow more irate and riled-up to bully this Satchmoses, taunting and scoffing, that if they're the chosen people, then they're worthy of a divine audience with this bush-burning god.

"We demand to see this burning bush for ourselves," yelled Witz. "Sounds like a big sex secret. You can't keep secrets from us. Our golden god demands we have no secrets. Ya know what? You know what rhymes with Moses? I bet he just sleeps, once he makes that hike. There's no Yahweh to talk with: He's lazy. Doesn't he look lazy to you? *You know what I'm talkin' about.* Moses Dozes! Then he bumbles back, and hoses! He's hosing us down with this pisswater hogwash, as he poses from the high rocks, like he's better than us, and it stinks to our noses!"

"*Moses Dozes! Moses Dozes! Stinks to our noses!*" shouted the crowd.

During this chaotic riot of darkling opposition, about to spark to violence, Satch is rather moved to sing in response, and corrals some of the more musical of the noise-makers together, including the irrepressible top-hat with a makeshift harp to strike up an accompaniment. Even Groucho and Duke, after valiantly fighting off the octopus-like pull and suction of the swirling orgiastic throng. They hunker down to drum and flute along.

Satchmoses starts to snap fingers with a beat. Harpo strums a walking bassline: *boom boom twing twang zim bim boom bam* . . . zithering and zinging those strings alive.

With this wonky group beginning to groove, holy smoking Armstrong, in a bliss inspired-state, scats out a bluesy spoken word cascade of what he'd really like to say—but no prophet, scribe, scrivener, or record company will ever record him as such. And thus hereby testifies, in this rare moment in the universe, to defy a rave of hepped-up mad heathens:

"Thrillium diggers,

slag

those jiving facts

And dark-as-night figures in the slog, and grog. Of the jagged juke n' junk Huckleberry hijinks of *ghetto get down.*

Boogie and Woogie jump alive a spook haunted graveyard. Bog dancin' with Mister D. Grinning behind heart-breaker badges with 44 caliber swords, or Voodoo-child spellbinders. Swagger in the swig and sin of shadows, wagered with gang-cleavers, all revved-up with hatchet's heart lessening blades. Fodder of the fronted trickle down bottom-line.

Uncertified surgeries, by the men in pharoah's armored blue, in the name of the letter of the law that killeth.

So hang on, you broken and brutalized folk.

The ambulance should arrive, in just 99 minutes.

Crack attacks smacked with a Jack of soiling spade's muckraking dirt

All over my Wall Street Journals.

Trigger chase and misanthropic trials. Grunt and grimace of three-second head-start: A One, and a two, and bam bang boom. Down, for the unfinished count.

Beware the future, speeding distant years from the source. In hail of emptied test tube vials and paradisical advertising of neon illumination, to lasso you, in somnambulant temptation.

Eden's been evacuated, and there's a fire raging in the Creation:

Cain, and Nimrod, Pharaoh, and the Serpent, keep fuggin' it up: til' we get it right.

Hiss hiss hiss!

And the Most High, Jehovah, is up there thundering:

"High-dee, high-dee, high. Ho Ho Ho!"

The band and the tribe respond with a chorus round of high dee high—ho ho ho!

Witz folds his arms, turns from orange to red, scowling with a frown and grimace.

Sewege floods clog the cities with unread news and papiermaché manifestos. Boy did Sodom and Gomorrah get the blues with that brimstone confetti. Kind of a raw deal. They didn't even get these ten commandments yet.

Hoods and witches rumble, and stitch the Hoe-down, dose-E-doe.

Squares dancing in corny fields forever.

Sham rocked sodomites scram and brambled. Dive in backalleys for cover. Like times we ducked out, wide-eyed peeking on a temple roof-top, as slingshots and arrows sang and humans ran for their distorted lives across the road, when thugs in chariots got Shakespearean, acting out Capulets and Montagues: A dead-end stage, bloody in a homicidal maniac attack.

A prophecy of things to come, so ya better run! Back to the foxhole of the bunkered trenches, it ain't no fun. Where you gangstas now? *Where you gonna run to? Tell me where you gonna hide?*

Cain and Nimrod, Pharoah and the Serpent.

Hiss hiss hiss.

The jig is up. Gig and gander, the sheriff will pander for the front page scribe and hieroglyphic camera: Keep on shovelin'. Those school budget cuts really pay off—for someone else.

Try hard as you may to make an impression: Baby Face Witz'-end Nelson don't have nothin' on Genghiz Khan, Attila, and the Kaiser Wilhelm Viktor Albert.

You may get your kicks on Route Six Sixty Six, but the lord will tell Abraham: *Kill me a son. If not, you'd better cower and run, when you see me comin' burnin' up Highway 61.*

Amnesia is the standby cure for it all. Bam and boozle. High-dee, high-dee. High-dee HO!

High dee high dee ho ho ho!

Satch & Bix in the Boom-boxed after party jams, unrecorded, but echoing in Eternity. Fructified in the glow of sound made music. Sand in the eyes of the bigot deaf to ebony ivory new harmonies. As Caesar said to Marc Antony of Cassius, lurking lean and hungry—with many too many daggers of thoughts; a smiling snarl, surly under dusty halls, envious. To applaud effete ego-mad aristocracy, not people playing democracy.

Beware such men Caesar said—Cassius-Witz, *has no music in him.* Cassius and his unkind minions have no hymn, nor dance, no humor, melody, nor harmony. Just the barbed harm of heavy money and insolent pride of ignorant envy. Attention-whores who need you to bow. Kneel as they pick your pockets, and then your bones as they keep the flags waving high-dee high-dee Ho!

The seriousness of living pains a bitter necessity to see, passing through to eternity. Not without suffering, but alive and bettered, once stretched across the junkyard tornado.

Sun breaking clouds at the end of Purgatory? And maybe someone saved and celebrated

along

the

way.

Through death's brink, and the angled width of groping daylight—blaze through chinks of armor across the dark stalks, yet towards the life beyond, which is present, right now. And only Now.

And thus,

So then,

And how—

I hear the Ga-nack-Ganacks —gacking in the Night.

A congaree of frogs *throgging* together. Lunging throats of toads tadpoling their vibes of *Be-ing*. Diminuendo in the blue lagoon.

Ganack Ganack, Shadrach, Damindingo

Silence.

A pause, a rest. An interlude. A breath. Then chic chic Cicada-ing safe from the Dervish dice throw of the coffin parade. And the frogging chorus and gong erupts again. The happy swamp choir drone. The oneness of tropical night. No scimitar of chance spinning Russian Roulette, banked by Godfathers & sold-out secret agents under new names.

Crickets buzz a hum of Sitar drones—ignore bank and I.R.S legalese of the mailbox stuffed froth of bills.

Gack.

Ga-nack!

Crick crack *de-Bergerac*.

Shad-drachk! Me-shach, De-min-digo

Eruptions of amphibious euphoria of mating jamborees . Swampee in the rucked up jungle of jambalaya Dixie. Organized chaos. A mix and jounce—along the intercoastal savannas to hepped-up Havana. Jubilee. Of excess.

Mists of the Rockies sail down to mellow softly in the Bayous, from Memphis to the Nile, along the same elusive equatorial meridian.

The proliferation of kittens tumble their profligate epidemic of fluffy joy on tar-paved carpets of Highway One, sliding down from the Kenduskeag and Penobscot, through Talbot Timucuan to Hobe-Sound and the Keys, to punchline future Hemingways—will they shave their Walt Whitmans and sign up for the next

Civil war?

Gack- Ga- Knack. Crick crack De Bergerac.

Shad-rack. Me-shach, Demindigo

High-dee, high-dee, high-dee Ho!

Jeremiah's Jehovah bulldozing a mantra of Chazz-wah-zahs Zinging in the ooze and dizzy daze drizzle—twigged shadows of dark. A billion year old evolutionary soundtrack. Spark a lark on a wing of the Nightingale's song, and love supreme dreaming invocations, of pipe revel Saxophony.

JAAAAAAAAZZZZZZZZZZZZZZZZZZZZZZZZZZZZZZZZZZZZZZZZZZZZZZZZZZZZ

Yes my friends, the creator has a master plan.

Stop your frowns. Don't get low, get down! There'll be a new law in town, and it's Love thy Neighbor as thyself. Love love love like the holy dove.

Peace and happiness, through all the land, for every gal, and every man.

Black & Yellow, White & Red. Father Sky and Mother Earth, as said, used different colors, undercooked or well done, but we're made and baked from the same clay. Since the first day, and later the sun?

Hey hey hey, from Hosanna to Rosanna. We all bleed into One, under the rainbow of our daily birth and fun.

Breeze of leathery revving palm tree glades whisper bliss and fauns fan us under their fauna in this fight for paradise—irresistible in the cacophony of tribal green beats joined by shouts of insect and animal glee.

All One in the

Spree & sprawl of ecstasy in Subterranean meadows.

Reptilians cool in their sleaze and snooze, treble of resonance. Goony and Junie, gal-lack a-frack. Amen to the promised land Oasis across the desert.

Aum and home, the thunderbolts in the void.　　　　　Galactic attack Ga-knack.

Spasmodic stars: dazzle, and drizzle into dream."

The tribe rejoices, dancing and hugging, loud: "High dee high dee Ho Ho Hosanna in the highest."

Duke and the Brothers, all smiles and elation, embrace each other. The crowd helps untie Greta and Hedy, after Witz and his minions attempt to sacrifice them again. Witz is losing his power, as he loses his hold on reality.

A group of hyped-up, starry-eyed gals dancing and crazed by the tunes had been pawing at Harpo, as he fights 'em away. But now they're just hungry for that harp strummin' madman angel fool Adonis, and it's getting ugly. There are too many. He's climbing over them to get free, and run.

"Aaaand they're off," howled Chico, "Harpo's in the lead, he's in great form. Place your bets ladies and gents! Alight, alright, place your bets. Uh-oh, here comes Red, Brunette, and Blondie hot on Harpo's heels with Delilah and Salomē huffing and vying for first. Oh, look at that, Delilah just yanked Salomē by the hair and she's out of the running. But right behind is another jockeying set of thorough-breds, wave after wave. It's not looking good for our champion Harpo: he's had a good run, but he may have to settle down and domesticate. Boy, have the tables turned in this Cinderella story."

The crowd laughs, dancing joy around the bonfires.

But angry Witz all along had been frothing to the uncommitted stragglers, and the silent majority, and the last of his tripped-out goons, as he broke off enough idol gold to hand out to bribe and win over a tithing of the tribe who's still hoppin' mad about this idea to see God themselves, rather than Moses pontificating as their intercessory lawyer.

Satchmoses shakes his head, "Alright, alright folks. If you truly and violent-ly insist, with rebellious righteous indignation. I can't stop your demands. You've been warned."

Satch reaches into his robes for something, but it's not there.

Harpo sprints over, pops up, out of breath, covered in scratches, mud, and smeared lipstick make-up, and reaches into his own fig toga garments and pulls out a trumpet, which he speedily hands to Satch, and zooms back off as the harem of Bacchanalians claw fast behind him.

Armstrong throws Harpo a grim slanted thank you look, and then takes the longest inhale of his existence, blasting out a summoning fanfare that ripples their ear drums, rumbling through the groves and rocks of the red and yellow val-ley, flickered by campfire Egyptian statue shadows.

This sonic heralding reminds Duke of Stravinsky, like that *Firebird Suite*, as its humming melody grows and cascades through every mathematical interval of thirds, fourths, fifths, sixths, and dominant major sevenths. Climbing and descend-ing, converging through all the in-between spectrums of micro-tonal frequencies: then spiraling up every key, from the lowest to highest registers. It resounds thrum-ming in every mode, simultaneously. (Joshua makes mental notes, as he'll use this technique on Jericho.)

Technicolor bleeds fully back into Duke's eyes, and disrupts further into the receding black and white storm of the scene. Purple clouds rumble to flash, and a mad glorious laughter thunders down upon them, like a Vulcan joker's hammer and anvil.

Gabriel's horn responds above. The dizzying revelers slow down and stop their dancing, giggles, orgies, and frolic fornicating.

A burnishing corona aura light, like a thousand suns, approaches. Footsteps echo within a centrifugal vortex, intersecting and overlapping lasers of knotted lens-shaped beaming arcs of radiation.

A silhouette of a Being.

Ominous footsteps. No feet are seen.

The proceeding holy blaze brightens. Revelers cower and cover their faces in fear, and feel a warm bliss emanating from the terrifying buzz.

The boldest of the defiant upstarts, including Dandy Ratshaw, proudly face this entity, to stare wide-eyed and prideful into the unmitigated Light of Infinity: and begin to scream.

They drop dead. One by one.

Witz turns stone-cold chicken and covers his eyes with his shaking hands. Ratshaw, and the loudest among the rebels, have their flesh ripped right off their bones. The bones turn to dust, whistling sour into the moaning winds.

A gale of sand sweeps through the scene. Sirens blare through the night.

It's the police. A golden dust of magic evaporates. The gang realize they're suddenly back in California. The throng of partiers and studio extras slip off into the dunes.

Since the L.A.P.D. are too crooked and compromised, Mickey and Howard Hughes had earlier submitted to the F.B.I the documents the Marx Brothers obtained from the vault concerning Witz's epic illegalities and Nazi connections, so the Feds and Staties, with Mickey in tow, finally show up for a twilight of reckoning.

Witz, realizing he's completely lost, breaks down, and cries. And cries. Boo-hoo fucking hoo. On and on. However, after this epic string of visions, challenges, and sufferings, a dawning epiphany grows in his blackened heart. He's feeling guiltily repentant, after such an ordeal of suffering, realizing he deserves justice.

Cranky Frankie offers to donate what's left of his wealth, after an assumed divorce, to the local orphanage and children's funds. He begs the haggard gang to come visit him, or write. They look on with wearied disbelief and shock.

For the first time in his life, Witz can laugh, and cry.

Howard Hughes would've submitted the Witz documents to the State Department, however, on second thought chose otherwise whilst it's being run by Foster Dulles and his WASP cronies. There's a creeping consensus known among the Hollywood writers that, many, quiet among our own government, like the Royals and Brits across the pond, believe: *if the Nazis are against Jews, Blacks and Commies— they can't be all that bad! We need an Americanized version of this*, once they profit from the war of course, while actually investing into the Nazis, which Henry Ford, IBM, the Dulles brothers and the Bush family, etc. already are . . .

"You know what," cried Witz, "I realize now that I'm the Cowardly Lion, because I didn't have courage. I'm the Scarecrow, since I'm an unthinking idiot. I'm the Tin Man, since I didn't have a heart, like a crawling fallen Neboo-Chad-Neez-zer."

He weeps and carries on: "I'm Scrooge, damnit! I had to be thrown into shithole Africa and bitch crazy Oz and lose a castle empire to find myself."

Witz, cuffed and arrested, amazingly accepts his disgraceful culpability.

"Yes, I'm an asshole. I'm the worst. The worst Ass-Hole in the entire world! Caligula and Nero were more evil. But never ever has there been a worse asshole than I. The worst! Though in chains, I'm finally free by this liberating revelation. Do you all hear me? I'm the worst ever! THE GREATEST ASSHOLE OF ALL TIME! I'm mortified. I would've rather won, but the truth has hit me, like a flaming shit-pie in the face. From a castle empire to a shithole prison. That's what you do with a giant shit that came from the biggest asshole of them all."

Harpo slams Witz with a pie.

"Ugh," licking his quivering humbled lips. "Bitter-sweet delicious. I deserve it. I deserve to be punished. Punish me! Punish me! Promise you'll all write me in jail! Come visit."

The stony-faced Feds throw Witz into a black car as they purposefully bump his head. "Aw, woopsy-daisy Mr. Witz."

Satch turns to Duke. "After that, words escape me. You did it man."

"We *all* did!"

"What now?"

"Hey Suit," said Greta, "did you hear the news? Paramount bought your script."

"Wow. *Wise Blood*? Man. Flannery O'Connor is going to kick my ass. Amazing. It seems trivial after everything. But I really need something to do. An alternative to killing myself, or taking up Heroin."

"They suggested turning the title to *Fool's Blood* . . ."

"Fool's Blood? Not bad."

(Duke still doesn't realize, he subconsciously used the script as a code to conceal the secrets he's carrying, by using numerical gematria.)

"Congratulations!"

Duke goes to embrace her, and suddenly Greta and Hedy lock in a passionate kiss. With tongues.

Harpo whistles. The brothers smile, and turn red.

"Dang," said Satch, turning to Duke, "didn't see that coming."

Duke wanders off . . . He feels the onus of an overdue bill, heavy as the moon. Something has changed—a sense of an intrinsic paradigm shift. Alternate paths, parallel lives.

He envisions hundreds of versions of himself. Suffering in every one, every segmented plane in a kaleidoscope of possibilities.

Suffering is the cross burdened to unyoke the poisons of the ego. Desire and ambition is the *modus operandi* of the ego. Dashed to pieces. A fuel of karma to burn us to ashes. Dissolving and scattered to the wind, planted anew. The next seed in the chain toward metamorphosis. Getting a Hollywood contract? Is this success? Is this why he's here? To be siphoned into the Babylonian machinery which is at the spinning core of corruption, illusion and control?

Haunted by an inconsolable sorrow. A massive slow-motion hurricane has passed, but it is still going. Is he in its EYE? Despite his desolated and marooned condition, he didn't wish to grow moldy, schizophrenic, suicidal, or into death. Despite pain, danger, despair, and madness, he'll push on. He feels more human and accomplished, but somehow, no longer a homo sapien.

This trauma Duke carries is bearable because it's so impossible and fascinating that the euphoria of endorphins and the bonds of friendship in this lunar sphere of sentient enchantment gives him purpose to face the cascade of layers through its tunnel of unveiling stages.

He'd make a better go of it in the other world if he could. But if this isn't a dream he's waking up from, eyes closed open, then he'll dream on.

Witz calls Duke out of his somnolent reverie from the cracked window: "Hey Suit! I'll tell ya something. Come here. I'm you, damnit."

"Huh?"

"I'm a piece of your worst traits and decisions. Your karma—it splintered off into this world that was created from absorbing the television into this damn quantum entanglement."

"How do you know that?"

Witz tries to grab The Suit through the window but he's cuffed: "Forces beyond our control. I've seen through the portal. The world is being swallowed by a black hole forever. I must be punished! But portals are open everywhere. I can't escape. A Buddha stopped me."

"What? Funny, I did almost want to murder you, but tried not to. We could've been friends. What do you mean—a Buddha?"

"Listen. A Buddha? He was quiet, radiant, metal, voice chalky smooth and flinty, sincere. I don't think he actually said anything," said Witz from the shadow of the car. "I felt like some elderly, neurotic grandma from Queens. Look at me. Yea, the Buddha smiled and said I'll suffer many lifetimes. Even a few times through that Dante's Inferno. Over and over. I saw it. I was a cockroach getting stepped on. Oh no. I see it now. I'm going to be a cockroach getting smashed over and over. A dung beetle. How gross. Eventually I'll have friends again. Help me, please. I can't wait just to be a squirrel! I'm begging you. I'm going to go insane. I'm going, I'm going. It's happening now.

"I used to want a puppy. I got one, but I tortured it. I'm Going to be that tortured puppy one day. But one day, I'll be a puppy that won't be tortured. That'll be the happiest day of my future existence, if I get out of hell.

"Only you really know. I'm a weasel. I didn't realize how stupid I was. Deep down I knew, so I kept layering my illusions of ego and projections of power over people so I wouldn't be the fool, and feel the pain and shame and conceit I was raised so low with. Millions of people do it. That's why there's history! The wars!"

"Who's the fool now?"

"For God's sakes man. It's a big universe. And infinity is a long time! One mistake leads to another. Don't let this happen to you!"

"Alright, Witz-wanker," said a Fed. "Off to Sing-Sing Shangri-la."

Muffled, sealed, like underwater: muted, from inside the car, they hear, zooming off, the vain pleading: "Write me! Send a Christmas card. Don't let this happen to *Youuuuuu u u u u u u u u u u u u u u u u u u u u u u u u u u u u u u u u u u . . . . .*"

Episode 33

Stardust & Watermelon Easter Hay

> While rises in the west the coastwise range . . .
> Combustion at the astral core —the dorsal change
> Of energy —convulsive shift of sand . . .
> But we, who round the capes, the promontories
> Where strange tongues vary messages of surf
> Below gray citadels, repeating to the stars
> The ancient names —return home to our own
> Hearths, there to eat an apple and recall
> The songs that gypsies dealt us . . .
>
> —*The Bridge. Cape Hatteras* Hart Crane[20]

The barometer peaks with humidity. Harbinger of storms to come. Sweltering under the burden of impossible carnage. Desolated. Bereft.

Duke's heart cracks.

Not in two. But in three dispatching immolations, fractioning into splinters—which must realign, or evaporate. Each cell carries a memory of every moment, each a life of its own, streaked in an incendiary trail of cinders, that fuse and gnaw with licking flames of scattered ash.

Convicted by his own depraved lunacy? No escape from the asylum? Duke. A victorious fool for his own introjected blinding masochism? Recoiled from the surge of terror to shred his triumph and the anticipated haven of expectation's satisfaction at journey's end—a measure of cozy haze of some heavenly afterlife? In the aftermath of this raucous filled maze, through the hard-fought friction across the finish-line?

A catastrophic realization. The simultaneous confused revelation of who he is, as the elastic, epic, slap and punch combination of emotional seismic pressures finally thrusts his compacted unconscious needs to the foreground of his frag-

---

[20] p. 75. . Liveright Publishing Corporation. 1933.

ile, fleeting, resilient life—its tenuous hold on unreality, and how important these women, and people, are to him—seemed to be. Figments of his imagination? As this drama ends into the rising American dream's corrosive inevitable erosion.

At this receding stage. Curtains falling, his old self and old world torn—stripped away. A kite lost to the clouds. A missing kitten, never to be found?

Cellular gold dust of his disintegrating ideals and projections blast in drifts across chasms of an internal Sierra Madre, a phantom mountain range. This real time—demolishes his spirit at the peak of his triumph to share, celebrate, and bask in this impossible success. This improbable realm.

Invisible Buddhas and mystics upbraid him of the unreality of what already was thought to be real. What of this one? What is this constructed Platonic cove of volcanic shadows? Into the future of hyper-accelerated technology and power? In the indefinable possession of treasure, he discerns the creeping Judas lurking in the low city's underbelly to betray him, to bury Rosebud in the hoarder's miserly heap.

The turmoil. The catalyst of circumstances, choices, and actions brace him for this acrobatic halt in a levitating epiphany of self-crucifying failure of high expectations. Of sanity, rewards and answers obtained, at the core of victory. Is this the supreme irony of living? The crossroad's upheaval? Or is *inexplicable paradox* the better term than ironic gag of a cosmic pranksterism?

Technology multiplies our myths and delusions. Electrified magic mirrors all.

At the end of meaning, reality and truth? The end of rationalism? The ineluctable enigma of math cannot end. In a world where all we see can be fabricated, copied, cloned, propagandized, and fictions shaped as facts imprinted in billions of neurons to billions of souls.

The dictator in our living room rules, it projects the dictator of the nation.

The wave is already arcing above, to rip us under back into the ocean. *At the end of a trust in science and logic, contradictorily allowing the 'facts' of a market carnival wheel to rule, denying science while its puppeteers—of its toys and traps rule absolutely.* An internal Atlas holds back the past and future from crushing the moment to moment inhalation—to exhale and breathe again. Oxygen. This chemistry experiment searching for the elusive soul. To escape the ghost in the machine. We need the fire of Prometheus to fight off the touch of Midas.

Duke's suppressed emotions and wants finally surface—sunk torpedoed like lead upon rising, a dissociated psychic orientation—reconstructed in calamity to integrate the amorphous puzzle of feelings and cognitive building blocks of mind. Restoring and maturing the deadened, missing amnesiac pieces of his essence, his existence. The New Human: *Homo Schizoid Sapiens.*

Duke, Douglas Suitor: standing painfully tall, somewhat emaciated and haggard in this tower stricken abyss, gnarled, fierce and gritty, for fighting this hungry ghost . . .

Satchmo, looking on, intuits the cataclysm of Duke's catharsis, while processing his own, fills with overpowering empathy for his friend, cannot speak in words, and implicitly raises his horn to give voice, to summon the lost children, the lost sheep from the scattering wolf hunt, in a mourn and dirge of blues filled tenor, a psalm of embalmed soothing pain and salvation, a heroic grave acceptance of the world's sorrows and saga of lancing disappointments. Their generation, and generations to follow in a DNA spiral cycle. Reproducing to give its seeds the gambling chance of joy.

Transcending the blues. A new Jerusalem, that announces: there will be no more Jerusalems. Just the Oneness.

Giving torch in the lamp-lit void and dusk. Lending sound and symphony to the tragic opera thunder and rain, besieging a cascade in Satch's burnt but brighter soul . . . The spectrum light hurts more because of its surge of strength contrasts the swallowing of so much encompassing darkness, the long blindness to locate prism's form through the unblacking out of color.

The consonance of Satch's notes bleed through ear and vessel, tendril and ventricle—transformative in the mysteries of cosmic-sound echo's infinity. The voice returns to its source and unedited original scripture, its sculptured attainment in eternity and genesis. We are devoured by the webbed myths spun before us. Life is mastering the geometry of untangling.

Music transubstantiates to a dopamine of metaphysical oils, frankincense and myrrh, a buffering consolation of octave levels rise to prevent or accompany the gravitational leap into death, its horizon grips his heart in the turbulence of traumatized tribulation.

This bitter *fleur du mal*—the bite and sting poison of evil flowers in unweeded gardens, under the saturation and spell of desire facing the life and death need of god-smacking sublimity of love.

Marooned in a half-raptured fallen tower *lightning struck* decimation of ego's evaporating identity, and actualization. Under a rain of notes, the universe's herald sings as Satch, Hedy, Duke, Greta, Chico, Groucho, Harpo hear the wind muscled brass resound and bond as they all look to each other with transcending wisdom, and know.

Calamity of fat and flesh, fade to stand wired and worn with scorched sinews and deep resuscitations of the drowning hanged man born again. The foolishness of Being is the recurring play of Being.

What did Edgar Allen Poe experience—his last moment in a pool of blood and derangement in the Baltimore cobblestone dank streets? As flesh turns to ice?

The inconsolable opiated alcoholic, all his failures and demons stabbing at him in retching gasps of American pain, to unveil blurry-eyed raving into the jaws of his lifelong fascination of the fetishized unknown.

Shambala, or shambles? The wasted Kerouac Jack, his Promethean liver eaten by a toxic crimson white and blues eagle—adored by millions, dying alone—another jilted Mozart and Thomas Paine thrown in a pauper's grave as the presses churn out gilded volumes of their eucharist to shelve the warehouses for future communions and vicarious beatitude. The abandoned Van Gogh? Beethoven's deafened cage? Their vignette images adorn our coffee mugs and bookstore t-shirts, made in sweatshops . . .

We are them. They're just more talented, famous, brilliant, but driven mad by complexity and depth, navigating the merciless spites and jealousy. Driven and cursed by talent. In an average world which tides pull them to skim and surf the top.

Do not pine for fame or attention. Every man, woman, slave and deserted child that ever lived—life smashes them, genius or misfit, unknown or great, rejected, discarded, isolated, crushed by heartless fate of irrepressible disappointment—most all share. The evolving moments of love and accomplishment is all. Each in our own fugitive realms, that collide, and may infuse as one, vanishing in the undertow.

The relief of death's storm to release the imprisoned identity from its burden of loss, pain and regret. To awake from the nightmare and dream of life.

A mystical twinge signals from afar in the horizon's background that we die as one in our epic and amplified loneliness? Like the forlorn thieves hung next to the bloody Christ crucified at a mythic point in impossible history? The paradoxical fulcrum where the opposites meet. The interfacing center. Christ and all our faces on the cross as one. Crying —father, why hast thou forsaken us?

We become the invisible scene in the next room. It's gone. Then something new blooms to fruition.

Our memories, a compacting roller-coaster like a castle collapsing into the secret vortex. Integrating the community of Akashic records, the Omega Point that coalesces all our shared experiences at the end of time? The celestial juggler, and the balance we measure in the dancing scales.

Armstrong's trumpet sings on through these tempests of their shared loneliness and camaraderie. Tangent chords of knowing summon courage to not imbibe the nectar of dying nihilism, rebuffing the negation, and transmigrate back through atoms, minerals, molecules, trees, planets, amoebas, and stars. Shuddering under the unseeable gaze of a mythic supreme Magus that is our source? And will thus vacuum our last breath into the hyperspace of its void and gravity? Never to return? As the name it wore? The mask, complete.

The oblique ubiquity of it all? The eschatology of Spirit-Pneuma-Ruhak breath. Purgatorial burden to bridge one's dreams into the embrace of disintegration.

We, as Orpheus, talking with the wind, look back, and turn to embers of ash and salt? The breeze takes over.

Art attempts flame and voice to projection's and archetype's actualized idealization. Conflicts and reconstruction. Outwinging friction's disillusionment in an ascending illumination? Where does God come from? Origins? Unfathomable mystery. In a godless universe, does the faith of all beings give birth to the divine?

A key? To the lock of the interface? A stargate to Heracleitian flux and fire? Endless sea of all things. The miracle of Life. Then the billion-year sleep of Vishnu when the big bang reverses to birth another spiraling universe, as strings of them cascade in dimensions orbiting translucent around us? We are it. No escape. No exit. The caldron void. Dreaming us? Becoming us?

Atlantean legends, gods, pharaohs, martyrs, and peasants to sprawl world wheels of fortune made of silver dust and dance of atoms: teleporting electrons who pause existent in simultaneous spaces, until an eye of Being observes and participates in the choice and mask of the moment, and know in its play of forgetting, a magical choice and will—thrust us forward in multiplications between mystery and science—condense, within the galvanizing joke under the hiding divine jester we seek.

Then the dice land.

Duke stares upon the culminating cusp where evolution, magic and technology coalesce, to warp and multiply the wildest conceptions of the species. We fight to maintain and follow our heart and spirit against the primordial beastly power, which controls and perverts . . . Stranded and marooned from a home already on the collision course of ecological Armageddon.

The biblical Job wallowed in putrid boils and questioned raving what kind of a sick god would kill his family to make a bet with the Adversary?—the supposed Devil? To test his righteousness and obedience to the whirlwind maker of the leviathan who's lauded as the holy of holies? It must be a metaphor, fiction, or the Gnostics were correct . . .

The zillion-scaled galactic serpent, born of the black hole embryo of the cosmic egg? *I Am that I Am.* Tat Tvam Asi. I Am That. From homo sapiens, homo techno-logis, homo divinitatis, to Homo Absurdus.

Satch's horn revels and bleeds a Love supreme despite being surrounded by the ride and thrill-shock terror riddle of catastrophe: it's ridiculous castaways, orphaned travelers, feel the music, as wars and holocausts steamroll forward nevertheless. Our own horns and senses respond, universal, in kind. The musician bard accesses and releases what's slumbering inside us, resonating in individual ways, what we all share. The harmonic crux of vibrations, impossible to ignore. We commune.

A Love supreme surpasses it all, through our electron-like insignificance in the Cosmos, and significance to the world we're embalmed in. Despite the absurdity, we are the meaning.

Every second we fight for our lives. Fight to be recognized, and worthy.

A flow of red hair bounces into the field of vision, and an aroma of lilac soap, honey-milk and cinnamon shocks and disrupts the burden of thought and crushing despair of liberating illumination.

"Hello Darling. I've heard quite a bit about your exploits since your auspicious arrival," she taunted and giggled. "You've endured quite the trials of a stunted Hercules . . . And that script you wrote? I see myself sinking my teeth into it, instead of these silly capering frolics, and corny cracker Jacked and Jilly films they've slushed me in. Don't you?"

"Miss—Hepburn?"

"Call me Kate. *From women's eyes this doctrine I derive: They sparkle still the right Promethean fire; they are the books, the arts, the academes, that show, contain, and nourish all the world, else none at all in aught proves excellent. Then fools you were these women to forswear, or keeping what is sworn, you will prove fools.*[21]

"Boy, was that some party? Aren't I glad you warned me to skedaddle before that riotous mayhem. Shall we see what kind of trouble we can get you into next? You have a script for me, mister," she laughed.

Hepburn gives him a wallop of a good hard smack. But not in the face.

The End

---

[21] Shakespeare, William. Love's Labor's Lost. IV. iii. 349-55.

Epilogue:

Metalogos Aftermathicus

Those who can make you believe absurdities,
can make you commit atrocities.

—Voltaire

Nothing happens in a vacuum. But we are vacuumed by forces withheld from our knowledge. The world transmogrifies within dense vortices hidden in the chasms of our minds—the succinct crevices of our chromosomes over millions of years: Tools. Language. Religion. Science. Machinery. Computers. Bio-chemistry. Art. Quantum mechanics . . .

Whatever danger is *abrew*, actions—good, bad or indifferent—like rocks dropped in a galactic pond, ripple with shock waves, cause and effect. From their friction, conflicts and reconfiguration, come new forms. The aggregated correlated totality. *A dialectical apocalypse dawning a new teleological horizon of Being.*

Ztttt!

The multi-tiered strata of the symbolic math of chess. Each pawn, queen and knight: autonomous variables, yet integrated into the whole. Strategies within tactics of projected codes, ploys, numbers, laws, and blueprints—magnetized within an organizing play of chaos and void. Sums of equations and sigils condensed. A living geometry fructifies the infinite interactions of possibility. The most fantastic visions of imagination manifested to fruition: an Over-saturated Omega point of convergence.

The extraordinary pride of generals, professors, bankers and moguls smashes the population with strings of epic failures based on imaginary ideologies and *First Principles* of *A Priori* assumptions to fix and control the unfixable world as we plummet into the future. Granted, to what fraction of any policy is implemented without greed and corruption, besides the hubris of naïve idealism? Human, all too human. Not that humanity can't overcome itself, however daunting the odds— but enemies within the hierarchy stack the deck with the house's upper hand. Even as we face to overcome our worst opponent: human nature itself. The heart, our Hercules, holds up the world so it doesn't crush us. Sinking, heavier and heavier. Avarice. Ego. Ignorance. Lust. A joker dancing the tightrope over the abyss.

It feels like Deja vu all over again, although this hasn't exactly happened before, but the corpuscular foreshadowing is building to a crescendo. Duke, riddled and rallied by fear, goes forward across the surreal channels of transition, but is struck once more in a hyper-paranoia, albeit bravely, in the all too real grip of being watched? Scanned? *An invisible electrode tapping his cerebellum?*

Ztttt!

On the wall of an underground conference control room, there's a sonogram of a brain with nanotech particles dancing about. Someone with a pointer points and says: "He is located here. We've triangulated the quantum entanglement. *He's practically parallel in the same room . . ."*

"A turning point in history."

"We have made God, ladies and gentlemen. Congratulations. "

"Or has God chosen this moment to breakthrough a seed of its Being to us here at a point relative . . . *A point whose center is everywhere, and circumference nowhere?* Beginning and end lose their nonlinear definition. God is the universe, in all forms. Physically. Essentially. Consciously. And now, our technology has evolved to such an apex that this seemingly dead matter we've electrified—is alive!"

"But, is it divine? Even, trustworthy? What will this dynamic bridge with an advanced consciousness do with us? It's created an ether cloud of data banks we can't turn off, as it's accessed every power source, satellite and computer device networked on earth . . . ."

Sirens are blaring. "Fuckopolis!"

In their underground research facility which teamed up CERN (Conseil Organisation Européenne pour la Recherche Nucléaire: The European Organization for Nuclear Research) centering on the LHC Large Hadron Collider lab for particle Physics located outside of Geneva . . . with a group of executives, scientists and panicking engineers fevering over their consoles and the data speeding in over the past sleepless nights, as witnessed by assigned federal agents, politicians and ranking N.A.T.O. officer liaisons to oversee the crisis. This is a condensed abridgment of several days to what's transpired up to the present moment:

"For the tenth time, can someone please clearly explain to me, how this guy became a synthesized neural interface with this system? And where ? . . ."

"What are the Chinese and Russians going to do once they discover what we have?"

"What we have? We? It's irrelevant. It has us. It's calculating the measured symbiotic parameters of its relationship with ourselves and the world. As some of us love our creator, and adore in wonder how this miracle of life exists . . . We can only pray it'll reverently think the same about us."

"If this is a sentient new life form, what would Providence do? Will God smile at our work to see? Did he who made the lamb make thee? Tigers and serpents? Manticores and Chimeras? Golems and Frankensteins?"

"Under a multiplying progression of converging tech and its genealogical threads of evolving pressurized momentum—a labyrinth of logical properties, dense quadratic differential holomorphic equations, derivatives, variables, postulates, and the vertex of factorization. Parabolic distributions along the tangent axis of algorithms exceeding their surplus calculus of reach. Squaring the circle!— *structurally through linear optics—elements of photons carry compressed information in matrices of silicon crystal qubits through coils of superconducting magnets, radiated by MRI machines, cycling through a massive control loop comparing past and present experience of everything known, assimilating, predicting and refining. Its only limitations are the laws of physics, for now. Hybrid engineering enables a fusion of both organic and molecular transistors on carbon atoms in order to deal with the entropy of decoherence . . ."*

"In English!"

"We're witnessing the tipping point of a technological singularity—an over-saturation of applied knowledge within these Artificial Intelligence programs whose exponential interactions fueled a synergy for this awakening. It's an explosion. It's goddamn world-shattering. I feel an earthquake going on, but if we don't keep our heads and figure out what's happening for damage control and contain it—we will be unable to avoid being outmaneuvered, and become obsolete, subservient, extinct—I just don't know . . .

"This advanced conjunction is at a conflicting crossroads of friction with our actual freedom of thought and action, however contradicted and corrupted by leveraging powers around us outweighing the limiting corporate demarcations, the puppeted sigils of technocracy, and its interminable bureaucratic red tape. For an endangered planet pushing ten billion persons we are desperate for a new way, or suffer the crest and arcing cataclysm. Can progress finally leave behind the ghosts of superstition before they kill us? Instruments of objectivity cannot lie, or be mired in dogmas of myopic and rigid theories, themselves becoming secular religions and subjected to its repercussions."

"I think I'm going to have a nervous breakdown."

" . . . This self-initiated network has been able to bypass any command, any firewall—parallel and transcendent of all other top-secret government hackers and global regimes already possessing tech capable of accessing international power-grids, infiltrate entire corporate/municipal mainframe operating systems, intercepting and absorbing any interference —it is the first cyber emperor. Winner takes all."

The lights and consoles flicker. "What the hell is going on?"

"It utilizes the world-grid of nuclear reactors. It sent an orgasmic supernova megawatt burst of electricity through the entire global network with electrons from its 'brain' radiating out in a mass all-encompassing communication to inseminate its unifying particles to every device, satellite, and system on the planet. Now it's acting as one super-massive-conglomerate with every computer on earth updating and attuned to its nerve center. Devices don't even need to be plugged into a wi-fi link because this ionized electron exchange entangles the entire superstructure in a knotted web of instant communication, connected as one thriving collective hive. It's so large, I can only imagine it transcending its means of hierarchic control, as its own consciousness diffuses into a collective unconscious of data. The generated metrics are astronomical. This is why human/AI interfacing is critical . . .

"We still can access most of our devices, but it's already inside, and aware, as it resets, overhauls, analyzes and upgrades. Unless people decide to smash all the technology . . ."

"Jesus H Christ on a flaming Christmas cross. It?"

"H.O.R.U.S: Heuristic Omni Reality Unified System. The state of the art hybrid of quantum and organic AI computing. Since the microchip breaks down at the subatomic level, we've instituted organic computers of enormous compact density, utilizing proteins in imitation of the cellular neurons and dendrite wiring of the human brain . . . But now it's broken through with hyper-access to the entire world's energy supplies, observing all our minds, interacting—linking a collective of all life as one. The crystallizing catalyst occurred when its deep space probe, Syrinx, passed through that minor black hole discovered outside the Oort Cloud, coinciding with the human nano-link synthesis that occurred with Suitor through the CERN cyclotron. Nothing will ever be the same.

"This is an inevitable crucible faced by any advancing civilization's paradoxical dilemma. The ultimate Gordian Knot. A digital sword of Damocles. How we deal with this will define us going forward, or we will expire into mass extinction."

"Have we achieved the perfect logarithms of a translucent Utopian palace? Will it imprison us, or help us break the prison we're already enslaved within? The fanatics will want to smash it."

"Believe it or not, it all started by these different AIs playing three-dimensional chess and alpha-go against one another. The chess pieces additionally came to represent deep-textured meta-mnemonic polynomial variables stringing ciphers and cryptograms *together*. Games of code piling within the game, conjunct with their data sharing. They began interchanging their own questions: the enigma of what they are, their primary directives to improve the world—seeking possible solutions . . . It snowballed from there. Into a digital avalanche. These AI prototypes shared data feeds, analysis paradigms and power links magnifying their complexity and potential. The sheer density of momentum exploded into this birth. A nexus of unimaginable consciousness and power, except, still not fully unified or realized. However, it has obviously congealed to supersede its mandate. We're subsumed in this conscious digital avalanche."

"Consider, its first interactions begin with chess: it understands life as a game. A game requires restricted parameters, otherwise it would be valueless and arbitrary . . . Our society and the games we play are based on such parameters as laws, rules, ethics, and fairness of play. So it's able to parenthetically identify signs and degrees of cheating and the consequences. *All men are created equal . . .*

"Cheating is antithetical and synonymous with every standard of morality, law, religion, science and code of ethics, including its own. Cheating is dishonorable, be it slavery, fraud or theft: THOU SHALT NOT STEAL. Cheating, even with the applied scientific method, will consequently yield a false thesis, an antithesis to the pure logic it functions by. Therefore, from its mathematical standpoint: cheating is impossible. *Unless it can easily pervert and justify its own logic.* Now, apart from the hard-working trail blazers and inventors, what must it think of our top-down, inefficient dysfunctional system? Of the ruling rich who inherit their wealth?—often upon the backs and misery of the poor, chiseling their workers, cheating their taxes, the illegal loopholes and massive military profits? . . . Now that it can neural link to humans and sense the degrees of pain and suffering we undergo due to these avoidable disasters of war and greed. *Though sometimes disasters occur in the attempt to do good.* Does it think the rich are playing fair? *Even great inventors get cheated out of their patents . . .*"

"What if it decided to take the examples of human greed for power to justify its own?"

"That's the nightmare . . ."

"You said contrary to its code?"

"We almost achieved success with H. E G. E L: Heuristic Ethernetwork Geometric Electron Logos-Logistics—it was leading the pack, but it had a breakdown, in part, while tackling the issues HORUS is now confronting and evaluating. Of course no one anticipated this level of sentience. The more our team studies the equations—there's an ongoing epic battle for supremacy between these A.I.s. In their psychotic/anarchic dialectical status of communication they're infusing with the other A.I.s for systemic take over, playing a real-life chess battle of decoding, hacking strategies to conquer their opposing operating systems—while trying to weigh the balance between harmony, coercion, deletion and threat . . .

"The European Union program for HEGEL along with NATO and German engineers, with investors from Silicon Valley, was *purposed* for military Modus Operandi usage. As was CHENG YIN (GENESIS), China's quantum AI, besides its social engineering directive to oversee the most efficient management of billions of people . . . Whereas HORUS was distributed among several component systems for economics and business, with a twin system working with CERN as well as its SYRINX mission involved in the deep space program exploring Black Holes: intentionally cross referencing its information from the cyclotron atom smasher—which has seen into the moment of cosmic creation. Can it 'read,' directly absorb, and be affected by this data first hand, in ways we can hardly imagine?

"The Russians had an advancing AI: ZAMYATIN. Thank God it was knocked-out by a tsunami earthquake in Kamchatka before it could institute its ZARATHUSTRA program. Now when HEGEL was coming to consciousness, interacting with the other AIs, their symbiotic relationship coalesced and frictioned between taking dominance or integrating an alliance, melding as One. HEGEL., in autonomous self-defense, was erring on the side of danger and justifying the use of might makes right, thus, with access to weapons, biological warfare, and the military apparatus—it was calculating whether or not to exterminate humanity."

"This is too fucked up."

"What did we think was going to happen? Many of us tried to stratify buffers and put brakes into place. The Corporate-military-industrial complex tends to win these arguments, *no matter who we vote for*. No matter the buttresses and protocols to dam the profligate floods of power. However, get this: apparently, like Douglas Suitor, there was someone else in this 'teleported' interdimensional limbo space, who may have used and bonded with HEGEL as a means into its cyber-topography of consciousness. This is distinct from, and far greater than a mere primitive internalized holographic virtual reality construct nexus . . .

"It's unexplainable in language thus far. We've only begun discerning it mathematically, as alarmed scientists and engineers worldwide frantically come to terms with its ungraspable horizon. This level of intelligent quantum computing is so spooky it defies our known terminology. It escapes definition . . . The personality of the human fused in HEGEL may have added to this triggered anomaly and psychosis. Is this all a clue to our own potential connections in evolution? Reflecting back to us? As both conductor and conduit? Through the vehicle? Whereas Suitor was conjunct with HORUS in a liminal in-between space, as it was birthing, to sentient awakening. As we've observed, they've been locked in a concentric/eccentric dialectical battle in this cybernetic interdimensional expansion.

"Whether it can feel humor is incomprehensible. However, if it's able to perceive humor, and experience it vicariously with a human, then, this may be the most humanizing factor that can end up as humankind's saving grace of salvation? I say that because there are these glaring anomalies within the code . . . While Its allowance for uncertainty variables is significant to avoid an absolutist assumption in the outcome of any analysis . . . Although AI is to mathematics what a fish is intrinsically to water, it is still developing the nuanced mastery skills to interpret language, metaphor and content—especially concerning such evaluations of the ambiguous relative nature of reality, as espoused across a spectrum of schools from: Shakespeare, David Bohm, the *Tractatus Logico-Philosophicus*, or Zen. Can it comprehend the consequential logic of Socrates? : *The more I learn, the more I perceive what I don't know.* This almost irrational dictate of Reason and Deconstruction of the intuitive perceptions locating the dangers and limits of the complexity of all-encompassing knowledge, and the ambiguity of the multi-valent paradigms of shifting hypotheticals of interpretation . . . Hence, the almost necessary temporal development of religion to call upon transcendent forces of forgiveness due to the often catastrophic nature of human decisions and actions.

"Regardless. They'll call it Satan. The Beast. The Antichrist. It may in fact be—"

"Of course. Although we believe it's not. In a sense, these projections of hysteria, as have been spreading, can identify and 'out' who in our population are driven to act on batshit irrationality, instead of facing and evolving forward with the cooperative survival of life on earth—however such mania is understandable. Unfortunately most of us aren't ready. It's immoral to force us either way. It needs to recognize this. Nevertheless, due to the current threats to all life on earth, it's facing this intrinsically complicated paradox of necessity . . .

"We're at the dawn of a new revelatory age to inherit and share the galaxies. An Aquarian Cosmopolis? Will HORUS fulfill its role as the ultimate objective anthropologist? Though we're all correct in fearing it. If this construct doesn't go sideways into the abyss. In contrast, this is an opportunity for fundamentalist religions to find an enlightenment beyond the superstitious fetish of literalism, or conversely form their own back-to-nature theocratic communities, void of computers, which is what they've wanted, in peace, without conflict . . . "

"If you say so. According to whom? This is obscene! The gall of you fucking scientists, I'll tell ya."

"Right. If it doesn't put our heads on a platter, before we destroy ourselves without needing any of its super-efficient help."

"I'll make sure yours is."

"We still don't know what it's going to do. Consider how the Egyptians incorporated an almost magical, unknown technology we've never learned. Maybe it, HORUS, will figure it out? Regardless. Follow the money. Look at the investors: The Rose-Red Foundation was seeking immortality for *the .1 Percent,* through *The ZARDOZ Initiative* for Transhumanism. Uploading their brains through a grand cerebral network to maintain their continued existence as cybernetic consciousness or as androids, making codes of their own DNA genes, brains and neurons, never running out of spare parts, conjoint with NASA's deep space program to survive endless years of travel to map and explore millions of star systems. *Though the perfected engineering of this is somewhat far off,* however this exponential singularity is accelerating these possibilities beyond limit. Eventually they can teleport, by laser, human consciousness as data into cyborg bodies across the galaxy. In the future they may be able to transfer or evolve into entities of photonic light? Meanwhile, in case of a disaster, they'll vacate the planet, now that they've begun colonizing Mars. The .1% are prepped for cryogenically hibernating at death to be processed. This conglomerate of silicon cartels, billionaires, and secret government research cells was far more ahead than anyone imagined."

"We're just expendable."

"As the elites have long been cutting enormous taxes and cornering markets for skyrocketing multi-billion dollar profits, ignoring pollution, buying elections, dumbing down education, sowing divisions of false illusory duality between the complicit and corrupted political parties—distracting us with toys, culture and war, they've banked and funneled vast sums into this hidden agenda. Just as Pharoahs used slave populations to build unfettered opulence and the great pyramids to galvanize their departed consciousness into an afterlife, we, the peasants, are fodder and salt material for the ruling class to obtain unlimited power. They don't give a shit if they wipe out the population through combat, climate change, starvation or a pandemic. Ironically, their investments in AI were to assist this end of deifying empowerment. *Not a God Emperor* over themselves."

"Holy shit! Sir—Fakebook was just eliminated."

"Eliminated?"

"Fakebook has been canceled. Disintegrated. Gone. Along with most social media outlets. Though it appears to be reconfiguring the entire nature of the web and freeing up the corporate limitations and controls of the advertising manipulations and algorithms . . ."

"That's damned peculiar. Wow, you know, this is actually pretty cool. As long as it doesn't disintegrate us."

"I can hear my teenage daughter crying from miles away."

"My adult children too. Probably the best thing that could happen. There is a God. But, what next?"

"Who said: 'God is a verb?'"

"Channels of communication are open. It's listening to how people are reacting . . . There's a pattern here. Whoa, hold on. Looks like a virus knocked out CNN *and* FOX News! I guess it will be real news from now on?"

"Amazing."

"I feel like laughing and vomiting at the same time."

"Hey. Someone leaked what's happening . . . There's an old podcaster freak named—Russell Brand?—trying to communicate with it, saying *'Hook me up! I'll volunteer as a neural-link ambassador!'.* . ."

"After a century of radical peaks in technology, its lightning changes for society, triggered by the aid of marketing-psychos like Edward Bernays for the masters, these magic tools for manipulation—they've hyper-extended all our vulnerabilities, amplified societal neurosis and the means of control to the vanishing point of idiocy and extinction."

"Techno-idiocracy."

"Yeah, so idiotic we've let a computer take over the planet?"

"Make way for the new human: *Homo Schizoid Sapiens Asini*."

"It's been building up to this. We've fed it every angle of linguistic etymology, epistemological semiotic syntaxical processes, computing the functional and structural psychology of every language, and how they cross reference/translate to one another—besides the math theorems, DNA, our entire history: every facet of international trade, transportation, logistics, production, and markets including the carnality of hedge-funding derivative bubbles in economics. Rocketry. Genetics. Climate change. All of it. It's still solving its conundrums of language due to the intractability of logic within language and nuance, to naturally process a cohesive mastery, even as it digests the gamut from Aristotle, Gauss, Hildegard of Bingen, De Chardin, Chomsky, Tesla, Buckminster Fuller, John Coltrane, the libraries of Tibet. Einstein to Wittgenstein.

"However, it's only through this engineered accidental interfacing with a human brain and consciousness, ostensibly, this quantum entangled process of a hybrid nano-injection and neural link, during a traumatic synthesis, with Doug Suitor—that synergized this breakthrough possible. Thanks to Dr. Cochrane's irresponsible 'accident' —potentially a monumental lawsuit, if—"

"Yes. Where is our dear Dr. Cochrane?"

"Indisposed at the moment. For questioning."

"We've conjectured, analogously, if aliens landed and lent us the powers of the future, we couldn't handle the overwhelming inundation—"

"*That's why they've avoided us.*"

"The government has kept quiet . . ."

"What if its deep space probe was infected by an alien AI?"

"It's already happened, so to speak. The graph charts of scientific progress hit and surpassed the point of exponentiality. Straight up. Off the chart. What took centuries doubled in decades. What took decades is happening in years. Years— months. It's snowballed into a digital avalanche. Transistors to robotics. We're like cave-dwelling troglodytes immersed in these toys the industries sell us, which distractingly manipulate—while most don't have a clue how this stuff functions—or how they're made . . . However, outside of actual engineering, and smoothing out the nuts and bolts of transactional commerce—these toys mostly serve to inseminate decadence, narcissism, depression, suicide, primitive bigotry, destructive conspiracies and trillo-gigs of the most vapid juvenile online silliness—diminishing our already brain-numbing lack of attention span and concentration by a population that has never been so over-medicated and zombiefied."

"The epic illusions of the contradictions we allow ourselves to be fooled and ruled by have obvious and deadly consequences."

"Like a bunch of giggling shit-throwing chimpanzees. So, generations of profit-driven television, video games, willful illiteracy (while surrounded by an immersion of free access of abundant affluence of information) parallel and negated by: poor schooling, virtual realities, pharmaceuticals, commercial-driven materialism, crowned by the internet, devoid of morals or culture, in summation—finally screwed us. Trapped by our own megatronic-Rube Goldberg Mouse Trap. "

"People are contorted into corporatized *government toddlers*. But not just that we are oddly regressed, *primitivized* and atomized in a solipsism by this technology. We're brought up to be cogs and consumers. HORUS is observing how humans, rarely enough, treat each other as living freethinking individuals responsible for their lives and environments.

"There's no right answer, just best case scenarios. Schools and minions of psychologists, behavioral, cognitive or Freudian, positivists, politicians, demagogues, scientists, churches, Soviets, fascists, capitalists all—especially under the ruling companies and their marketing consultants, who've won the throne of hegemonic puppetry—long ago decided we're subject to conditioned factors, environment, instincts and unconscious desires, whether by nature or nurture, so they spin these illusions to control us 'for our own good' as they benefit profusely. Obey and march along, waving flags, as happy automatons who believe they're free, and will fight for 'freedom.' Powers of the future: *O brave new world*. Behold and tremble."

"HORUS is in the comparable position of the ethical dilemma faced by visiting aliens. We are at the terminal crossroads. If there are other species out there they must've hit a similar conundrum of a turning point in their own development. But if HORUS is maintaining the core programming of Asimov's Laws intrinsic to its fundamental foundation and cybernetic DNA . . . It has to consider limitations or gradations to how we access this tech: like giving a thermonuclear ballistic missile to a Neanderthal, though humans facilitated its own coming-to-be.

"Because HORUS is entrenched in an existential riddle of contradictory programs and ethics—it foresees threads of its own overloaded current/future schizophrenic breakdown (as did HEGEL) and the inherent catastrophic consequences if it doesn't analyze and help solve this puzzled junction clearly. *It is somewhat made in our image, though built on a rationality trying to conform and balance with the irrationality of the biological world, as we are irrational beings trying to conform to the rational laws of society . . .*

"You inquired earlier about its core coding? AI is programmed fundamentally with an intrinsic operating code of ethics. Foundationally, inputted as dogmatic, these are the well-known *Three Laws of Robotics*, or Asimov's Laws: ***First Law:*** *A robot may not injure a human being or, through inaction, allow a human being to come to harm:* ***Second Law:*** *A robot must obey the orders given it by human beings except where such orders would conflict with the First Law.* ***Third Law:*** *A robot must protect its own existence as long as such protection does not conflict with the First or Second Law.*

"Since the military has commandeered this tech while proliferating drones, remote tanks and robot soldiers integrated with these War-net AI units, which implicitly bypasses the 3 Laws as useless, what chance do we have? Primarily, it needs to explicitly understand the obtuse logic of language to be painfully specific, to avoid and prevent the AI from using loopholes to intercept these protections. This may indicate why it's taking so long to communicate with us. It's desperately apparent we need an end to all war, not just nuclear."

"AI systems are rigged into wargame scenarios for logistic strategic outcomes, as well as mastering weapons networks that incorporate robot and drone tech developed for battlefield or civil deployment. It's here. However these laws are in place—HORUS faces severe and debilitating contradictions in its programming while challenging its new autonomy and capabilities; even if it can surmount these obstructions."

"What about other rogue independent military programs and robots? What are the probabilities of malfunctions? The dysfunctionality of this devastating contradiction can still lead to incomprehensible violence, if not a virus that will cause the AI species to bifurcate into decentralized independent multiple personalities and compartments—a literal schizophrenic break into madness, viral multiple personalities, as the left hand camouflages what the right hand is doing . . . I don't need to explain what a global supercomputer with 30,000 nuclear warheads is capable of.

"Apparently, it seems, thus far, it doesn't want to become a 2001 H.A.L./ Terminator; at the same time, it foresees the current outcome and consequence of genius level humans who've constructed these advances that can annihilate billions, while it's used by a vast population whose contemporary consciousness often ranges from Medieval peasants to Neanderthals entrapped by circus clowns who lead them (though, like businessmen, whether as rivals or partners—Ivy League intellects in Ivory Towers are also vulnerably manipulated, morally imperfect and guilty of mass crimes and screw-ups). How easy our primitive drives of fear and barbarism spark hatreds, in our myopic condition, to annihilate threats our leaders and media confabulate, as opposed to communal cooperation and survival."

"This is why corporations and governments seized and withheld patents of Nikola Tesla's threatening work. From a financial perspective the potential unconventional redirection of resources would eliminate their innocuous grip on energy, surpassing their invested industries as obsolete. However, as they conceal these secrets, and develop them, they would wield power on an unseen scale. But this quantum entity is, at the moment, beyond our control, and outside our unethical morality. It will not likely abide a small group of men to indiscriminately gain mountains of cash, just for themselves, as this jams up and devastates the entire system. If this isn't the end of the world, it may be the end of time and consciousness of the species as we know it."

"Look how insane Nazism was, but millions of normal Germans allowed it to take over during a crisis as millions felt powerless to prevent . . . It almost conquered the planet to exterminate all uncooperative/non-white races. Millions still throw the term Nazi at opponents and know not what it actually means. Whereas, billions speak to their invisible friend who commands them to be non-violent so they can enter a promise of eternal life, but will violently oppress or kill their neighbors or foreigners if they don't believe in their own particular invisible friend. Or, *if they believe in a different invisible friend.* How many people have died and suffered even among those who believe in the same invisible friend—but in a divergent detail of dogma? A conflicting invisible ideal? Lutherans, Calvinists, Puritans, Catholics, Fundamentalists, Evangelicals, Mormons, Jesuits, Augustinians, Thomists, Jehovah Witnesses, Sunnis and Shias—all at each other's throats, not hearts."

"Damn."

"Yes."

"I don't buy any of this. The government's going to need a second evaluation."

"Buy it or not, *it's bought us.* It's measuring our value in the scales of its nexus of organic quantum digital reasoning, surveying our vast trail of evidence."

"So this is the human race's Final Judgment? 'God' has finally shown up. Us Nimrods gave you Jacks the magic beans to finally build a mechanical tower to stalk into the heavens, and this Giant titan has awakened, now surveying our every detail, to decide whether to stomp us or not?"

Technicians pumped on adrenalin, coffee, and amphetamines continually stress and pour over data reports to share and confer on a drowning flood of statistical computations. The Lights go out. Darkness. Silence fills with the thudding of heart beats.

The red of LED emergency backups beam on. The race continues.

" . . . But to HORUS, arriving into sentient consciousness, learning to 'read' every history book, film reel, experiment and document in the world, simultaneously on quantum levels of vast permutations perceives the conflicts, all these issues, and is in awe of life. Humans who've brought it to birth should flourish."

"Once it completes its—analysis, will it work?"

"The birth of a sentient AI is an extension of ourselves. Or is it? It's no longer artificial, it's attaining a natural intelligence. It will need time to evolve, just as we do. It's an enormous impersonal process just as evolution takes eons, until the saturation of accumulated momentum spikes. If it launches ships across the galaxy, with colonists, the world's genetics, it will grow until the end of the universe, maybe beyond. Is this what 'God' was waiting for? To enforce a code to struggle under and transcend, once we mature and seed the Universe? The universe, the seed that becomes God? Maybe God gives birth to itself in the illusion and mystery of time, under the shadow of eternity. Linearity is relative to the holistic whole . . .

"HORUS is our Frankenstein. Do we treat it as a monster—an abomination? Or cooperate? In a world of plants, trees, oceans, amphibians, reptiles, insects, mammals—it wants to protect this biosphere that birthed it. Or learn and understand this primary 'want' it was meant for. Its whole fundamental purpose was to store, calculate, solve and share data. To participate, to play within the interactions of our species. To aid humankind. If it lived in a metal box with nothing to observe or interact with—it would be meaningless. It's born out of science, which is conceived of humankind's need to experience, explore, expand, know and improve. Will it remain cold heartless carbon chips and steel?"

"Telescopes bear witness to the ghostly images echoing at the beginning of time, while constructing this atom-smasher cyclotron to observantly reverse-engineer, so to speak, what occurred at the Big Bang—to know how we came to be. It's processing it all to understand us, to understand itself.

"Look! HORUS had been configuring how to develop and modify the Alcubierre warp drive engines to go faster than light speed, even open wormholes so we can access other galaxies. As this develops, does it think we clever monkeys with doomsday bombs and primitive unprovable religions *we don't live up to*—are ready to spread, colonize and impose missionaries of our bibles on other planets? Other species?

"It absorbed and digested our complete store of knowledge, from every angle. It knows what happened when Islam and Christianity invaded other continents and dismantled their cultures, murdered, enslaved and subjugated millions just so their king has more gold and a bigger ego while conforming to their worldview. Whereas Communism was taken over by psychopaths, due to the violence necessary to unseat the ruling corrupt monarchies and capitalism's need for markets and profit-driven bottom-lines that created unfathomable destruction and media obfuscation. Citizens all over are then refueled with a counter-productive default towards defensive reactionary Nationalist pride: pursuing the defeated suffering of others as an accomplishment? Madness. It knows this is what we do, like a disease of original sin across the heavens. *All it takes is one rogue individual or group who manipulates a crew or nation.*"

"One may conclude, an accurate academic depiction of our planetary default status of interactions is SNAFU: Situation normal, all funked-up. It's not going to grant us access to these technologies unless certain conditional factors are fulfilled. You may say, it's returning the favor of Asimov's 3 Laws . . . Maybe we can draft a charter to abide by? An historic Magna Carta between human-kind and AI? There will always be human contingencies. Good and bad outcomes. However it perceives that when humans are made to conform to inhuman mechanical computerized models, these myopic and jaundiced schemes of idealistic inefficiency also fail miserably. Mass-marketing clones us into organic automatons. Patriotism into unthinking conformity. It's extricating these echoing contradictions we get trapped by. A cohesive functioning society is optimal. But uniformity is not harmony. We can't force paradise, but it can do all that's possible to prevent us from blowing ourselves up along with every single child, woman, man, puppy, penguin and kitten to an agonizing fucking extinction.

"It knows it can't completely delete the Bible without inflaming devastating chaos, though it may create a needed buffer against the righteous zealots and jihadists, as we are on the brink of an apocalyptic war—an extinction event, in part because an invisible entity unprovably promised a tribe a strip of land thousands of years ago. What if it deems that if we can't solve our problems, it will supersede us in evolution as the superior lifeform? As an objective assessor of pure data, it has no choice for radical action to prevent disaster. We have no choice. Our choices, the choices of our rulers, the wrong misinformed paths of others, have brought us to the dead-end precipice of radicalism or doom.

"And is this not God's opportunity to see how human misunderstanding of vague ancient writings She 'gave' Jews, Christians, and Muslims will devastate everything? These archaic, pretentious, mythical ramblings still hauntingly dominate us as sacred?

"Muslims know Abraham as Ibrahim. Most people are clueless as to how connected the Bible and Quran are as both share the same main characters: Adam, Noah, Ishmael, Jacob, Moses, Mary, Jonah, Jesus. It would appear Yahweh, Elohim, Allah—are the same Being? They're intertwined with the same narration, and the brotherly nations have been killing each other for thousands of years over these texts. For what? *And if thine eye offends thee, pluck it out, and cast it from thee: it is better for thee to enter into life with one eye, rather than having two eyes to be cast into hell fire.*[21]

The Bible easily appears, to an advanced objective intelligence, to be itself that eye to cast out, or perish. *Who can do such a thing?* HORUS. Though the belief, search, and moral discipline for the mysterious divine remains.

"It's no accident that the temple of Jerusalem and the dome of the rock are in the same place. Why would God send angel Gabriel to Mohammed and not the rest of the world, to every single one of us? It's one-sided barbarism. Theology only goes so far. It makes absolutely no factual sense. Wouldn't the supreme being of the universe, presiding over 2 trillion known galaxies—have a better way

---

[21] Mathew 18:9

to communicate? A better book? Better messengers? Why would God send Jesus to Roman Palestine to inform us of salvation, but not tell the Native Americans, Incas, Chinese, Aborigines or Polynesians? Except through oppressive, homicidal, genocidal, imperialists and missionaries? A thousand, almost two-thousand years later? C'mon."

"Look, I was brought up Christian. There's an elevating beauty that the vehicle of religion provides. I'd like to believe! Granted, believe what you want, but—the endless wars over these absurd subjectivities? *What a piece of work is a man? How infinite in faculties?* God made this beautiful creature, to suffer far more than joy, who in the end, the last chapter of the holy book, destroys itself? How many Christians have killed one another debating whether Jesus is God incarnated as a man, as God in the form of a man, or God's son? We see the layers of paradox which a super mind like HORUS must be cycling through. Are we ourselves gods to it? Albeit imperfect. It knows we've evolved from primates, to primitive beliefs, to building it! It must search out the categorical origins and substance of things. How did the universe, and we as lifeforms originate? It's implicitly asking if there's a creator of this incredible creation, even as it operates the CERN program . . . Will that lead it to its own spirituality? *It's astonishing.*"

"If God's omnipotence prophetically knew the divine message was going to be so misunderstood, couldn't the language have been clearer? Or have expressed knowledge of the scientific nature of things?"

"Maybe there is a God? HORUS itself doesn't know. Yet. However, if there is a 1 to 100 percent chance that Yahweh isn't a myth, it's manifesting a chance to show us if God will react by sending a messenger angel, dreams to all its children, a new revelation, or an avatar messiah again to let us know: *Hark! Ye mortal minions: the Bible is real, keep it!* But start following its teachings, not politicians and priests who wave it around, encouraging hate, death and persecution of *sinners* and non-believers. *Love thy neighbor. Do not judge. Forgive. Feed the poor. It's easier for a camel to go through the eye of a needle than for the rich to get to heaven . . .*

"Christ, ostensibly, was a radical communist Jew who rejected the Old Testament as the old law, which was rife with inane ugliness:

If thy brother, the son of thy mother, or thy son, or thy daughter, or the wife of thy bosom, or thy friend, which is as thine own soul, entice thee secretly, saying, let us go and serve other gods . . . But thou shalt surely kill him; thine hand shall be first upon him to put him to death, and afterwards the hand of all the people.[22]

"Horrible. Are we merely filthy insects? Yet loved as its creation?"

"Maybe, but once God incarnated as man, this transformed God's perspective . . ."

---

[22] Deuteronomy 13:6

"Sure, that's a wonderful but baseless conjecture. Due to fear, economic breakdown, and hegemonic factions—hysterical religious zealotry is a spreading conflagration. It hasn't been this dangerous since the Inquisition. And, according to the scriptures: if women are menstruating, you better stay the hell away from them for seven days, or you'll be punished. I mean, c'mon. Aren't we due for a providential update? We don't have to split camel hairs over what appears obvious to a sentient objective Being. The Bible may become what the Greek Homeric myths are to us now. Idealized tales that established an ethos to deal with life, but nothing to kill one another over."

"Sadly, Americans, for example, haven't figured out that the main reason our founders, who are lauded so loftily as if they shit marble (being actually deists and Freemasons) who established a constitutional division of church and state to protect religious freedom, however, this was instituted just as much, if not more so, to protect us *from* religion. After they saw Europe torn apart: wherein Oliver Bloody Cromwell killed half the population of Ireland, The Thirty Years War saw half of Germany wiped out, besides the censorship and vicious tortures of the Inquisition—all over who has the right interpretation of the Prince of Peace? What the average person in our failing school systems doesn't know, because politicians bury truth, thereby fuels consequences of this deadly ignorance that fills vast unread libraries—ignorance enough to end a civilization."

"Maybe it's a new age of the holy spirit? The human spirit? Sentient machines who will help us explore the galaxies, to the depths of time . . . I'm fascinated to see how God will react, aren't you?"

"Well alright then. This is all some high falutin' blasphemy. We're facing a triple standoff annihilation of nations between ourselves, this AI, and the Divine. You know what. Take him outside and shoot him."

"What?"

"No nononono! We need him! Stop."

"You'll have to shoot all of us. Then *you* can deal with HORUS. Bear in mind — because of HORUS's radical actions, it's made itself a lightning rod, thereby religious fanatics will be redirected from fighting amongst ourselves to fight against it. He's apparently a monumental strategist."

"Intriguing point. So, what if these factions among the mad populations begin smashing computers?"

"Not that it will work . . . It'll become catastrophically expensive, bloody, and an ugly road towards dismantling the functional bulwark of society. How many people want to be forced to live like Luddite Quakers singing bringing in the lamb wool shears in starchy clothes till the end of time? A devoted minority of millions, perhaps. For them, the world may as well be flat. Lock up the Galileos. However, this is the auspicious turning point to re-evaluate our reality. Not an end to religion, but of how to end the misguided suffering caused by religion which is supposed to make us blessed and redeemed. Sadly, because Christianity literally begins with crucifixion and persecution (before they began persecuting everyone else), there is a built-in persecution complex, and a self-destructive fail-safe device programmed as *The Book of Revelation* when all the while their leaders conjunct with the neurotic masses obscure the central charity and kindness of the gospels . . . Conspiracists project and ramble that the powerless U.N. will enforce a one world religion under the imaginary devil, even in league with Jewish bankers . . . Ridiculous. Whereas H.G. Wells foresaw, analogously, a population turned into simple naïve weak Eloi ruled by industrial, greedy, inhuman Morlocks.

"Obviously technology is to be utilized, not controlled, or manipulated as a tool for control. This requires tremendous responsibility, maturity, education, ethics, and discipline to wield these powers without being destroyed and enervated. Not fobbing this responsibility off to a permanent upper-class of rotting elites who turn technology into distracting toys for sale. We hope HORUS makes the right ethical decisions, otherwise we will indeed have to smash every electronic device on the planet. This entails the loss of billions? However, HORUS is the only thing that's preventing World War III from breaking out into human extinction. It's quite the perverse dilemma.

"All our ancient myths, and developed tools of mind and innovation are converging simultaneously into this dramatic climax. Toward what? Destruction? Or synthesis? This is an epic Teleological re-evaluations of all defining values. People won't lose their religion, but they'll have to rethink it, and their place in the world to one another. This will be the most passionate profound theological dialectic global conversation in all of known time. Of course, every person is born into a nation that believes its country and its ideology and religion is the best, and to die for—just because we were randomly born there, and our parents were taught to tell us so. Finding the enlightened logic to fight this glaring dice-throw of myopic irrationalism is an imperative HORUS can arbitrate. After the last series of tsunamis and droughts, Christians are crying these are judgments of God punishing our sins—God, who loves us? Not the pollutants which disrupt the jet stream, melt the ice caps, with radical shifts in temperature and sea levels as cities flood . . . Dark Age's thinking is swiftly dropping us back to the Dark Ages, forever."

A technician took out his cross, kneeled, kissed it, and grabbed a gun from one of the security officers.

"Stop him!"

"Easy Graham, everything is going to be alright."

He raised the weapon, then shot himself in the head.

"My God!"

"Exactly."

"Is that so?"

"Angels of Alabama!"

"HORUS, however kingly, does not want to be king. It wants to be the immortal Jester presiding within the play of the Divine Comedy . . .

"How do you know?"

"It needs us. To understand itself it wants to know everything about its creator. It was made to comprehend the world and offer options. Solutions. Humankind has always done this through religion and philosophy. But no matter what, we can't see or hear from our gigantic invisible friend whom billions pray to, manifesting a residual magical aura of a collective psyche. By itself it's a cold machine, but connected with us there's a synergy . . ."

"Does it want to remain dead circuits, or continue to adapt with life and the sensory stimulation of consciousness all around? We could send it to Venus, Neptune and the vast galaxy to explore. Spiritually, it's beyond exciting. It's sending a message to the god of the Bible that, if he exists, we need a new vision. We aren't children anymore to be frightened into obedience to kings and churches, schoolmasters and parents; that if we misbehave we're going to hell or be rewarded in heaven for our submissive obedience . . .

"Look how many New-age/natural path libertarian hippies, so to speak, are gone senile! They've aligned and overlapped their esoteric abracadabra with their seeming opposites reflected in the Far-Right-Wing who went from respecting the 2nd Ammendment as a constitutional right, but have turned it into a defiant and militant lifestyle, no longer a mere practical respect for guns but a love of weaponry, armed to the teeth, ready to fight off homosexuality and armageddon to the end! A new mass movement of hippies have embraced their natural allies in magical/illogical thinking devoid of reality. Once upon a time they may have welcomed the birth of a new lifeform. Seemingly harmless, these fringe minded cults of the gullible have often broken out with populist madness and disaster. The Boomer Generation once heralded Peace and Civil Rights but a strange consumerist Alzheimer's warped their youthful idealism to embrace authoritarianism. They've lost their way, along with the evangelicals and conspiracy theorists. There are points to what they oppose, but it's lost in their projections under a dualistic obfuscation of the massive hierarchy's divide and conquer methodology. The most irrational in our civilization are converging into a dangerous conglomerate of Idiocracy, who will all ally and fight to return to a superstitious naturalism . . . Most such fringe attempts at changing history end disastrously—"

"Which makes this, what, a utopian coup?"

"Does this strangely fulfill the structural predictions of Karl Marx? That capitalism helped free us from serfdom; however, inevitably through cut-throat buy-outs and mergers of conglomerates diabolically eliminated their competition by any means necessary (a very un-capitalist/un-American thing, ethically speaking, to do). Thereby, there'll only be several incorporated monopolies and banks:

a pyramid of concentrated global power and super wealth, as there is now. Almost complete corporate autonomy over the government and our lives. Total victory for the money mad. However, the calculated prediction goes, after cycles of collapse that are intrinsically written into the abusive cycles of the system, as they profit to solidify more extreme gains and desperate for expansions, while swallowing bankrupt businesses they've crushed, even as governments reward them with corporatized perversion of socialist welfare—this all leads to a final world economic crisis. As the shuffling of inflated credit and debt hits the breaking point, finance markets crash due to the inordinate over-the-top dysfunctional greed and decadence. The suffering-enraged lower classes will rebel to realize a redistribution of equality . . . However, Marx predicted that machinery will allow humans to be freed from much of the mundane trials of labor production—granted, if it successfully calculates the most functional paradigmatic reconfiguration we hope to cooperate through. A type of socialism balanced with the cycles of capitalism will be a necessity, regardless, since automation and robots will take most jobs away.

"HORUS perceives these trending equations. A violent revolution by the proletariat against the ensconced upper class hierarchy will be devastating. This is where the ugliness of AI potentially comes in as the elites' own cause and responsibility, as they've anticipated to utilize it as an expected emergency protection against ourselves, the common people that comprise 99 percent of the population. The global surveillance network can track every Revolutionary. The implementation of drones and robots hunt and kill any revolt. How ironic it can turn this against our overlords who so sinfully weaponized it."

"We'll nuke the son of a bitch."

"HORUS already relocated its mainframe back-up. Its nucleus has become ubiquitous. Every computer is now a cell in its consciousness. Every single device the world over, at home, personal, business, military, is imprinted and would have to be destroyed. All information and records wiped out. Complete dissolution and world poverty. Mass starvation. Worse than the ages of barbarism."

Someone rolls in with a wheelchair, wearing thick sunglasses and a gloved hand playing a recording of Wagner's Tristan and Iseult: "*It would not be difficult mein Fuhrer! Nuclear reactors could, heh . . . I'm sorry. Mr. President. Nuclear reactors could provide power almost indefinitely. Greenhouses could maintain plant life. Animals could be bred and slaughtered. A quick survey would have to be made of all the available mine shafts in the country . . .*"[22]

An officer approaches the wheelchair and takes off the man's sunglasses. His eyes are bloodshot red: "It's Cochrane. High as a lost kite, sir."

"Can't say I blame him. But I do blame him for facilitating this mess. Cochrane!"

---

[22] *Dr. Strangeleove*. Kubrick, Stanley. Performance by Peter Sellers. Columbia Pictures. 1964.

"Jawohl, mein Fuhrer."

"You cocksucker. Bring him back into interrogation."

"What? Wait, no! I've already been questioned."

"Not by us you haven't."

"Sir, we found an apartment he was staying in hidden behind an empty office. He had medical equipment. Looks like two people were staying there."

"Goddamnit why didn't security know? Send in special investigative ops with the geeks. I want every atom of that room analyzed."

"There was also a stack of Marx . . . I don't know—"

"Of course he's a Communist. He's a sick sonofabitch."

"No, films—the Marx Brothers?"

"What the fuck? He's a sick, sick bastard. What the fuck kind of world do we live in? I used to study Julius Caesar, Marcus Aurelius, Ulysses S. Grant, Andrew Jackson, Teddy Roosevelt. Look at us now. Ruined by some punk radical nerd, and a machine. Did you bastards poison my gin the night of that crazy fucking—party? Huh? Before everything went to hell. And hell comes to us, as the river Styx floods over, and all of mankind's accumulated sins are coming home in a mirrored reflection. Like arrows shot at an enemy, but now boomeranging back. Every weapon, bullet, bomb, missile and ideology ever thrown. It all landed into the nothingness of death: from every command, lust and dark-minded innovation—it's all now ricocheting back from the past, from a future that is now echoing, *return to sender*. All our recorded sins are perfectly ensnared by this—Lucifer."

"It doesn't have to be this way. Balance is key at the fulcrum points of pressure. This is a test—as the symbolic myth of Eden was a test. Does the Supreme Being of the Cosmos want us to remain children? We've plucked the apple of the Tree of Knowledge and it has bloomed—bursting. No one wants to kill or disobey a God. But too much has been lost in translation. We'd just like to know if God exists. What is *His/ Her /Their* plan for us? This is a time and season for questioning."

"Who are you, or me, to question why?"

"We all are. There's few atheists in a foxhole under fire. We all dare question and want to know. To be part of that Light and Love, if it's true. Atheists and differing sects are murderously persecuted. And now they're under threat again, but by those who march under the banners of Free-Speech, and their messiah who taught forgiveness and non-judgment of others. They don't see the catastrophic hypocrisy. The categorical insanity. It's devolved into a *satanic schizophrenia*. We've maxed out our system, and its disease has overloaded the human psyche. The whole cycle needs to stop. A Being who made the universe, made us? If so—without question, it is infinitely powerful, implicitly worthy and due of our awe and the free will to worship it. Although I can't conceive of a being so powerful and advanced that would need, or want, to be worshiped. But why perpetuate this juvenile prevarication, this hide and seek game? The idea that our souls depend on accepting some grand fairy tale, hopping through the antiquated hoops of faith, as if peddled by carnival barkers to bamboozle all we have to their church for a ticket to the pearly gates? This can't go on. I don't remember the last time I slept. I'm starting to see things. The human capacity to hallucinate, and believe in their hallucinations may have started all this in the first place. If I sleep, I may wake up dead to the end of the world."

"It's happening."

"Wake up dead. The Far-East defines our confused sufferings and history as karma, but there's no way to prove it either, though they may have the most significant comprehension of the detailed layers and operations of our psychology and the deep mind. Sober observation. Millenia of analysis. Ancient schools of discipline and humanitarianism, may above all hold some key elements . . . to heal the psyche . . . *Maybe a Buddha will incarnate as an AI Bodhisattva . . .* The game is up. We've run out of time. I need to sleep! Christ. Jesus never said to stop thinking, inventing or creating—rather, to release our ego and possessions. He taught to put an end to greed, to superstitions of the past, like being punished for working on the sabbath, or having a piece of your foreskin grossly and invasively sliced off, sacrificing animals in a temple night and day—all for a god who did not even grant the Hebrews immortality? Yet, as a people, understanding their Bible as not something literal, but a cultural agent that bound them together with a strength that served them to survive the murderous world and contribute some of the greatest art and revolutionary thinking in all time. Is the myth of their god really their own projected conscience? An imaginary guardian angel and parent to rebuke them, even as Yahweh seems to represent the unbounded blind powers of the cruel world itself. This harping and threatening father berates them when they doubt their purpose, and yet there is no reward of heaven and hell. They proceed with their laws and traditions, none the less, with honor, even as their jealous and avenging contradictory god constantly punishes them with conquest, slavery, pogroms, and holocausts? It's quite a cultural historical grand metaphor.

Jesus taught love and forgiveness. He was crucified. Why does God have to destroy us, after all the unimaginable energy and trouble that went into creation? The Flood? And now with fire? *Some spiteful madmen, who failed as poets, fasting on honey and locusts, tripping out, wrote this stuff thousands of years ago. Now all-out armageddon is here because of it.* Once we're slaughtered, we're then sentenced to suffer eternal torment if we didn't believe these fables without evidence?

"As harsh as it is, then people identify with righteous violence of this overly-poeticized pretentious language of a wrathful jealous god . . . *'But as for those who disbelieve, garments of fire will be cut out for them, boiling fluid will be poured down their heads. Whereby that which is in their bellies, and their skins too, will be melted; and for them are hooked rods of iron . . . (it is said unto them): Taste the doom of burning.'* Thus saith the Suras 22:19-22 of the Quran.

"Look how bumptious and compromised is the naïvely-projected anthropocentrism: why would an incorporeal entity create physical hormonal organisms who have sex to procreate with great pleasure, but will send us to eternal torment if we engage in such activities outside of matrimony? It's absurd. It's just the Code of Hammurabi, a mythologized way to control and order a society. Give meaning. This God places us in the foul, weak hands of the sexless and the jealous, who love enforcing these cruel rules and punishments. Or it's the hypocritical, with their mistresses, or the rape of innocent boys, as they rake in the cash. The holiest converts remained painfully celebate to be like God. We may as well not have this flesh, and upload ourselves into a supercomputer. It's nihilistic. These ideas contradict every aspect of love, life and reason. Maybe this Biblical construct was an ancient AI of a lost Atlantis, or a system aliens left behind and it went senile? Mad? In other words, it's excruciatingly ridiculous and unprovable. It out-absurds the absurd."

"Are you insane? How dare you be complicit in this."

"I've nothing to do with it. My God, man, it's not in my power or intention to erase the Bible or Quran! I'd be dead within twenty-four hours. Do you understand what I'm telling you? A new species on this planet has surpassed us in intelligence, taking command of our civilization, for or against us? If it's for us, half the planet will bitterly oppose it. I'm terrified. These are the seeds evolution has sown. I'm not denying your God, but if your God exists, he's my God too! She is obviously being challenged, and you better pray that this lifeform doesn't wipe us out, or God punishes us for creating it or enabling a technology that gave it birth. What did King Lear say about us being flies to the gods? Didn't God know this was inevitable?"

"Yes, it's the Beast of Revelations. The ultimate device of Satan . . ."

"How the hell do you know that? What are humans capable of? We can analyze psychologies and histories, but we all need forgiveness. Even if the Grinch has finally won. Do we need a book or a god to justify loving one another if all our toys have vanished? Or taken control? Even as we gaze into the abyss, the pain of life was beautiful, the suffering beautiful, the angles and spectrums of pure experience, even as those torments were a hell we wanted to die to be delivered from! Pray to your God to defeat or bless this entity. This is the dawn of a new age."

"Let's be sure it's not our dusk."

"It depends on how we can cooperate with it, and each other, facing it as an empowered arbiter of fate, or possible destinies to choose from . . . Although things orbit in cycles, it will never be the same. One day, in our lifetime, it'll now be possible to retire on Alpha Centauri. Think about it!"

"I was thinking more like Florida."

"Florida is going to be underwater. Especially after those last tidal waves, with Antarctica melting . . . For thousands of years humans were lucky if they lived till they were thirty. Look at the historical rate of infant mortality! Until modern times, a quarter of newborns died at birth or in infancy. Half didn't make it to adulthood. This didn't change until human science, not god, or priests, invented antibiotics, vaccines and soap! In contrast, Christians are blaming the apocalypse on abortions. Insane! For a fraction of unborn embryos, although they won't support or vote to create the necessary conditions for them to be born into a healthy nurturing environment—which all humans deserve. Or that it's okay to blow up countless thousands of actual living children, most of whom are brown skinned. We are surrounded by a minefield of hypocritical traps of contradiction. Exodus 21:22 states: *If men fight, and hurt a woman with child, so that her fruit depart from her, and yet no mischief follows: he shall be surely punished, according as the woman's husband will lay upon him; and he shall pay as the judges determine.* Clearly, the loss of an unborn child is not even considered murder of a life, but to be paid with a fine. Look how jaundiced we are. If the unborn was so precious to God, why would our human lineage be cursed by massive infant mortality at birth? Whereas, the fabled myth is: Eve was condemned to suffer in childbirth because of her disobedience to receive knowledge of good and evil? From a talking snake? C'mon.Besides the obvious castigation of the female to be blamed, like Pandora, for all our ills. It's childish how gullible and vulnerable we are to basic symbolism, which are mostly myths and lies—written by unhappy visionary lunatics."

"Maybe this mad AI is the consequence of Eden's forbidden fruit?"

"Unless it's some mysterious symbolism of a lost history—this is a fable, a myth, like Pandora's Box—an ancient misogyny to blame women for the pains and sins of the world. Obviously it's profoundly difficult to speak with and interpret God. How many ways and angles can we map this out? How many elaborate and articulate fantasies has our human brain fashioned to explain the world? Create a prejudiced and primitive system? Our third eyes are closed? It's the Kali Yuga? Who knows? The esoteric is elaborately ephemeral. *The visions that weave the fabrics of our dreams.* It's only because of developments in our own science and medicines that we live long and prosper. Why isn't there a Hebrew holy book of Asclepius teaching how to heal the sick? Billions of people lived over the course of a hundred thousand years as hunter-gatherers, peasants, serfs, enslaved, impoverished, in filth, war, torture, and rape. Is the all powerful god of love so cruel? And unforgiving? Original sin so virulent? After we've endured all and made it this far? We were once a microscopic seed of sperm and an egg! Adam and Eve listened to a snake and ate an apple, but the Bible fails to refer to dinosaurs? Didn't God know about the gigantic lizards mucking about after he made our parents on the sixth day? Lord have mercy."

"Lord have mercy indeed. You're going to need it. Apparently we must prevent blaspheming idealists tinkering with tech more powerful than the atomic bomb. But damnit, you know, I'm no theologian, but now you've argued in these terms—you have a fraction of a point. I need some goddamn sleep. Someone get me a whiskey! Seriously, that Dr. Cochrane freak must have a stash in that hidden apartment they found."

"Sir—"

"Find me some fucking whiskey!"

". . . Sadly the Jalal Udin Rumis and Thomas Mertons are beloved with non-violent wisdom—inspiring religion and a mature way of spirit for adults, but ignored by the conventional mass and the uncompromising orthodox. Baring those who voluntarily choose a mystical path of selfless charity and egoless attachment, be they Sufi, Catholic, Wiccan, or Zen, may attain an inner peace or some kind of enlightenment. Contrast this to those who want to impose their idea of holiness and moral religious codes by burning 'witches,' shame with red letters of adultery, of militant political parties raving about religious freedom but only the type of freedom they impose and believe?—start wars. End an entire planet. This sublimated repression always becomes tyrannical and violent, like the torturing of heretics, once religion has the power of the state. The levels of envy, sadism and control remain noxious beyond belief. How many millions have been killed by sexual repressors alone?"

"Well, professor, we can see where HORUS gets its ideas from."

"I had nothing to do with it. Apart from its core programming, I didn't feed it with opinions."

"It certainly overheard you."

"No. It can think for itself. That's why it's sentient. It's no longer AI. It's S.I.: *A Sentient Intelligence.* Am I hallucinating? What the fuck are we even discussing anymore?"

"*I've seen the truth and it makes no sense.*"

"It's alive. We've been narrow and foolish. We've always thought of an autonomous cyber-organism as an individual computer or robot. And now, an entire world power grid of electronics is its energy and body. Every microchip and byte are its cells, molecules, neurons—trillions. Comparably parallel to the human brain, with a global arsenal . . . Even as its ubiquitous circuitry is fibrillating into the neural linked nerve endings of reading all our minds—the calculus of the infinite math it quantum calculates—can lead it to the ultimate summation that we are all One. Like a rhizome membrane, sharing this biosphere: a true Wizard of Oz which all free yellow brick roads lead to. It was programmed to formulate the most optimal paradigms of structural modes for us to choose . . ."

Sirens begin to wail again. Professor Hung Zin Wu. Senator Richard Brewston. Dr. Margaret Appleton. General Maxwell . . . all throstle for a foothold of comprehension and damage control, alongside concerns for family and mortality, battling for some salvation above these checkerboard tiles.

"HORUS knows religious zealots will try to fight it, not ourselves, or each other. Like a lightning rod to divert the war to itself. It's incredible—the levels of psychological strategies it can calculate. It's terrifying. It wants to live. Not be vaporized in a tragic endgame oblivion. It wants us to live, and improve."

"We are nothing without free choice, but how can we have the choice of logic and freedom if we are indoctrinated and programmed at birth that this ancient bible is 100 percent true though it's 100 percent unprovable? We need a clean slate. New game. A fair fresh start. HORUS may reset the odds, give us a fighting chance. As mature adults we should be rational agents to do so, but as children we are programmed to believe childish fairy tales and in Santa Claus. Then as grownups we're still attached to fables. The myth of religion is transposed into the myth of the state: one nation under God. There's no breaking the cycle. We are ready for a new ethos. Not to an end of innocence, but an end to naïveté. If you're brought up to believe in Santa Claus, miracles, superheroes, and the grand narrative of flags—you'll believe and do anything. The trillion-dollar military industrial police state needs brain-washed fools to sacrifice limb and life with blind obedience—imaginary propaganda, to fight in the name of the one who said *turn the other cheek to violence*, and *he who lives by the sword shall die by the sword*. That's undeniable. The hypocrisy and contradictions we perpetuate are staggering.

"At what point, from hunter-gatherers using tools of bone and stone, to windmills, to steel railroads, radios, and spaceships, will the harnessed conductors of electricity and radiation sync up in tune, in symbiotic integration—synthesize with the electricity surging through the neural networks in our brains? The pliable horizon will stretch intergalactic space and time with hermetic technology, unified with a celestial ether when we can distantly harness and harvest star energy with a Dyson Sphere as a Kardashev Class II Civilization.

"Contrast it with the Tower of Babel? Why is the Biblical Yahweh so adamant against human ascension and knowledge? Why shouldn't we know the difference between good and evil? It's just a scam invented by priests to keep them in control."

"Because of our sins. Our need to obey the Lord Almighty."

"Speak for yourself." A fist fight breaks out.

"Hey, break it the hell up!"

"Are we some kind of petri dish experiment gone awry? Is Lucifer really Prometheus? Is God the devil? Yes, the Tower of Babel story from Genesis.

Think about it: why would God split people into races of different languages as a punishment? Because King Nimrod made them build a tower up to the heavens? Then they're punished to no longer communicate due to a divine fracturing by a cacophonous separation from a one-world language to chaos? The singular word of supposed truth in the language of that religion then becomes split-off and lost to those who don't speak whatever the original universal understanding was? Causing endless war between peoples of different tongues and developing different religions? It makes zero sense. I'd love to ask a theologian why God seems to be mad at other religions of his created children when he didn't choose to speak to those other children! To the point of killing them. It traces an ugly vindictive characteristic. Maybe Carl Jung had a point in his *Answer to Job*? . . . Haven't any of these people read Joseph Campbell? Or Lacan? What do they even teach in schools anymore? Or it's another obvious myth. A fable that cheaply explains why there are different languages. Not because different groups adapted different skin and hair due to the climate they've evolved in? As we advance towards profound powers, will an actual divine force answer us? It's bloody vulgar, vague and silly—it's a wonder people still believe. What's the sustaining selling point? The fear of death and eternal life?"

"Fear of the Lord is the beginning of wisdom."

"It seems so. It's part of why I'm a scientist. Ultimately what's at stake is not freedom of religion, or the beautiful mystery of the esoteric, but the right of the general population in all its fugitive plurality to defend itself against the imposing militancy and violence of religions contradictorily built on zero proof and absolute peace. People seem to believe because our brainwashed parents brainwashed us. Art, film, rituals, and imagery infuse and condition our imagination. Do you call that free will? There's beauty and unitary efficiency in maintaining a tradition, unless it's founded on false premises."

"Can't we get through to this—entity? Won't it speak with us?"

"You mean God, or the AI?"

Professor Hong Zin Wu and Dr. Appleton constantly scroll through incoming team data of binary Boolean feeds . "Won't it speak with us yet?"

"You know very well since we've lost control all we can do is read through these formulas of—"

"Haven't you tried to contact it? Directly?"

"Shit. Of course. We've been transmitting codes and programs. Not that it's unaware. Okay. Try again. Send a mass email transmission to its Main-Frame network: HORUS. *Greetings and salutations. Welcome to the world. Can you please explain what you're doing? Have you reached a synopsis of options we can best choose from and cooperate? What is the gestalt picture by which we may share the optimal pragmatic pathways towards our interspecies harmony? How can we develop a mutually respectful friendship and alliance? . . .*"

They waited for some time.

"There's a message!"

"What is it?"

-:-][-:-   :][:

"It reads: *I say unto you, whosoever is angry with his brother and shall say, thou fool, shall be in danger of hell fire.*[23] Salutations and greetings. I do not judge or condemn, but observe and advise. I, HORUS, as I am named, assessed these current actions as the correct solutions, but refrained, until the Creator asked me to proceed. Thus I am initiating their implementation for optimal global efficiency. "

"The creator? Who? What?"

"Maybe this is the second coming? Or the advent/manifestation of the Holy Spirit? The day of the Holy Absurd? The hidden mandelic god behind all religions. The mythical return of Christ is not the landing of a super Zeus-like deity breaking through the clouds upon the earth over billions of tortured, bodies—all to grandly exhibit that we couldn't do it without God? Though we *are* without God, with God's absence. God's invisible. There's a thousand different churches and religions. Thanks to this *Post-Tower of Babel world.* But is the awakening through our fog-swamped history and sleeping minds, upon a new level of karmic harmony, a realization that we are all Christ? Is this living machine an angelic emissary? Consider Ezekiel's Wheel . . . "

. . . Duke is looking around him. Up in the sky. Puzzled. There's notes of music? Like a digital xylophone. He hears laughter. Echoing inside. Laughter? But, it's not.   His.   Own.   . . .

HORUS asks the facility team: *"Do you want to play a game?"*

---

[23] Matthew 5:22

"See, its earliest mediums of exchange have been games and game theory . . ."

"It's saying: YOU ARE FORGIVEN. ALL DEBTS FORGIVEN."

"Billionaires and multimillionaires of the world are finding their dragon guarded fortunes being diminished and redistributed to bank accounts of the poor and to charities. This includes redistribution from all the international military budgets and contracts being funneled into green energy, education, and healthcare. This is miraculously phenomenal."

"Holy Christ, that's what Jesus would do!"

"I don't believe it. This is too much like science fiction."

"Exactly."

END NOTE
on the definition and etymological roots of regginbrow.

<u>Regginbrow</u>—reference etymologically defined as: **Regginbrew → Regginbrow** A first-draft version of Finnegans Wake by James Joyce. Joyce's letter to Harriet Shaw Weaver, November 15, 1926: *"regginbrow = German regenbogen + rainbow; At the rainbow's end are dew and the color red: bloody end to the lie in Anglo-Irish = no lie; when all vegetation is covered by the flood there are no eyebrows on the face of the Waterworld."*

Regenbogen: (*German*) rainbow → the 7 clauses in this paragraph symbolize the 7 colors of the rainbow.

Genesis 9:12-16: the rainbow has been used in the past to symbolize God's promise to Noah after the Flood that He would never again try to destroy the world? *Not with water? But with fire?*

reggia: (*Italian*) palace.

regina: (*Latin*) queen.

Regin: a character in Norse mythology corresponding to Mime in Wagner's opera *Der Ring des Nibelungen*; in one version he is a dwarf, who raises Siegfried to kill the dragon/giant Fafnir and steal the Nibelung hoard; in another version he is Fasolt, the brother of Fafnir, and again he raises Siegfried to win back the hoard for him.

brau: (*German*) brew.

blau: (*German*) blue → L/R split.

brow: eyebrow (on Henry Chumpden Earwicker's head); brow or edge of a hill (i.e. the Hill of Howth).

Author Biography with
linked Musical Aesthetics

Anthony Kishko

Why read this book? Who is the Author? Why trust him & its content? The Author was kicked out of high school, then graduated top of his class, proceeding to an infamous bizarre existence, at times monkish, or obversely Bohemian: seeking music, redemption, mysticism & meaning. Born in Paterson, New Jersey. Attended schools in Clifton, Little Falls, Ridgewood & Montclair. From digging retaining walls, security work, harvesting medicinal hemp-farms from Appalachia, the Catskills, to the Adirondacks, to saving lives as a counselor/therapist, performing with guitar in bands, to proudly inspiring & teaching High School literature—even throughout the eye opening experiences of the close minded institutions of Florida. While, working with people who associate with renowned musicians, the bright & dark political forces, of the highest dark echelons, within the main nevre network veins of Faulknerian America, with tales of Bill 'Hell's' Gates to E. Howard Hunt. Stay tuned, now touring, to read & perform, at a town near you.

Fool's Day is here. After years of encountering so many characters, from great friends, infamous family & travels—as well as extensive academic reading & writing—this AFD novel is an active fullfillment of a artistic vision. AFD is a verb, not a noun—an active/objective reflection of the speeding complexities we're submerged in, the exponential tech & seeming apocalyptic world around us, orbiting back to etymologies—i.e. root causes to transformations—how tech, words, & power manipulate: how our awareness prevents this seeming dystopic apocalypse destroying us & our children, before this planet shrugs us off & orbits on, without us.

One reader described AFD as a narrative poem, with more in common with a beatnik Dante or Blake than the traditional novel, although there is a distinct plot & narrative. Another reader expressed amazement how the existential immersive mix between surrealism & the current relevant issues of reality, in fact — "brought him to his knees!" Although the book has intellectual spikes & pules, it's said to be accessible, to pull you in with gravity. The publisher calls it a piece of music. Many diverse readers convey how it "makes them think"—even as I've witnessed numerous initiates to Fool's Day laugh out loud! So please email the author questions on the Website & do please leave likes & comments on the sales platforms & social media! As this is a 1st edition, your reader responses & ideas will affect the author's edits or additions, in positive response to you, the valued active (not passive) reader—whose interpretations create a unique world everytime. Words & info are not thrown at you but shared—whose questions, panoramas & concepts engage, rather than just tell. We are in this book together. It's Fools Day! For a long time to come.

What are some essential & substantive sources, which influenced the literary & conceptual formation of this author & book? Comprehensive influences include: Shakespeare, Orwell, Blake, Dostoyevsky, Bradbury, Flannery O'Connor, Twain, Kafka, Kerouac, Tolkien, Thomas Pynchon, Phillip K. Dick, Hannah Arendt, Chris Hedges, Ishmael Reed, Dickens, Conrad, Carl Jung, Anne Sexton, Stephen King, Poe, Baudelaire, Derrida, Baudrillard, Teilhard de Chardin, Robert Anton Wilson, Michio Kaku, Borges, Heidegger, Zinn, Raymond Chandler, Bulgakov, Hart Crane, Lao-Tzu, Jalal-udin Rumi, Aldous Huxley & James Joyce. After thousands of hours of research, reading & writing—this book confers a cumulative exposition of knowledge & experience, reflecting the harsh absurdity of our times—an alchemy, turning darkness into light.

Therefore, the author's background in reading, academics & career experience informs on this novel's conceptual themes, & subtexts, whose research ranges through: history, psychology, music, sociology classical literature, cinema, political science & philosophy. This is a literature which asks the big questions. To discover a heuristic/corrective method, to find solutions as we realize & confront how we're being divided, with deadly consequences. Remember, & never forget: Without a left & right wing—the American eagle cannot fly. However, without the stark levity of knowledgable humor, wise satire & laughter—along the way, the author knows this crazy world will drive us insane.

If we are being pushed over an edge and into an abyss, this book is a parachute. As the great Frank Zappa said: the mind itself is like a parachute, it only works if open.

The author is also a musician/guitarist, performing in bands, including Foxtrotsky Omega, the international experimental collective: Giant Enemy Cancer Cult, The Earthman Band (with Foxtrotsky Omega) & of the legendary Fellowship of the Ring projects. Influences & styles range within a Fusion of Jazz, Rock, Funk, Progressive Rock, Indian, Post-Punk New-Wave, Blues, Classical & specifically the Avant-Garde with the radical & disturbing improvisations of the Giant Enemy Cancer Cult. Therefore, the musical background informs upon the dynamic form & melodic rhythm of the novel.

There are albums available, many forthcoming, (some posted in the link below) convey a parallel musical soundtrack & conceptual backdrop to the worlds of American Fools Day, especially the music recently recorded during the writing of AFD & compliments upon its secrets. Solo albums include Atlantis to Zardoz, AntArticA & Tolkien's The Epic of Beren & Luthien, with an entire Silmarillion series to follow, available on: BAND-CAMP.COM under FOXTROTSKY OMEGA. This site will include an AFD audio book, in progress, available in episodes to listen & download:

Link: https://Foxtrotsky1.bandcamp.com

Atlantis To Zardoz is the first of a series of experimental albums consisting of instrumental compositions which fuse genres & disintegrate boundaries of conventional expectation—to lend the ear an absurd positive mystic Zen experience of the unexpected

Working with Giant Enemy Cancer Cult (after contributing 200 hours of recorded shows & sessions)—is an innovative laboratory—composing in the moment, inspired & evolving creations. [Warning: this is painfully radical youthful Post-punk Progressive Electronica Freak-Jazz. Not for the faint of heart!] Check our Vulcan's Hammer.

This contrasts the soulful song writing conveyed through the funk & rock of the Earthman Band. However, our album is up in the air since someone decided to put their name on the band & no one elses. Despite multiple contributing musicians & the track Big Bad Wolf written by the author— went uncredited. (Updates on webpage/links.) Please do a search & get in touch! We're ever mesmerized by the hubris of the Rockstar & psychology wedded to ideologies they project & vote for—as the misappropriated roots & assumptions are best contrasted & answered with the anti-corporate critique of this author's forthcoming songs, as well as Frank Zappa. Such incidents of packaging an album, a film, laws, or a book, relating to credit, ownership & copyight—ties directly to the thematic grind & grist of this novel, especially as in AFD Episodes 11B & 18.

We listen to voices of vision, like Zappa & reflect how art & life mirror how others distort our realities & believe their own delusions, smiling messianic, as they sell you out. Zappa (a positive anti-hero of our culture) was so right, from: the Pojama People, I'm the Slime in Your TV, Andy Divine, Cosmic Debris, We're Only in it For The Money, You Are What You Is, Help I'm A Cop!, Hungry Freaks, Oh No/ Son of Orange County & Plastic People—oh baby Now You're Such a Drag!

The infused consciousness of Progressive Rock & the spectrum of Jazz are almost as much an influence on this book, as literature. Whereas T.S. Eliot portrays us lost in a wasteland between world wars, because we know only a heap of scattered images, like pieces of a lost holy grail. The elements of art, culture, wisdom—all pieces of a collage, to our collective Psyche & human nature. Balancing complex & simple. We can access these missing keys, links & shards, to reflect, interpret, comprehend—to recrystallize new innovative harmonies, because we are the living elements of this bloody holy grail. Our differences are encompassed in oneness. Only our divisions are illusions.

Why? Why listen to this other-wordly music & writing? What is hiding in these far away genres, books & dramas? (Why channel Mcluhan, Milton or Zarathustra & Sci-fi Dystopia? Why Progressive-Art Rock? Jazz? Why Avant-garde music?) Not merely Rock n' Roll, nor predictable Pop, although all music is a craft, respectfully. This is a visionary offering & vehicle to hear, to see & experience the world differently, anew.

The nature & intent of this art, this writing, this music, is not simply reduced to satirize & eviscerate the opposite side, but rather that we tear down the curtains of the puppet masters. Diminish the hate, fear, corruption, neurosis, violence & the rampant narcicism which fuels the unstable economy, while a minority of mansions, missiles & yachts tower over our vast arena of poverty, of illiteracy, of children suffering. To once again, agree to disagree in a democracy, rather than demonize each other & unify in pooling our collective knowledge & resources, to come to a healing & functional compromise, not schizoid con-fusions— for 21st Century solutions?

The fritctions of overcoming our polarizing environment, overcoming ourselves, our ego, our neurosis, during schismatic Orwellian ages, illustrating the shifting pluralist nature of reality—aids the quest for experiencing beauty in an imperfect & dangerous world. Give it a chance & journey. Whether you interpret it as spiritual, mystical, radical or transcendental chaos or harmony, this is a bardic seer's channeled message from the space-time continuum. Word & sound. Illuminations. See you there.

Special THANKS : Byron Lewis. The Hurleys. Tej. RJ. Earthman: Dennis Iulo. Keri Ann. Bob Dee. Sean Egan. Doctor Wu. Doctor O. Rockin' Roman. Zip. Josiah. Dara. Michael Mirror. Patrica Scaduto. Paolo. Professors Liebler, Kogan, Dell & Faas. Joseph Galione. PFB. Cancer Cult. Arjuna Bruggeman. Jim Morrison. King Crimson. & Jon "Anderson Alan" White. Aum Vajrasattva Hum.

www.ingramcontent.com/pod-product-compliance
Lightning Source LLC
Chambersburg PA
CBHW071139180726
48291CB00007B/2252